FOREVER IN HIS HEART

"Conaire . . ." Deirdre shivered with more than the embrace, with more than the lift of her hair by the wind, suddenly chilled. "Something . . . something is happening."

Aye, something was happening. Something he'd battled against, something he knew was folly, yet something he'd not had the strength of will to escape from—something he'd taunted in the arrogant thought that he could fight it—the gods, his fate, the power of the love o' this woman. Now she stood in the circle of his embrace, her head beneath his chin, with the wind tangling their tunics. The rage of a passion long suppressed surged against the bonds of reason, until a webbing of a hundred thousand fissures spread through his resolve.

"I have dreamed this." She traced something upon his chest, then she blinked up at the sky, at the silver of the sun. "I've dreamed of this very day."

"Aye, woman." His palm burned against her flesh. "I've dreamed of it, too, a long, long time ago."

"Kiss me, Conaire."

He looked down upon her in the time between the times, and he saw the face of Brigid.

Seven hundred years of waiting.

His head dipped toward hers. He felt the rush of her breath against his lips.

Even an immortal could not struggle forever . . .

LISA ANN VERGE

TWICE UPON A TIME

ZEBRA BOOKS
KENSINGTON PUBLISHING CORP.

ZEBRA BOOKS are published by

Kensington Publishing Corp.
850 Third Avenue
New York, NY 10022

First Printing: September, 1994

Printed in the United States of America

Author's Note

It was in a small, firelit parlor in County Cork where I first heard the Irish language spoken. My husband and I had journeyed to this home to meet his distant relatives—descendants of the brothers and sisters left behind during the potato famine. Our tongues loosened by a warm meal, good companionship, and a bit of local whiskey, we told stories and recounted family histories—in English—all while a game of hurley blasted from a small television—in Irish.

There was something doubly anachronistic about hearing an ancient language wheezing from tiny speakers, while we jabbered in twentieth-century English around a charred old hearth. Our hosts could speak Irish, but they admitted they rarely used it in everyday life. And here's the pity of it: Only about 40,000 people in the world are fluent in Irish, mostly in and around the rugged western coast of the Emerald Island. English has long supplanted Irish as the island's first language.

Ah, but what the Irish do to the English language! The lilting quality of their speech, the colorful expressions they use—both derive in great part from the richness and rhythms of that ancient tongue. In many ways the Irish have won the battle to save their language: They have stolen English and made it their own.

I've done my best to recreate the musical cadence of "Irish" English in *Twice Upon A Time,* so that you, the reader, can hear the magic as I still do. Occasionally, I used an Irish word. Since, to an English speaker, some Irish words do not sound like their printed appearance, I've decided to include at the back of this book a short glossary which includes pronunciations.

May you, too, fall in love with the music and magic of Ireland. *Fad saol agat.*

Long life to you.

A Faery Song

We who are old, so old and gay,
  O so old!
Thousands of years, thousands of years,
  If all were told:

Give to these children, new from the world,
  Silence and love;
And the long dew-dropping hours of the night,
  And the stars above:

Give to these children, new from the world,
  Rest far from men.
Is anything better, anything better?
  Tell us it then:

Us who are old, old and gay,
  O so old!
Thousand of years, thousands of years,
  If all were told.

—William Butler Yeats

Prologue

France, 1223 A.D.

It was a time for dying.

The ocean roared against the craggy shelving of a crooked talon of cliff, boiling up a mist as dense as steam. On the scrubby ledge, gnarled crosses bristled like defiant warriors against the black-bellied sky. A clump of villagers huddled in the lee of a thatched-roofed church. Nearby, a priest braced himself at the head of a grave, and muttered wind-stolen words to the wooden cross speared at its head.

Conaire stood apart from the others. The salty wind lashed his brooding form. Cold fingers of seawater seeped into his tunic and drained the heat from his blood. He thrust his chin to the gale. His cloak flapped around him like the wings of a great hawk.

The priest ceased his chanting, ceding the battle to the hiss of the coming tempest. The grave diggers gouged their shovels into the red brown earth, as the priest made the final sign of the cross. The villagers mimicked the motion, then rustled like a great flock of ravens rising to the dawn.

Aye, that is always the way of it. Conaire curled his chill-stiffened fingers into his palms. *Go, then. Go to your hot stew and your loaves of thyme bread. Go sell the fish rotting in baskets on the shore. There's never time to mourn the dead, while the business of the living continues.*

His footsteps crunched across the gravel. The grave diggers paused, their shovels dribbling clods of sod. Conaire pitched to one knee and clutched a handful of soil. He crumbled it between his fingers and sifted it into the pit.

Sleep easy, my old friend. May the sun shine warmly on your face.

The church bell clanged from the bell tower. The discordant chime bellowed through the fog.

If you find her where you are going . . . tell her to wait for me at the doors of Tír na nÓg . . . one more time again.

The villagers' gazes weighed heavily upon his bent head. Aye, 'twas long past time for their suspicion and fear, he supposed. He should have known better than to linger in this tiny hamlet until all his seafaring friends lay scattered in the ground beneath him, their flesh eaten, their bones dust. But *she* had taught him too well; a healer could not leave a single man suffering. So he had stayed to ease the pain of the passing of the last of his aged companions into death.

Yet still he lived, *still* he lived—if one could call such an existence life. No warm hearth crackled for him in the hamlet at the base of the cliff. No soft-voiced woman peered out a crack in the door, or strained her ears for his footfall. No grandchildren sprawled on the hearth to plead for stories. And now, there was no longer anyone with whom to swap tales while the rain seeped softly through the thatched roof. No one with whom to reminisce about voyages to Venice and Rome, to Syria and Egypt, no one with whom to share a simple meal or a simple memory.

'Twas a good time to die.

Conaire heaved his broad-shouldered frame to its full height, not bothering to stoop and waddle, as he had for so many years. Let the wind scour the ash from his hair. Let the sea mist cleanse his face and hands of soot to uncover his unlined skin. Men saw what they expected to see; if today, they finally saw him as he was, there was naught he could do to disguise the truth. 'Twas the way of the world.

His fog-soaked cloak snapped behind him, as he turned his back to the villagers and strode into the swirling mists. The milky vapor engulfed him in an odd, welcoming warmth. He paused at the tip of the cliff and squinted down toward the white-capped sea carving the shores of Marseille. Above, rain-burdened clouds jostled in the sky. Soon, he thought, the twilight between light and dark would come—soon, the mist would be neither rain nor seawater, nor river nor well water. It would be the time between the times, as the Druids had once taught him, when the walls between the worlds grew as diaphanous as mist.

He nodded once to the glory of the ocean. He would choose a sea-death today. He would row his fishing boat out into the tempest, and challenge the water's fury. He closed his eyes, imagining the course of his coming death. The sting of liquid salt gorging his lungs. The flex and stretch of his muscles as he struggled against the inevitable suck into the ocean's womb. The last white-hot flash of agony, before the blood stopped pulsating in his temples and an unearthly warmth and darkness cradled him in silence.

He would see the light. He would approach it, drawn irresistibly to the glow of love and warmth and joy, like the welcoming arms of some primordial mother. He would hear the birds singing softly and the outline of a tree would emerge—a silver tree bathed in golden light. And he would know that this was *Tír na nÓg,* the beloved Otherworld.

Then he would hear the bells, tinkling like fairy music. He would race toward the chimes, race toward *her,* thinking *this* time it would be different—for hope was a tenacious plant which grew back no matter how many times it was cut. But just when he glimpsed the edge of her robes, just when he saw the tips of her fingers, outstretched for him, just when he detected the fragile scent of rainwater and honeysuckle that had always clung to her hair . . . the door would slam shut.

Then he would awaken, buried in the chill earth, with dirt clogging his nostrils and a winding sheet stifling his movements. Still smelling her, still sensing her presence, clinging to the feeble threads of the memory until the screams of his earthly body stripped him of the last fiber and left him with a different agony. Cold. Hunger. Pain.

Wretched life.

Conaire swathed his cape around his body and spun away from the edge of the cliff. He plodded through the cemetery, past the half-full grave. He no longer mourned the dead. His old friend had slipped through the door to a land of warmth and peace and pleasure. Now Conaire mourned for himself, for the hell the gods had forced upon him—the loneliness, the deceit, the fear in the eyes of men. It would always be like this. He would fool himself that he could be like other men, but then another lifetime would pass, the lies would begin, his disguise grow thinner, his friends die one by one . . . and he would try, once again, to leap the precipice that kept him from where he belonged, only to find himself bound to life again, forced to leave for another place, another existence, like a dozen lives before . . . all the same.

All but one.

A bolt of lightning cracked open the sky. Rain pelted his shoulders like angry tears, sluicing down the long-dried riverbed of his face. He had relived that single life until the fabric of the memory frayed like a storm-chewed fishing net. He wished he could forget. But the memories seized him in moments of distraction. Such was the wretched fate of a man whose soul lay in the grave.

He would never—*ever*—lose himself like that again, no matter where the road took him in the years ahead. For now he understood: He would have been better off if he had never known her—if he had never given away the full of his soul.

But it had been his first life, and he had been too young and too ignorant to guard his heart.

He had loved before he knew he was immortal.

And thus forever alone.

Part One

Erin (Ireland), 513 A.D.

One

"What's this? Are ye hiding from me, on such a fine, soft morning?" Brigid searched for movement between the crowded trunks of the gnarled oaks. "No sense of fair play, have ye? You can see me—but to my eyes, you're no more than will-o'-the-wisps." She tilted her head in challenge. "Now, an honest race . . . that would be more sporting of ye than playing hide-and-seek in the glade."

She raked up the hem of her linen tunic and darted deeper into the forest. The chill mists of the morning kissed her cheeks, and dusted droplets of dew through the blaze of her wind-whipped hair. The dawn nudged away the black folds of night, spraying the glade with uncertain silver light. Silence hovered over the woods, but for the patter of her swift feet and her soft, private laughter.

A secret smile curved her lips, as she sensed that she was no longer alone. She pretended she didn't notice their presence, for they were shy creatures, uneasy with her brazenness. She skimmed along, playfully avoiding the slick surface of protruding rocks and the moss-edged pools of rainwater scattered along the forest floor, her ears perked for the tinkling of their voices. Her unbound hair clung to her face and shoulders, and swept heavily along her back as she teased the creatures deeper into the woods. Soon, they grew bold enough to dart from the shelter of fern fronds and nestle in slim tufts of tall grass bursting from the bases of tree trunks. She heard their light footfalls amid the litter, pattering like raindrops trickling off the hollow palms of fresh leaves.

Brigid lifted her skirts and whirled, laughter bubbling out of her. "So you've come, have ye?" She spoke her challenge to the skies, so as not to frighten them away. "I knew you couldn't resist, not on a day like today. Come, let's see how swiftly you can race with me to Lough Riach!"

She bolted down the slope, setting her sights on the iron-gray surface of the lake gleaming through the dense fencing of trees. The air tickled her throat with sea salt. She sensed the *Sidh* quick on her heels, tumbling and rolling after her as fast as their fairy wings could take them. She bounded from tree root to tree root, squealing as she sprinted through a puddle and splattered her legs with mud. Her thick woolen cloak, sopping with gathered moisture, dragged upon her shoulders. Without a thought she twisted the brooch which pinned it around her, until the cloak tumbled upon the grass. She dashed forward, lightened, exhilarated because she knew she was winning the race.

"There! I've beaten you all!" She gripped the rough bark of an alder, which leaned over the peaty depths of the lough. She whirled, her cheeks flushed. "Shall we race again?"

A bush shivered, then stilled. A single leaf drifted down from the boughs. Empty mists eddied on the forest floor, and the predawn forest rang with silence.

Her smile faded. She tugged a strand of red-gold hair off her cheek and planted her fists on her hips. She had been too bold. Now they had hidden again, as skittish as field mice beneath the shadow of a hawk. She tilted her chin stubbornly. She had done nothing wrong—the air had sung in her ears and the wind had blown beneath her feet, and they had raced with her like birds! When would they learn that she was not like the others? Brigid of the Clan Morna was not afraid of the *Sidh*—and the *Sidh* had no reason to be afraid of her.

"You're like frightened old women, ye are." Brigid crouched

by the edge of the lake. She peered across its slate-smooth surface to the fog-shrouded outline of the opposite shore. "And with me, *me,* who's known ye for near one-and-twenty years, aye, since I was still on me Ma's breast! It makes no sense, I tell ye."

So she sat, as quiet and still as she could, waiting impatiently for the little people to return. Och, for the days of yore, when these creatures mingled with mortals as boldly as if there were no veils shimmering between them. But she was wishing for the stars, she was, for she had no memory of when the worlds intermingled so intimately. Since the churches and monasteries began sprouting atop the open altars of the Druids, it was as if the doors between the worlds had been sealed with stone and daub. Without the flux of air and light between them any longer, they drifted apart. Now, it was only in times like this, in the misty uncertainty between night and day, when the veils thinned and the *Sidh* dared to peep through. 'Twas her own good fortune that she could still sense the Otherworldly rustling and hear the *Sidh's* muffled voices beyond the shroud. Most of humanity had long been struck deaf and blind by the foreign priests.

She closed her eyes and took a deep breath of the charged air, summoning her wavering patience around her. Och, here she was, chiding the *Sidh* for their skittish ways, when it was *she* who had lost her senses, to be prancing about like a fey child long before dawn, so far from the protection of her hut. All night she had tossed and turned, as anxious and fretful as a caged thing, and this morning she'd woken with a fire in her blood, with no sense to it at all. She'd sooner stop the rain from falling, or the wind from blowing o'er the hills, than sit quietly in her smoky hut among her herbs and her spindles on a morning such as this.

The *Sidh* gathered again, restless and eager, their presence as vibrant as the buzzing of bees. Brigid opened her eyes and imagined she could see them, sparkling like tiny stars as they swarmed around her.

Aye, she thought. *Something is going to happen.*

The knowledge had hovered on the edges of her consciousness for days, as elusive as a fairy-child in the shadow of a church. The more she concentrated on it, the more swiftly it faded, but the certainty still tingled in her fingertips.

"So you've returned, have ye?" She slapped her hands free of soil as she stood up. "I won the race—and fairly, I did. It's a prize I'll be getting from ye—and a fine one, too. I'll have no more of your mischief. 'Tis high time for you to be showing me what's been putting this burn in me blood."

She waited. Nothing. Nothing but muted, tinkling laughter that faded into the sound of the wind winnowing through the leaves. Suddenly, a vision flashed through her head; a vision of a glen full of foxglove.

"Och, 'tis cruel, you are, to toy with me like I'm nothing but a cringing old priest." She strode back to where her cloak lay on the ground, then whirled the dew-drenched garment over her shoulders. "But if it's foxglove you'll be giving me, then so be it. I'll not have anyone—of this world or t'other—saying Brigid of the Clan Morna's an ungrateful wench."

The mists swirled close around her. Out of the silence, a feeble ringing sounded in the wind. The tenuous music beckoned her deeper into the woods, leading her unerringly to a fresh-bloomed thatch of foxglove. She plucked her fill and absently knitted the blossoms into a long chain, but the haunting melody did not stop. The high, thin sound thickened and grew louder, until she could distinguish the distant beat of drums and the hollow whine of reedpipes. 'Twas fairy music, played within a fairy castle, siphoning through the veils to lilt on earthly air.

"Aye, there's more to this than a bit of foxglove, there is." She tucked the fragile chain of blossoms in a calfskin bag that hung over one hip. "So, will ye finally lead me to the door of the Otherworld, then? Will ye finally welcome me in?"

The melody was vaguely familiar, part of an ancient, sacred ceremony—Brigid couldn't remember which one, for her priestess-training had ended when her mother died, leaving her with only a partial knowledge of the old ways. But Brigid's thighs and her arms, her feet and her fingers, the curve of her back— they all remembered the dance. She whirled deeper into the forest, kicking the frayed hem of her linen dress up with each step, swaying her way closer to the strain.

Then the music suddenly stopped, as if an iron door slammed shut in a mead hall.

Her skirts wrapped around her legs as she missed a step and faltered. Disappointment washed over her like a cold winter rain. Would they always lead her so close to their world, allow her to scent the perfume of their smoke-fires, only to slam closed the door? Would she always be left on the threshold, alone?

"Nay, lass, don't stop."

The unfamiliar voice echoed around her. She swirled and scanned the woods. She realized with a start that she stood in the midst of a perfect circle of aged oaks, which thrust out of the wild disarray of the forest. 'Twas a sacred altar of the Druids, overgrown and tangled with honeysuckle vines and thick with underbrush. Between two of the hallowed oaks loomed a man's hazy silhouette.

"Who goes there?" The grass rustled beneath her feet as she skittered backward. "Come forward and let yourself be known, by the gods."

He swaggered out of the uncertain mist. His purple, knee-length cloak hung loose from impossibly broad shoulders and swirled around strong, leather-bound legs. Just at the edge of the circle, he planted one booted foot on the risen root of a tree. He tossed the folds of his cloak over one shoulder, revealing a richly embroidered linen tunic stretched taut across his chest—a chest which bore the musculature of a man used to swinging the iron sword slung from his hip.

Och, this was not a *man,* though he had the shape of one. To call this creature a man was like to call a chieftain's best hunting dog a common cur.

"What's this?" she demanded. "Why did ye sneak up on a lass with nary a 'good day to ye'?"

" 'Tis not yet day." He made a sparse gesture to the indigo sky beyond the lacy bower of branches. "The night still hovers over us."

"Just because the moon's still showing her face in the sky, doesn't mean it's fitting to lurk in the bushes and leap out at a woman like ye did." She yanked her skirts up from the damp grass. "My life nearly left me body at the sight of ye."

"But your wits stayed sharp as a nettle, I noticed."

"A tongue is a woman's only weapon, it is."

"Sheathe it, lass. You've no reason to be afraid o' me."

"I'm *not* afraid." She knew better than to show fear. Men could smell it like a pungent oil on a woman's skin.

"No? You've the look of a startled fairy-child—any moment you'll disappear into the mists."

"I'm afraid of no *man.*" If this man had wanted to do her harm, he'd have done it by now. And she'd no need to fear for her maidenhead. She had known since her first moon-blood flow that she was destined for something greater, and no one could change the roll of fate. "You did appear out of the air, ye did, but I'll not be darting away like a rabbit seeing the shadow of a wolf."

His lips curled back to show a jaw full of strong teeth. She examined him boldly. He spoke the Irish, but with a strange and unfamiliar accent. A warrior, he was—the scratched and beaten bronze scabbard of his sword told her that. He had the boldness of a king. Yet she knew that no human warrior, much less a king, would wander unattended through the woods at such an hour, and she heard no others about.

Her heart gave a sudden leap. Her mother had once told her that the *Sídh* were just like humans, so much so that if one of them dared to nudge aside the veils, you could pass him in the woods and think him as mortal as yourself. Staring across the distance that separated them, she wondered if this magnificent creature was not of this world, but had somehow wandered through a tear in the veil to emerge bathed in Earthly light.

"Who are ye?" She jerked her head to the woods around them. "What business have ye in these lands?"

"You don't know me, lass?"

"Nay." She squinted at his features in the dim light. She knew every man within a day's ride of Lough Riach, for she had tended most of them through sickness or war wounds, and no woman could forget a man like this. He was not handsome. The bones of his face thrust bold and arrogant against his skin—a sculpted, mercilessly square jaw; high, prominent cheekbones. His brows, as black as a beetle's back, slashed uncompromisingly over deep-set eyes. His hair was his best feature, for it flowed full and thick and rich with auburn highlights to his shoulders. Yet it didn't seem to matter that he did not have the refined features of the most handsome of men. A life force crackled around him, like the heat and light and sparks of a raging bonfire.

She shook her head once. "Nay. I've never seen the likes of you."

"I'm a cattleman, from a clan to the north." He spread his arms regally, as if they stood within the circular walls of the royal *ráth* at Tara, and not in the midst of the woods. "I'm traveling to Clan Morna. I've a fine bull, the finest in Connacht." His eyes gleamed with merriment. "I'm looking to set him free on a new herd o' fresh young cows."

"So you're a common *bóaire,* are ye?" Her brows arched. Dim light gleamed off a braided golden torque set around his neck, a sign of great wealth and power. A fist-sized, silver, jeweled brooch cleaved to the breast of his cloak. If this man was a simple cattleman, then she was the legendary Queen Maeve herself. "Your cows must be bringing in a fearful amount of milk this season, *bóaire.*"

" 'Tis a potent bull I have, who sires many calves." He lifted his booted foot from the tree root and strode into the circle of trees. "You, lass, who are you?"

"You don't know me, do ye? Can ye not tell who I am by me trappings?" She spread open her heavy woolen *brat* to show the full length of her worn and mud-bespattered tunic underneath, the hem so tattered it revealed the full length of her calves. She twirled, letting the hem of her *brat* whirl around her shins, then she dipped low and bowed her head in mock obeisance. "I, sirrah, am the King of Morna's much-beloved daughter."

Her head was lowered, so all she saw were her dirty leather shoes and the crushed grass, but she sensed his mirth as one would sense the rising of the sun upon one's face.

"The moment I laid eyes upon you dancing like a fairy-sprite in the mists, I told myself, no common bondswoman, she. Nay, no smith's daughter. But what is the King of Morna's much-beloved daughter"—his lips twitched at the words—"doing dancing alone in the woods so early in the morn?"

She straightened and shrugged. "A king's daughter can do as she pleases."

"Have you no husband to keep you abed?"

"Husband!? Nay, and I'll be thanking the gods for that. What need have I for a husband to cook for and clean after and treat me like a slave?"

"A woman who dances like you shouldn't lack for company."

"I like me own company, thank ye very much."

"Then for whom did you dance, *bean sí?* "

Fairy woman. Och, she felt like one of the *Sídh* now, full enough of restive energy to raise her arms and fly. It had been so long since she'd had company she could actually *see,* someone she could speak to who would talk back! Was this why she had been wound as tight as wool around a spindle these past days? It felt like it, indeed—for lightning raced in her blood and thunder trembled in her bones. She wondered, fleetingly, if he were one of the legendary warriors of the Fian.

"I dance for myself, *bóaire.*" The soles of her feet tingled. She pranced a few light steps and whirled to the tune of her rushing blood. "I dance for me and for the glory of the morning, no more than that."

" 'Tis glad I am of that, for I've no stomach for killing before dawn."

Her dance stopped mid-step.

"I'd have killed the man—mortal or not," he explained, gripping the hilt of his sword, "who dared to deny you to me."

Anger inundated her edgy excitement. Och, the arrogance! Did this creature think, just because he found her unprotected in the woods, dancing alone, that she would fall into his arms like some loose-winged fairy sprite? Nay, not Brigid of the Clan Morna, by the gods. "There will be no killing here. No man can lay claim to me."

"Then the men of these parts are all blind or fools."

"The men of these parts know better than to give me trouble, they do." She was too proud to tell him that she had not lived among the villagers since she was banished from the tribe seven years ago. Instead, she shrugged one shoulder, letting the neckline of her tunic slip over the rounded limb. "I am my own mistress. I go where I will, say what I will. And I dance for whom I will."

His low and seductive laughter ignited an unfamiliar heat in her belly.

"You're laughing at me, are ye?"

"Nay, lass." He edged around the clearing, his sword gleaming dully in the growing dawn. "I'm pleased that you danced for me."

"I did no such thing!" The folds of her *brat* snapped as she showed him her back. "How like a man! Like a rooster who thinks the sun rises just to hear the sound of his crowing."

"You've a temper as fiery as your hair, wood sprite. 'Tis good. I like my women as bold as they are beautiful."

"Your women?" She slanted him a glance. "Is that what you're thinking now?"

"You'll be thinking it, too, by and by."

"Och, only in your dreaming mind! Such a big man ye are, all puffed up with your pride!"

" 'Tis true nonetheless."

"Is it now?" She scoured his form with her gaze. "And what would a king's daughter be doing dancing for a common cattleman?"

"Bondswoman or king's daughter, a woman so full o' passion must have a powerful need o' a man." He eddied one step closer. His bold gaze dared her to back away. "You *did* summon me here."

"It's a wonder your head doesn't explode with your arrogance. This meeting was not my work—'twas yours."

"My strength lies in my sword arm, not in magic. Had I the power to summon such a one as you, *bean sí,* I would have done it long ago."

Secretive tittering bubbled from the outskirts of the ring of oaks, and suddenly she knew for sure who had brought them together in the strange, misty morning. "Och, there's a bit of mischief afoot."

"Be it mischief or not, it's glad of our meeting, I am. I've a powerful wanting for you, lass."

His words robbed her of speech. No man had ever uttered such sentiments to her. Even when she had lived among the tribe, ripening into a woman, no man had ever courted her with pretty words. She had been feared as much, if not more, than her own priestess mother. She remembered many a day working in the corner of her hut, endlessly carding or spinning wool, listening enviously, head-cocked, to the flirtations of the others just outside the wattle-and-daub walls. For all his boundless arrogance, this man before her treated her like a woman, and not like a carrier of a plague. Her heart swelled at being *wanted,* even if only for a swift tumble in the dew.

She toyed with the herb sack hanging from her hip. Suddenly, she stopped and dug her fingers into the calfskin. Realization struck her dumb.

"What say you, woman?"

She glanced up. He had trailed a wide circle around her, like a warrior assessing the wiles of an unbroken horse. The enormity of the discovery descended upon her like the slow seeping of honey into a slice of barley bread.

The key to the door of the Otherworld lay in her hands.

"Come," he coaxed, his voice as soft as fox fur. "The day is fine, and my blood as hot as fire. Lie with me in the dawn."

She barely heard his offer. Possibilities whirled in her mind. Och, it would be glorious to go to the land of the *Sídh,* to live among the fairies. Perhaps her destiny lay therein, and not in the silent loneliness of these woods. It would be glorious to belong to one world, instead of forever living on the edges of two.

All she had to do was coax this warrior-king willingly to her side . . . and then capture his soul.

She lowered her eyes, as she had seen the other young girls do, when she was living in the *ráth.* She eddied around him, wary, weaving her web of enchantment. "A bold one, you are," she murmured, "to speak so plainly to me."

"I won't simper and grovel and spout false praise, like a poor bard at a king's table."

" 'Twould be a fine change from your swaggering. If your

loving is as blunt as your speech, sirrah, I'm thinking ye'll have
no more art than a bull."

A slow grin blossomed on his face. "What the bull lacks in
art, he makes up in other ways."

Her steps faltered as color washed her cheeks. "Can ye not
get your mind off your dangle for more than a moment?"

"It's nay more a dangle, but a sword at the ready."

She glanced at the iron sword lying against his thigh, and
ignored the other bulges of his body. "I wondered why a 'common cattleman' saw fit to carry such a mighty weapon."

"What matter? I wield it well."

"Too sure of yourself, I'm thinking."

"I always get what pleases me. One way or the other."

She tossed her head, feeling her hair flow like liquid fire down
her back. *Come closer,* she thought. *Come into my web.* "Would
ye take what's not freely given to ye?"

"Aye, if I'm wanting it badly enough."

As arrogant as a cock, he was, brash and bold and sure. She
could not suppress the smile which tugged at her lips. He looked
upon her as if she were a tasty morsel to nibble on before breaking the fast. Och, she should be frightened; she knew nothing
of him, and he stated his intentions boldly enough. A woman
could lose her soul, if she drew near such flames. But it was *he*
who should be frightened. For beneath the folds of her cloak,
she tugged at the ties of her calfskin sack and let the chain of
foxglove spill into her hand. Such a chance as this came once
in a hundred thousand lifetimes.

"You should not pluck a fruit before the branch willingly
gives it up," she warned, filling her palm with the knotted blossoms. In the ebb and flow of their wary circling, he had wandered
behind her; she refused to turn to him and thus show her fear.
"The taste of unripe fruit grows sour in your mouth."

"I like a bit o' tartness in my women."

"Do ye now?" She made a careless shrug. "Seems to me you've a belly full, then, and you've no need of me."

"At the sight o' you, lassie, it's like I've never touched a woman before."

"Och, you're quick with the answers, ye are." She turned her face to him as he rounded to her other side. "But I'm having none of your nonsense."

"Has no man ever sung your praises?"

"Not in so sweet a voice—but I'll listen to none of your deceiving. The emptier the drum, the louder the noise, and your rattling is near to deafening me."

He threw back his head and laughed, exposing the thick column of his throat. His laughter echoed through the woods, startling the *Sídh,* who hovered silent on the periphery, into utter silence. 'Twas a roaring bellow, fearless and full of mirth, the laugh of a high king or a war god. His eyes sparkled when he looked again upon her. "I'd wager a field full o' cows that many a man has been bloodied from tangling with your thornbush of a tongue, *bean sí."*

She tilted her chin, too proud to admit the truth, pleased nonetheless with his statement. "I see nary a scratch on ye, *bóaire."*

"I am not like other men." His gaze ran swiftly from her tousled red-gold hair to her muddy feet. "As you, clearly, are not like other women."

"And what would you be knowing about me, when ye've only just laid eyes on me?"

"Not nearly enough, but be sure o' this: Before this is done, I'll be knowing every sweet bit o' you."

An image flooded her mind, a forbidden, earthly image of the two of them wrapped in each other's limbs, his muscular arms around her, his hips pumping languorously against her spread thighs. . . . Her body tingled with prickly heat from the scalp of her head to the soles of her feet.

"Aye, lass." His voice dipped low and throaty. "It'll feel better than you can imagine."

In her momentary distraction, he had drawn swiftly and silently closer to her, so close that if she reached out, she could touch the fine weave of his knee-length linen *léine*. Her breath caught in her lungs. Coming so close to this man was like drawing close to the sun. His presence blazed upon her. Every blade of grass, every drooping leaf, stilled around her. She could no longer hear the patter of dew from the trees. It was as if the drops hung suspended in air, waiting for the meeting of these creatures of two worlds.

A thought flashed through her mind, swift and disconcerting. It was one thing for mortals of this world and the immortals of the *Sídh* to converse, it was another altogether for them to reach across the veils and touch. Now that the worlds had drifted so far apart, surely such a thing went against nature, surely such an act would ripple the smooth fabric of life and have consequences beyond the wrinkle of the moment. Hesitancy seized her by the throat. Her fingers froze over the chain of foxglove.

"Tell me your name, lass, or I shall kiss it out o' you."

Something rough and husky vibrated in his voice. There was an old saying, that to give a man your name was to give him a part of your soul. She felt the gossamer threads of her own web turning in upon her.

"I am called Brigid."

"Brigid." He rolled the flavor of the name in his mouth. " 'Tis a fitting name. The name of a goddess."

Suddenly, the distant clang of monastery bells pierced the air. The clamor reverberated through the deepest shadows of the woods. The *Sídh* disappeared like smoke dispersed by a sudden wind. Brigid's heart constricted—*Och, those wretched bells must* not *drive him away!* Her uncertainty dissolved. Swiftly, she seized his wrist and twined the chain of blossoms around it three times. She gripped the loose ends tightly until the last echo of bells vibrated into silence.

'Twas done. He remained, earthbound, before her.

Bemused, he turned over his hand and looked upon the bracelet. "What magic is this?"

"A chain of fairy foxglove." The blossoms looked pitifully weak around his muscular forearm, too fragile a chain to bind such a giant to the earth. "You're bound to me now. 'Tis an enchantment as old as time. You must do my bidding."

His chuckle jarred her ears. "You don't need spells and flowers for that, Brigid. You've put such a fire in me blood, that I'd willingly do your bidding, for no more than the price of a single look from you."

The breeze gusted, lifting her hair from her nape and blowing a rogue strand across her cheek. She did not raise her face, for a new suspicion blossomed in her mind. She felt the mist of his breath on her head. He radiated warmth and strength; he smelled as crisp and clean as any newly-bathed mortal man.

"Look at me."

The leaves rustled in the oaks, the grass and gorse beneath her feet crackled, though she didn't move. The clouds above shifted, growled, and released a spattering of rain. With a quiver in her heart, she lifted her lashes and dared to look upon him.

Something jolted her from within, like the strong kick of a full-term babe within the womb. White-hot lightning arced between them. Brigid curled her fingers over the chain of foxglove. The clear, silvery depths of his eyes were as familiar to her as the morning mists, as the expanse of the white-bright winter sky. She would have known this man anywhere, though she'd never laid eyes upon him before—not in this life.

"What enchantment is this? What are you? Fairy? Sprite?" He scraped his finger down her neck to rest on a throbbing pulse. "Nay, no sprite, this. Warm as any woman. Flesh and blood and passion."

He reached for her, and the foxglove chain slipped out of her hands. His touch burned, och, it burned, but it was not the searing, forbidden embrace of creatures of separate worlds. This was an Earthly fire, and she knew in that moment that all her enchantments were for naught. This was no gossamer creature of the Otherworld. His hands were tight on her shoulders, hard and determined and possessive. A warm tingling rushed through her blood, the liquid swell of an unfamiliar and glorious longing.

"You've the Sight." His eyes, those eyes of silver, burned like crackling lightning. "Aye, you have the power—your eyes could drain the soul from a man."

Her eyes. Dread flooded through her. He was a man. And she had forgotten her wretched eyes.

She struggled away from him, breaking the contact, stumbling back to glare at him at arm's length. "Are you the one who's afraid now, *bóaire?*"

"I'll never fear a wee bit o' a lass, even if she wields the power of ten Druids."

"Ye won't be fearing that your cows will leave off giving milk, or I'll strike ye blind or deaf, or bring a powerful storm to muddy your way?" She waved to someplace deep in the woods. "You won't be fearing that I'll steal the seed from your wretched bull?"

He made a gesture of scorn. "Why would you waste your power on such mischief?"

She said nothing; she could not tell him that the people of Morna blamed her for every calamity that struck the tribe.

"Aye, now I understand why you dance alone. The men of these parts are cowards. And Christians, too, I'd wager." He scraped his sword out of the scabbard and held out the gleaming length. Swirling, pagan designs etched the metal hilt. "Me and mine—we've not blinded ourselves to the ways of the world. And I fear nothing."

She knew it was true. He still dared to stare deep into her

eyes, unflinchingly. She clung to his gaze, waiting for his mask to fall and the true extent of his horror to show, but still, he met her gaze, unwavering, and a strange hope blossomed in her heart.

The *Sídh*, always full of mischief, had toyed with her by giving her foxglove and then leading her to this man. A chain of fairy foxglove would not bind a human to do her bidding. But there might be a gift in this meeting after all—for this was the first man she'd ever known, besides her brother, who could hold her gaze for more than one terrified moment.

"Who are ye?" she asked, huskier than before. "What are ye doing here?"

He sheathed the sword. "Aye, it seems neither one of us is who we claim to be."

" 'Tis not an answer, that."

Suddenly, she heard a voice in the forest. She started and scanned the circle of trees.

"My men search for me. I have been away too long." He thrust out his hand, wide-palmed and strong. "We are well met, Brigid. Come with me."

She skittered back from the sight of his hand. Her gaze flittered like a bird to the forest around them. She'd face one man; she'd not face a whole army. "I'll go nowhere with ye, not yet."

"Aye, you will. 'Twas fated, this meeting in the mists." He beckoned her with a regal curl of his fingers. "I command you to come with me."

She glared at him. "Speak to me like that, and I'll have none of ye."

"You'll have more than you've bargained for, lass."

Her retort died on her tongue, for the voice called out again, joined by others, louder, closer, and she heard distinctly the name of the man they summoned.

Conaire.

She dug her fingers into the furrowed ridges of the tree bark.

She froze and stared at the man with new eyes. His braid of a torque captured the first golden rays of the sun.

Suddenly she knew who stood before her.

Och, cruel gods, so cruel, to give and then snatch away . . .

"Conaire of Ulster." She spit the name at him. "You've come to claim Morna, haven't you, cur of the Uí Néill?"

A corner of his lips curled. "Finally you know my name."

"Aye, and a curse upon it!"

She swirled and raced into the dying mists, her feet slipping over the dew-cooled grass. She grasped her skirts in her hands, hiking them away from the length of her scratched and muddy legs. The thunder of her heart pounded in her ears. She waited for the clench of his hand on her neck.

But he didn't follow. He called out to her—a sharp, angry bark. The possessive sound of her name on his lips lingered in her mind long after the echo faded into silence.

Steel clanged against steel. Stark morning light flashed like lightning off two long, lethal blades. Conaire roared with each swing of his heavy sword, the bulk of his frame absorbing the powerful impact of blade against blade before he pulled back, whirled the weighty weapon over his head, and swung anew. Sweat stained the wool of his tunic and dripped off his chin, but his legs stayed as firm and immobile as century-old oaks. His barrel-chested adversary staggered under each mighty blow.

"Are you man or child?" Conaire swung anew, and his opponent's knees buckled. *"Fight,* damn you."

Blades clashed. The warrior stumbled back. Mead sloshed onto the sleeve of his *léine* as Conaire barreled through the crowd of observers to relentlessly drive his opponent against the shoulder-high rock wall of the ring-fort. Still Conaire slashed, fiercely, his teeth bared. The iron of his weapon shattered beneath a blow. His opponent slipped and skidded in the mud, ducking the splinters of hot metal flying through the air. Conaire thrust the jagged edge of his broken sword against his pale neck.

"Yield to your better, swineherd."

The fallen warrior huddled against the wall, his breathing harsh. He opened his hands in defeat, and his sword clattered to the ground. The people of the Clan Morna who had paused in their work to watch the sparring of their new *rí ruirech,* or over-king, stood silently, while Conaire's men cheered and drunkenly sloshed their wooden cups of ale. Conaire tossed his broken weapon aside and tested his opponent's for weight and balance. A rivulet of something hot and wet slid down his face, and pooled in the corner of his mouth.

"Who will spar with me next?" He scanned the surrounding crowd, searching among the artisans, the cattlemen in their bright green woolen cloaks, and the dark Pict slaves in their rags and chains, for the sword-bearing warriors of the Clan Morna. Even the most powerful-looking among them averted their eyes like maidens on their first foray to the Lughnasa fires.

"You'll not find another to fight ye, Conaire of Ulster." The king of the Clan Morna spoke from a stump near the entrance to his hut, flanked by two black-robed priests. His long, white hair blazed like snow against the folds of his purple cloak, and his blue eyes glittered more harshly than the enormous jeweled brooch lodged at his throat. "You've bested three of our finest warriors. 'Tis plain to see why the Uí Néill chose such a strong champion to do their warring. It's no wonder Connacht and Leinster have lost so much land and cattle to that clan these past years."

"Fat, your men are, as fat as autumn cows." Conaire wiped the sword on his mud-bespattered tunic, then hefted it to the ready. "Is there not one among you who is not as weak as a woman?"

"My men do be valuing their swords too highly to challenge ye." The old man gripped the cross hanging around his neck, as

Conaire fixed him with his wild-eyed glare. "You have lived up to your reputation, Conaire *dochloíte*. No small comfort it is, to know that my son died fighting a man who is as invincible as his own legend."

"Had I known," Conaire snapped, "on that day when I fought for the Uí Néill, and your son for the enemies of the Uí Néill, that he'd be the only worthy opponent in this tribe, I'd have spared his life, just so I'd have some sport when I came to claim Morna as my own."

The old man's shoulders stiffened. "My son's blood ran with the pride of generations of chieftains. He served Morna honorably. He would not have allowed you to dishonor him in such a way."

"Then I would have told the High King to grant me the overlordship of some *other* tribe. Your clan was not the only clan to fall that day to the Uí Néill." He scanned the gathered warriors of Morna, all immobile but for lowered and thundering brows. There wasn't a one of them Conaire feared on the battlefield. He silently taunted them, sneering at their striped and checkered cloaks, their dyed eyebrows, and their oiled and frizzed hair. He and his men were as safe here as if they were on Tara hill with the powerful Uí Néill clan, or home among their own Ulster tribes.

He shoved his sword in its scabbard. "Cowards, all o' you. I rule nothing but a tribe full of women, children, and *cowards*."

He snatched his cloak from the pile of stones that formed the outer fencing of the large *ráth,* and whirled it over his shoulders as he headed out of the enclosure. His footsteps pounded hollowly on the wooden bridge laid over the shallow ditch, then drove deep imprints into the muddied earth.

Conaire marched up the hill at a pace fast enough to match the thunder of his heart. By the Club of the Dagdá, was there no man in the whole province of Connacht to give him a fight worth the time? 'Twas plain to see why the Clan Morna did not resist when he and his Ulstermen rode over the rise three days ago to claim the overlordship due to him—all the clan's finest warriors had died proudly, on the battlefield. All that remained were timid girls draped in the torques and scabbards of men.

He crushed dandelions and thistles beneath his leather-bound feet. A breeze topped the rise and thrust cool fingers through his hair. The wind swept away the stench of blacksmith's fires and the fetid odor of livestock rising from the *ráth* nestled below, near the shores of Lough Riach. He filled his lungs, then exhaled to get the stink of other men's fear out of his nostrils.

The whole rolling green expanse of his new kingdom lay before him. Herds of plump cattle dotted the lush hillsides and grassy valleys. Mirror-smooth lakes and trickling streams glimmered from behind clusters of apple trees, laden with unripe fruit. A herd of sleek, red deer grazed fearlessly near the protection of the woods. All this was conquered without a fight; all this was his. He scanned the bristling northern forest emerging from the next valley, the dense woods through which he and his men had traveled. Therein lie the true burn in his blood—therein hid his next conquest.

A woman with hair the color of burnished gold and skin like cream. A woman whose chin tilted like that of a queen, and whose tongue could slice a bard's wit into ribbons. A woman whose eyes knew all the secrets of the world. One brief encounter in the pre-dawn light, and her angular features, the reedy length of her body, the deep, husky timbre of her voice, all clung to his memory like the scent of honeysuckle. His loins had burned for her for three days.

But she had disappeared into the mists, like some creature of the Otherworld.

A twig snapped behind him. The steel of his sword rang as he wrenched it from his girdle and whirled to face his pursuer.

A wooden cup tumbled to the earth, spilling amber liquid into the ground.

"Aye, now look what you've done!" Aidan, Conaire's second-in-command, grimaced at the waste, and glared at Conaire through narrowed hazel eyes. "Now there's only one cup o' heath mead, and you'll be wanting that, I'm sure!"

Conaire sheathed his sword in one swift, angry move. "You'll lose your head one o' these days sneaking up on me, foster-brother."

"I'd say it's not the sneaking that's got you strung as tight as a lyre. 'Tis spoiling for a fight, you are."

Conaire grabbed the brimming cup of ale. He quaffed the potent brew in one gulp and thrust the empty vessel at Aidan's chest. "That old king spread his arms for us as a whore would spread her legs; I trust him not—there's a battle yet to come."

"Wage it when it comes, then." Aidan squinted into the cup, then tipped it upside down to gulp the remaining drops. "Here and now, there's ale a-plenty, and many a widowed Morna wench looking to share her pallet."

"You grow soft in this place."

"I'll grow as fat as a bull, if I've my way of it. The old king's free enough with his food and ale and women."

"Like a calf led to slaughter, you are." Conaire paced, while the tip of his sword traced thin furrows in the ground. "The women are probably poxed, the ale poisoned, the food rotting and wormed. You could choke to death on the false kindness."

"I don't see you refusing the food nor the ale," Aidan remarked, "though there's been a powerful lot o' wondering why you haven't mounted any o' the bondswomen. I lost a fine bit o' cattle wagering that you'd be halfway through the tribe by now."

"They're all as dry as winter grass."

"She plagues you still, doesn't she?"

Conaire's jaw tightened. His abstinence had not gone unnoticed, but he thought the reason for it might. He kept searching the saucy-eyed bondswomen who served meals in the mead hall, for one with red-gold hair and swirling green eyes—in vain.

"By the gods, we searched for her 'til the sun was high." Aidan's cloak flapped with the waving of his arms. "We found naught a thread, not a whisper of her passing—"

"She's hiding in those woods."

"Aye, perhaps so, but a fairy can hide in many a place and drive a man mad with wanting . . ."

" 'Twas no fairy I saw." Conaire seized Aidan's flailing arm and dug his fingers into the ruddy flesh. " 'Twas a woman, as much flesh and blood as you or me."

"Dancing in the woods? With no one but the will-o'-the-wisps and the *Sídh?*" Aidan tried to wrench his arm away, in vain. "See sense, Conaire. No man saw her nor heard her but you, not even the footsteps of her passing, and the ground as wet as a bog."

Conaire pushed him away and sent the man reeling. He and Aidan had known each other since they were boys, had fought beside each other in a hundred battles, had made a thousand cattle raids, wenched and drank and sparred together. Such closeness brought privileges—but now Conaire had no patience for it. Since he had first laid eyes on the lass, his blood burned to find her again.

"She's got you by the rod, she does." Aidan stumbled to his feet, the butt of his sword clanging against his leather and metal girdle. "The people of the clan say she doesn't exist."

"She is of Morna—else she would not have run away when she heard my name." He sneered down at the circular *ráth,* the fields extending beyond it like the spokes of a wheel, the scattering of tiny thatched huts. "They make the sign of the cross at the mention of her name. 'Tis proof she exists, in one form or another."

"Well, unless the old badger is hiding some of the women in the food caves, there's no mortal woman here who looks like the wench you saw." Aidan squinted at him. "If there were, I'd have found her by now, for you know 'tis I who can sniff out the fairest wench in any tribe."

Conaire's eyes darkened to black. "If you value your head, walk a wide circle around her."

"Aye, she has bewitched you, if you be threatening your own foster-brother over a woman." Aidan glanced at Conaire's forehead. "Well, bewitched or not, I'll not be fighting a wounded man."

Conaire sensed the blood running down his face, but he did not deign to touch the wound.

"Two-fingers' width over, and that shard would have blinded you in one eye." Aidan grinned, revealing a wide gap in his yellowed teeth beneath his drooping mustache. "The laws forbid a blind man from ruling. That would be the end of all those dreams of high kingship."

" 'Twould be the last of your hopes of drinking wine in the mead hall of Tara hill, as well."

"Aye, which is why I sent for a woman to tend you." He jerked his head at an old woman who labored her way up the slope. "I've a great thirst to spend my old age drinking on the hill of the high kings of all Erin. I've fought at your back for too long, Conaire—I've no liking to see you defeated by a stray bit o' sword . . . or by some fairy enchantment."

Conaire's *brat* snapped behind him as he swirled away. He peered off toward the forests, willing it to bring forth its secrets, to bring forth the woman who haunted him both awake and asleep. " 'Tis no enchantment."

"Aye, 'tis. She's running from you like no other woman has, and so you're wantin' her all the more." Aidan slapped him on the shoulder. "Conaire, I know you well. We shared the same wetnurse's teat, we did, and that when we were too wee to fully enjoy it—"

"No man knows me, Aidan. Not even you, the blood son of

my foster-father." Conaire turned the full intensity of his gaze upon him. "You know the name of your father—but who is mine?"

Aidan choked on his own spittle. "Begorra, what are you doing, asking me such questions? You know not even the Druids of Ulster can give you the answer to that. Your mother took the secret to her grave."

"And no man has ever claimed me his son."

"Your father might have died before he saw you rise to power." Aidan leaned toward him, disbelief raising his brows. "Is this what's been rattling in your head these past days? Can you not put a stop to it? We've talked o' this all our lives, until there's no more talking to do."

"I'll talk of it," Conaire growled, "until I know who lay with my mother in the circle of the Samhain fires—"

"Do not speak o' it." Aidan waved his arms to hush him. "Are you mad? Are you beginning to believe what they all say o' you?"

"Aye, perhaps I am." Conaire clutched the hilt of his sword, flexing his hand over the fit. "Know you of any other reason why no other man has ever beaten me in single combat, why no wound has ever bled me dry?" He clutched a handful of his auburn hair. "Why no gray hair has ever grown on my head, nor lines wrinkle my face, though we are of an age, foster-brother?"

"And how would I be knowing why a man is cursed with age and another not? Mayhap it's all the ale you drink, or the meat you eat, or the women you tumble, that keeps you looking like a man o' five-and-twenty winters." Aidan planted meaty fists upon his brass-studded girdle. "And it'll be a fine day when you forget all the babble of ignorant sots, and stop looking past the length of your sword arm for the reason for your good fortune."

"*She* knows."

"The fairy?" Aidan sputtered. "That knock on the head has made you daft."

"I saw it in her eyes."

"Well, if it pleases you to think this creature knows the mysteries o' your birth, then I'll not be talking you out of it." Aidan sank down to the ground and squinted at the woman who approached. "Thank the gods you're here, woman. Stitch 'im up and stop 'im from sputtering any more dribble."

With a swirl of his cloak, Conaire sat upon the ground and with a single, royal gesture summoned the old woman to tend him. She swabbed at his temple with a damp piece of linen as he gazed northward, brooding.

Mayhap Aidan was right. What else but an enchantment, this queer burn for one woman? Before arriving on the shores of Lough Riach, he had tumbled willing bondswomen as often as most men took meals—and then went on to think of more important things. There were tribes to conquer, cattle to steal from clans too weak to hold them, battles to be won . . . a world begging for the tread of his feet. Three days ago, he had won a hard-earned kingship. Yet while the bounty of the lands of the Clan Morna lay spread out before him, all he could think about was finding and possessing the woman who had wrapped foxglove around his wrist in the misty light of the morning.

He tugged up the sleeve of his *léine*. The chain of blossoms crumbled around his wrist. He fingered the dried leaves until a few fell to dust.

The old woman cackled. "Now I know why ye scorn the ladies of Morna so, my lord."

The old woman grinned, showing a single, gnarled tooth in a cavernous mouth. One eye, quick and roving and as bright a blue as the springtime sky, crinkled at him. The other remained milky, glazed over, and fixed.

" 'Tis an old enchantment. Older than myself, my lord." She paused in cleaning his wound and scratched a nit in her head of scraggly gray hair. "When I was a lass, too many years ago t'count, we used to wrap a chain of fairy foxglove 'round the arm of the man we wanted as a husband, though 'tis said it was once used to capture fairies and the like. There's no more talk of that in these parts."

Conaire passed his gaze over her. A simple iron pin held her dun-colored, threadbare cloak closed against her breast, marking her of no consequence in the clan. "Who are you, woman?"

"Me name's Glenna." She pointed a gnarled finger toward the south. "I live in the last hut, beyond the copse of trees."

Conaire saw the hut, isolated and alone, some distance from the rest of the settlement. He had made a point to search it, but it had been empty.

"I was out with the cows when ye searched." She re-wet the linen cloth and wiped new blood off his face. "I hear tell you and your men follow the old ways, my lord."

He tugged on the foxglove. "What do you know of this that my Druids don't?"

"That chain binds you to the one who caught you—ye must answer her every demand."

Aidan rose from his dozing with a yelp. "D'you hear that, Conaire? Guard your cattle, lest the creature, wherever she hides, steals the last calf away from you and trades it for thread and cloth and golden baubles."

"Must be a fool of a lass, to hide herself from a man as fine as ye, my lord." The old woman wiped a fresh drop of blood off his jaw. "There's not a woman in the clan who'd balk at sharing your cloak."

"This one wants more than his cloak," Aidan interjected. "She's stealing his wits, as well."

"Fie on you," the old woman retorted. "Do you even know the lass?"

"Do you?"

"I know every woman in the tribe. Brought most of them into the world. Mayhap, if ye describe the lass to me, I can bring her to ye."

"Aye, you old witch," Aidan sneered, "and soon you'll be promising pots o' gold—"

"Red-gold hair she has." Conaire seized the old woman's gaze. "She's seen no more than twenty summers. Her clothes were those of a common bondswoman."

"Her eyes," the old woman whispered, "did they swirl like the green depths of Lough Riach?"

Conaire paused, remembering the sight of her amid the bower of oaks, remembering the way her gaze sucked and tugged at his senses.

"Aye, I feared as much." The woman squeezed blood out of the wet linen. "I know her my lord, if ye met her in yonder woods."

Conaire's hand shot out. His fingers wrapped around the old woman's arm.

"Mercy, my lord! Me bones are as dry as sticks."

He stood up, dragging the woman with him. The stench of cows and sour milk filled his nostrils. "Tell me her name."

"Oh, my lord, 'tis forbidden to speak it—"

"Her name."

The old woman sank to her knees, trembling. "She's called Brigid."

Aidan stumbled to his feet. "By the gods. . . . So she's not a fairy."

"They call her *cailleach*—witch," Glenna sputtered.

"Bring me to her."

"I don't know the manner of your meeting, me lord, but she may not be welcoming ye into her home."

Conaire scowled down at her.

"She's the king's daughter," she blurted. "And you, my lord, have killed her only brother."

Two

Brigid's eyes danced with mirth. She twitched a willow switch at the weasel-like creature crouched at her feet, teasing the sleek, black pine marten with a tuft of hanging fur. The little tree-cat swatted at it. With a flick of her wrist, Brigid made the fur jump. The tree-cat leapt back, uncertain, its back arched and its black eyes bright and wary. Then it crouched belly down in the dew-laden grass, ears perked, watching.

"Don't ye want it, *maoineach,* my precious?"

She flicked the bit of fur over the marten's head. The creature shot up on its hind legs and cuffed it. He tumbled on his back, then twisted his sleek body to all fours to bound up again in pursuit of the elusive tuft. Brigid twirled in a little circle around him, mimicking his movements, her laughter riding on the gentle breeze.

"Silly little tree-cat." Brigid dipped down and scratched the marten behind its pointed ears. The half-wild creature succumbed to her touch, his beady eyes fixed on the elusive fur. "Since you were a wee, wounded little kitten we've been playing this game. A body'd think you'd have the sense to know by now that it's not mouse."

Brigid's fingers stilled in the creature's glossy pelt. The sun slanted down through a break in the lush greenery to pool in a little clearing in front of her hut. Though the gentle rays warmed her hair, a cold prickle of foreknowledge tickled the nape of her neck.

Och, she was being foolish. No one disturbed these woods but she; the birds still chattered their summer melodies in the boughs above. Had someone approached, surely she'd have long heard the intruder crashing through the brambles and hedges she'd laid along the path by the stream.

"Och, I've less sense than ye, I have," she muttered, as the pine marten leapt from under her hand and embedded its claws deep into the tuft. "Don't I know well enough how men run from me eyes? 'Tis folly to think that *this* man is any different." She lowered her voice. "And it's a fool, I am, to even be thinking on it. It's disrespect for the dead."

Fur rasped her leg as the pine marten squealed and raced away into the woods.

"Good morrow to you, Brigid."

As unpredictable and uncontrollable as it was, her Sight never failed her. She straightened and wiped the palm of her hands on the ragged cloth of her *léine* as she turned to face him.

He stood slope-shouldered on the shadowed edge of the clearing, like the sight of the sun burning through a cloud. The golden swirls and vines embroidered on his knee-length tunic shimmered against the fine linen. A curious, jeweled brooch girding his three-colored cloak glistened boldly against the scarlet, blue and green woolen folds. Those folds draped his right shoulder, exposing the wide gold band which encircled the powerful bulge of his upper arm, gleaming the same red-gold as the thick twisted torque around his neck.

The brassy sunshine dappled over him as he swaggered deeper into the clearing. "No words o' welcome for your new over-king, lass?"

She folded her arms across her chest and granted him her profile. "I've no words at all for the likes of ye."

His laughter mocked her. "Aye, you do. Your head's near to bursting with them."

"I'll not have me tongue cut out of me head for saying such things to my *rí ruirech.*"

"I've got better plans for your tongue than that."

Her eyes narrowed as he entered the shade of her hut. Three days of playing cat-and-mouse with the warriors he sent to search for her hadn't deflated the swell of his arrogance. " 'Tis brazen and shameless, ye are, to speak such a way to me, when you be knowing who you are, and who I am."

"I am the same man, and you the same woman, as the morning I watched you dancing in the mists."

"Then, you were on to telling me you were a common *bóaire,*" she retorted, "passing through the woods. I did not know then that you were the wretched Ulsterman who led the Uí Néill against me brother Niall."

He planted a hand on one of the posts of her hut, flexing the bare length of his corded forearm. "The wind must carry the news, if it found its way so deep into the forests."

"Did you think I wouldn't know such a thing?" A flash of memory assaulted her, of the last time she saw Niall striding around this very clearing, so full of pride, swinging his sword, with his cloak whirling around him, his blue eyes glowing as bright as the sky. "Me brother could not stop talking about ye before he went off to battle. 'I'm going to fight Conaire *dochloíte,*' he said. Conaire the invincible. He swore to cut ye down with one stroke, he did."

"I remember him. A wild sword-swing he had."

"Do ye remember killing him?"

The post groaned as Conaire unburdened it of his weight. "Three tribes of Connacht and ten of Leinster fought against my Ulstermen and two hundred of the Uí Néill. Any man could have swung the deathblow."

Unwittingly, the memory of Niall's death-vision rose. She saw him on the rain-drenched battlefield, his hair matted with blood and gore, his arm outstretched, and his white fingers curled around the hilt of the sword of Morna. Now, she recognized the giant form casting a shadow over Niall's corpse. "I've ways of knowing things without a body telling me."

"Then 'twas fated, his death."

"Knowing what happened and knowing 'twas fated doesn't soften me to the man who swung the deathblow, Conaire of Ulster."

"It was I who wielded the sword, aye, but 'tis your father who bears the blame. Your father chose wrongly when he threw in his lot with the Leinstermen who plague the Uí Néill like fleas on a hound's back."

"Och, no man of Morna's afraid of the Uí Néill." Her chin rose to the treetops. "Me father fought with Connacht when the Uí Néill stole the High Kingship of Erin from the kings of Connacht. We've no love for you and your kind here."

"If your father had kept his peace, High King Murchertach would have not sent me to defeat the Leinstermen, nor have sent me here to carve a kingdom from the defeated. 'Twas your father's folly that caused your brother's death—"

"Nay, 'twas *ye*." She turned her back to him, to hide the tears shamefully pricking her eyes. " 'Twas as if you thrust the sword through me own heart."

"He died a warrior's death, woman." Frustration threaded his words. "He died face-forward, his sword clenched in his hand."

"I should be grateful to ye for that?"

" 'Tis a prouder fate for a man than rotting away with hunger or old age."

She knew it was true. Niall had been a warrior. A warrior could ask for no better death than at the hands of the champion of the Uí Néill. But that was a man's code, a man's comfort, and she drew little solace from it.

"If I could take the stroke back, woman, I would. Aye," he nodded, as she turned to glare at him. "Your brother was the only one in the whole o' the clan with any fire in his belly—"

"Now you insult me tribe *and* me brother." She jerked her skirt away from him, though he was nowhere near her. "He'd sooner spit in your face than accept your pity."

"Then no man could have stopped him from dying that day on the field, and my sword was naught but the deliverer of the gods' will."

His words rang true, but she did not want to hear them. She had known Niall's death was fated long before he went to war. She had cried hot tears when the vision first came to her, but she knew no gnashing nor wailing could change the course of events. Since she was a wee child, she'd learned to use the foreknowledge to prepare for what was to come. Like the flooding of the valley one spring, when she had known barely ten summers. Like the Uí Néill cattle thieves, who tried to steal an entire Morna herd on the southern slopes. Like her and her mother's banishment from the clan. Her mother's long and lingering death.

Then she admitted that it was not the loss of her brother that made her so angry at Conaire. She had bade her farewell to Niall, a tender parting the gods allowed because of the vision. 'Twas the warring of her own spirit that made her bark and spit like a fevered dog. This man came to Lough Riach a conqueror of all she held dear—an arrogant, murdering warrior. She should hate him. But hate was not among the strange emotions born that morning in the sacred grove, emotions even now shimmering between them like the brilliant rays of the sun.

Forbidden emotions, they were, for she was destined for another.

"If the sweetness o' my tongue can't smooth your ruffled feathers, lass, then I'll appeal to your woman's soft nature." He nudged a swollen wound on his temple, clogged with congealed blood. "Some one-eyed hag told me you are the best healer south of Cruachan."

The wound blossomed on his head purple and tender. It

needed a good soaking and stitching, if it were to heal properly. Anger flashed in her—*I should let it fester and rot, I should let him go about life with a scar marring his wretched face*—but the fury came and left like the flare of a comet across the sky. She was a healer to her core; she could not deny his request.

"King or no king, I'll not be healing ye for nothing." She dared to meet his unnerving gaze. "There's little goodness for you in me heart, and soon the winter'll be here, and I've no liking to starve."

"Name your price. The over-king of Morna can pay well for your services."

"Och, I wager he can, paying me with me own clan's cattle."

"I'll pay you with me own heifers, or whatever you'll be taking for the healing."

She crossed her arms and peered at him through narrowed eyes. He was a tall, broad-shouldered man, and she could think of a hundred things that he could be doing with those brawny copper muscles around and about the hut. Since Niall left for battle, the pile of firewood had sunk near to the ground, and the thatch lolled off the back of her roof like an idiot's tongue. She'd not had a taste of fresh boar since Niall's last hunt, and her mouth watered at the thought of another batch of honey mead. Och, she'd make this man pay a king's share, she would, and she'd feel no shame in it. 'Twould be an *eric* for the death of her brother—and she'd add a large honor-price on top of the fine. 'Twould be the only justice she'd ever get for the loss of Niall.

She gestured sharply to a well-worn tree stump by the door of her hut. "Sit down. A lass could get dizzy looking up at ye. I'll think on a proper price, I will, while I clean your wound."

She brushed past him and felt the rumble of laughter in his chest. Elbowing him away, she stepped into the shade of her hut and stopped inside the door. It was as hot as an anvil in the clearing—beads of sweat slithered between her breasts and pooled in the hollow of her back—and the coolness of her hut set her skin a-chill. She tugged down a few dried herbs which dangled from the roof of her hut and spiced the smoky air. She tossed a cluster of twigs upon the hot stones in the dying center hearth fire, blowing upon them until the branches caught flame. She set a pot on a tripod above it, as curls of dusky smoke rose and slipped out the smoke-hole in the roof.

She emerged into the sunshine some time later, and wordlessly handed him warm porridge sprinkled with purple sloes and a bladder which contained the last of her precious mead. She might have little to call her own, but she was a Celtic king's daughter and would give food and drink to any who came to her door. He devoured the offering with gusto, as she crushed some dried herbs with mortar and pestle and tried to thread her one precious silver needle. She wondered if he even knew what he was eating, or if she could have served him grass and muddy lake water just as well and saved her stores.

On the third try, she finally threaded the needle. Och, she felt like a field mouse under a hawk's nest, the way his gaze followed her every move. Jabbing the pin through the sleeve of her unbleached linen *léine,* she grabbed a wide, wooden bowl and headed toward the stream. She returned through the thin woods, carrying the bowl against her hip, full of the cool spring water. She wondered what magic this was, that a man's eyes could probe her as palpably as the branches brushing her legs.

Some of the water sloshed and dampened her hip, and she cursed beneath her breath at the icy flow. "Have ye no better thing to do, than burn holes in me back?"

"Any more holes in your *léine,* lass, and you'll not be wearing it at all."

Her chin rose a fraction. She had no sheep, and the people of the clan Morna were reluctant to part with the wool the women worked so hard to card and spin, even for the price of her healing. It was her Ma's dress she wore, and Ma gone these past five years, and she'd had none to replace it. She placed the bowl on the ground, crouched beside it, and threw the crushed herbs within.

"How did ye find me here?" She stirred the mixture vigorously with a yew-wood stick. "With me working day and night to keep the path hidden from the ignorant, I thought no man'd ever find it who wasn't led."

"You gave yourself away with your talk and your laughter."

She frowned. 'Twas an old habit, talking to herself in the midst of the woods. She craved the sound of a human voice, even if it was only the echo of her own. "And what made ye so sure you'd be welcomed here, wounded or no?"

"I have a way o' making myself welcome to women."

"Och, still braying like an ass."

He chuckled and tossed the empty bowl of porridge at his feet, then wiped his mouth on his knotted forearm. " 'Tis no wonder the people of Clan Morna fear to speak your name. You've more barbs than a hedgerow."

"Aye, and good for me that I have, I'm thinking. Is that how you found my hut, then, charming it out of a loose-skirted bondswoman?"

"There's only one skirt I'm looking to get under, lass."

"Aye, well don't be getting your blood up, for rags or no, this *léine* is stayin' down and about me legs."

"Is it now?" With an arrogant flip of his wrist, he tugged his fist-sized brooch off his brilliant cloak and tossed it in the dirt. The fine wool slithered down his broad back to pool around his hips. "I wouldn't wager any cattle on that."

She felt the heat of his body like a Lughnasa fire, and though they sat a good three paces apart, she could smell the man-scent of him; sunlight and sweat and steel. "Are ye going to tell me how ye found your way here, or are ye going to blather about until your lips hang loose from all the work?"

He lifted the mead-skin high and sucked the bladder dry. She saw the gleam of the golden drops clinging to the dark bristle of his chin. " 'Twas easier to defeat your clan's warriors on the field of battle than find out who you were. I had to rip your identity from the throat of some one-eyed hag."

"Glenna? Why would that gentle soul be hiding me name from ye?"

"The same reason why every last man in Morna denied that you existed—even when I held my sword to their throats."

The stick clattered as it fell into the bowl. The herb brew sloshed over the rim.

"I'll be wanting to know, Brigid, what the king of Morna's only remaining child is doing living in rags alone in the woods. And I'll be wanting to know why it's forbidden to speak your name."

"So it's grown as bad as that, has it?" She dug her fingers into a ragged swath of stained linen and dunked it into the cloudy herb mixture, sloshing it around with more force than was necessary. "Och, that explains the honey, then. I suppose it was too much to expect them to give it out of the goodness of their hearts. I suppose I'd sooner see cows fly than see them change."

"You're speaking nonsense."

"I've got you to thank for a pot of fresh heather-honey, Conaire of Ulster. Your sword put the fear of the gods in them." She lifted the linen and wrung the water out of it. "Yesterday I passed by the sacred pool near the shores of Lough Riach, and wasn't there a pot of the finest honey you've ever tasted, just waiting by the edge? Now, if it were Lughnasa day, or Imbolc, or Beltaine or Samhain, it'd be no surprise at all, for on those sacred days they all sneak out from beneath the eyes of their priests and lay their mutton and mead and cream by the pool, as they did in the old days, though I think they've all forgotten the reason for it."

"Nay, they haven't." Conaire squeezed the leathery neck of the mead-skin. "They bring gifts to appease an angry goddess."

"They bring gifts so I won't make their cows leave off milking, or curse their unborn children with twisted limbs or blinded eyes, as if I would ever do such a thing, even if I knew the way of it. Their fear has fed me for seven years."

She approached him with the damp linen. She felt his perusal upon her body like the kiss of the sun. She brushed his blood-matted hair away from the cut. Her fingertips tingled as she touched his skin, as she threaded them through his hair which gleamed like the warm, rich wine the priests craved so, and which felt as soft against her palm as the finest brushed wool.

Och, had it been so long since she had touched another human being, that she had forgotten the feel of a man's skin? The heat and bristled texture of it, the faint, salt-sweet scent, the swift pump of blood close beneath the surface? The dampness of clear sweat slicked her fingers, as she traced his smooth brow. His eyes gleamed up at her like the smoky surface of a shaded, sacred pool—and words barely born faded and died in her throat.

A faint buzzing filled her ears. His exotic, broad-boned features, the deep dent in the middle of his chin, the reddish stubble on his cheeks . . . they all faded away like a reflection in a smooth pool grown turbid. His eyes captured her, compelled her into silence, so she did not protest when his hands boldly encircled her waist.

His voice rasped low and husky, as his hands explored the narrowness of her rib cage. " 'Tis a strange man who fears a lass like you."

"The priests are strange men," she heard herself say, even as a voice in her head screamed, *pull away.* Until now, she did not realize how her body craved human touch—she was starved for it. "With their fasting and their scorn o' women and their heads shaved like the bearded full moon."

"Aye." His palms rasped down her curves to settle on her hips. "No Christian I'll ever be. I'd sooner cut off my own sword hand than live with no meat nor ale . . . nor women."

Something in the way he said the word brought her to her senses. *Women,* is it? Well, Brigid of the Clan Morna was no common, loose-skirted slave for him to plow and seed! Mercilessly, she pressed the damp cloth against his temple, knowing the bitter herbs seared the raw flesh like a hundred branding irons.

She took a measure of pleasure out of his shocked and sudden stiffening. " 'Tis no compliment to those who follow the old ways to have ye acting like the only bull in a new herd of cows."

He squeezed the flesh of her hip. " 'Tis no wonder they banished a woman like you from their sight. Beneath these rags you've a body men would kill to possess."

" 'Twas not the priests who banished me," she said sharply, stanching the rush of her blood. "They made me own father do that."

She turned away too abruptly, for she heard the tearing of the worn fibers as his finger caught in a rent in her tunic. She ignored it and crouched down by the bowl, steeping the linen and wringing out the blood. She sensed his anger against her back, like the heat of a raging brushfire.

"Your father is a fool."

Water splashed into the bowl and splattered on her skirt. "Speak *not* of me father so."

"Only a coward listens to the fears of lesser men."

"And what do you know of it? The strongest man can lose his hat in a fairy-wind. The foreign priests wield powerful magic. How else could they sweep over Erin like a scourge?"

"Fire worship still rages in Ulster."

"I don't believe ye." For surely, nowhere on the sacred soil of Erin had the priests failed to riddle with their crosses. "And if it's true, then the priests have not found their way to that wretched place, then."

"The Ulster chieftains suffer the priests' presence in their mead halls only to hear about the world beyond the great sea— no more. They don't grow Christian."

She returned to him and pressed the newly soaked linen

against his wound again, staying away from his greedy hands. The news unarmed her. So long, the Christians had controlled the people of Morna. Not since her grandmother's time had the old ways been common and open, and long had the fires of the festivals died on the hilltops—but for one of her own, which still raged in defiant silence. The news filled her with yearning. There might still be a place on Erin's sweet green grass where she might belong.

"Never would I, nor any other king of strength," Conaire continued, "let the priests grow so close, that I would betray my own blood."

Strong, fighting words, these, and she could not stop her heart from surging at the sound of them. No man—not even Niall—had ever spoken so, and it warmed her soul to hear a man rail against the injustice of her banishment . . . but even as the emotions swelled in her throat, she crushed them, for 'twas her father Conaire scorned, her beloved Da, who was naught but a victim of the priest's water magic, and then the guilt washed over her for her disloyalty, for the man she tended was an Ulsterman, a sword of the Uí Néill, the murderer of her brother—and her father was her blood and her king.

"You know nothing of it." She slung the linen toward the bowl of herb water. The needle flashed in the light as she tugged it from her sleeve. "You were not there when Da lie near to death on his pallet; you were not there when the black-robed priests forbid me Ma from tending to him."

"I know better than to listen to men who know not the taste of women."

"Mayhap there's power in keeping out of a woman's thighs, Conaire, and you should heed it well." She jabbed his purple, angry wound with the needle and drew the linen through. "Those priests did their water ritual upon Da as he lay ill, when he had no defenses against their magic." She pierced the other side of the wound. "When he awoke they told him he was a Christian, and there was naught he could do about it, and if he broke the rules of their God, his soul'd burn in hell for an eternity."

"He lost his soul, he did, when he sent away his only daughter."

"You'll be telling the will of the gods, now, will ye?" She felt his skin grow warm beneath her hands from the effect of the herbs, and she squeezed the edges of the wound together. "Da laughed at them, he did, and scorned them, just as you do. But didn't a bloody flux affect the cattle that year, and didn't pellets of hail as big as stones fall from the sky and ruin the barley as it lay in the fields, and didn't the people of Morna begin to die with some strange affliction?"

" 'Tis no more than might happen any year—"

"Is it now?" She tugged on the thread to bring the flesh together, wondering how he could sit so calmly when she knew her ministrations stung like a hundred thousand bee stings. *"That* year none of the old Druid enchantments worked to save the people. And the priests began to whisper that it was because Da continued to sin, that the wrath of their God was upon Morna."

Conaire made a sound of disgust. "And what was his sin? Eating a fresh haunch of lamb on a holy day? Drinking too much o' the mead, as a king should?"

" 'Twas nearly as simple. Me Ma was Da's second wife, and their ways say that a man can only have one at a time."

"Aye, and fools they are. What are all the maidens and the widows of the warriors to do, if a man could only have one wife? How is one woman to run a king's house by herself? And how's a king to run a kingdom without sons?"

"You'll be asking *me* to explain the Christian ways?" She jabbed the needle in rhythm to her anger. " 'Twas but an excuse, I was onto thinking, for always it was upon me they cast their fear. I had the devil in me eyes, they said. It was I who had cast the furies upon them all."

"Have some pity on them, lass. 'Tis a hard thing for a man to look at you, and be forbidden to touch you."

The needle slipped from her damp fingers, and she fumbled to retrieve it. The buzzing of the bugs nestled in the warm grass rose suddenly, filling the clearing, and the odor of crushed summer grass tickled her throat.

"Whatever it was," she rushed on, "they demanded I be banished with me Ma. Me father resisted them, he did, for as long as he could. But soon all the clan cursed and spit upon me Ma and myself. Da had no choice but to cast us out—"

"A man always has a choice."

"A man, aye, but not a king. A king is responsible for the health of his tribe."

"Your father is a coward."

"Enough!" She bit the thread clean through with her teeth. Only a king can know how heavy the mantle of kingship weighs on his shoulders."

"I am a king. And had I a daughter, I'd not leave her for the wolves."

Her lips tightened. How many times had she wondered why Da had submitted so easily? How many times had she wondered why her father never sent word with Niall to her on Samhain's Eve, nor on Beltaine Day? Och, this Ulsterman was setting her mind racing, he was, and he had no right. Her father was under the influence of those black-robed strangers, and he feared to make any gesture of love to her, lest they cast some curse over his people. It was always the way—she forgave Da for it, for she remembered the tears on his face the day she and her mother left the *ráth* forever. And now this warrior-king was setting her mind a-muddle with his fierce, fighting words.

"You are a king but three days," she said tightly, dabbing the fresh beads of blood with the corner of her sleeve. "And you, Conaire of Ulster, have no children to sacrifice."

He pushed away her hand, shot to his feet, and kicked the

empty bowl of porridge so it clattered along the packed earth. His eyes sliced into her like silver daggers.

"Who spoke such words to you?" His sword rang and vibrated as he drew it out. "I've killed men for daring to say those words. *Who told you?*"

In her frozen surprise, Brigid supposed that such was how a man looked upon the field of battle, with blood lust hardening his gray eyes to pewter, the sun setting his hair aflame, and his cloak whirling about his shoulders, with his raised arms so taut that the blue trails of veins throbbed upon the corded muscles.

"Tell me his name, Brigid."

His voice boomed through the forest, and she found herself thinking of the famous Ulster King Conor who owned a magic shield, which roared like the stormy sea whenever he was in mortal danger. And she wondered why, in the face of such fury, she felt only awe.

"Would ye strike at me heart, Conaire, for the truth it whispers to me?"

His chest heaved. He lowered his sword as his blood lust ebbed. "Then 'twas your Sight which told you."

"Oft I don't know what it tells me, until I speak the very words." She shifted her eyes to his long, gleaming sword. "I'll temper that, though, for I've no wish for me or mine to feel the bite of your steel."

"I would never strike a woman." He sheathed the sword. "Since your Sight told you I have no sons, your Sight can also tell me why."

She lifted her hands to her hips. "Now you'll have *me* doing the work of the gods, will ye?"

"Nay, but I'll have you tell me why neither of my two wives—fat, healthy women, both—has never borne me a child. Nay—worse—neither has ever taken with child." He glared beyond the treetops to the hidden horizon. "And though I've plowed every fertile field from Ulster through Connacht, never once has a woman, high-born or low, come to me swelling with my babe."

" 'Tis common knowledge," she snapped, "that if ye seed too thinly, the rain'll wash it away, and you'll never have a good harvest."

"Mark me, it's not for the trying that I fail." He swung around, his sword clanking against the studs on his boots. "I've foster-lings a-plenty living in my ring-fort in Ulster, but none of them are my flesh and blood. A king needs sons, else he's naught but half a man, and there are whispers enough about the strangeness of my birth."

"There's many a man conceived around the night fires of Samhain," she argued, "who knows not his father's name."

"You know, then, of my birth." His gaze was long and con-templative. "Were you of my tribe, woman, you'd have the Druid's seat of honor by my right hand."

"I have told you nothing ye don't already know."

"Tell me when I will have a son."

"Do ye think the visions can be had for the asking?" She jabbed the needle into the neck of her tunic and sloshed the herb-water onto the lush green grass. "I've no more control over them than you. Me Ma died long before she could teach me the full of the old ways, and now they are lost to the world. My visions come when they wish: an apple won't fall until it's ripe."

"I'll kiss it out o' you, then." He crossed the distance that separated them in two long strides. He clutched her shoulders. The bowls in her hands clattered to the earth. "If the visions don't come, then at least I'll slake this burning in me blood since the first I laid eyes upon you."

"No!"

He stopped a breath away from her lips, his eyes aflame, her chin pressed against his tunic. She smelled the honey mead upon his breath, the sweat and salt of his skin. Something inside flared as hot and molten as the smith's ore in the fire pit, but she forced her legs to straighten.

"You'll not force me, Conaire."

"You feel the slow burn, lass. I see it in your eyes."

"I'm a king's daughter," she said through clenched teeth. "No man will treat me like a common slave."

" 'Twill be nothing common about our mating." He pressed his loins against her. "I'm hard just at the smell o' you."

"Aye, and so would be any man too long in war, I'm thinking."

"Yield to me, woman. I'll stoke that fire in your belly, as I stroke the secrets between your legs—"

"Those secrets are *my* secrets, to be given when I please." She struggled away, stumbling once bereft of his strong hold. "I'll have a proper wooing, I will, or I'll have none of you at all."

She could not believe she had spoken the words, but there they hung, lingering on the air. She was toying with sparks in a hut full of winter-dry hay, she was, when she knew that this man was not the one for whom she was destined. Yet, something had made her state such a thing; perhaps the gods had sent this man—the only man she'd ever known who wasn't afraid of her eyes—to ease her aching loneliness, while she waited for her destined lover.

"Aye, I'll woo you, lass. After I've had a taste o' you."

He reached for her, but caught nothing but a fistful of air. She swirled in the midst of the hot sun, feeling the glow of her hair around her. Their gazes clashed. She knew very well that she was defenseless before such a mighty warrior. She knew that as her over-king he could command her to submit to him, and in her outcast position she'd be a fool to refuse. She knew, too, that if he took her in his arms again, she would melt like butter, for she craved human touch as a thirsty man craves water.

She wanted him—she was forbidden to have him—yet he was the only man who could ease her loneliness.

The words bubbled out of her; she knew not where the courage came. "Patience is the price, Conaire."

"The price for what?"

She jerked her chin toward his wound, freshly bleeding red. "It's a scar I've saved ye. You're in me debt for the healing I've done. My price is patience, it is."

A muscle flexed in his cheek. "So that's to be the way o' it."

"Aye."

"I'm not a man to wait for a pleasure that can be had here and now."

" 'Twould do ye well to keep that rod in your tunic," she argued. "You may find the food is sweeter, when ye've not been gorged upon it."

A reluctant grin blossomed on his face. "With that tongue, you're a better swordswoman than all the men o' Morna."

"Aye, and a better tradeswoman, too." She planted her fists on her hips and hid the hope in her breast. "What say ye, *ri ruirech?* Do ye have the honor to pay the price?"

"Aye, a wooing you'll get, lass, if that's what it will take to have you." He swept up his cloak and whirled it over his shoulders, then scooped up his brooch lying in the grass. He pressed the warm metal into her hand. The garnets riveting the pin to the circle of etched gold sparkled in the light. "My first gift to you." He touched her cheek with one finger. "We'll see, when this wooing is done, who is the more hungry for the other."

He strode out of the clearing, his cloak flapping. His fearless, arrogant whistling cut through the thick verdure, and mocked her long after he disappeared from sight.

Och, this contemptuous warrior wasn't worth the bother, she thought, glaring at the shivering branches of his passing. She'd welcome him to her hut, she would, but she'd welcome him only to suck dry the last bit of his knowledge of the world. It'd been too long since she'd heard of what passed during the *feis* at Tara last year, or at the latest fair in Cruachan. She yearned to hear of what new churches the priests had built, and of the intrigues of the high court of kings at Tara. In the end, Conaire's vanity would be his downfall, for a dozen moons would pass before his pride allowed him to realize that she'd never yield to him. And so she'd stave off the loneliness for another passing of seasons.

She flipped the brooch into the air and caught it in her sure grip. *Whistle while you can, Conaire of Ulster. 'Twill be I who'll be the last to whistle.*

Then, without a whisper of notice, a cloud passed over her eyes.

Brigid blinked once, but the gray vapor persisted. The misty fog blurred the edges of her vision, whirling like the smoke of peat fires, gathering and thickening until the blackened haze cut off the brilliance of the midsummer day.

From what seemed like very far away, Brigid felt the brooch slip between her fingers. She was not afraid. She was familiar with the swift and unexpected blindness. She had had this vision every year since the onset of her moon-blood cycles. The revelation always plagued her with the coming of Lughnasa Day, the midsummer Celtic festival—the sacred night of the fires which she would celebrate at the next new moon.

The earthy scent of moss-drenched moisture billowed from the gray haze. Tall, silvery forms shimmered through the fog, then differentiated into a cluster of oak trees. The grove's living warmth reached out and caressed her, for oaks were the king of trees, giver of shelter and warmth and worshiped above all others. Blue green light filtered eerily through the vaulted verdure to cast an uncertain glow upon her bare skin. It was an uncanny twilight, like the kiss of night and day, and high up, in the star-studded skies, an unearthly moon-sun burned metallic and white hot.

One of the trees swelled, then birthed a shadow, which unfolded into the silhouette of a man. Brigid stretched out her arms and welcomed this creature of spirit and flesh, for she knew that she and he were a part of one whole, and that what was to occur within this ring was an old and sacred ceremony. He approached. The creature's dark *brat* shimmered with golden crescents, like the cloak of a powerful Druid. The heat of his breath fanned her cheek, redolent of rain and dew. His large hands rasped on her bare skin—was it the furrowed texture of bark she felt? Was that his crescent-sprinkled cloak she felt brushing against her, falling to the earth beneath their feet, or was it the whisper-soft brush of shedding leaves? He caressed her nakedness, urging her to open herself to him and let him ease this growing ache in her body, this lonely void in her soul. And she knew that some greater fate lay in this glorious mating, for she sensed around her the bated breath of men and gods, the stillness of the earth-sun and the wary watching of the Otherworldly moon . . . as if this coupling forged the last link in some mystic chain . . .

Then the scene began to dissolve into mist, and like every other time, she fought to stay within the circle, to stay with the creature who filled her heart. She wanted to look upon the face of her lover, to finally see the beloved features that always swirled in darkness. She struggled to probe through the veils that kept this last bit of knowledge from her . . . but inevitably the shadowy images receded, lost to her.

The smoke obscuring her vision thinned to filmy whorls, and then dissipated altogether. She found herself standing in the sunshine in front of her sagging hut, staring at the honeysuckle that edged the moss that clung to the thatched roof.

The brooch winked in the grass at her feet. She picked it up and turned it over and over in her hand.

"You'll be left the hungry one, Conaire," she murmured, the wisps of the vision still clinging to her. "For me maidenhead is fated for one not of this world, for one far greater than ye."

Three

Aye, he would give the lass a wooing to rival the legendary wooing of Étain.

Conaire descended upon Brigid after a mid-morning squall, while the raindrops still tumbled from their cradle in the leaves to splatter intermittently onto the earth. He unfurled at her feet two cloaks worthy of a king's daughter; a saffron *brat* which lay on the damp grass like an unbroken carpet of blooming gorse, and a heavier, striped cloak, dyed crimson with madder from Gaul and bluish-purple from the liquid of dog-whelk shells from the west of Erin. He draped a length of blinding white linen dusted with gold over her shoulders, then wound about her arm the finest woven gold braid that could be had in all of Erin.

"I would have you dress," he told her, "as befits a woman of your birth."

As the days passed he showered her with baubles; carved hair combs made of bone, jewel-encrusted balls to fasten to the fiery plaits of her tresses, enameled rings, a girdle of links hung with tiny, clustered bells, ankle-rings of swirling silver, *ruam* with which to color her cheeks, and other such things he imagined a woman would crave. Yet she never wore the riches, even when he visited. And each time he handed her another gift, she'd turn it over in her hands, comment on the fine workmanship or an unusual design, then put it aside, as if it were no more than an empty horn of mead, and ask him if he'd like some heather honey and barley cakes.

Once, he clutched her by the waist and drew her slim warmth against his loins. "My hunger's not for food," he growled, burying his face in the honeysuckle and rainwater silk of her hair.

She struggled with a wiry strength, her eyes roiling with rich green thunder. "Have ye forgotten your price already?"

"Have I not been patient enough?" He nudged the jeweled cup crushed between them, frustrating his efforts to draw her closer. "Doesn't a man deserve more thanks than this for the gifts I bring you?"

She jerked away. A heavy weight clanked against his chest, then thudded to the grass. "Take your metalwork, you scheming deceiver. D'ye think I can be bought like a hosteler's wife?"

And so he whirled away and raged back to the ring-fort to plow his war chariot like a madman across the fields of his kingdom, the reins of his two foam-flecked horses as taut as a harp's strings. He tested the flex of his spears until they snapped beneath his grip, nicked two blades into jagged edges fighting in the muddy *liss* of the ring-fort. At night in the smoky mead hall, Conaire swilled enough hazel mead to drown two men, then barked at bards for tales only to cut them off, or summoned his harper for music only to bellow like a hound when the lyre twanged not to his liking. Slaves and Ulster warriors alike trod wide circles around him, and whispered behind their hands the suspicions they dared not to say aloud.

But Aidan dared. After a mad morning race across the fields with Conaire, he slid down his horse's heaving side with a *thwump* of his cloak and approached his king. Conaire hunkered on the hurdle of one of the animal pens, sharpening his sword with a whetting stone.

Conaire spoke without raising his head. "You're as slow as an old woman, foster-brother."

"Aye, but me horse is alive after the race, which is more than I can say for that beast o' yours." Aidan glanced over the hurdle to the sweat-soaked stallion, its proud head bent in exhaustion as two Briton slaves lathered its steaming coat. "You'll not bring the lass around by killing your own horses—"

Aidan swallowed his words as the cold tip of a blade chilled his throat. Conaire's eyes shone as deadly silver as the sword beneath his chin.

"They're *my* horses to kill."

"Look at yourself." Aidan felt the blade tickling his words. "Holding a blade to your own foster-brother, and all for a woman."

" 'Tis a sparring I want." Conaire pulled back the blade, leapt off the hurdle, and landed flat-footed and ready. "Fight me for the champion's portion of the stag I felled yesterday."

Aidan crossed his arms across his checkered *brat*. "I'll not fight ye."

"Growing old and growing into a coward, are you?"

"I'll not fight a man who snorts and paws the earth like a bull with the smell o' a cow in his nostrils."

Conaire grew like an angry god. The blade found its niche in Aidan's throat again.

"Every man down to the meanest slave knows she's stolen your manhood. 'Tis as plain as the nose on your face." Aidan knocked Conaire's sword aside and ignored the sting as the blade nicked his palm. He faced Conaire, eye to eye. "You're bewitched, ye are."

"There's no stink of magic in this."

"All the worse, then." Aidan stanched the throbbing wound on his hand with his fist. "You'll not shake free o' it by destroying another war chariot or killing your horses or killing *me.*"

Conaire glared, the fury banked in his eyes. His hand clenched over the hilt of his blade. 'Twas no getting away from it, this angry, endless rush of thwarted passion. He'd never before felt the like. Many a time he'd been tempted to ask his Druid if he were bewitched, but he wanted no man laughing into his beard over his failure to bring this woman to his pallet.

"Go back to her, Conaire."

Conaire whirled with a flash of blade. "She wants none o' me."

"There isn't a woman alive who wouldn't give the last tooth out o' her jaw to have the Champion of the Uí Néill in her bed."

"She's spurned my gifts."

"Then you've yet to find what it is she wants." He sucked on his hand and glared at his king. "Be off with ye, *now,* before the bards start a-singing songs about their poor, witch-befuddled king, and paint you with such shame that you can no longer show your face in all of Erin."

So Conaire mounted another horse and took the narrow path bowered by oaks and yew to the pebble-strewn stream, and followed its gurgling path deep into the woods. He dismounted when the path grew too narrow for the horse, left the beast near a sweep of sweet summer grass, then shouldered his way through the verdure to the golden clearing glowing just beyond the ancient, gnarled limbs of a thick oak.

He elbowed a leafy bough out of his way, and saw her standing outside the door of her hut.

Her hair shone like polished brass upon the saffron wool of her *brat.* Her tunic, bound with the brooch of his clan, caught flecks of sunlight and scattered the rays like stars. A faint tinkling filled the clearing as she approached and the clappers of a hundred tiny bells chimed on her girdle. Her long, white neck arched like that of a swan, as she looked up and drew him into the swirling iridescence of her eyes.

"I've been expecting ye, Conaire."

He took in the sight of her like a man starved, his hands clenched into fists at his sides.

She spread her arms, exposing more of her pure white *léine* beneath the yellow glow of her cloak. "It's been many a season since I've felt such fine stuff against me skin."

His gaze fell to her breasts, small and high. Through the fine linen he saw the pucker of her nipples, and he found himself wondering what it would be like to draw one raspberry-colored tip into his mouth, to feel it harden against his tongue.

"Why?" The word rushed to his lips, harsher than he intended. He jerked a hand to her clothes. "Why now?"

She shrugged and fingered the tight weave of a linen sleeve, staring up at him with eyes whirling as iridescent as the inside of mollusk's shells. "Because ye came back."

There was no knowing a woman's mind. Only when he came empty-handed to her door did she accept all he had given her. He was of no mind to puzzle it out; 'twas enough that she accepted the gifts and did not tear him to shreds with her tongue. And it made his head soft, to see her draped in cloth he'd given her with his own hands, even if he wanted nothing more than to rip it off her body.

"They say you've bewitched me."

A corner of her lips twitched in sad mockery. "I've worked no charm. I know not the way of it, though the people of Morna would have you think otherwise."

"Tell me why am I here, then, when every bondswoman in Morna has offered me room on her pallet to flush me mind o' you."

"Me Sight doesn't teach me the queer ways of men." Her cheeks stained an angry pink. "Blame not *me* if ye find no pleasure in a whore's arms."

He seized her shoulders and squeezed them—hard. "What do you want o' me, woman?"

Her eyes flew to his face, and in one brief moment, like the clearing of mist to reveal the whipped surface of a storm-lashed lake, he saw a raw flash of passion. But just as quickly it was gone, masked in murky shadow.

She jerked out of his embrace and stumbled back. Tilting her chin, she smoothed her hands over the length of her *léine* and gestured toward the hut, where a crude yew board bristling with pegs lay in a pool of sunlight. "I want no more of you than this, Conaire of Ulster: Play me a game of *fidchell*."

"*Fidchell?*"

"Aye. 'Tis an old battle game. Surely an Ulsterman served his first food on the tip of a sword must know the way of it."

He stiffened. "I know it well enough."

"Good." She turned with a flap of her cloak. "It's been many a moon since me brother and I played . . . me palms have been itching for someone to challenge."

So *fidchell* they played as they sat on the sun-warmed grass with thrushes warbling in the bushes and late summer bees lazily buzzing swirls in the air. As he stretched on his side, one arm draped over his raised knee, three days of unceasing activity began to take its toll. A heavy languor settled over him, dulling the sharp throb of his bruises, and he wondered if she had crushed some herb in the new beer she offered him to make him so drowsy. He cared not; he let the lassitude wash over him. Between games, she placed before him a meal of new whortle-berries with sweet clustering cream. As the juice of the berries ran down his chin, he found himself speaking of things he shared not even with Aidan. It was to prod her Sight, he told himself, as he spoke of his priestess mother, of his search for a father with his own face among the men of Ulster, his determination to earn a kingdom by sword, since his lineage was unknown to him and thus he could not claim a kingship by blood. She listened as intently as a child listening to her first bard's tale in the shadows of the mead hall.

The playing of the game seemed to please her, so the next afternoon he arrived with a *brandub* board, made of mother-of-pearl with smooth, enameled pieces in dark blue and rich green. She ran her cool, white hand over the board in silent reverence, and then tilted her head and challenged him to a match.

"For wagers," she added, settling down in the yellow pool of her *brat.* "Niall and I always played for wagers. The loser would milk the cow or go amid the thorns to seek rowanberries."

"I'm not a boy to play for trifles." He tossed his sword in the grass by his side and ran his gaze over her body, as he wanted to run his hands—and wondered for the thousandth time when she'd grant him the liberty. "The sweat of a cow's udder won't be found on the forehead of the *rí ruirech* o' Morna, it won't."

"It's a proud breed you are, to scorn honest labor."

"It's a warrior, I am, not a slave." He leaned down on the bulk of his arm. "If we be playing for wagers, let them be worthy o' the name or let's not do them at all."

"So that's the way of it, is it?" She pulled up the first piece and rolled the smooth enamel between her fingers. "Let the winner decide the price of losing, then."

His blood rushed, for she had lost the two games of *fidchell* they had played the day before. He met her gaze and held it. " 'Tis a dangerous weapon you put in me hands, lass."

"Every sword has two edges. Are ye willing to risk the weapon turned upon yourself?"

He dropped the dice into her cupped palm and set himself to the task of winning. As the afternoon progressed, the dappled shade beneath the nearby oak tree stretched until it licked the edge of the board itself. Conaire grudgingly admitted that the lass knew the lay of the board, and knew the way of the pegs with craft and stealth—better than many a man he'd played in Ulster. But he was shocked when she plucked out his last peg with a throaty laugh.

"For a man of such famed skill in war, Conaire, this battle game seems to have gotten the best of ye."

He stared, stunned, at the lay of the pegs. "It's not natural, that a woman should know so well the way o' battle."

"I'll have you know that me grandma fought with the men of Morna against the Uí Néill before I was born. She was the finest swordswoman in all of Connacht."

"Did she teach you *brandub?*"

"Nay." Brigid wrinkled her nose. "Me brother taught me. He used to practice with me, before he played with the other boys. It's not fitting for the king's son to lose to sons of common *bóaire.*"

"Nay, nor for a king to lose to a woman." He rose up on his hand. "So what work will ye charge me to, lass? The first three trials o' the sons o' Tureen?"

"It's woodcutting I'll set you to. My stores are low, and winter not three moons away."

"Woodcutting?" He roared to his full warrior's height. "You have the champion of the Uí Néill to do your bidding and you set him to cut wood?"

"Aye." She calmly gathered the game pieces from the grass and pegged them in the board as she scanned his broad shoulders. "Ye've the strength for it, don't ye?"

He spread his callused, broad-palmed hands. "These hands know better the feel o' a sword hilt, lass. I'll find you a boar to slay, a wolf to kill." He waved toward the hut. "I'll summon slaves to do such work—"

"Nay. 'Tis ye I'll see with an axe in hand." She gathered her cloak in her hand and rose to her feet, tossing the length of her gleaming hair over her shoulder. " 'Twill do you good to sweat like a common man. You've altogether too much arrogance, ye do."

"A man earns his pride—"

"Will ye be having me think that the men of Ulster do not pay their wagers, Conaire? That the over-king of Morna is not a man of honor?"

She said it with a triumphant twinkle in her eye, and a smile lurking at the corners of her lips. He strode to the hut and snatched the heavy-headed axe leaning by the woodpile, then marched out deeper into the woods. Stripping off his cloak, he took to the woodcutting with ill humor, but he chopped until the pile of logs topped the roof of her hut.

He sank the axe blade into the last piece of timber, as sweat soaked the embroidered neckline of his tunic. He turned to find her hovering over a pot of stirabout.

"Another game."

She lifted one pale brow. "Is it the thatching you want to be doing now?"

He dropped his weight down in the flattened grass on one side of the board. "Another game."

She sighed and took the bowl of stirabout off the fire, a grin lurking about her mouth. "Och, it's a fine thing to have such a strong man to do me bidding."

His mood darkened more when the game ended, for he found himself twisting prickly hay in his hands and braiding it into ropes, with the stench of rot and moss in his nostrils as he strapped the heavy thatch upon the roof of her hut. Below, in the slanting light, she frolicked about like a calf in springtime, weaving herbs into the thatch to keep away the fleas.

Conaire cursed as the rope of thatch slipped through his hands and left a spray of splinters in his skin. Her laughter mingled with the tingling of the bells on her girdle.

He frowned down at her. "Fine spirits you're in now, lass."

"Aye, for you're as clumsy as a woman ten moons gone with child." She covered her smile with her hand. "Perhaps 'twas a mistake setting you to the thatching. This poor work won't even keep out the sun."

"It will serve you right, for setting a warrior to it."

"Nay, it's worth the soaking me pallet'll get with every rain, just to see ye huffing and ruddy-faced and all a-twisted with fallen pride."

He growled down at her, but at the sight of the mischievous smile gleaming behind her hand, he suddenly realized how ridiculous he must look, draped in his tricolored cloak, his gold torque beaded with dirt and sweat, clinging to the rotted thatch of a hut and snarling like a dog. 'Twas right, she was, to be laughing at him so, a king brought so low by a woman's wiles. At least seeing him work stole the barbs from her tongue and loosened its root, for she'd been as voluble as a child all day. His lips stretched in a rueful smile.

"When you're finished with this, Conaire, we'll play again, so you can get your chance at vengeance." She clutched a handful of herbs from the pile at her feet, and massaged them into another length of the thatch. "I've butter to churn and berries to collect and roots to dig—"

"My next gift to you will be a slave."

"And what do I need with a slave," she teased, "when I've you to do me work for me?"

"You don't think I'd be such a fool as to play you again, do you?"

"Aye, I do." Her cloak slipped off her shoulder with her shrug, exposing the pearly flesh of her collarbone. "Have ye no courage, Conaire? The way of the dice surely won't always be with me—"

"The way o' the dice had naught to do with it." He pulled tight the sinew with which he tied the thatch to the roof. " 'Twas magic you used."

The rope sank as she stopped her work. "Are ye accusing me of cheating?"

His gaze slipped over her slowly, lingering on the shape of her legs beneath the caress of her tunic, the golden bracelets that encircled her right upper arm, the cascade of hair over her shoulders, the tilt of her firm breasts. He met her eyes and knew she felt the smolder in his gaze. "The price o' my winning would have been high, lass."

Her cheeks blossomed with color. "I'll have no one say that Brigid of the clan Morna has no honor—I use no magic in the playing."

"Maybe no chants, but it was magic, of a sort. A man can hardly concentrate on war or war games, when there's such a sight near to lull him into distraction."

"Och, listen to ye." She tossed her head, and the golden balls clattered against one another. "As if it's me fault ye can't keep your eyes to yourself. What would ye have me do? Play with me *brat* over me head?"

"Nay. I'd rather lose at *brandub."

Her smile stilled, then slowly grew, intensifying with the color in her cheeks. She bent down to clutch another handful of herbs, hiding her face from his perusal. "Och, you'll have plenty of time to do that . . . if ye'll stay for another game."

And in that moment, as she lifted her face up to his, the sun illuminated the hope lurking in the depths of her swirling green eyes. Conaire suddenly saw clear the working of this woman's mind. He'd been so fevered for the wanting of her, he'd not seen the simple truth before his very eyes. The lass had lived in these woods since she was barely a woman. She was as lonely as a swan who'd lost her mate.

The next afternoon, he strode into the clearing and surprised her bent over a bubbling cauldron. The brilliant folds of his cloak wiggled and whined beneath his arm. He released the load and out shot a fox-colored creature who planted his huge wet paws on Brigid's shins.

"One of the bitches had a litter a while ago," Conaire explained. "This one's just weaned. My gift to you."

She lifted the wolfhound pup in her arms and buried her face in his fur. Out lolled a wet pink tongue which tasted her from chin to temple. Brigid laughed, and the sound glittered like fairy music in the clearing.

"Precious, he is." She ruffled his fur by the scruff. " 'Tis the finest gift ye've given me, Conaire."

The expression she granted him had more force than a hundred sword strokes. He wondered at her power, that she could make a king of warriors, a king's champion, feel as awkward and ungainly as a newborn colt.

That afternoon, as the sun shone like an ember between the leafy boughs of oaks, he rose to his feet and drew Brigid up with him, leaving the sleeping pup in a warm circle of trampled grass. A softness cushioned Brigid's mouth, but an uncertainty lingered in her eyes.

"Come back with me," he said.

"Back?"

"Aye. To the *ráth* of Morna." He traced the curve of her cheek, kissed golden with the last cool rays of the sun. "You've never heard the harp strings of my bard, nor his stories."

"Och, and there's a fine thing," she said, quietly, without venom, "having me, of the tribe Morna, a-sitting and listening to some Ulster bard rave about Connacht defeats."

"My bards know also the sorrows o' Deirdre, and of the trials of the sons o' Tureen."

The knowledge gave her pause. "Do they know the story of the swans? Of the children condemned to live on the earth for hundreds of years?"

"Aye. The Children o' Lir." He rubbed the pad of his thumb against the pulse leaping in her throat. "They tell that tale better than all the rest, with not a warrior in the whole of the mead hall left with a dry eye."

The light that had entered her eyes when he gave her the wolfhound pup flared bright, brighter now than he'd ever seen before. Aye, he wanted this lass by his side, sharing the champion's portion from his dish, drinking mead from his horn, her ears filled with the strumming of gilded harps. He cupped his hand around her neck, then slid his other hand around her waist, and gripped the hollow of her back. Her spine yielded to him as he felt himself stiffen against her.

His head filled with the scent of her, sweet honeysuckle and clean, tart rainwater. "You need only to say aye, lass, and there'll be a place for you by me side."

She arched her neck higher, so the bristle of his chin scraped her forehead. A tress slipped off her shoulder to tumble down her back. "Will ye bring me back here, Conaire, after the stars have risen?"

"Nay."

He'd never bring her back to this sagging hut of warped wattle and caked daub, to live alone as an outcast. He'd wrap her in fine, brushed wool the color of jewels, lay her in pallets stuffed with gosling's down, and have bondswomen wash and brush and plait her hair, until the color rivaled the sunlight. He'd summon every bard in all of Erin to fill her head with tales, her days with laughter, just so he could gorge himself on the sound of it.

And aye, aye, he'd taste his fill of her. He'd feel her soft, open thighs against his loins, feel the tight, heated wetness of her core, feel her young, firm breasts pressed between them. He'd feel her long, supple body thrashing in passion with his every stroke, and he'd coax cries from her until she grew too hoarse to cry out anymore.

A hot rush of blood filled his loins. " 'Tis long past time you laid down with me, woman."

Her silence filled his ears. Above, a breeze tossed the leaves and exposed the fragile spines to the dying crimson rays of the sun. For one, brief moment, he sensed her softening like the crumbling of a riverbank in a flood.

Then she drew away from him, and it was as if the night wind snuffed out the last of the sunlight.

"I cannot go, Conaire."

His hands, empty of her warmth, curled into fists. How long could a starving man survive teased with the scent of food, before his need broke all bonds?

"Aye, you can go with *me,* if you willed it."

"Nay—"

"I am the over-king of Morna. No priests and no petty chieftain can stop me from bringing you in."

"Aye, but what would I be, if I went with ye? Not a member of the clan. Not an Ulsterwoman." The point of her chin tilted higher. "They will think me your whore."

"I'd kill the man who dared—"

"—to speak the truth?" The bells of her girdle chimed as she stepped out of his reach. "Though you see me as naught but an outcast, Conaire, I was born the daughter of a king. I'll not be shaming me clan, nor meself, in such a way."

He stood in the clearing with his chest heaving, his palm flexing over the hilt of his sword. He knew not the way to battle with wisps and mists—give him an enemy to fight, and he'd dispatch him before sweat could bead on his brow. But this was a war with a woman as lithe as a fairy-child, and as mercurial as the winter wind. Each time he thought he held her in his arms, he found himself holding nothing but eddies of air teased with the fragrance of her—and craving the feel of her full in his arms all the more.

"Go now, Conaire." She swept up the puppy and hugged him close to her breast. "Go now and do not come back. For here's the truth of it: I can never yield to ye."

"You *will* never yield—"

"Nay, I *cannot.*" Her lashes swept down, casting faint shadows on her cheeks. " 'Tis shameless I've been, teasing you so. It's been so long since a man has looked at me without fear in his eyes, that I dared to trifle with ye."

A roar clenched in his chest. "Who or what dares to challenge my claim to you?"

"No less than fate itself." Her eyes rose reluctantly to his face. "I've known this all along: My destiny is with another."

The hilt of the sword burned against his palm. So that was the way of it; the lass was bound by the message of her own visions. His fingers clenched in anticipation.

Suddenly, he had an opponent to fight.

"You'd best practice your *fidchell* tonight." He whirled toward the break in the woods that led to where his horse grazed. "For come tomorrow, we'll be playing again."

"Are ye a fool, Conaire?" She followed him through the clearing, clutching the pup to her chest. "Don't ye understand? You cannot win."

He swirled and brought her up short. "Do you think I became the *rí ruirech* o' Morna by leaving the field of battle?"

"This is no mortal foe you face."

"If it is the gods I must battle, then so be it." He grasped a handful of her hair and watched it shimmer through his fingers. "I'll be here when he comes for you. One-on-one combat will determine the winner. And you will be the prize."

Four

The cow lowed as Brigid dragged her hand down the beast's slick udder. A thin stream of milk steamed into a lathe-turned bowl. The cow stamped her back hooves, circled her snout in the air, and flicked her ears. Her eyes loomed white.

"Easy, now," Brigid murmured, petting the cow's prickly side as she aimed the last of the rich milk into the froth. " 'Tis near done, we are."

The wooden bowl scraped against the ground as Brigid slipped it from beneath the sagging udder. Hitching the rim into her waist, she leaned the weight of the full bowl into her hip. Wind burrowed under her hair and tinkled the golden balls which weighed down a scattering of narrow plaits, then gusted again, stronger, as if to set the balls pealing anew.

She smiled a secret smile and struck the cow on the rump. The beast bolted down the hill.

"Aye, ye'll find sweet summer grass on the banks of the lough," Brigid murmured, "but on a day such as this, ye'll not shake the fairy wind from your nostrils."

She headed up the winding, weeded path, the milk eddying in the bowl as if invisible fingers dipped and toyed with the foam. The breeze chilled the damp spots on her *léine* from underneath, for these gusts leached through the dirt from the very womb of the earth and billowed around her knees. Mists curled up from the sod, wound about the furrowed bark of the trees, then dripped like thin mother's milk to the turf. High in the oaks, the leaves rustled as if a thousand birds nested deep in the verdure.

Brigid kept her eyes to the lichen-coated rocks of the path, while the Sight writhed within her like a caged thing. She caught snatches of acrid scents, then lost them before she could find the source; strange, unearthly images glimmered on the path before her, then dissolved into fog. The dawn had long ceded to the brighter grays of morning, yet the *Sídh* still roamed thick. 'Twas why she loved Lughnasa—and Beltaine, Samhain, and Imbolc. On such days, the walls between the worlds thinned, the veils separating human from inhuman mingled and parted, and the fairy folk pushed back the ache of her loneliness for the span of more than a few hours. Brigid sensed the closeness of the Otherworld like the heat of a kiln's stones against her cheek.

A finger of sunlight broke through the haze and buttered the dew-laden stones of the path. The fairy wind ebbed with the tender onslaught of sunshine. Brigid felt the first prickle of certainty the Sight had granted her all morn.

Conaire would visit today. *Again.*

The very air she breathed sizzled through her blood and set her skin tingling. She stopped in mid-stride as a heat swelled like the tide within her to burn the tips of her ears. Conaire once spoke of enchantment, but 'twas *she* who welcomed her brother's murderer and her father's nemesis to her home; 'twas *she* who trembled each night with hot and cold, like a woman beset with the ague. 'Twas she who each day eagerly awaited the sound of his footfall on the path . . . and found herself beset with a young girl's dreams.

She hitched her skirts over her free arm and set her mind back to the path. 'Twas foolish, she was, wanting what couldn't be. 'Twas dangerous to tease destiny, for her fate still lay with the fairy-lover of her dreams. And even if Conaire somehow bent fate to his bidding and won her as his prize, 'twas folly to yearn for what he offered her. Though highborn she was, no Ulster over-king would take an outcast to wife, a woman with one cow to her name, when beautiful daughters of rich men a-plenty preened and pranced for him in Morna. Aye, Conaire wanted her—desire raged like a flooded river in his eyes—but she feared it was the piquancy of the chase that lured him here each day. She was naught more than another tribe to conquer, another herd of cattle to steal, a woman promised to a formidable opponent, and thus a woman wanted all the more. For despite all his bold threats to battle her lover from the *Sídh*, Conaire had offered her nothing more than a warm place in his bed.

Och, but the spirit of Niall forgive her, she *wanted* Conaire here. How he filled the clearing! His laughter shook the very trees. He crossed wits with her with the same bright, teasing ease which he would cross swords with a foster-brother. She felt like a flower closed against the world—and Conaire was the sun, coaxing her to open up, tempting her to show her face to his warmth; and even as she struggled and fought, she felt herself bursting into full bloom.

A flash of red fur bolted from around the hut, tumbled down the slick path, and wrapped itself around her legs with a low, frightened moan. The trembling wolfhound pup lifted liquid eyes to her face.

"Hush, precious." Brigid dipped down to absently trail her fingers through his coat. "It's naught but the whispers of the Otherworld; they mean no harm to ye."

The pup trotted around her ankles as she poured half the milk into the butter churn standing behind her hut, and half of what remained into a wide-necked bladder she had tucked into her girdle of bells. She tilted the bowl to her lips and let the warm froth slide down her throat. The pup yipped piteously, until Brigid lay the wooden bowl on the ground and let the wolfhound noisily lap up what remained of the rich froth.

"The light o' morning becomes you, lass."

Conaire leaned on the corner of her hut, his arms crossed and a lazy smile on his face. For a moment Brigid wondered if he were just another specter conjured by her unruly Sight, but then the boughs parted with the force of the wind and bathed him in a bolt of light. His auburn hair glistened with moisture, as if it were newly washed, and the ends twined against the twisted rope of gold encircling his strong neck. Garnets flashed from his fist-sized brooch, and from the pounded gold girdle cinching his tunic at the waist. His brilliant scarlet *brat* flapped against his calves with the force of the breeze.

A glow warmed her face. She bent over to pick up the bladder of milk sagging on the ground, so that her hair would slide forward and veil from him her shame. "A brave man, you are, to be walkin' about on Lughnasa morning." She hugged the milk-warmed skin to her midriff. "Did you not fear you'd lose the path and wander into the Otherworld?"

"Perhaps I have." His treacherously handsome smile widened, as he slid his gaze down the length of her body. "No fairy-queen could weave a stronger enchantment than who I see before me."

"Och, you've the mists in your eyes." She flipped a scattering of gold-tipped plaits over one shoulder, trying in vain to stanch the swift rush of pleasure she felt at his compliment. "You'll whistle another air, Conaire, once I've set ye to your task." She gestured to an axe whose blade was buried in one of the logs of the woodpile. "Ye'll be needin' that today."

"More woodcutting then."

"Aye."

"That proves your magic, to have a king rising at the crow of the cock to do a slave's work at a maiden's bidding."

"Do I hear a bit of complaining in your mouth? It was you who demanded another game yesterday eve."

"Aye, and I'll demand another again, I will." His shadow fell upon her with all the power of a Druid's hand. "Fate will be upon us both soon enough. 'Tis only a matter of time, before the dice turn my way."

"Don't be holdin' your breath. I'll not have ye passin' out at me feet for lack of air."

Her skirts raked the debris on the ground as she brushed past him, wondering how he could treat the inevitable battle with such levity, when it would undoubtedly mean his death. Och, but she understood little of the way of warriors, and the day was too fine and bright to dwell on that which she couldn't change. Better to continue on as they had these past days, blindly pretending that nothing had changed; that fate, in the end, would somehow turn a kind face.

She rounded the hut and escaped into its smoky interior. She tugged a flagon half-full with mead from its hook on the wall, and replaced it with the bladder of milk. She tossed the mead in a basket of woven rowan bark, added the *fidchell* board, then dribbled in hazelnuts and yew berries and a loaf of barley bread. Conaire's shadow darkened the doorway.

"Are you mad, woman?" Conaire hefted the ball of fur balanced on his forearm. The puppy licked his froth-flecked muzzle and lolled out his tongue. "You're feeding milk to the spawn of the most ferocious wolfhound in Erin?"

She looped the basket over her arm. The air thickened with Conaire's presence within the small confines of the hut—suddenly, she needed air like a drowning woman.

"The pup wanted it," she said. "I'll not deny him."

He turned aside as she passed out of the hut. "I brought the pup to defend you, and you raise him on cream and honey."

"Defend me? Och, there's a sight. It's only you I need defending from, and he licks your boots as if you're his sire."

"There are other dangers in these woods."

"Aye, and I've avoided them well enough these seven years." She tugged on the axe handle, but couldn't tear it free. She glanced at the pup in his arms. "Will ye be cutting wood with the wolfhound, then?"

"Not much good he'll be at that, or anything else, until you start cutting his teeth on raw meat." He tossed the pup to the grass and jerked the blade out of the wood. "Feed such a wild creature milk, and he'll grow as tame as a lamb."

"Then perhaps you should have a sip." She twirled and headed towards the forest higher on the hill. "Of the two of ye, it's you who more needs the taming."

His bold yelp of laughter echoed through the clearing. The sound buffeted away the lingering mists. The sunlight poured down around them like amber rain, and Brigid wondered why it always seemed that Conaire carried the daylight upon his shoulders.

"You'll be hoping in vain, lass." His grin split wide and white, as he settled the axe handle on his shoulder. The pup yipped and leapt around their feet as they padded into the forest. "I'm no young pup to be sweetened with a bit o' milk."

"Is that the truth now?" She let her gaze boldly run over him. "Och, you're not so far from your nursemaid's breast that ye can't be curbed, I'm thinking."

"It's been one-and-thirty summers since I suckled from a breast for *milk.*"

"Listen to ye!" The innuendo robbed her of breath. "If you've one-and-thirty summers, then I'm the Morrígan."

He swept down in obeisance. "Hail, raven-queen of war."

"Och, enough of you!"

"Do you think a man could rise to a kingship without seeing ten, fifteen years of battle?"

She squinted at his smooth skin, stretched fresh and young across his wide-boned face. No lines fanned out at the corners of his startling grey eyes. No gray salted his rich auburn locks. Yet she had been hearing about Conaire of the Uí Néill since she was a little girl. How like Cú Chulainn, that legendary Ulster warrior who once battled against Connacht. Though the warrior of yore had lived barely thirty summers, he had never grown a beard.

Cold fingers slithered up the back of her neck. 'Twas said that Cú Chulainn had been the son of Lúgh of the Long Arm, a god and one of the *Sídh*.

"You're not the first to think me too young to hold a crown, but I've battle scars enough to prove my mettle." He petted the hilt of his bronze-sheathed sword. "And the iron to prove my words, if anyone dares to question me."

"The years have barely touched your face."

A gleam lit his eye. "Aye, and there's no less life a-burning in me for the wear of time, either."

Brigid led him higher on the hill. "It explains a lot, it does, why ye keep comin' back here. There's no bringing to heel an old and grizzled hound."

"Haven't you yoked me well enough?" He swung his free arm wide. "What else would bring a man out on such a morning? You've got me doing your bidding as easily as a Briton slave."

" 'Tis your honor that sets you on my path so early. I beat you in *brandub* yesterday at sunset, I did, and ye've yet to pay the price."

"Aye."

"You see? You can put reins on a horse, but that doesn't mean ye can ride him."

"If you'll be wanting a ride, lass, you'll not find me bucking you off."

"Och, and there you go again!" Fire flared on her cheeks. "All the milk from all the cows on all of Erin couldn't tame ye."

"You don't want a man who can be tamed, lass. You and I both know that."

Their gazes met, and her bones softened like beeswax left in the midsummer sun. Och, he had no right to stare through her with those clear gray eyes. Ruthless, he was, to seek her out and seduce her, when a thousand women would go willingly to his pallet, when he knew she was destined for another, when he knew, he *knew* that her heart yearned for more than just the merging of their hungry bodies. Could he not see how she lived on the edges of the world? Could he not see how strongly she ached for a place she could belong—a place she could call home?

Could he not see the danger?

"If it's wood you want, lass, we've passed enough good oak for that."

She shook her head. " 'Tis a special wood I seek. You've a pyre to build on the top of this hill."

"A Lughnasa fire?"

"Aye."

"There's no need o' that. My own Druids are lighting fires near the ring-fort."

"And what good will that be, with the priests a-peering down upon them like ravens?" She hitched up her tunic as the path steepened. "Your men will go, but *my* people fear the priests too much to dare."

"Then they'll not come here."

"Aye, they will. Just as they have come every year. They may be Christian-bred now, but their Celts' blood still hears the call of the fires."

She stopped and peered around the bristling young tree trunks, until she found what she sought. "There." She dropped the basket upon the moss. "That yew and oak, the ones twined with woodbine. 'Tis the sign of the gods' blessing. Those trees must be sacrificed for the fires."

Conaire's mantle slipped to the moss with a soft *whoosh*. His glittering brooch thudded atop it. "Let's be done with it, then."

The yew and the oak had trunks no thicker than the span of a man's hands. With five or six swift strokes of the axe, the oak creaked, snapped, and thudded to the forest floor. She sensed an anger in the stiff line of Conaire's shoulders as he whirled around to the yew, and there was a fierceness in the swing of his bulging arms, but she held her tongue; 'twas disrespectful to speak at the cutting of such glorious trees. When the yew crashed to the earth, golden light flooded down from the hole left in the verdant canopy.

She gathered Conaire's discarded cloak and brooch, as he tucked the saplings one under each arm and headed to the height of the hill, raking the earth behind him with their crowns. He tossed the wood across an open plain, and snapped the branches off as if they were naught but kindling.

His eyes flashed a dangerous, stormy gray as he bound one clutch of sticks. "You should have found me another task, Brigid."

"Och, and here I was, thinkin' I've finally found humility in ye." She settled in the shade, and the wolfhound pup trotted over to curl in her lap. "A man as bold and brawny as you should have no trouble with a bit of tree."

"It's not the woodcutting I object to, nay, not no more." He tossed the bound branches aside. "For you, I'd do it. But I've no liking to do work for the likes of the people o' Morna."

"I'm the last of the Druid blood, as thin as it is." She shrugged and scratched the wolfhound behind its ears. "It's my duty."

"You owe nothing to them." He tugged the yew into the sunlight, his back running dark with sweat. "They've exiled you and scorned you and called you *cailleach.* Yet you still light these bonfires, so the cowards can sneak to the hill like thrice-wed men seeking their bondswomen's beds."

He set to the other trees' branches with fury. Slivers of wood flew as he snapped off bough after bough. Her ears rang with his words; her heart fluttered with the meaning. Och, how good it felt to hear another say what she dared not even think! Barely before the thought was born, Brigid lowered her lashes in shame at her own disloyalty. Morna-born she was, and cast out or not, she could not deny her own blood.

She tilted her chin; this Ulsterman knew neither his mother nor his father. If he could not understand the blood bonds of kin, then she'd argue another way. "If I don't do this, Conaire, then no one will. The ancient rituals will die on this soil."

"They'll not die." A branch snapped in his hand. "Even in the shadows of Patrick's church, in Armagh, I've seen highborn warriors make sacrifices in ancient pools."

"*That,* that is worse," she argued, "for the Christians take the sacred places from us, and make a mockery of them."

"I'm no Druid," he growled, "and I've no tongue for such things." He hefted the axe in his wide-palmed hand. "This I know: The priests are but fleas on Erin's back. They are weak, and thus they and their ways will die."

Brigid ran her hand over the pup's soft coat and held her tongue. Conaire was a warrior and held close a warrior's code; the weak would die and the strong would survive, the good and the right would always emerge champion. But she lived amid the gray mists, and knew the uncertainties of the world. Strength did not always lie within the thickness of a man's arm. And fleas, in multitude, could kill the hardiest wolfhound.

Conaire finished chopping the wood, then wrestled the piles into two bristling pyres. Silently, she handed him the flagon of mead. Grasping it by the neck, he uptipped the flagon and swilled his fill of the potent, golden fluid, while rivulets of it ran down his neck to drench the sweat-dampened linen of his tunic. She smelled the faint, salty perfume of his sweat. A pulse throbbed in his throat. She imagined she could hear his heart beating strong and sure in his chest.

"I've paid the price." He thrust the dripping flagon into her hands. "Now, lass, we'll sit to another game."

She met his clear gray gaze. He'd not taken a blade to his face this morn; a sprinkling of dark bristle prickled on his jaw and shadowed his upper lip. Sweat glistened on his brow, and flecks of bark and tiny slivers of wood speckled his skin. She yearned to run her fingertips over his cheek . . . just once, just to taste this man's skin. She flattened her damp hand over the fine linen of her *léine*.

"Another game, then." She pulled away from the blinking blindness of him and headed toward the yellow bolt of her *brat*, spread on the grass in the shade. "I've plenty of tasks awaiting a man's hand."

The ash tree stretched its boughs above to guard them from the mid-morning sun. Burrowed in the leaves, two blackbirds lilted their full lay. Brigid dropped the flagon of mead beside her, vaguely thinking that the skin was still heavy, though Conaire had surely drank the most of it. When she pushed aside the woven basket to make room for her legs, two ripe red apples rolled out from behind it.

She bit into one of the crispy apples, savoring the sweet tartness of the fruit. She held it out to Conaire, as he made the first move on the *fidchell* board.

He examined the apple, but did not take it. "What magic is this? There's not an apple tree in all of Ireland that has dropped its fruit yet."

She lifted a brow. "Isn't there?"

"Aye. And I'm in no mind to be caught in your web of enchantment again." He nudged the board with his hand. "I'm planning on winning this game."

"I can't have ye playing on an empty stomach." She took another bite with relish, and he narrowed his eyes suspiciously at her. She shrugged. "It matters not to me. I'll keep the apples to meself."

He glanced at the other apple, lying in a saffron bed of folds. The pup sniffed it hesitantly.

Conaire snatched it up. The flesh crisped as he bit into it. "I suppose it won't help to scorn a gift from the gods."

A light breeze swept over the hill as they played, bringing with it the faintest perfume of heath. The quicken and holly rimming the open slope of the hill quivered and rustled, but every time she turned, there'd be nothing there but the sway of a low bough or a tremor of a bush. 'Twas too bright now for the *Sidh* to be dancing in the shadows, even on Lughnasa day, but she sensed their presence around her. She wondered what made them so bold.

Then, in the distance, above the chattering of the birds, the sweet sound of lyres drifted high on the air. She glanced at Conaire, but all his concentration focussed on the *fidchell* board. She strained her ears, listening to the hollow echoes of revelry in the Otherworld, as the fairy music surged and ebbed. The sound grew so loud she could hear voices raised in shouts and laughter; she could hear the stamping of dancing feet and the slosh of liquid as the *Sidh* sipped honeysuckle nectar from cups made of foxglove blossoms.

"It seems your magic has worked against you, *bean sí.*"

The music stopped; the chattering of blackbirds above deafened her. She blinked blankly at Conaire. He was grinning, and a light gleamed in his gray eyes.

She leaned over the board. "My turn, is it?"

"Nay, lass." He lifted the apple, which was still whole, though she knew he had taken several bites. " 'Tis *my* turn now."

Color ebbed from her cheeks. Her pegs were scattered all over, many lying upon the saffron *brat*. She had not remembered making a single move.

Her eyes flew to his face. "You've won."

"Aye."

The sunlight dimmed, as if a high, thin cloud passed across the sky. She sank back on one hip and narrowed her eyes. "There's mischief afoot here."

"You'll not be trying to go back on your word now, lass."

"Nay. I'll keep my word."

She had no choice; the time had come to pay the smith for the magic he had forged into the blade. Och, but not yet, *not yet*. She felt the darkening of the wind around them; smelled the first wispy, salt-sweet breath of the Otherworld. If they tempted fate on Lughnasa day, the gods themselves would rush through the thinning veils and put a halt to it. Och, but she wanted Conaire's company, if only for one more day, just one more day of light and laughter . . . she wanted Conaire to *live!*

She tilted her chin and looked him straight in the eye, and tried to veer him away from the inevitable. "Well, Conaire. You'll be wanting to know about your parentage, then."

"My parentage?"

"Aye. Surely that is why you've been coming here all this time, doing a slave's work and wagerin' at *fidchell*." Her gaze slid away. She chose her words carefully, for all she had were suspicions—nothing revealed to her through her visions—but if she were clever, she could draw his interest away from slaking his desire and bringing upon them the fury of the gods. "Your father . . . it's knowledge of him you'll be wanting."

His body tightened. A bluish pall fell over the hilltop; a furtive, shifting breeze fluttered the hem of his tunic.

Abruptly, he rose to his feet, then whirled his back to her, his bronze sword sheath banging against the metal bosses of his girdle. "A full moon ago, such a thing I wanted more than anything." His eyes snapped to hers. "Now, you remind me of that which I'd completely forgotten—something I've searched all of Erin to know for one-and-thirty years."

Her lashes swept down in shame. " 'Tis too great a thing for a man such as you to forget—"

"Aye, but I have. Your eyes . . ." His hands curled into fists. "They plunder a man's senses."

"My eyes have been faulted for worst things, they have, but I'll take no blame for your own forgetfulness." Her back stiffened. " 'Tis enough that ye remember now, when the time has come to have your questions answered. If that be your price—"

"*No.*"

He swept away the *fidchell* board with a swipe of his hand.

The pup leapt from a sound sleep as the wooden pieces spilled atop him.

"Look at me, woman." Conaire pitched down before her. He seized her by the chin and probed her eyes. "It's lying, you are. Lies don't sit well on your tongue. You know nothing—nothing but suspicions—and I've had a bellyful o' those." His grip tightened. "You cannot delay the inevitable, not anymore."

Air gelled in her lungs. A trembling began in her belly and spread through her body, rippling out to her tingling fingertips. The time had come, and though her body rushed with sensation, a strange peace settled upon her mind. Her fight was over. She had tried to save him. Whatever powers manipulated them like the pieces on a *fidchell* board had brought them to this. No one in *Tír na nÓg* nor on this Earth could change the course of her path.

Yet he hesitated, devouring her with his gaze, lingering on the play of shadows in her hair, the curve of her cheek, the gape of her *léine,* and lower . . . then returning anew to pierce her gaze with his own.

"Speak." No tremble warbled her voice. "Tell me the price I must pay."

"The price . . ." He traced her jaw and hesitated as the pad of his finger pressed the vulnerable flesh of her lower lip. ". . . is a kiss."

His body stilled like a hunter crouched in the tall grass. She saw the surprise in his eyes, as if he, too, could not believe he had made such a simple request. But Brigid knew, instinctively, what would happen once they kissed. Even a single embrace could unleash powerful forces.

A strange, shimmering shadow fell over the land. It was like the blurring of her sight before a vision, yet Conaire stood clear and vivid before her. She did not stop to question the fading of the light—'twas Lughnasa day—it was their taunting and teasing that brought down the magic like a shroud.

She leaned forward, the long, weighted plaits of her hair slipping over her shoulders to brush his thighs.

"A kiss, Conaire, I can give ye."

And all the voices of the forest hushed around them. The wind faltered until it no longer scattered dried leaves over the bare rocks that jutted out here and there from the carpet of grass, like the bare bones of the earth. The *Sídh* stilled their restless rustling behind the bushes and trees. The blackbirds paused mid-note, the high tones of their songs ringing in the air.

Conaire plunged his hand into her hair, weaving his fingers deep in the fiery tresses, digging his fingertips into the nape of her neck, and drawing her face toward his. Brigid braced her hands against his solid chest. Hunger flared in his eyes like a bright silver flame, just as his lips descended to meet hers.

"Nay, Conaire."

Her fingers came between them, stopping his lips only a wish away from hers. His breath fanned her cheek, and the hot fury of his wanting tightened every muscle in his body. She saw, for the first time, the sparks of gold scattered like dust in his gray eyes, lights that glowed sharp with desire.

" 'Tis I who am to give you a kiss," she whispered, tracing the firm, moist texture of his mouth, "not the other way 'round."

And so she trailed her fingers down the short scar on his chin, felt the stubble that roughened his jaw, traced the jut of his high, wide cheekbones, discovered with a sense of wonder the sun-kissed color of his skin, and the auburn tips of his dark brown lashes. His hair was as soft and thick as fox fur against her hand. He made a strange, grunting sound deep in his chest, and the vibrations reverberated through his body, so his muscles quivered like the plucked strings of lyres. Something quivered in response deep inside her, vibrating to the same pitch. Touching this man was like teasing a wolf, for she sensed the wildness in him, seething just below the surface. She drew closer to him, to escape the sudden coolness of the wind, until the warmth of their bodies gathered between them. She slipped her other hand around his neck. She pressed her nose beside his, let her eyes flutter shut. She resisted, still, the same way one would resist tasting a newly baked loaf of bread or the very first haunch of fresh lamb after the autumn slaughter. Nothing, she knew, would ever be so glorious as the very first kiss.

She smelled the warm, salty man-scent of him, felt the stubble of his beard raze her lips as she gently, oh, so gently, pressed her mouth against his upper lip, tasting his skin where the sweet juice of the apple lingered, then slipping down to press upon the corner of his lips, and then, and then . . .

'Twas as if the bonds of her body fell away. Their lips, their breath, their spirits mingled. A sound rumbled up from deep inside him, deeper than the man . . . from the core of the earth itself. He dragged her against him until only two thin layers of linen separated them, until the fury of a hundred Lughnasa fires couldn't rival the heat raging between them. And still they kissed, their lips joined and moist, the texture of hard and soft, of demanding and yielding, all so new to her and yet it felt as if nothing that had come before had ever been right . . . and as if finally, on this hilltop, she had been born.

He pulled her away, his eyes white with passion. He gripped her shoulders and squeezed them—hard—as if to prove to himself that she was made of flesh and blood, and not some fairy wraith, set to disappear out of his life as soon as he determined to have her most. "What enchantment is this," he asked hoarsely, "that can bring a warrior to his knees?"

She traced his cheek with her hand, trying to catch her breath. *"Speak to me, Brigid."*

She trailed her trembling fingers over the hard muscles of his chest to feel the thunder of his heart. "It's magic, it is, though 'tis not of my doing. I've not the power to conjure such things alone, *mo rún.*"

His head jerked up, as if he had just noticed the eerie pall that hung over them. Shadows around them softened. Vivid green grass and blazing yellow gorse and bright pink heather bleached into gray. The wind breathed cool on their skin. On the slate-gray surface of the Lough, a flock of ducks suddenly took flight.

She clutched his tunic, trembling still from the force of the kiss. Magic seeped into the air around them like the tartness of distant rain. Her stomach clenched—*Let him not come, not today, for no mortal man can survive one-on-one combat with a warrior of the* Sídh. Her fingers dug deeper into his tunic. She wanted Conaire—*Conaire*—no other, man or god.

Then, suddenly, the light filtering through the ash leaves above them shifted and narrowed. The dappled shadows thinned and curled until pale crescents of light peppered Conaire's tunic, like the *brat* of a revered Druid. She traced one of the tiny slices of moon as her heart swelled in her throat.

"My . . . my vision," she murmured. "Tiny crescents on his cloak . . ."

He did not hear her. He jerked up, bringing her with him. He stepped out from the cover of the ash tree, grasped the hilt of his sword, and squinted up at the sky.

"By the club of the Dagdá . . . Look!"

She followed his gaze, her breath short and knotted in her throat, but she knew what she'd see, for she'd seen it a hundred times before in her vision. The sun hung in a cloudless sky like a two-day-old moon. A blue green light deepened upon her skin. Soon, they would be plunged into an uncanny twilight. Soon, this unearthly moon-sun would burn metallic and white-hot in the sky . . . for the moon eclipsed the sun, and her vision had come to pass.

"The moon passes across the sun." Conaire watched the last glimmers of light bead around the edge of the black disc of a moon. "The time has come, Brigid."

The last bead of light hovered, then died. The world plunged into deep blue darkness. High in the sky hung a black disk threading pearly, translucent light into the star-prickled sky. On the horizon, a dark orange glow hovered.

Brigid stared at Conaire. The midday twilight tinged the planes of his face silver. She gazed upon his features, so new to her, yet as beloved as if her soul had known them for a hundred lifetimes. The shackles of her own guilt fell away; it did not matter that this man had killed her brother in battle; it no longer mattered that he had conquered her tribe. He and she were fated long before his name had fallen cursed from her lips.

Stubble prickled her palm, as she lifted a trembling hand to his face. The memory of the vision swept through her mind; the gray mists of her stubborn ignorance parted, finally. Now, now, she recognized the salt-sweet taste of his kiss, now she recognized the swell of her secret lover's arms; now she recognized the scent of the Otherworld which clung to his skin. The answer had lain before her all these weeks, as plain as the moon, but she had not had the courage to see it.

She curled her fingers into his hair. "Och, Conaire, I've been so blind."

"What is it?" He unclenched his sword, his gaze sharp upon her. "Tell me what you see."

It was a command, but no anger or insistence reverberated in his words. In this eerie twilight, in this meeting of night and day, in this merging of the worlds, the barriers they had held against each other crumbled into dust. There would be no more games between them.

"All me life I've been plagued by a vision—a vision of a man. My lover." The words surged to her throat. "I ne'er knew his face, but I knew I was destined for him. The Sight is wary and uncertain when it grants glimpses of one's own fate. I did not understand the full of it until now." She glanced at the black disk glowing in the sky like hot metal, then back at Conaire's face. " 'Twas you I saw in my vision, *mo rún*."

"Not some creature of the *Sídh?*"

" 'Twas fated we meet, Conaire. Long, long ago."

Her stomach clenched, for there was more she knew, now that the prophecy's knot was unraveled. She knew why Conaire was not like other men . . . for now she knew whence his father came. She held her tongue. There would be time enough, in the passing of the days to come, to ease him into accepting the truth of his lineage.

"In my house, lass, you will have a place of honor." A muscle flexed in his cheek. "In my house, you will be queen."

Her heart rose to her throat. His silver gray eyes burned with new intensity.

"Brigid of the Clan Morna." He clutched her wrists, where her hands lay flat against his chest. "Be my wife."

In the sky above, sunlight burst forth from a tiny spot on the edge of the black moon and rushed like water around one half of the disk. Her soul soared high, high, as light as air beneath the wings of a sparrow. With the uttering of those commanding words, the loneliness which had always clung to her like a dark cloud melted away, filling the void with joy and hope and sunshine.

Conaire's wife. Queen of Morna. No more would she live alone in these woods, dreaming of the impossible. She'd have a strong, mighty husband, she'd have children, she'd live among the people of Conaire's tribe—people who followed the old ways who surely would not fear her. Then another thought came to her—a memory of her father's tearstained face the day he was forced to banish her and her mother from the clan. In her joy, she dared to hope for yet another miracle.

Conaire's fingers tightened around her wrists. "Speak, woman, or I'll kiss the aye out o' you."

She gently tugged her wrists from his grip and stepped back from him, tilting her chin to meet his gaze. "Tonight, in the sacred circle of oaks, by the light of the Lughnasa fires . . . I will become your wife."

He reached for her. "I'll not be waitin' for fires, lass, I'll be making you my wife *now—*"

"I'm the daughter of a king, and I will be a queen," she said, skittering back. "Will ye have no ceremony to the joining, and all your people a-wondering about it?"

"There'll be enough ceremony," he argued, seizing her and pulling her flush against him, *"after* the bedding."

She stopped his kiss with her finger, then lifted her lashes to meet the hunger in his eyes. Daylight lit his features, etched in thwarted passion. "Before we marry in the old way, you must go back to Morna. It is the custom. You must ask for my father's blessing upon this union."

"Your *father,*" he stated, his voice raw with frustration, "is my *subject.*"

"Och, I know the patience will choke ye like a rope, *mo rún.*" *But this is a chance I cannot forfeit, a chance for my father to take me back without shame.* She traced his lower lip, and her fingertip trembled. "I ask you to do this, Conaire, my husband . . . do this for me."

Five

The bellow of bagpipes shook the rafters of Conaire's newly built mead hall. Golden ale splattered on the fresh reeds, as drunken warriors stumbled up to dance. The red-faced pipers clattered the reeds and elbowed flat their bulging leather bags, their fingers flying over the crude pipe-holes, while all around them men jostled and drank and played dice on the paving stones, and sweaty bondswomen hipped their way through the crowd, bracing platters of fresh-roasted boar.

Tonight, the king would take a queen.

Behind the woven wooden screens which walled off the king's living quarters from the rest of the hall, Conaire sank his teeth into the champion's portion of the boar and tore off a greasy shank of meat. Attendants hovered, fastening his leather belt studded with garnets, strapping on his gold arm-bands. A bondswoman teetered on a bench behind him, yanking a stag's-horn comb through his gleaming wet hair. On the third snag, Conaire released a roar which sent her scrambling to the ground.

"Enough." He tossed the haunch toward a platter, sending platter, haunch, and all skidding across the paving stones to crash against a wooden cask, still steaming with bathwater. *"Out, all of you!"*

Aidan sprawled across the mountain of pelts on Conaire's pallet, brooding with a horn of ale braced on his belly. "What's all this murderin' noise about?"

"My wife'll be after thinking I'm a woman," Conaire sneered, jerking his hands through his damp hair, "with all this primping and preening."

Aidan's teeth curled back in a snarl as his gaze followed his foster-brother's pacing. "A wee bit o' the marriage shakes, have ye? Not a horn of ale ago ye were grinning like a wolf and announcin' your marriage to all who'd hear. Don't be tellin' me the fairy magic has worn off already?"

Conaire ripped open the laces at his throat. "You'd be liking that, I'm thinking."

" 'Tis no secret I've no liking for enchantments." Aidan rolled to his side, then held up a hand against Conaire's fierce glare. "Don't be lookin' at me like that. Your rod's ready to jump at the smell o' her. You should have wed her and bed her this very afternoon, but you left her there. *You*, who has never waited for man nor god. Is it a wonder I've a powerful dark feelin' about all this?"

"And I thought 'twas the ale which made you as dour as an old goat since I rode in from the woods." Conaire jerked aside the woolen curtain and gestured to a bondswoman laden with a tray of mead. He swung a horn toward his foster-brother. "Take this. I will have more from you than frowns on the day o' my wedding."

"Ye've had enough o' me best wishes," Aidan muttered, rising to snatch the cup, "at the two other weddings o' yours I've witnessed."

"Aye, and look what that's brought me." He braced a foot against a bench and peered impatiently out at the revelry at the other end of the hall. "Nothing but a lass who weeps at the sound o' my footsteps, and a stringy princess of an Ulsterwoman."

"And two and twenty fields o' the finest grazing land an Ulsterman's ever seen, a hillside full o' cows and a bull to rival the bull o' Connacht, and a seat in Tara's mead hall." Aidan sucked mead off the droop of his mustache and spit out the shank of hair. "What does this creature o' yours bring ye? Nothing but the clothes on her back, and whatever wicked enchantment she holds over you."

Conaire belted down the honey-mead in a single gulp. Aye, aye, perhaps he was bewitched; for now, out of the magic of Brigid's presence, he could think of no other reason why a warrior, the Champion of Ulster—a *king*—bowed without a battle to her foolish request; and left the woman he would make his wife standing alone on the hillside, while he stood burning for the taste o' her, waiting like a common slave in his own mead hall for an underling's arrival.

Conaire thrust his empty horn in Aidan's belly. "You'll be singing another song when you lay eyes upon her."

"She could be as fair as Deirdre o' the Sorrows and it wouldn't matter, I tell you."

Conaire barked an incredulous laugh. "Is this *your* mouth I'm hearing these words coming from?"

"Beauty never boiled a boar, or spun thread or wove cloth—and rarely does it bring cattle and land—and 'tis *that* you marry for." Aidan jerked his chin toward the tumult in the hall. "If you'll be wantin' beauty, find a bondswoman. There's enough o' them itchin' to share your bed."

Conaire jerked closed the woolen curtains. "You'll be making a feast o' your words, when you lay eyes upon her. I'll wager a bull upon it."

"I'm a bull richer, then. I'll not be blinded by the beauty of a *cailleach.*"

In the midst of Aidan's words, sunlight thrust golden fingers through the cracks in the wooden screens. The clatter of dancing feet ceased with a stumble, and the music wheezed quiet as a shocked silence fell over the mead hall. Aidan's last word carried like a shout. Its ugliness lay between them, writhing like a strange living thing.

A blood-red flush worked its way up Aidan's face and flooded over his scalp. His gaze slid away. He fingered the door curtain aside and peered toward the light. "Well, ye've no more waitin' to do. King Flann has arrived."

"You've been spending too much time between the legs o' that Morna girl." Conaire snatched his sword from where it leaned against the screen, and rasped it into the loop hanging from his belt. "That Christian girl o' yours knows naught of my *wife*."

Aidan's jaw hardened; his throat worked, but no words fell from his lips. Conaire frowned as he whirled his mantle over his shoulders. 'Twas not Aidan's way to judge a woman so quickly—'twas not Aidan's way to think much o' women at all, out of bed.

"Come, no more of this." Conaire slapped Aidan's shoulder, propelling him into the hall with the force of the blow. "Stand behind me now, Aidan, as my witness and my brother."

The excited, murmuring crowd parted to make way for Conaire's arrival. With a scrape of bench and clatter of pipes, the musicians stumbled off the small, raised dais, retreating as Conaire stepped upon it and swiveled to face Brigid's father.

King Flann stood in the wispy gray light of a smoke-hole, in a circle littered with gnawed meat bones and sticky pools of spilled liquid. The hem of his blood-red woolen cloak trailed into the crushed rushes, caked thickly with mud. His breath wheezed through his throat as he braced himself upon a polished wooden cane, for the path between the King of Morna's ring-fort in the valley, and Conaire's ring-fort under construction on the height, was steep and rocky. Deep blue jewels flashed between his gnarled knuckles.

The old king lowered his eyelids in greeting, no more. Conaire chose to ignore the slight. The fragile, old husk of a man looked as if one good, stiff wind would shatter his bones into powder. With a flick of a finger, Conaire commanded a bondswoman to offer his guest meat and mead. King Flann lifted the flat palm of his hand as she stumbled forward.

Conaire's nostrils flared. "Refusing my hospitality, King Flann?"

The elderly king made a sparse gesture to the two black-robed priests flanking him. "We fast today."

Conaire nodded for the bondswoman to step back into the shadows. Strange ways these Christians had, denying themselves food in a time of plenty. At least now he could dispense with the formalities.

"I've summoned you here to celebrate with us this night."

Flann's features crumpled as if he'd gulped a cup full of four-day-old milk. "Do ye mock an old man? Your Lughnasa is a pagan feast, of no interest to a Christian."

"And what of a wedding feast?" Conaire's brows shot together. Surely the old man knew. Conaire had made no secret o' it as he rode into the *ráth* today. "Is that of interest to a Christian?"

The old king shrugged his shoulders. "Aye, a marriage, of course. 'Tis a sacred thing, that."

Conaire frowned and glanced beyond Flann, to the two Romans hovering in the shadows. One dodged Conaire's gaze and nervously fingered a wooden cross hanging around his neck. *Cowards.* Conaire had suffered the priests' presence in his kingdom because a conquered people took comfort in their presence—and he cared not what gods a people worshipped, as long as they remained loyal to *him.* Now, he stilled the urge to skewer them for delaying his union with his bride. The wretches had kept the truth from the old man, and thus he'd be the first bearer of the tidings.

Conaire elbowed the folds of his cloak behind him and hitched his hands on his hips. "I'm to be wed this night."

"Wed? Again?" King Flann's brows raised, and crumpled a river of wrinkles into his forehead. "Such a marriage as that will be a pagan thing, taking a third wife while the others still live—"

"I'll be wedding your daughter."

The revelers jostled in nervous curiosity. Flann raised his head and peered oddly at Conaire through sunken blue eyes. Smoke from the fire on the far end of the hall whirled and eddied around the smoke-hole, casting a wavering light between the kings. Conaire waited for the old king's well-wishes, his thoughts already halfway to the sacred circle of oaks.

"D'ye have nothing to say, man?" Aidan surged forward. "The king honors you and your clan, by choosin' to marry your daughter, though he'd no help from ye—"

"You are mistaken." The jeweled chains about Flann's neck clanked as he shook his head. "I have no daughter."

A frisson of shock rippled through the crowd. Somewhere, a cup clattered to the floor. A bagpipe, accidentally crushed, wheezed a discordant breath. Conaire dragged himself back from a distant place, and glared at the old king in disbelief.

"Is it age rattling your brains," Aidan hissed, "or are ye simply a *fool?*"

The old king tightened his grip on the head of his cane. "I have no daughter."

"Think again." Conaire pushed Aidan aside, anger simmering in his chest like a pot of water set to boil. He swaggered off the dais and towered over the old king, who stared at some unfocused point beyond the hall. "Think hard, Flann, and mayhap I'll forgive the lapse as a cruel trick o' your fading memory. Brigid, you called her when she was born to your second wife. Niall's sister, and your only living kin." He lowered his voice to a pitch which had raised the hairs on many a man's neck over the years. "Tomorrow, your banished daughter will become queen. I'd advise you to bless the union."

Aidan's voice rose from behind Conaire. "Only a fool would spit in fortune's face, Flann."

The old man stank of decay and musky herbs, and the pink flesh of his scalp shone through his thinning mane of hair. Conaire stilled the urge to shake him; he was naught but an ignorant old man, mired deep in the ditch of his own digging. He cursed him, still, and he cursed Brigid for forcing this duty upon him, and for clinging to a young girl's distorted memories.

"I have no daughter."

The crowd rumbled and staggered back, farther away from the two kings. One of the priests grasped Flann's sleeve, but the old king raised a regal finger, and the priest released him. Conaire glared down at the old man's pink pate, wishing the king was worthy of a challenge, for his palm itched for the feel of his sword hilt, and his muscles burned to swing the heavy steel.

"What is it, Flann?" Conaire flexed his fingers and glanced at the old man's knotted throat, wondering if it were worth the effort to choke some sense into him. "What can you not bear? The thought of a pagan wedding under a moonless sky? Or the bitterness knowing I shall have what women I please, while you must send yours away?"

" 'Tis pity I have for you and yours, for your souls will burn for eternity."

"Nay, nay," Conaire continued, his lips curling in scorn, " 'tis the thought of my dark *pagan* blood mixing with the blood of a daughter of your own loins. Aye, aye," he nodded, " 'tis the thought of my son with my face and my gods and *your* crown—"

"She will bear no sons." The aged king jerked his head up and met Conaire's glare. Flann's red-rimmed eyes burned, like twin holes in a dead husk of a charred tree, revealing the embers still flaring with life within. "Thirty-one summers you've seen, *King* Conaire. No child of yours has ever taken root—no one ever will."

Conaire's sword rang in the room; a woman's scream pierced the shocked silence. The priests lunged for their king as Conaire swung, but Aidan clamped both hands on Conaire's arm, and, carried by the momentum, flew in front of him, knocked Flann into his priest's arms, and stopped Conaire mid-swing.

Conaire bared his teeth as Aidan scrambled to his feet. *"Out of my way—"*

"Would ye kill her father," Aidan snapped, "as well as her brother?"

The words penetrated the blood-red haze of his battle lust. He shook off Aidan's grip and stepped back, his heart pumping, his chest heaving with thwarted murder, the hilt of the sword scalding his palm.

The priests helped the old king to his feet. Dirty rushes clung to his blood-red cloak, but the old man stood chin upraised, not deigning to wipe them off.

Conaire pushed Aidan aside, and stood so close to King Flann that his words left spittle on the old man's hair.

"For my wife's sake—for the queen—I grant you your worthless life." Conaire scraped the tip of his sword across the king's golden torque. "Heed me: You are forbidden to speak to her, to speak *of* her, even to lay eyes upon her—except to crawl like a dog begging for her forgiveness. If you disobey me, I shall tear out your heart while you still live, and feed it in pieces to the wolfhounds before your dying eyes."

Conaire whirled on his heel, strode the length of the hall, and hacked the woolen curtains of his chamber aside. Aidan followed, as the rumbling in the room rose to a roar and the priests hurried the old king out of the hall. Conaire speared his sword into the mountain of pelts.

"You're bewitched for sure," Aidan said, moments later, from the doorway, "to let a man who said such a thing live and breathe."

He curled his hands into fists. Blood lust still thrummed through his veins. "For a woman gifted with the Sight, in this, Brigid is blind."

Aye, Brigid . . . waiting for him in the circle of oaks. A muscle flexed in his cheek. He wondered if she sensed this moment, if she saw it with her Sight—if, even now, she stood trembling, alone, the illusions she'd nurtured for too many years shattered around her. He seized his sword and slung it through his belt loop. Brigid no longer needed a father. Tonight, she'd take a husband.

Conaire shunted aside the ripped woolen curtains. "I'm going to her."

"Now? Alone?" When Conaire did not answer, Aidan followed and clamped a hand on his shoulder. "Listen to me. She's Flann's daughter, no matter what that old fool said this night. Think, man." Aidan stepped in front of him and his sour-ale breath blasted in his face. "Ye cannot gallop alone into the dark o' the woods with anger blinding you like this. You're going to wed the sister o' the man ye killed on the field o' battle, the daughter o' the man whose kingship ye stole. How do you know they're not in league, the two of them—"

"You've the fears of an old woman." Conaire yanked off his foster-brother's hand. "And I've a bride waiting, which neither god nor man will keep me away from any longer."

The swift and impassioned pounding of a horse's hooves rumbled up from the earth. Brigid sensed his approach with the bare soles of her feet, long before the silhouette of a rider loomed on the hill, against the amber blaze of the Lughnasa fires.

An edgy gust of wind buffeted her torchlight. A needle of wood pierced her thumb, as she tightened her grip around the gnarled shaft. The torchlight was no more than a spark compared to the glare splashing down the hillside from the raging pyres. Yet the shadow of the rider did not hesitate; he swaggered his body off the beast, snatched the reins, and with a flap of his cloak strode down the hill, following the light which winnowed like golden fingertips through the fencing of tall oaks, toward where she stood within the sacred circle.

Her husband had arrived.

Her blood swelled hot; her breath thickened in her lungs. The furtive, midnight breezes caressed her skin as warm as a baby's breath, yet suddenly she trembled with cold. With a swirl of her cloak, she began to pace, casting wary glances with each pass at the descending, broad-shouldered shadow. Och, the *Sídh* danced boldly tonight, sparkling around Conaire and silvering the twisting path with Otherworldly moonlight. The music of the fairy wind sluiced through the hollow reeds of Lough Riach, and thrummed high in the air. Her ears roared with the rattling, with the giggling snatches of voices, with the tinkling bells and wispy aromas of Otherworldly roastings. She could not *think* with such a din; but she knew 'twas more than the flux of magic and the shifting of the worlds which churned her thoughts.

She sank the torch through the pelt of grass, deep into the yielding earth, then rasped her hands down the length of her saffron *brat*. Aye, it was the moon-dark tides surging in her Celt's blood—hotter and hungrier than ever before. The hollow of her palms, her throat, the shadows beneath her cheekbones, the taut arches of her bare feet . . . all the empty places tingled, as if scrubbed with crushed nettles. 'Twas a power deeper and stronger than a mere woman's will which seized her tonight. She closed her eyes and sucked in a lungful of the tart-sweet, midnight air, letting the flux and flow of the tides inundate her senses, letting it lead her through the mysteries to come.

And so it was when, moments later, she heard her husband's husky, welcoming words.

"Who do you dance for, *bean si?* "

The dew-drenched hem of her saffron cloak slapped her ankles as she whirled to a sudden stop. Only then did she realize she'd flattened a circle of grass about the shaft of the torch with her dancing. She swiped away the hair plastered across her cheek, as a looming shadow separated from an oak. Conaire paused on the edge of the sacred circle, one foot braced on a knotty, risen root, the light blazing his hair into fire.

"I dance for my king, and my husband." Sweeping her heavy mane over one shoulder, she bowed down in obeisance. "I dance for you, Conaire."

" 'Tis glad I am o' that."

"Aye, I thought you might be." She straightened and tilted her chin. " 'Tis the last merry dance I'll be leading you, I'm thinking."

His face was swathed in shadows, but she sensed his amusement like a sweet, warm glow. Then it ebbed into something hotter, something heavier. The anxious wind faded, like a bellows breathing its last. A fern swayed; a knocked pebble sputtered across the ground . . . then an unearthly stillness seized the air.

And suddenly, Brigid felt as if she were rising above, looking down upon the two of them, sensing a strange familiarity in the dusting of stars smeared across the sky; knowing with stark clarity that this night was planned by some higher power, before there was time or men or reason. And in the brief moment of wisdom, she wondered whether this was a vision of the night to come, or whether this evening, this act, was simply elemental; if she sensed no more than man claiming woman, a ritual as old as time, as simple as the rain falling, as necessary as air and water—or some greater joining, some repeat of a union blessed in an earlier life, and here, finally, come together again. As quickly as the vision came, it slipped from her grasp, and she stood still in the circle of oaks.

Then all thoughts of the world around her ceased . . . for Conaire loomed over her, blocking out the world. A shock of hair shaded his brow, but could not dim the golden sparks in his silver eyes, burning hotter than any Lughnasa fire. Impatience thrummed from the taut muscles of his body like the strum of a hundred thousand lyres.

She grasped her brooch—his first gift to her—and tugged it off. Her cloak slipped off her shoulders and pooled at her feet.

The cool night air tightened the blue woad, where she had painted the ancient symbols of fertility upon her thighs, belly, and breasts—the only covering she'd worn beneath the saffron cloak, now puddled like melted butter around her ankles.

A hiss of surprise was all she heard before he swung his iron-muscled arm around her waist and thrust her against his chest. She bent back for him like a water reed to a gale, sensing with some deeper wisdom his man's need to lay claim with the force of his hands and his lips, what had been denied to him for so long. He palmed her chin with a calloused hand, rasped his warrior's, rough-edged fingers down the column of her throat, then grasped the swell of her breast as she arched with a muffled groan into the hot cup of his hand.

Her breath soughed harshly through her lips. The moon-dark tides flooded her senses, blinding her, deafening her to all but the man who held her upright in his grasp. She moaned in protest as he dragged his hand away from the rigid peak of her breast to explore further. He swallowed the sound with the hungry rasp of his lips.

'Twas not the gentle kiss of the afternoon—nay, not this heated mingling of flesh. He nudged her mouth open to suckle her lips, her tongue; to draw out the pith of her soul. She fisted the linen of his tunic. His arm dug into her back—were it not for his hold, she knew she'd slip to the ground, as fluid as a raindrop off the sloping hollow of a fern.

Just as suddenly as he had grasped her, he tore his lips away. "You are mad, woman." He grasped the bones of her hips and hiked her against his loins. "Have you no sense at all, what you do to a man?"

"Nay . . ." The threads of his fine linen tunic nipped at her swollen, heavy breasts. The hollow of her loins yearned for his heat and his hungry strength. "Teach me, *mo rún.*"

"By the gods . . ." His fingers dug into her hips, as his gaze traveled over the white arch of her throat. "An innocent bared for the slaughter." With rough hands he clasped the spare flesh of her buttocks and flattened her against his loins, forcing her to stop her mindless gyrating. " 'Twill *be* a slaughter, if you do not stop this teasing, woman."

She knew she should cease her wriggling—for his shoulders tensed like rock beneath her hands as he struggled to restrain a power she knew nothing of—all for her sake. But her thighs trembled and passion churned in her blood. All sense of self-preservation had deserted her the moment he'd touched her. Now, his arousal pressed solid and thick against her belly, throbbing, and her body ached to draw his sap of life deep into her womb.

"Is there no ceremony?" he asked gruffly, jerking back as she raised her mouth for a kiss. "No words to be spoken?"

"Och, Conaire," she said, pressing so close the jewels of his belt bit into her belly, "you'd think *you* were the virgin, with all your talk."

He seized her and shook her; then he lifted her level with his gaze. " 'Twill not be an easy fit—and I am not a patient man."

The wind returned, breathing through the boughs above them with a sweet, high sound, like the sighs of fairy-children. Brigid traced his clean-shaven jaw with her fingers. Aye, rough-edged he was, but a gentleness lurked in this warrior's heart.

"There's a price to pay for every pleasure." She tugged off his fist-sized brooch and tossed the jeweled ring toward the torchlight, as the heavy wool *whooshed* off his shoulders. "Love me, my husband. In that, you will make me your wife."

The violence of his kiss forced her head into the bulwark of his shoulder. Her eyes fluttered closed; his tunic smelled of wood-ash from the mead hall, the nubby texture of the fibers imprinted on her bare skin. Dizzy with his kisses—hot and wet and ravenous and ceaseless—she wound her arms around his neck and plunged her fingers beneath the rope of his gold torque, holding on to him so as not to collapse at his feet. She had never felt the quivering shock of human lips pressed against human lips—och, she'd been alone so long!—now she feasted upon the sensation, until every nerve on her body throbbed raw and exposed.

Linen snarled as he fumbled to shed his clothing, then gave way with a tear. She tried to help with his belt, but her hands trembled so that he yanked them up with a growl and planted them on his shoulders. He pushed away from her to rid himself of the tangle, but her groan of protest froze in her throat as the naked, white-hot flesh of his chest seared her from loins to breast.

There was a blindness in his eyes as he hooked her knees and pressed her down in the circle of flickering torchlight. 'Twould be enough to strike fear in any woman's soul, to have such a broad-shouldered, lean-hipped tower of roped muscles pressing her against the ground—but she was as blind with passion as he. All was a muddled storm of sensation . . . the damp grass beneath her, the heaviness of his body upon her, the strange pulsing of the earth against her limbs. Their lips joined, merged, separated, explored, then came together again. His calloused fingers rasped over her tender nipples; she broke the kiss and gasped, then choked upon her own moan as he lowered his head and sucked the rosy, swollen tip of one breast into his hot mouth.

It was not enough; 'twas never enough. The more he touched, the more she craved his touch. She raked her fingers through his hair, pressed his head closer. His teeth scraped the taut, aching nub, as he slipped his hand between her thighs and yanked the willing limbs open to the brush of the night air.

She arched off the ground with the first rough, unfamiliar invasion of his fingers. He murmured something, something harsh and vibrating with frustration, but she could not hear for the roaring of her blood. He touched her again, gentler now, but 'twas not enough—she needed more and told him so, tilting her hips against his hand and sweeping her fingers down the length of his chest, seeking his root, seeking some distant fulfillment.

He throbbed hot in her hand, but she'd barely closed her fingers around the thickness of him, before he jerked back and stopped the deep stroking of her womb. His knees nudged hers apart, and he rolled between them. His hands tangled in her hair, spread out over the grass like liquid fire, and his lips joined hers again, and again, eager, ravenous, undeniable . . . while below, at the core of their bodies, the hot tip of him pressed deep against her loins.

Then, he froze.

She dragged in a ragged breath. It was all happening so fast, so fluidly, in a moment they would be one. Och, she ached at this unexpected stillness. He brushed the faint grimace of frustration on her brow, and she blinked her eyes open.

Perhaps the torch flared, or perhaps 'twas naught but the muddlings of her overwrought mind, but it seemed in that moment as if the arched canopy of leaves above them shone brilliant and gold, and it seemed as if a hundred thousand birds sang amid the boughs—but 'twas only a passing thought, for her gaze fixed upon Conaire, lowering his head toward her. 'Twas as if he sipped from some sacred chalice, as he brushed the barest of kisses against her mouth.

Then he lifted his head. He had stanched the blindness with the sheer force of his will. Now his eyes blazed the purest silver she'd ever seen. His own thoughts fluxed clearly in those eyes, and suddenly she realized that he, too, came to this place an innocent, for however many women he had lain with in the past, however well he knew how to rouse a woman's body, before this night, before this moment, he had never given of his soul.

But soon the silver of his eyes clouded with need. He kissed her again, greedily, and then again. She slipped her hands around his back and held him tight. She felt his control snap.

His knees jerked, spreading her legs wide open. The burning shaft sank deeper, and she thought she'd die of wanting, if he did not soon fill her womb.

He groaned and stretched his length into her. She cried out, sharp and loud, but 'twas not from the tear of pain—like the swift bite of lightning upon the land—but from the glory of the heat of him filling her up.

He pulled back and out—she raked his shoulders with her nails to take him in again—and he plunged deeper, and still their bodies moved, and moved, his breathing harsh in her ear, his words unintelligible—the unfettered murmurings of his soul. Something coiled tight within her with each powerful thrust, and she thrashed her head, this way and that, the night dew soaking her hair and bathing her cheeks. This was the joining, this was life—she was the moist, welcoming soil beneath the drive of the falling rain. She felt herself buoyed up, up, up— with him, against him—until they could rise no more, and with one choked cry, she tore open just as the throbbing heat of his seed filled her.

Long after the torchlight flickered and died, she lay quivering beneath him, his head heavy on her breast, while the starlight blinded her.

Morning nudged away the veil of night. Brigid nestled deeper in the warm cocoon of Conaire's embrace. In the woods around her, she sensed the stragglers of the *Sídh,* rousing from their fern-canopied beds of moss to stagger about like servants woken too early to work, plundering through the chill, shifting Earthly mists into the warmth of the Otherworld. Not until the coming of Samhain three months hence would the walls grow thin enough again for human and inhuman to mingle so freely. The growing weight of the wall pressed against her skin like a fog, muffling the wavering fairy voices drifting through the mists until she heard them no more.

Above, on the hill, the ashes of the Lughnasa fires simmered and popped. A single blackbird cawed to its mate high in the canopy of boughs. In the distance, Brigid's cow lowed mournfully.

She blinked her eyes open. Conaire's chest stretched out before her, rigid muscle covered by battle-scarred skin. *Her husband.* The warm salt-sweat scent of him clung to her hair. In the growing light of day, she dared what she'd no sense to do last night; she let her gaze linger upon the form of the chosen one, keeping still so as not to wake the sleeping giant.

Och, look at him, sprawled out on the grass, as naked as a newborn, but for the folds of cloak twisted haphazardly across his loins. Any other man would look vulnerable so exposed, aye, but not Conaire—nay, not a man so broad-beamed, thick-thighed, the muscles of his body rock-hard even in slumber. Och, she'd never known the like of such a man. 'Twas a wonder he'd not broken all her bones with the blind fury of his passion last night.

Her skin grew hot at the memory. Lazily, she tilted her head back against the ball of his shoulder, and glanced up at his face. In slumber, his proud features relaxed into the laziest of smiles. Brigid's own lips twitched. Och, a warrior he was, aye, 'twas true. But in the cool light of morning, this king of kings had the look of a boy who'd outplayed all the others at hurley.

In the distance, her cow lowed again, a broken sound—a pleading cry to be eased of the sagging weight of her udder. The world beckoned, there was no more hiding within this sacred circle. Carefully, she slipped out of Conaire's arms. And winced.

Aye, there's no avoiding the price of pleasure, she thought as she pushed the tangle of his cloak off her legs. Cringing, she eased up to her knees, then slowly straightened against the sore protests of her thighs. She walked gingerly to her cloak, pooled on the grass where she'd first dropped it.

"Nay, lass."

His words were but a whisper; she turned to look at him as she gathered the cloak from the ground. His smoky eyes, heavy-lidded, watched her from behind the veiling of his lashes. She had a sneaking suspicion that he'd been awake all along.

"Leave the cloak, wife. I'm thinking I like the sight o' you better without it."

She jerked the wool tight around her. "I'm thinking ye've gotten an eyeful already."

"Aye, that I did."

Heat flushed her face; in the rage of their passion last night, she'd not had a moment for shyness. Now, in the growing light of morning, she remembered that her body was thin and angular, her breasts small—and so she covered herself against the scrutiny of a king who'd undoubtedly slept with a hundred thousand softer, fairer, fuller-bodied women.

She sidled a glance at him. A slow, lazy grin had spread over his face.

"Och, look at ye." The words tumbled out of her, with a rush of pleasure in the knowledge that he found her body pleasant to look upon. "There ye go, grinning as bold as a cock."

"It's a queer man who wouldn't, the morning after his wedding." The grin widened into a leer. "A stranger one still, to be morose with such a woman standing naked before him."

"Have you no mercy, Conaire?" She fisted the slipping folds at her throat. "Will I not be having a bit of privacy, now that we're wed? Must ye leer at me, as if I were a haunch of mutton?"

"It's pleased I am, to see you up and walking about."

"Did ye think I'd be laying about at this hour?" She searched the flattened grass for the glint of her brooch. "There's food to prepare and a cow to milk—"

"There'll be no more milking cows for the queen of Morna."

She found the brooch and swept it up. She jabbed the pin through the folds. "Are you offerin' up yourself, King Conaire, to ease that poor beast's pain?"

" 'Tis well known to you, lass, that I can be coerced." He stretched his arms under his head. The blanket inched down, over the rise of his swelling root. "But I'm thinkin' you'll have none o' me today."

"Och, listen to ye." She slipped one arm out of the folds of the cloak, and ran her fingers through her tangled hair. "You'd like me to be limping about like a three-legged dog, so you could swagger about full to the neck with pride."

"Nay, I'd rather you bartered your charms for the price o' milkin' that cow."

"I'll be doing no bartering today." She swept a brazen glance over the half-naked length of him. "Of the two of us, it seems 'tis I who fared the better after the night. *You're* still lying on your back like a worn-out old hound."

"Does this have the look of a man too tired to love you, lass?"

Conaire jerked the cloak off his loins. Her face flushed at the sight of him so engorged in the broad daylight.

"I see you're all puffed up with pride again." She lifted a teasing brow. "A soul would think you'd have more dignity, a man of your age, a king, thrice-wed."

" 'Twas my first wedding, last night."

"Och, you're fibbing. You've two other wives, don't I know it."

"The others don't matter anymore."

A teasing rejoinder died in her throat. He was a warrior, too hard-skinned to ever utter sweet words to a woman—she knew better than ever to expect such a thing from him—this was the closest she'd ever get to a declaration of love.

He held out his open palm. "Come here, wife."

Another day, another time, she might buck at the command in his voice—she was his queen, not a bondswoman to be ordered about—but now she craved the strength of his embrace. In the end, she knew, they would both be slaves to one another.

She opened her cloak like the wings of a great bird, and let it billow over them as she sank into his arms. His fingers swept into the tangle of her hair, lifting it up, weighing it in his hands. His root throbbed against her thigh.

His fingers tightened in her hair. "You have two days."

She lifted her head from the snug cup of his shoulder. He slipped one of his hands between her legs. He'd barely parted her nether lips, before she jerked at the soreness.

He removed his hand. "Two days to heal, no more. It should be enough, for the best healer south of Cruachan." He rasped his lips over hers, wiping away her wince with his kiss. "After that, I warn you: No more reprieves."

She released a throaty laugh. He kissed her again, deeper, until he pulled away with a coarse curse.

In the distance, the cow lowed insistently. "I must go to her now. 'Tis cruel to leave her so."

"We'll ride to the beast." He rose with her and gestured to where his horse stood, head-bent, amid the mists. "Aye, a horse, lass. Did ye think I'd have the queen of Morna walk into her own *ráth* the day after her wedding?"

"Morna?"

" 'Tis where we're going, after you milk that wretched cow." Conaire snatched his tunic from the ground and elbowed his way into it. "You didn't think the king and queen would live in a hut in the midst o' the woods, did you?"

She watched Conaire as he tugged on his boots and swept his cloak over his shoulder, kicking around the flattened grass in search of his brooch, wondering how he could act so calmly, when he'd just set her whole world to rights again. If they were off to Morna . . . The hope she'd almost not dared to hold burst in riotous full bloom. "Da . . . Da blessed the union, then."

Conaire straightened, saw her face, and his visage darkened like a sudden winter storm.

"No." He shook his head. "No, lass."

The tender bubble which had swelled so swiftly in her chest exploded with white-hot pain, spearing shards into her heart.

"Damn your father to the fires of his Christian hell." His gray eyes shot sparks, like the pounding of a blacksmith's anvil. "He denied you, Brigid, there's no softening the truth. He wants none o' you."

She dropped her gaze and stared blindly at the crushed reeds beneath her feet. *He wants none o' you.* What a fool she was, hoping for the impossible. It seemed that nothing had changed with the passing of the years, that her father's heart had hardened to stone instead of softening with time.

" 'Tis the priests." She spit the word. "They always had such power over him—"

"How long will you be blinding yourself? 'Twas your *father* who cast you out—no other."

She turned away and seized the shaft of the torch. Conaire could not understand; he knew no father nor mother; he knew not the strength of the bonds of blood. Nor had he witnessed the tears upon Da's face—the priests flanking him like ravens— the day she and Ma were exiled from the clan. Conaire would have her shut Da out, but love was not to be tamed so easily. Love bound her to both men; perhaps, someday, Conaire would come to understand the futility of fighting it.

She mocked a careless shrug as she yanked the torch out of the ground. "It's the aged branch that's hardest to bend, I'm thinking. There's no use bothering about it." They'd be in Morna but a short time, and then she'd be rid of the place and the man. "It's Ulster I'm thinking on, and Tara hill. 'Tis no doubt I'll find a better welcome there."

"You'll find welcome enough here."

"We'll not stay long enough to wear it through, then." The torch furrowed a trail in the grass behind her, as she headed out of the circle of oaks. "The Uí Néill will not take kindly to their champion hidin' away in the west—"

"The Uí Néill will find another champion." He seized the torch, forcing her to spin around to face him. "This is my home. And yours. We'll not be running away from it."

She glared at him and shook her head in disbelief. Och, he

did not understand. She could not live within the *ráth*. Surely he didn't think he could bring her back to the same people who'd cast her out, to a father who still denied her.

"I am king here." He speared the torch deep into the earth. "In this place I will build a clan of my own: The Uí Conaire. 'Tis what I have fought for all these years."

Something heavy sank inside her, dragging her spirits deep into the mire of fear and foreboding. She should have known, she should have seen . . . Deep within this warrior's heart hid a yearning for family, for heritage, though he knew the wanting not by that name, but as a lust for kingship.

She cast about for another solution. "There'll be other kingdoms you'll conquer—"

"Aye, but 'twill be done from the *ráth* I build for you, on the hill o'ershadowing your father's."

"Have ye no sense?" *Och, Conaire, are ye blind, blind, blind to the ways of humankind? You cannot force men to stare into their own fear.* "I cannot live there."

"You are the daughter of the king of Morna, and I am his over-king. It's where you belong."

"It's talking, ye are." Her voice trembled. "Talk cannot turn a poisoned mind."

"You are my queen, and my wife." He threw back his powerful shoulders, and the expression on his face was that of a king who would get what he wished—of a man who'd never been thwarted. "I'll hear no more talk o' this, woman. Come. Today I bring a queen to my people."

Six

Brigid kneaded the greasy shank of wool to coax more slender thread through her pinched fingers. Her wrist cracked with stiffness and cold, as she rotated the spindle to turn another length of yarn around its swelling middle. The first chill howl of winter prowled outside the circular hut she and Conaire shared within the *ráth* he'd built atop the drumlin. A gust blasted through the plugs of moss in the wattle and daub, buffeting the fire. She shrugged deeper into her mantle and squinted over her work.

Suddenly she started upright. The spindle clattered to the paving stones, trailing a winding, red river of wool across the floor.

She rounded the carved wooden screen that separated the sleeping area from the main room of the hut. A dark-haired bondswoman, bent over a simmering cauldron, froze like a hare caught unawares by a fox.

"Stoke that fire." Brigid checked that the spits and ladles and other cooking utensils hung neatly on the wall, that none of her weaving or sewing lay about the floor. She toed the rushes for freshness. "We'll be needing food. Fetch two of the moorhens caught this morning, and put them on to boil. Mead, also—plenty of mead. And bring some barley cakes and honey."

The bondswoman tilted her head toward the gape of the smoke-hole, her mouth slack, painstakingly figuring the time of day by the slant of the cold gray light.

"Don't be counting the wattles." Och, couldn't the foolish girl sense his approach? Couldn't she feel the rumble in the earth, the welcoming growl of the sky? Even the pup sensed it, for he lifted his head, sniffed the air, then sprang up and nosed his way out the door. "We've no time for idleness. The king is coming."

Brigid reined in her impatience as the half-wit set diligently to scratching the threadbare linen over her inner thigh, her head cocked for the sound of Conaire's approach. Och, it must be like blindness to be without the Sight. It was if the grass itself stiffened to greet Conaire, and yet this woman still stood, hearing nothing but the bleating of the penned sheep and the curses of the workers, as they wove blackthorn bushes atop the wooden hurtle fences which ringed the fort. Aye, Conaire had been gone for six nights, battling Leinster cattle thieves on the southern border, and aye, he was not expected until the waning of the moon—but to Brigid, it seemed that only a deaf person couldn't hear him galloping across the fields toward the *ráth*.

"Will ye stand there and let the day slip away?" Brigid seized two sticks from a heap against the wall and tossed them beneath the boiling cauldron. She snapped the fringed hem of her tunic away from the scattered sparks. "Off to your tasks. You can't cook a moorhen by boiling it in your mind."

The girl set to work with a confused frown creasing her brow. Och, how the wretched people of Morna mock their queen, Brigid thought, as she slipped behind the screen to don a clean *léine*. She'd been served by a dozen bondswomen since Conaire first brought her here. The only one who had dared to remain in her service was this girl-child, as daft as a mule.

But she'd not think of that, not now. She'd not think of the deafening loneliness of being an outcast in the midst of a lively village. Conaire would be here soon, to fill this wretched, smoky, dark place with light—to push back the oppressive stench of fear. She clutched a comb carved from the antlers of a king stag, and tugged it through her hair until the tresses crackled. *Six days*. 'Twas the longest he'd been away since their marriage.

Already, the suffocating burden of these heavy walls began to lighten upon her shoulders.

As she slipped the last copper ring on her finger, the wolf-hounds in the fort began barking. Soon after a cry went up among the men.

"The king! The king!"

Brigid rounded the screen in time to see the bondservant splatter a long-handled spoon into the cauldron. The half-wit turned on her, her mouth slack, a vague crease on her brow. Brigid did not look away; she had ceased hiding the truth long ago. It was not the first time, nor would it be the last, that the Sight would come upon her unawares. She would not have Conaire come thirsty and hungry into a cold house, simply to halt the frightened whispers of Conaire's people.

After a clatter of hooves, the door burst open. Conaire strode in. Firelight flashed off his sword, off the gold arm-bands encasing his biceps, and the thick torque around his neck. Rainwater dripped from his dark mane of hair, and ran in rivulets over the tight weave of his purple *léine*. He shook himself off like a great shaggy dog, then swept his hair off his face, and grinned . . . and it was as if the winter melted away under the hot breath and brilliant sunshine of Beltaine Day.

In two strides he was before her. With a growl, he hefted her up by the hips.

"They've been feeding you well, wife." He shifted her weight in his arms and cast his gaze over her. "You're growing as sleek as a young mare."

She smiled, secretly. "A mare grows lazy and fat when her stallion is away."

" 'Tis more o' you to hold on to, I'm thinking." His grin spread wide and white. "A pity I'll have to work it all off o' you."

"By the gods!" The wattle-woven door battered in the wake of Aidan's entrance. "I should have known it, when I saw you gallopin' up the hill as if you were chased by the Morrígan herself. And alone, no less, with not a man at your back! Begorra, man! Are ye mad, riding through these lands unprotected?"

Conaire did not glance at his second-in-command. His smoky gaze swept over her face, her hair, lingering with promise on her lips. "Is there something you'll be wanting, Aidan?"

"A bit o' dignity'd be welcome." He stomped around the fire to glare at his king. "Your sweat doesn't have time to dry upon her skin before you're back, with your sword up and ready again." When Conaire didn't release her, Aidan waved his arms in a violent circle. "Have ye no sense, man? Put away your plough and come to the mead hall. A king sees to his house, before warming the queen's pallet."

Conaire spread his palms flat against her buttocks, watching her lips soften, her lids grow heavy with desire. "Has there been trouble in my absence?"

"Nay, not a bit o' it, and if ye doubt it, there's an empty stretch of mud outside that's begging to be beaten by me boots—"

"Then I'll see to my king's duties later."

Conaire slid his hands further over the curve of her rump, until his fingers pressed intimately between her buttocks. She gasped—and then managed a husky laugh as Conaire buried his lips in the hollow of her throat.

"By the gods, can you not take your hands off her for a moment, man?" Aidan gestured to the half-wit bondswoman cowering against the wall. "She'll be off with tales before you get your woman to bed, and the poets have no more need o' fodder, I'll tell you that."

"Have ye no better thing to do?" Brigid asked, a tone of steel ringing in her voice. Aye, she, too, had heard the songs the visiting poet had composed, rising from the mead hall in the wee hours of the morning; but there was no reason Conaire must know of them, not now, not while that poet and his attendants still lodged in the *ráth*. Conaire was too proud and too hot-tempered to suffer such insolence in his own house—and the murder of a poet was a sacrilege beyond measure.

So she turned her head against Conaire's, so her husband would not see her face, then flashed Aidan a look of warning. "Must ye stand there like an angry, old goat, whilst a man makes love to his wife?"

Then Aidan did what men rarely dared; he glared straight into her face, thrusting his shoulders back in defiant boldness. Rigidly, he held her gaze, just long enough for her to see the hatred which seethed in his hazel eyes.

"*You'll* not silence my tongue," he snapped, "not while poets sing songs o' scorn about my king."

"Hush your blatherin' tongue." She stiffened in Conaire's embrace, and wondered anew how far Aidan would go to drive a wedge between them. "Have ye no sense—"

"So the poets dare to mock me, do they?" Conaire lifted his head. "Let them." He cast Aidan a lazy, half-lidded glance. "Their words cannot dull the blade o' my sword. Nor cast a shadow on my triumphs."

Aidan took a step toward them. "I'll tell ye something for nothing, Conaire—"

"Do you think I rode my horse through a storm to be standin' here dripping wet talkin' to you, Aidan?" Conaire jerked his head toward the door. "The men follow, with fifty head o' cattle we stole back from the Leinstermen. They'll be hungry and cold. Be off and see to your duty." He turned back to her, his voice dropping low and husky. "And I'll see to mine."

Brigid felt her cheeks burn with the anger of Aidan's gaze; but she did not glance at him in triumph, as she knew she very well could. There was no triumph in discord between the two people who loved Conaire most.

Then Aidan was gone, and the bondswoman, too, and Conaire's hungry kiss pushed away all other thoughts.

It was ever like this, when Conaire first returned home from a long journey. Later, later there'd be time for the long, slow loving, for . . . imagination. Right now, all that existed was the simmering, demanding heat of his kisses; the swift and hurried yanking of clothes, the throaty laughter truncated in gasps of pleasure as their naked skins finally touched. He lifted her up, and she melted against him.

That morning, she'd brushed the wolf pelts on their pallet into crackling softness. Now as Conaire lowered her upon them, the hairs stood and reached for her. Conaire covered her with the whole, hot, naked length of him. Her body softened where he grew hard; her hips tilted with that unspeakable yearning which only abated for brief moments, a yearning she'd reveled in during the long, glorious nights of the months past that they'd spent upon this very bed. He spoke husky, urgent words—harsh words of wanting, of needing—a warrior's language of love. On the walls around them, firelight flared amber and gold.

His rough hands trailed hot, liquid magic over her limbs. She opened her lips to him, and devoured the tart scent of fresh air and open woods which clung to his breath. Mist and rain and dew shimmered on his skin, and she dared to trail a path over his jaw with the tip of her tongue, sipping the nectar. How warm he was, radiating heat like the sun itself, driving back the winter with the sheer force of his presence. How hard and powerful the thundering of his heart, as he sought the welcoming entrance to her body's deepest core. How he filled her . . . oh . . . the intoxicating tightness, then the throbbing rhythm, the timeless rocking, the ripples of sensation racing over her skin, like the sizzling shock of hot summer rain. And she gripped him, tears pricking the back of her eyes, for sometime during her three-month stay in the *ráth,* Conaire had become more than a beloved husband, more than a lover. He'd become her sunshine, her moonlight. Her only taste of freedom.

For a brief time in his arms, she soared.

Later, when the fire had died to embers, he rolled his weight off her body and drew her into his arms. She released a long and contented sigh.

A smug rumble of laughter bubbled in his chest. " 'Tis glad I am I pleased you, lass."

"Aye, well it's good for you ye did." She settled her head in the niche of his shoulder. "Six days is too long for a man to be goin' off and leaving his wife."

"Is it now?"

"Aye. A queen has naught else to do but spin and weave and sew." *In this dark little hut, alone, with the cruel whispers of children filtering in through the walls.* "A wife gets to thinkin' of what she's missing."

He caressed her breast lazily. A slow smile spread across his lips, as her nipple peaked in his palm. "Is that complainin' I hear coming from your mouth, and you barely three moons wed?"

"Och, you didn't marry a complacent little pup, I'll have ye know. When I stop complaining about your absence, that's when you should worry, I'm thinking."

"Is it not enough that they call me spellbound?" Conaire traced circles around her engorged nipple. "Would you have them thinkin' me as befuddled as a mule?"

She touched the bristle of his strong, square jaw, uneasy with the slight edge in his words. "Are ye listenin' to the mutterings of fools now?"

"It was my intent to raid north to the eastern borders until Samhain, lass. Yet here I am, bounding to my wife's lap as soon as I came within a half-day's ride."

"It's glad I am of that."

She ran the palm of her hand beneath his chin. He looked up at her from beneath a shock of hair. His easy smile faltered, for that strange, glorious feeling drew taut between them again, as it did whenever they lay together, naked in body and soul. It was a tender emotion born in the fire of passion, nurtured by the fluid of time, blossoming in the sun of their companionship. She knew it as love, for such a river of emotion flowing between two people could be nothing else. And though Conaire surrendered to the currents, sometimes she saw in his eyes a certain wariness of this strange magic over which neither he nor she had any control.

"Aye, it's glad I am of that," she repeated, rasping her nails lightly over his throat. "I'll not let ye leave my bed 'til Samhain, if I've my way of it."

"That is a gift I cannot grant you." Conaire abandoned her breast and traced a line down her abdomen. "The Leinstermen still attack to the east. I came here for the night, no more. Tomorrow morning we ride again."

Her heart sank—low, low, so low. The shadows Conaire had driven away gathered in the corners of the room and hung like wet fog. "Those wretched Leinstermen." She jerked up and tugged a pelt around her chest, to hide from him the depth of her disappointment. "Why don't ye just let them steal a few head of cattle—"

"No man will live to steal from me or mine."

It was Conaire the king who spoke; there was no countering his words—she knew it even as she tried. "You said yourself, Conaire, that they were nothing but fleas."

"If I allow them go unchecked, others will join them."

"So you'll be going off again, and leaving me here, with Samhain Day only four nights hence?"

"I'll be back by Samhain, wife." He rubbed his callused thumb down the indentation of her spine. "My men wouldn't take well to sleepin' under the stars on the most magical night o' the year. And I've no likin' to waste the surging of the moondark tides."

His words did not cheer her. It would take no more than a winter storm to delay him, and then he would not be here to preside over Samhain. Aye, the Druids would have the ceremony, but she'd not be welcome, for even the Druids cast strange, frightened glances her way. More importantly, without Conaire, she could not announce the news, nor make her special request, as she had planned these past weeks.

He rubbed a spot tight at the base of her spine. "It was you who once told me that a king is not a man."

She frowned at him. Aye, she remembered it. She had been talking about her father. She pushed the painful thought away. She did not want to think about her father, who'd she'd only seen once, from afar, during her whole stay in Morna.

"Och, it's a fine thing to be using a woman's own words against her." She batted him with the end of the pelt, then rose up from the bed. "Go off to your warring, then. I'll not be missing a bit of ye, I won't."

"And where do you think you're going, wife?" Conaire hefted himself on an elbow and reached for her. "I've only one night to make enough memories to fill the days to come—"

"Never mind that." She brusquely tossed her unbound hair over one shoulder and shimmied into her tunic. A lump swelled in her throat. "There's two moorhens that'll be boiled to bones if I don't see to them, and I know by the rumbling of your stomach that you've another appetite to fill."

She passed beyond the partition before he could respond, and fumbled with tossing sticks beneath the dying fire. She was cursing the half-wit who'd not finished plucking the moorhens before dropping them into the pot, when Conaire seized her from behind and whirled her to face him.

She closed her eyes, but it was too late. The wretched tears she'd struggled to control had long trailed hot and wet down her cheeks. Och, how she hated these tears. How she hated the unpredictable flux of her emotions, how she hated to show Conaire such weakness.

"It's more than my leaving that's caused this." His fists tightened around her arms. "Who dared to cause this, Brigid?"

"It's no one," she managed through her tight throat, "who'd you'd want to hurt."

"I'll kill him."

The truth swelled in her throat, until she had to bite her lip to keep it from leaping from her tongue. "Conaire, don't you understand?" Surely, he knew enough of women . . . "Are ye blind?"

"Nay, I'm not blind." He seized her hand and twisted it palm up, tilting it so she could see the calluses in the light. "Do you think I don't notice that a single half-wit serves you as bondswoman, that Aidan's fur rises when your name is spoken, that no footprints mark the mud before our door, but mine?" He found his sword on the floor and hefted it in his grip. "Three months you've endured their ignorance without tears—now I will have the name of the man or woman who caused them."

"How like a warrior," she muttered, "to think you can battle away all sorrows."

"Brigid—"

"I'll tell ye, then, for you're like a dog with a bone once you've got something in your head." She took his hand and flattened it over her abdomen. "Here's the man who's causing these wretched tears, since you'll be wanting to know. Your son, Conaire. He'll be born on Beltaine Day."

An odd silence engulfed the room in the moments after her blurted announcement. The fire crackled, the boiling water rumbled in the pot. His gaze fell to their joined hands. His pulse pounded beneath her grip, and warmth surged as he curled his fingers, ever so slightly, into the faint swell of her abdomen.

"It was to be my New Year's gift to ye." She released his wrist and wiped her tears with the back of her hand. "I was going to announce it before everyone, I was, at the Samhain ceremony. Now it's all spoiled, all spoil—"

Her words suffocated in the bulk of his shoulder. He drew her up, up, into the yielding warmth of his embrace.

But this . . . this was not the iron-armed embrace she'd long grown used to, the choking hold she always had to squeal to be released from. This embrace was careful, controlled, self-conscious. It was a gentle pressure, the kind of touch a pup might expect from its mother's jaws.

She tilted her head back. She'd expected war cries of triumph, horns of mead raised to the sky, a new, arrogant swagger to his walk. Not this quiet, not this unusual solemnity. Then she met his gaze and sucked in a swift breath—for the currents that always flowed between them suddenly surged, gushed, and she knew he'd finally surrendered.

"So, wife, you give me a babe for Samhain." A smile—boyish, almost bashful—tilted the corner of his lips. "Did you think to make a fool o' me? I planned to give you naught but a gold torque and a handful of jewels."

There it lay, like a golden chalice before a thief; the opportunity she'd known would come after her announcement. Guilt stabbed her, and she wondered anew if there were something evil in using her pregnancy as a means to an end.

"I'll not be saying no to baubles, husband, but there is something else . . ."

"It is yours."

Her heart fluttered; and for a moment she smelled the honeysuckle blooming in the woods, she felt the crispness of last year's leaves beneath her feet; she felt the kiss of the fresh wind on her cheeks, the loving warmth of the *Sidh*. Then she stanched the hope: for Conaire spoke without thinking.

"I would have this child born in Ulster. Or Tara. Or anywhere else," she added. "But I'll not have him born here."

She lowered her lashes in shame. She did not want to see the disappointment on his face. She knew he'd expected her to ask for some exotic rarity which he could acquire through wealth or travel or hard work. He had spent the past months building a strong ring-fort and all that went inside it: a feasting hall, animal pens, weapons' sheds, a strong-walled home just for the two of them. He had spent a season building a dream. Now, she wanted to leave it.

She shouldn't have asked. But a wave of homesickness overwhelmed her as she remembered her little hut in the woods—remembering the way the honeysuckle climbed over the ill-thatched roof. There, in that isolation, she'd never been as lonely as she was here, surrounded by people. She would suffer the isolation, if she were alone. But she would not have her son born in this place, where hatred and suspicion and fear rumbled up from the very earth beneath them.

"We're off to Tara then, after Samhain." He splayed his fingers wide over her belly. "My son deserves to be born in the hall o' kings."

Her eyes flew to his face. That odd, youthful smile lingered on his lips. Her throat parched; she felt again the wretched welling of tears.

"Nay, no more o' that." He thumbed a tear off her cheek. "Had you asked for the club of the Dagdá, I'd have torn away the veils and wrestled it from the god's hands myself."

"Och, listen to your nonsense. I've done nothing that I haven't took pleasure in meself."

"Aye, 'tis true, but you've given me more than a babe, lass. His chest swelled. "Tonight, you've made a man o' me."

Brigid huddled near the fire, absently sweeping a polished stone over the swath of linen draped on her lap, to work the last lumps and ridges out of the weave. She hummed softly as she worked. Now and again her breath caught, as she remembered the delights of the past evening with Conaire.

Suddenly, the cold, white glare of mid-morning flooded over her. She squinted up to see her bondswoman hesitating in the open doorway.

"So you've come, have ye?" Brigid had not seen the half-wit since yesterday, when Conaire had ordered her and Aidan out of the room. "Good. We've ten women's work to do to prepare for the journey to Tara."

The linen slipped like fluid through her fingers, as she swept it aside. A draft whirled in and chilled her ankles, when she rose to her feet. "Come, come, don't be standing there as silent as a stone," she said, "you're drainin' the heat from the room."

" 'Tis . . . 'tis the king here."

"The king? What foolishness is this?" Conaire certainly was *not* here; she'd have sensed his presence. "The king left with his men before the break of dawn, he did. Now come, we've linens to launder."

Still, the bondswoman didn't move. She poked one finger into a burn hole in her tunic, then glanced furtively over her shoulder.

Brigid followed her gaze and noticed the silent, shadowy shapes gathering in the misty whiteness. Then a long cane jutted out from the edge of the doorway, and tapped the girl out of the way. The blinding sunlight lit upon a head of snow-white hair and streamed gossamer rays around a form draped heavily with golden ornaments.

There was a moment, as she stared across the room at the regal figure, when some practical part of her mind thought—ah, 'tis King Flann of whom the girl speaks—and she felt nothing more than any woman would, set upon suddenly with a guest of high birth, wondering if she had enough mead in the *souterrain,* or if she should slip beyond the partition and tend to her hair.

Then her heart murmured, against her will, *Father . . .* and a bitter fluid seeped into her blood.

"Aye, aye." His voice was little more than a croak as he bowed his white head. "With all me failing senses, I can feel the unwelcome wind which blows from ye, child."

She flinched at the endearment, then flushed with anger that he had the audacity to use it. Many times during the first weeks in Morna, she'd daydreamed about her father coming to her, just like this. The daydream would always end with him falling to his knees and pleading for forgiveness—and her falling before him and letting their tears mingle in reconciliation.

Those dreams had died a hard death.

"Perhaps I should not have come."

Words surged to her throat, fierce and hurting words, but they lodged and choked her. In the end she stood and said nothing, and silently cursed the part of her—the flesh and bones and blood—which still tangled her in the knotted net of emotions which came with kinship.

" 'Tis so, 'tis so." The cane upon which he leaned trembled. "I ask but one thing, before I leave ye in peace. The path to this *ráth* is steep and long. You'd not refuse an old, weary man but a few moments of rest by your fire?"

She stiffened. He'd made the request humbly enough, but it grated on her ears, for it reminded her that though she was this man's abandoned daughter, above all she was a queen, Conaire's queen. It was her duty to show hospitality to all who came to her door, yet here she was, letting one of her husband's under-kings stand in the draft of the portal. She felt oddly like a child who'd been gently rebuked.

"Sit."

The word came out harsher than she intended.

He drew back, out of the portal. "Perhaps 'tis best if—"

"Is it marring the honor of this house that you're after," she asked, "by refusing my hospitality?"

He closed the flap behind him and worked his way toward the fire. He concentrated on the rushes as he planted his cane, took a few steps, then planted his cane down anew.

She had only seen him once, from afar, during her whole stay in Morna. She'd recognized the bushy head of white hair he'd had even seven years ago, she'd recognized the gleam of gold at his throat, wrists, neck, and in his hair, for Da had always decked himself in the richest of finery. Now, without the glare of morning light, she saw that though his clothes hadn't changed, the figure bearing them had. Seven years had shriveled him like a dried apple. He creaked down into a heap by the fire, as if crushed beneath the weight of his thick woolen cloak and all the gold and gem-encrusted ornaments of his position.

This was not the robust king she remembered. She wondered how many splotches on his skin were due to the loss of Niall, how many weary creases to the usurpation of his power. . . . Then she whirled her back to him and snatched an empty horn from a peg on the wall, despising herself for the pang of pity.

"I'll bring you mead, and some herbs to restore your strength, if you've the courage to take them."

A few minutes later, he reached up to grasp the horn she thrust at him. His fingernails, in which he'd once taken so much pride, were cracked and cloudy.

" 'Tis a terrible thing," he murmured, noticing the direction of her gaze, "to grow withered and old."

"To be old and withered is no shame; you'll get no pity from me," she countered, hardening her heart. "A long life is the gods' greatest gift."

"Mayhap for some." He bowed his head and contemplated the gentle sway of the golden honey-mead. His scalp shone pink through his thin hair. "But all the bitter seeds a man has sown through the years, they come to harvest in his old age."

The bells on her girdle jarred discordantly as she turned away from him. He'd come too close to the raw edges of the wound. "Sow no anger and you'll reap no evil—is that not one of your own priests' platitudes, King Flann?"

"Aye, I know I've brought upon meself the ravens that pick at my flesh."

"What's this then?" She snatched her spindle whorl and scooped up the basketful of wool, then planted herself, straight-backed, on the bench near the wall. "Careful, King Flann. You'll have me thinking you've a heart in ye."

He lowered the horn and fixed his blue gaze upon her. "I did what I thought I must, child. A king cannot always be a father . . . or a man." He cupped the horn in his palms and stared into the liquid anew. "And not all of us can cast our eyes into the future and see what is best."

"King Conaire has gone warring to the east." She snapped the spindle as she twisted out a length of thread. "Whatever petition you wish to give him must wait until Samhain—"

"You know it's you I came to see."

"Do I now?" The wool bunched and knotted between her pinched fingers. She kneaded it fiercely. "Then perhaps 'tis you who has a touch of the Sight."

"Mock an old man, aye, do it, if it soothes your wounded vanity." He slammed down the horn of mead. It cracked upon the hearth stones. He stared at the cracked bone for a moment; and then, with a weary sigh, pushed it out of his way. "It was foolish of me, to expect no anger between us."

Indeed, she thought, the hurt burning in her breast, *Indeed.*

"Perhaps it is best that we speak not of the past." He waved vaguely toward some invisible thing behind him. "Of things that cannot be changed."

"Then it's for sure we've naught to discuss."

"You'll choke upon such bitterness, child." His hand fell upon the soft heap of linen lying beside him in the rushes. "You must give it up, lest it spread like sickness."

He caressed the smooth sheen of the linen cloth with trembling strokes. She did not like it—the sight of his ragged nails scraping the linen. She faltered in her spinning. She watched him as he tugged the cloth closer, as he ran his hand around the edge, as he bunched it into an oblong shape, like that of a swaddled infant.

"I cannot remember," he murmured, "when last I touched a babe's swaddling clothes."

A coldness washed over her. It was for the babe, he had come. For the child—her son.

The spindle clattered on the paving stones. She yanked the blanket from his hands.

"The herbs have done their work, I'm thinking. Be off to your own hearth fire."

He did not meet her glare; he never could before, and part of her thanked the gods for his own foolish fears, for now he would not see the bite of hurt beneath her anger.

"Child—"

"I'll be hearing no more of that."

"Aye, aye, I've no place to call ye that, that I know." He worked himself to his feet, leaning heavily on his cane. "Those seeds I sowed . . . the vines that sprouted have choked off all me hope with ye, I see that now. Of all women living, it's you who've I've wronged the most."

She stood stiff and unyielding, even as someplace deep inside began to bleed.

"I'm a brittle old man, and I've no more pride in me to bother about." His gaze fell upon the blanket, wrapped in her hands. "Your child will be all that is left of the line of Morna. He will be the grandson I stopped hoping to see. I'd be asking you but one small thing—"

"The child is mine and Conaire's—you'll have naught to do with him."

"Will ye be sowing more bitterness then? Will ye be making the same mistakes as me?"

No. I'll not be sending me own son away. I'll never deny him—as you have denied me— The words swelled to her throat, but with the heat and anger rushed the scald of tears—och, these wretched tears, simmering so close to the surface these days— and so she choked down the words and turned her back to him.

She'd not let him see her bleed—for then he'd know her weakness; and he'd call her daughter, all for the child, all for the babe. She was naught but a vessel for his dreams of immortality, for if she'd not conceived a son to carry on his line, Flann would never have appeared at her door.

The years slid by her. For a moment she was a child again—in the time when she still had a child's eyes—and her father sat cross-legged in the feasting hall, close to the hearth fire, the stones of his brooch glittering in the red orange glow. She had snuck into the feasting hall, while her mother nursed Niall, but she did not belong among these laughing men, the Druids in their pale cloaks of strange symbols, the lawmakers with their serious expressions. She hid in the shadows, watching, until someone found her and tried to usher her out; but her father caught sight of her and beckoned. Then he took her in his open arms and settled her in the folded wool of his cloak, absently brushing her red-gold curls.

He'd petted her like a lapdog. And now she wondered if he had ever loved her at all.

"Aye, I see it was a hopeless thing," he wheezed, "coming here to ye."

She did not answer; she closed her eyes tight to squeeze back the pain. A cool draft kissed her cheek, and at first she thought—*good, he is leaving*—but as she opened her eyes, she noticed that no cold mid-morning light bleached the firelight from the room. The breeze came from nowhere, and it churned the steam from the cauldron of boiling water into little whirlwinds. The moist-rich fragrance of moss burst in the air like flowers in sudden full bloom. She had a moment of dizziness, as if she were transported of a sudden into the midst of the sacred circle of oaks . . . and she wondered why a fairy wind visited her now, when in all these past months of loneliness she'd ached for the scent and she'd never caught a single whiff.

"To think I was hoping to stop you from racing off to Tara

hill . . . To think I could talk you into staying in Morna until the child was born, so I could gaze upon his face but once . . ."

She only half-heard Flann, for a more compelling sound snared her attention. A low moan filtered through the creases and cracks in the wattle walls. 'Twas a mournful sound, soft and sorrowful, broken by muffled sobbing—as weak and reedy-thin as the wailing of the wind. But she was not fooled; she'd heard this Otherworldly dirge before, but never did it float so thin in the air, and she wondered if it was the vaulting of walls around her which hushed it so, or because the person for whom the *bean sí* keened hung onto life by the thinnest of threads. Twice before, she'd heard this lament, but louder and brash and screeching. Once for her mother. Once for Niall.

The anger drained away from Brigid like mead from a torn bladder, leaving nothing but hollowness and pity.

She turned to face Flann, but the room was empty. In her distraction, he'd left her alone.

She tucked the soft linen under her arm. She would go to him, reconcile with him in some way, before she left for Tara. She'd no love for Flann, but she'd not have his last memory of her be one of anger and bitterness. The *bean sí* had sung again, for another member of her family.

Her father would be dead within a week.

The deeper Conaire rode into the woods, the denser the forest's canopy became. The meager moonlight which filtered through the boughs soon paled and faltered, until naught but gleaming threads of opalescence pierced the webbing. But he knew the way well; he nudged his mount faster through the pearly white mists creeping over the forest floor. Beyond this wood, through a few more valleys, lay the lands of Lough Riach—and Brigid.

A slow grin crossed his features. The wind sang high and wild through the trees. Dry leaves scattered down, buffeted by contrary breezes. Twigs crackled beneath the cover of fog; tree trunks creaked and leaned. The scent of moss sifted up from fissures in the ground and billowed in the air. Aye, the worlds brush close against each other this Samhain's Eve. How his men must tremble on that windswept hill they'd insisted on camping upon this night, while he made his way back to Morna alone. But Brigid. . . . Aye, how she would love these woods. Tomorrow, he would take her to that grove of oaks, where they could feel the magic of the New Year growing like grass out of the ground, and then celebrate life in the season of darkness.

A war cry pierced the night. Jerked out of his musing, Conaire tightened his grip on the reins and scanned the black shadows around him, cursing his inattention, cursing the constant rustling of the woods which had dulled the edge of his warrior's senses.

Then the screeches rent the air. Swords flashed, where once there was darkness. Black shapes loomed between the trees, then hurled themselves at him as he scraped his sword to the ready. His sword found steel; still more steel; then cold fire sliced the flesh of his thigh. Warm blood bathed his leg. His steed screamed and bucked, then reared around and flashed its hooves. Conaire swung his sword wildly at the shadows, but there were too many and their greedy hands yanked him off his heaving mount. He roared his own war cry, and knew even as he stumbled somehow to his feet, even as his sword found flesh, even as blood lust brought on the fighting rage and the figures reared away from the lethal arc of his sword, that it was all but over, all but over, for he'd felt the taste of steel in his belly, and the acid burning of his life's-blood oozing over his skin.

One of the men laughed, hacked Conaire's own sword out of his grip, and placed the blade on Conaire's throat. The rancid stench of turned meat blasted Conaire's face.

"King Flann thanks ye for fillin' the witch's belly." The man twisted the blade. "He'll be raisin' his grandson now, to take his

Seven

A frigid wind scoured the hillock, grinding smooth patches of rock which jutted through the scrubby rug of grass. On the drumlin's rounded height, the pregnant swell of a royal burial mound pulsed black against the winter sky. Four white-robed Druids hefted a bier upon their shoulders, and carried Conaire's still body deep into the tomb. The women's keening vaulted above the howling of the wind.

Brigid stood apart from the others. The wind wrestled with the weight of her saffron *brat,* until it wrenched the wool from her white-knuckled grip. The yellow folds battered her legs, jarring discordantly the bells upon her girdle. The gusts whipped hair across her face.

She let the damp tresses blind her. She needed no eyes to see, for the funeral ritual unrolling before her was naught but a strange, vivid dream. For though the wind howled o'er the land, though the cold earth sucked the last dregs of warmth from the soles of her slippered feet, Brigid stood as still as the ancient stone columns which rimmed a nearby hill. From the moment she first laid eyes upon her husband's pale, waxen skin, she'd become an observer, detached, silent within some deep, calm place inside herself. 'Twas naught but an illusion, those deep gouges in his belly, those lifeless gray eyes. Conaire couldn't be dead.

For if he were, the ground would tremble beneath her feet; the skies would tear open and thunder, the very stones would scream at his passing. She herself would have hovered over his death scene like Morrigán the Raven; she would have felt the slice of steel through her own flesh. The Sight could pierce through all veils, and it had never failed her, not with Mama, not with Niall, and never, never with Conaire, who was spirit of her own spirit, heart of her own heart.

How vivid it all seemed. Even from her quiet place, she smelled the salt-sea upon the westerly wind; she sensed tremors of cold shaking her stony body. *Trickery,* she reminded herself. Above the western horizon, snowy fingers of translucent clouds cringed back against the purple of the encroaching night. There was the cause of this waking dream; Samhain approached. 'Twas the trickery of the *Sídh,* the flux and flow of magic in the furtive wind, which caused such strange nightmares. Soon she would awaken and discover that the bondswoman had let the fire dim to embers, and that Conaire had stolen the wolf pelts from her again.

Suddenly, amber torchlight pooled around her.

" 'Tis a woeful day, child."

She heard the rustling of a long cloak across the grass, and smelled the musky oil scent of his hair, and wondered what her father was doing in this dream.

"Weep, child." He curled a bony hand into her shoulder. "Weep as a woman should, and keen as a wife must."

Och, wasn't it like her father to chide her in his sly little way, to remind her of her duty, even in her dreams. Well, she'd have none of it. Then she thought, *soon I will awaken, for it's Conaire's hand on my shoulder, surely. Soon he'll shake me from my tossing and turning and end this strange nightmare.*

"Don't you understand me, woman?" The fingers dug deep into her flesh. "You cannot stand here as mute as a stone, while your husband lays dead in his tomb."

He is not dead. You and all the others are caught in this sticky magic web of a dream, too. Can you not smell the magic in the wind, or have you long lost the nose for it? Can you not tell that Conaire is but sleeping?

"By the *Dagdá* isn't *this* a foul sight."

Och, and now Aidan, she thought, as she glimpsed through the tangled netting of her hair the warrior striding purposely toward them.

"Aye, 'tis enough to make a priest take up arms, it is," Aidan continued, mud splattering on his tunic with each stride. His hazel eyes blazed from black, sleep-starved sockets. "So the daughter has reconciled with the father—and King Conaire not yet cold in the ground."

His anger penetrated to her calm, silent place. Och, how full of hate, Aidan was, and how it flowed off him like waves of heat from glowing red cooking stones.

"It's often the folly of an old man," her father said, "to wait too long to right his wrongs."

King Flann's hand slipped off her shoulder, and Brigid felt a strange urge to seize it. *No, no, Conaire, wake me from this madness.*

"Have you nothing to say, woman?" Aidan's voice cut through the howling of the wind. "The greatest warrior who ever lived has died—though the world would not know it, by the stillness of his wife's tongue."

She blinked at him from between the shanks of her windblown hair.

"Did your witchery finally wear thin?" Aidan's lips curled back in a snarl, as his gaze fell to her belly. "Or is it just that ye've no need o' him anymore?"

Aidan's tongue was unfettered now in this odd fairy place of her imaginings. Here, Conaire no longer stood between them. Here, she had no tongue to answer him back. He would say everything he bit his tongue upon in Conaire's presence these past months. For a moment, she wondered if Aidan had commanded the Druids to bring this dream upon them both, just so he could speak his mind without fear of reprisal.

Och, Aidan . . . You cannot bear the thought that he might love me more than you, can ye?

It was as if he read her thoughts, for suddenly his hatred blazed into flames. "He loved you not, woman. He had an eye for that cleft between your legs—aye, that he did. But 'twas no more than that between ye."

"Hush, man!"

King Flann stepped between them. From her distant place, she noted that her father's step could be spry when he wished it.

"It is his wife to whom you speak—"

"Wife." Aidan spat the word at her feet like a cherry pit. "You married him long enough to get yourself a belly full o' child, didn't ye?"

Absently, she ran a hand over the slight swell of her abdomen.

"Those cursed eyes o' yours won't blind *me* to the truth, woman." A muscle jumped in Aidan's ill-shaven cheek. "Conaire ne'er sired a single child upon a hundred thousand women—it doesn't take a fool to know it's not *Conaire's* child in your womb."

Aidan, Aidan, the bitterness twists your mind.

"Enough." Flann straightened, giving form to the sagging bulk of his fine woolen *brat.* "Have you both no respect for the dead?"

Aidan looked upon Flann as he would look upon a stubborn clump of manure clinging to the hem of his cloak. Flann gestured to the burial mound with a tip of his torch. The Druids filed out of the portal, without the bier. Aidan whirled his back to both of them and bellowed for his horse. The crowd rustled like a great flock of birds, glancing uneasily eastward, where the first dusky fingers of Samhain crept over the land.

Her father's moist breath warmed her ear. "You must keep

your senses clear, child. Aidan is Conaire's foster-brother. The men will choose him for king tonight, 'tis no doubt."

Would it never end, this foolishness? Would the dream grow still more raveled?

He seized her arm. "You must think of the child, the child who will be king someday. I can help you, if ye'll let me."

She turned to him and let the wind scour her hair from her face. The shadow called Flann stumbled back. His yellowed skin paled to moonlight. The torch slipped from his grip. She saw it fall, and she knew then what she must do to end this Druid enchantment. She reached for the head of the torch and grasped the flaming bulge as it tipped toward her. For a brief moment she looked down upon the fire in her grip and felt the corrosive singe—and then a scream launched from her throat.

Her knees jarred against the hard earth. The torch clattered and rolled a few paces away. She clutched her wrist and stared in horror at the taut, reddening skin of her palm and fingers. Through the blurry haze of pain she thought—*Aye, now it's over, and I'll wake to find the ashes of the hearth fire on me hand*— but she looked up, and the icy wind froze the tears of pain on her cheeks. The villagers' faces turned toward her, bathed in the red orange glow of the setting sun. Her father stood pale-faced against the dark robes of his priests. She cried out *no,* but 'twas a choked word, hoarse and half-swallowed, and rose up to her knees to see the burial mound stark against the red-streaked sky.

The agonizing blistering of her hand faded into nothing . . . for this was not a dream.

Conaire is dead.

No. No no no no no no no—

She launched to her feet and slipped upon the grass. Mud soaked her shins as she raced to the burial mound. She shoved the women away from the opening of the tomb. Her fingernails pierced flesh. She screamed at the women to cease their wailing, to leave, leave, leave the king in peace—let him sleep in peace.

The keening songs died in shrieks. The woman stumbled to their feet and scattered away. Brigid saw herself mirrored in their eyes—her hair uncombed, falling to her hips, her clothes still streaked with her husband's blood, her eyes wild, deep-socketed, heavy with the flux of madness. She glared out at those who lingered. She did not attempt to hide the crazed ebb and flow of her fury, but screamed for them to join their cowardly clansmen fleeing over the eastern hill to the safety of their hearths, then pointed to the east, to the encroaching night. Even the Druids in their white robes blanched and stumbled away, until she stood alone on the hill, the pregnant surge of the burial mound silent behind her, the others fleeing homeward.

Then she turned her back and stared into the gloom of the tomb, and surged toward the dark depths, intent on searching for Conaire among the dusty, old bones of long-dead kings, intent on lying down and pressing her body against him to impart some of her living warmth into his cold form, and to hear his heart beating again in his chest—for he was *not* dead—then, in that moment, the last ray of sunlight disappeared beneath the western horizon.

Samhain rolled over her like a dark wind. A salt-sweet, humid fragrance billowed from the yawning opening of the tomb, like the sleep-laden breath of the earth. She stumbled back from the power of it and remembered it was sacrilege to enter this tomb. These ancient burial mounds were the doors to the Otherworld; they were sacred places, not to be breached but by the highest of Druids—and the dead.

Something cold thrust icy fingers through her veins. Perhaps she was mad. She grasped her temples and collapsed to her knees. *No no no no no no no.* He was *not* dead; her heart screamed it, though her mind battled with the evidence of her eyes.

Vaguely, she sensed the change in the world around her; the softening of the wind; the warm mist spraying up from the fissures of the earth, the faint drizzle sifting down from the darkening sky, the odd tilting of the dim horizon, the hushed whisper of the parting veils. One of the Druids had left a torch sunk into the earth in the lee of the burial mound; the fog dispersed its amber glow around the entrance to the tomb.

The low moaning of the *bean sí* rose above the faintest howling of wind. Brigid jerked and looked around her. The fairy-woman floated near, just beyond the circle of light. Brigid glimpsed the swaying of the creature's snow-white limbs, the floating of her gossamer gown. The faint keening worked upon Brigid's whirling thoughts like a lullaby upon a child. A *bean sí* always sang as a warning—thus the one for whom she sang still lived.

Conaire was *not* dead.

Brigid sank to her knees. Och, she'd known the song of her heart rang true. The *bean sí* had wailed these past three nights, the same weak, airy sound—and she'd known it was the death-song of an old man or a young child, not of a warrior. Not of a king. Conaire's *bean sí* would gnash and screech and shatter the very walls between the worlds with her shrieks.

Brigid wrapped her cloak around her and drew close to the torch, pressing her back against the wall of the burial mound. The *bean sí* continued her song in the darkness outside the circle of golden light. Brigid let it lull her into sleep, knowing that somehow, in this season between the seasons, in this most magical of nights, light would rise out of darkness, and life out of death.

Brigid woke to the heat of a human hand on her shoulder.

Laden with golden regalia, Conaire crouched over her. The first pale fingers of dawn streamed across the sky, streaking red the auburn shag of his hair. His breath fogged on the crisp morning air. An uncertain mist clouded his gray eyes.

"Mo shearc." He tugged a damp strand of hair off her cheek, then wrapped it tight around his finger. "I'll not let you fade away like the other shadows o' this night's dream."

She threw herself against him. "Och, ye'll not be rid of me so easily."

His arms banded around her—warm, hard, tight. Otherworldly mist clung to his cloak, but beneath the layers of wool and linen soaked with the sweet, cloying fragrance beat a heart, strong and sure.

"Aye . . ." Laughter rumbled in his chest. "None o' the pleasures o' the fairy lands can match the feel o' you in my arms, woman."

"Is that where ye've been, then," she said, cursing her shaking voice, "sipping nectar from bluebells, whilst your wife waits for you to come home for Samhain as you promised?"

"Aye, it was the fairy lands, I'm thinking . . . but it all fades now." He shrugged his mighty shoulders then separated from her, to scan the full of her face. "It's your fault, woman. I suspect my head was so full o' the thought o' you, that I paid no mind to the wandering o' the path through the mists."

"Always ready with an excuse, you are."

"It will teach me to watch the path next time I race to your side on Samhain's Eve."

She dug her fingers into his arms, as a silence fell between them. His gaze wandered inward. Och, he did not fully understand. 'Twas the way of things, it was said, that a vagueness clung to a man after leaving the Otherworld, and the memories dimmed soon after, so in a thrice he would think he'd done nothing more than dream, and in that way too much knowledge of the world beyond would not seep through the doors, and the powers would remain secret and safe from all but those who truly understood.

But this was no dream. The world had witnessed his entombment. She'd have to tell him the truth. 'Twas a truth she should have told him months ago, when she first realized who he was. But she had put the task off for another day, and still another, for she did not want to destroy Conaire's happiness. Now she could delay no more.

A morning wind swept away the last of the night's mists, and set her skin to shivering.

"You're chilled to the bones." He rose to his feet and glanced around the rocky drumlin. "When we return to the *ráth*, lass, you'll be telling me what we're doing out here so early in the morn. Where's my horse?"

"There will be no going back to the *ráth*, Conaire."

"Would you be staying here," he asked, jerking his stubbled chin toward the burial mound, "when we've a kingdom waiting for us?"

She winced at the word. There'd be no kingdom for either of them, not anymore. Now, they would be hounded to the ends of the earth.

"Do you remember nothing of the nights past, *mo rún?*"

Her soft question gave him pause. He probed her features, while the breeze toyed with the hem of his dusty cloak. A wary uncertainty lurked in the depths of his gray eyes.

He angrily shrugged his shoulders, as if the ignorance clung to him like a sopping wet cloak. "I'd rather be knowing the truth with a horn o' mead in me hand and a blaze o' fire at me feet." He seized her hand. "Come—"

She shrieked and yanked her hand back, then stared down at her palm, as if flames leapt from the skin anew.

"By the *Dagdá*." Conaire snatched her arm and glared at the oozing, blistered mess. His fingers cut her circulation from the elbow down. "Who did this—"

"*I* did it," she cried through a taut throat. "I did it last night. I seized the head of a torch to rouse myself from a nightmare." She raised her lashes and fixed her gaze upon him. "Last night, I stood on this hill while the clan buried you in this tomb, Conaire."

He swayed back a little, then an indulgent half-smile began to play about his lips. He ruffled her wild mane of hair. "Lass, you've been out in the cold too long, I'm thinking, and the pain o' this wound has stolen your wit—"

"If I could close me eyes and make the truth disappear with the morning, I would." She took a deep breath as the pain ebbed. "Look to your own wounds, and try to remember whence they came."

With her good hand, she jerked up the sleeve of his right arm and ran a finger down the jagged knitting of a deep slash, healed as if he'd received it weeks—not days—ago. Conaire raised his forearm up to examine the scar more closely, then his gaze drifted to the fine linen tunic he wore, and the beaten golden belt slung around his waist. Absently, he ran his hand along his abdomen, and Brigid saw his fingers pause over the layers of linen wrapping she'd wound around his chest, so the congealed blood of his wounds wouldn't stain his fine clothing.

"Leinstermen." One eye twitched with the return of the violent memory. "A flock o' them."

"Aidan and the others," she whispered, "found you near a stream in the western woods."

"Your father sent them to kill me." The memory flared in his eyes like a flame, while the heat of fury flushed his skin ruddy. "He wanted the babe—my son—raised as his own."

Father.

A shock bolted through her body. She remembered her father's soft words of only days ago . . . and recognized them suddenly as the whispers of a twisted and desperate man.

A shudder rippled through her. When it passed, with it went the last remnants of the little girl who yearned for the love of her father.

"Brigid." His gaze drifted to the opening of the tomb. "This thing . . . it cannot be."

She drew her attention from the pain of betrayal shuddering

away inside her. 'Twas Conaire she must tend to now, as he grappled with the truth of his heritage.

"I'll have no magic in this." He shook his head, fiercely. "This is not the way of men. A warrior dies by the sword—"

"And so you did."

"Then what is this?" He pounded his chest with flat and angry hands. "How can I breathe, how can I live? Such is not the way o' the world."

"Do you think you know the full of the way of the world, then? Do you think any man does?"

"I'll have no magic—"

"I willed you alive, aye, I did." The hurt resonated in her voice. "But it was not my wishes which dragged you living and breathing from that tomb—you of all men should know that."

The wind picked up, snarling his *brat*. He whirled away from her and stared at the burial mound, his shoulders taut and thrown back, as he struggled to understand what knowledge came to him in snatches of memory.

"Such things that I saw . . ." He curled his hands over his head and yanked upon his hair. "No sooner do I remember them than they are gone from me like mist."

"It is the way of it. You'll remember less as the hours pass, until you'll vow it was naught but a dream."

"Perhaps it was."

"Listen to me." She approached him and placed her good hand on his back. "Have you not sat in the feasting halls of your people more times than a man can count, and listened to the bards recounting the history?"

"What has that to do—"

"Listen." She splayed her fingers against his stiff, unyielding back. "The *Sídh* live among us, even now, as they have since the world began—only their world and ours are drifting apart, and the doors between them are hidden and more difficult to find, so some of our people forget that they are as real as we

are." She traced the swell of his arm as she stepped in front of him. "As real as *you* are, Conaire. Have you not guessed the truth, after all these years?"

He jerked his shoulders to shake her off. "Will you be spouting the idle talk of old women?"

"You were conceived by the Samhain fires—"

"You said yourself there's many a child born ten moons after the fires, who knows not his father's name."

"*That* I said before I knew you were the man of my vision."

His jaw locked; his nostrils flared. "You've kept secrets from me, woman."

"Aye, and well I have, for by all your talk, you'd not have believed me until now." She shrugged deeper into her cloak to shield her body from the cold morning wind. "I told you once, the Sight is vague when it comes to seein' one's own way. The day I discovered you were the one of my fate, I saw through the mists of obscurity. Do you not remember that you were prepared to battle that man of my dreams—that man of the *Sidh?* That man was *you,* Conaire. Your father was one of the *Sidh.* In your veins runs fairy blood."

A muscle flexed in his cheek. "You're speaking madness."

"Madness, is it? Cú Chulainn himself was the son of the god Lúgh—born of a mortal woman and a fairy man. He, like you, was an Ulsterman.

"That's but a tale told to pass a cold night by the fire."

"There are grains of truth in all the old stories." She patted her own chest. "It is said that my own mother's mother carried fairy blood in her veins—and thus it runs even in my blood, diluted though it is."

Still, he shook his head. "The world is not as it was."

"The world will always be as it is, Conaire, and the ways of men cannot truly change it, no matter how hard they sweat about in trying." She tugged her *brat* tight around her body, telling herself that it was nothing but Conaire's stubbornness which made him disbelieve so many of the ancient truths. Soon, he would accept what and who he was. "Well-matched, we are. We belong to a more ancient time than this, you and I. Me, born with the Sight which men have come to fear; and you . . . you born of fairy blood—immortal, like one of the *Sidh*."

The words were spoken. She backed away and wrapped her cloak more closely around her, shielding her throbbing hand from the pinch and pull of the cloth. She found a dry, rocky spot near the edge of the burial mound and huddled down upon it, watching Conaire's stiff, thrown-back shoulders as he stood grappling with the revelation. She could do no more; acceptance would have to come from within.

She tore a length of linen from the hem of her tunic and wrapped it tightly around her hand. The red orange dawn faded into a gray winter sky, and the wind gusted to sweep the last vestiges of magic from the face of the earth. Brigid shivered; her cloak was soaked from a night in the damp mist and drizzle, and now there was no Otherworldly magic to keep her warm. Through some echoing hollow of valley and hill, through a trick of the thin morning air, she heard the high, sharp voices of the clan Morna rising from the *ráth*, far beyond the ridge.

As she tucked the edge of the linen taut around her hand, she turned her mind to worldly things; to the future that stretched before them, to the child who fluttered in her womb. She lay her bandaged hand on the soft tumescence of her abdomen, feeling, for a moment, a stab of sorrow for the fairy-blooded child she would birth into this unbelieving world.

Suddenly, Conaire dropped his cloak off his shoulders and strode to the opening of the tomb. She rose trembling to her feet as his determined steps brought him right to the gaping opening, for if he entered those dark caverns and stepped through into the Otherworld, she could not follow. But he faltered near the portal, as if some invisible force billowed out of the door and warded him back. She watched his fists curl tight and whiten.

Eight

"Are ye mad, Conaire?"

Brigid's words rang in Conaire's ears. He ceased his headlong, mindless dash towards the eastern horizon and swiveled, then strode to tower over her.

"Mad? Aye, perhaps I've a touch o' it."

His head still swirled with gossamer images. He could not shake the perfume of exotic smoke-fires from his nostrils. Vague, sylphlike forms slipped through his memory, then dispersed like mist. The melody of a sweet, high singing haunted him, for the remembrance of it came in short bursts, then faded into silence. Even when he looked upon Brigid, with her swirling eyes and her swirling cloak, it was as if a sparkling mist hung between them.

He gripped her arms and felt again the firm warmth of her—aye, she was human, she was real—he could hold onto her until the clinging fingertips of the Otherworld faded.

"Aye, it's a bit o' madness," he repeated. "I've a belly full o' wounds that should have left me dead, and I've a wife giving credence to the gossips o' my youth—and I'm finding myself believing her."

Her shoulders softened in his grip. "Och, Conaire, I thought—"

"That I'd deny it? Nay, woman." He gazed beyond her, to the swell of the burial mound, to the door to his father's house. "Now I know why I've the look of a man of five-and-twenty winters, when I've seen nigh forty; now I know why my sword slices so true."

He gorged his lungs with morning air. The names of warriors of the old tales rang in his head: *Cú Chulainn, Finn MacCool, the Fenians, the three sons of Usnagh.* Aye, since his youth he'd listened, rapt, to those tales of honor and glory, and held those names up like mirrors, hoping to find the most meager of reflections within. He'd long felt the burn of a different fire in him, brighter and hotter than all the other men he'd known. Now he had a name for it: 'twas a streak o' fairy blood burning in his veins.

'Twas true, what he'd suspected all his life; he was destined for some greater fate.

"Why are we standing here, freezin' in the dawn on some ancient sacred place, when I've a kingdom to see to? Come." He pulled her along. "To Morna we go—"

She dug her heels into the clay. Her eyes shone bright and wide, too achingly green amid the grays and browns of this rocky drumlin. A rogue tress slipped across her face, bright as blood against the paleness of her skin.

"There will be no going back, Conaire."

"You're speakin' foolishness, woman—"

"Only yesterday eve the people of Morna buried you in that tomb." She gestured to the full length of him. "Do you think they'll be risin' with shouts of joy, when they see you walkin' and breathin' like any mortal man?"

"They'll be falling to their knees."

He heard her gasp, but his mind was already over the ridge, beyond the *ráth,* to other kingdoms, to the kingdom of all Erin.

"Don't be a *fool!*"

Her cold, angry words drew him to his place. She stood like some fairy-wraith, her thin body swathed in wool, and her hair billowing around her head, tossed by contrary breezes, her bandaged hand held like a babe against her chest.

"They'll destroy you, Conaire."

He laughed, a sharp bark which reverberated over the land. "They *can't.*"

"There are many ways to die, while even the body lives."

"What would you have me do, woman? Hide like a coward from the ignorant?" He gestured to the east, his steps following the pull of his senses. "There is our kingdom." He spread his arms. "This is our *world.*"

"They are blind, ignorant, and full of fear. They will destroy what they do not understand."

"This is not so strange a happening," he mimicked, "Cú Chulainn himself was the son of the god Lúgh—"

"Don't mock me."

"I am who I am. You, my wife, should welcome this, for I am proof of what no man has ever proven, that your ways and your beliefs are true."

"*They* will call this my witchery, the devil's work—even as you first did."

"They will see sense soon enough, as *I* did."

"There's no teaching the dull and closed-minded." She seized his arm and tugged it, willing him to tear his eyes from the horizon. "You must trust me, Conaire, for I know what it is to be different from others . . ."

"I'm a warrior, woman. I'll not race away from a battle." He loosened her grip and seized her shoulders. "Have you no courage for this? You are my queen."

"You'll rue this day for as long as you live, for I know the way of men."

"Men's wills are like reeds in the lake; they bend with the wind—I shall come to them like a storm." He dragged her full against his body, crushing the soft curves of her, the new and tender fullness of breast, the hard round of her growing belly. "You bear the seed of kings, wife. You will stand beside me— proud and defiant—for you are vindicated."

Her lips, swollen and red, lay open to him. He seized their bounty, and took, and took—for this was woman, *his* woman, who'd given him all: his manhood, his heritage. She would see sense. He held her head steady in his hand until he was drunk on the taste of her, salt-woman and morning mist. Her damp hair screened their faces from the eyes of the world, and cocooned them in the honeysuckle warmth of her skin. He supped on her until the rigidness of her shoulders eased, and her spine melted against his embrace.

The sap of life rose in him, hot and undeniable, and she yielded to him with the softest of moans. She blossomed beneath his kiss, all sighs and surrender. His knees scraped against the solid earth. He braced one hand on the cold rock and eased her down. Beneath her tunic lay hot skin and moist eagerness, living flesh whose spirit no fairy could match. The moon-dark tides raged as they'd never raged before; there was no art to this loving, no tenderness, for she bucked beneath him as eager as he, their loving naked beneath the great, gray, rumbling dome of the morning sky. He sought the core of her and filled her with the hard, hot length of his need. She cried out at the union; the void filled, the yearning quenched, for this was the joining of spirit and flesh.

Heart still hammering, Conaire pillowed her head on his arm and gazed down upon his woman. He thumbed her cheek where the bristle on his jaw had razed her pink, then kissed the hollow beneath her cheekbone. Her breath came hot and fast by his ear.

"Yield to me, woman," he whispered, pressing their joined bodies still closer. "Stand by my side at Morna."

"I'll stand with ye, my husband." Her arms tightened around his shoulders and her body jerked, as if with a sob. "So be it."

Brigid plodded beside her husband, feigning an effort to match his long, purposeful stride. Conaire marched onward, oblivious to the oppressive gray fog which rolled in around them; his firm steps plowed a path straight to the looming shape of the *ráth* in the hazy distance. She battled with the urge to seize him, stop him, rage until he saw sense; but she knew it would be in vain, for she knew deep in her bones that each jarring step brought them closer and closer to doom.

She'd never raged against the Knowledge before, but now the price had never been so high, nor the outcome so easily preventable. But from the moment Conaire had lain with her atop the rocky drumlin, she knew there would be no swaying the will of this king. When he raged over her like the power and fury of winter storm, filling her with him, then stared down at her, his gray eyes glowing brighter than any metal forged in fire—willing her to acquiesce—she wondered if perhaps he *could* mold fate in his strong hands; if the brute force of his own shimmering personality could sway the hearts and minds of a whole people to see the world in a new way. In his all-loving embrace, she found herself believing the unbelievable.

She had surrendered, knowing better, and knowing, too, that one mere woman could do nothing to stop the wheels of fate.

Now she silently mourned as she plodded toward their destiny, for she sensed that for all his eager lovemaking, she'd lost a part of him this day. She'd surrendered him to a dream of greater glory. She supposed that was the way of it for the wives of great men; they never owned the whole of the man, for part of his soul belonged to conquest, with all its masculine camaraderie and honor and glory—things that women were blissfully denied, and thus could not fully understand.

And she wondered why they'd been brought together at the hot fires of Lughnasa, only to be torn apart on the cold morning of Samhain.

The pounding of horses' hooves emerged from the mist. Brigid scanned the ridge and saw the murky shape of a rider and two horses cresting over it. Conaire stopped, legs spread, directly in the rider's path.

She recognized the rider; one of her father's loyal men, stern-faced and dependable. *Come to fetch me from the door of the tomb, no doubt. Come to fetch the bearer of my father's heir.*

Sighting a figure beyond his horse's head amid the roiling fog, the rider reared back his horse and opened his mouth to rage, but his lips fell slack. The wispy fog parted and cast a single ray of sun upon Conaire's glowing regalia.

Instinctively, Brigid moved around Conaire and pressed against his side. The rider's bulging gaze fell to her, then back to Conaire—who stood, chest thrown open, grinning.

"Back to Morna for you," Conaire bellowed. "Have the *ráth* readied for my return."

With a spray of earth and a flash of crossing hands, the rider was gone before the words were full spoken. He and his horse stumbled with haste and disappeared below the slope.

With a reckless laugh, Conaire followed the path of uprooted earth. He paused when he realized that she still stood where he'd left her.

"They are waiting for us, wife."

Her feet felt as heavy as lead. *We have but this moment, husband, before all will change.* Even as the thought passed her mind, she realized that it was too late; everything had changed already.

"Have you no mercy, Conaire? Dragging a woman with child clear across the kingdom?" She hefted the hem of her cloak from the clay, her hair falling across her face to screen the hot bite of tears. "I'll come at me own pace, I will."

The mischievous mist granted them teasing glimpses of the circular fortress, as they worked their way down the slope toward the newly built *ráth*. Amid the thatched-roofed dwellings, dark figures swarmed, then streamed out through the opening to head in their direction. Conaire stopped on level ground, his foot resting on a boulder, waiting with an arrogant tilt of his jaw for the arrival of his people.

She closed her eyes against the sight of the crowd racing up the hill, but she could not ignore the rumbling of the earth beneath her feet, nor the shouts carried to her amidst the fog, nor the sharp rattle of a horse's hooves. She forced her shoulders straight; her chin high. For all the good it would do in the end, they mustn't sense her fear.

Aidan rode far ahead of the clan. His horse's hooves shot sparks off the rocky ground as he urged it crudely up the slope, then skidded it to an abrupt stop, splattering clumps of wet sod at their feet.

Aidan's knuckles whitened upon the reins as he struggled to control his heaving horse, his eyes fixed in disbelief on the figure before him. "By the *Dagdá.*"

"No horn of mead for me, foster-brother? You come empty-handed to your king's side?"

"Foul magic!" Aidan's burning hazel gaze swung to her. "Not even in death could you let him be, could ye, witch?"

"Easy, foster-brother." Conaire lifted his foot from the boulder and planted it firmly on solid ground. "I'll forgive you much for the shock o' this, but I'll not let you set loose your tongue on my queen again."

Aidan's stallion sensed his fear; he stamped and skittered back, flattening its ears against its head.

"I expected," Conaire continued, "a better greeting from you, Aidan."

"Cease this!" Aidan tore his gaze from Conaire to glare at Brigid. "He died a warrior's death, yet you reach your rotten fingers beyond the grave and drag him out of *Tír na nÓg.*"

"You stupid fool." She scanned him with scorn. "You've known Conaire all your life, and never saw the truth."

"I knew enough to curse the day you wove your spell of enchantment around him."

The wind picked up and snapped Aidan's *brat* over his shoulders. A white rod gleamed where it was tucked into his belt—the white rod of kingship.

"You did not wait long," Conaire said, with dangerous softness, "to get yourself crowned, foster-brother."

"Fetch this creature away, witch," he commanded, "or you'll see his blood run red anew—"

"Enough!" Conaire's voice cut sharp through the morning air. "Shake the mead fumes from your head and look upon me."

"Would that this evil were nothing but mead clouding my sight," Aidan growled. "Would that it were madness—"

"We joked about this often enough. How many times did you mock me as a child o' the *Sidh?* It should be no shock to you, of all men, that the legend is true."

The words gave Aidan pause, but only for a moment. He shook his head fiercely, as if to shake off enchantment. "It's the witch speaking—"

"Och, such foolishness!" she blurted, stepping beside Conaire, sensing a fissure in Aidan's rock-hard anger, sensing a chance in the wind. "Last night you were after accusing me of killing me own husband, and this morning you're after accusing me of bringing him back to life. Don't you think I know me own mind?"

"You've a witch's mind, bent on evil." Spittle sprayed his mustache. "Aye, you know your own mind, woman. You couldn't control him in life, could you? So you had him killed, and then resurrected this creature to take his place—"

"By the spear of Lúgh! 'Tis the power of the gods you'll be putting in me hands!"

"—now you'll have me giving the king's rod to this mockery of a man, and you'll rule this kingdom through him—"

"I'll be the one," Conaire growled, "to take that rod back."

"It's a fine show of it you do, woman, to have your own creature acting as if he has his own will."

"You'll be tasting the strength o' my will, foster-brother."

Aidan seized the hilt of his sword. "I'll not be muddled by your witchery, for I touched my king with my own hands yesterday, he stretched out like the warrior he was, cut down in glory. Before me now I see a witch's minion dressed in the king's clothes, ready to do your bidding—"

"Your king," Conaire argued, striding toward Aidan, "stands before you."

Inside, she screamed. *No, no, Conaire! Can't you see it in his eyes? He fears you, he fears this, because he does not understand. He sees not his foster-brother, but a body come alive by magic and evil.*

"Nay, not *my* king." The sound of drawn steel rang through the air. "My king died yesterday. I know not who *you* are."

Aidan swung his sword once, a great silver arc that sliced the front of Conaire's tunic. Conaire spread his arms and froze in his footsteps, then stared down at the rent slashed across his chest.

Brigid clutched her heart. Aye, there was more than one betrayal here this morning.

Then, a low, angry buzz began in the air, like the humming of bees near the hives outside the ring-fort. It surged; grew loud and more distinct, until she realized that the buzzing was the hum of a hundred voices; the vibrations of the approaching crowd.

"You should be afeared, witch." Aidan pulled his wild-eyed glare from the shape of the tall king. "It was arrogance to return here, thinking we'd bow down to this creature o' yours. There will be no escaping for you now, or for this wretch."

Suddenly, the slope vomited people. Waves and waves of them came—their bare feet hard on the ground, their arms upraised, their voices sharp and harsh. Her stomach tightened. She felt the shimmering rage of the crowd like a wave of heat.

Conaire backed up until he stood in front of her. His sword

rang as he pulled it out and embraced the hilt in two hands. Legs spread, he glared at the crowd.

Like a wave of water hitting a wall and tumbling back upon itself, the crowd stopped at the sight of their king, in all his gleaming regalia, standing before them with his breath misting on the cool air. For one brief, trembling moment, as she heard the people of Morna gasp into utter silence, Brigid sensed that many of them looked upon her husband with his golden torque gleaming and the sunlight crisp on his long, auburn hair, and his silver eyes as sharp and clear and bright as a winter's sky, and struggled not to fall to their knees. A thin line separated reverence and fear.

For one brief, trembling moment, she wondered if Conaire *could* conquer their fear. For one sweet second, she dared to hope for a different world, for a place Conaire could mold to his will, a place where the *Sídh* could run without fear even in the light of day, a place where Druid fires light up the night, a place where he and she would be honored for their gifts, and not hated. She pressed close against his back and dug her fingers into the hardness of his arm.

"Kneel!" Conaire's voice cut through the silence. "Kneel at the sight o' your king."

Gasps rifled through the crowd, murmurings which grew higher and more frantic. She saw hands flashing in the sign of the cross, and she began to hear the whisper of *witch, witch, witch* . . .

"I am their king." Aidan kicked his horse closer to Conaire, his chest thrown back, his gaze scanning the crowd of people. "They'll kneel to no wisp o' magic. For this—" he gestured to Conaire with the tip of his sword, "—is the devil's work."

She felt the shock ripple through Conaire's body. Such were Christian words, aye, and Aidan had spent much time among the Christians of her father's house, even sleeping, it was said, with a Morna bondswoman. It had come to this then: Aidan had chosen the new religion, the new world, and thus stood forever opposed from his friend and his brother.

Conaire glared at Aidan. "You've been spending too much time between the legs o' that Morna girl, foster-brother."

"You," he scowled, laying his sword out inches from Conaire's face, "are no brother of mine."

With a high, sharp cry, someone amid the mob threw the first stone.

It struck Conaire on the face. Droplets of blood oozed out of a welt a sharp edge had sliced across his cheek. It was as if the scent of blood filled the air.

"The unholy creature bleeds." Aidan raised his voice to the crowd. "What has died once, can be killed again."

The second stone hit her. She stumbled back, stunned, but Conaire's hand curled around her arm, dragging her up, lifting her behind him, even as he knocked Aidan's sword away. Something wet slid down her face. The buzzing surged; shouts rang out; stones hailed upon them.

The madness was unleashed.

"Stay close."

Conaire's sword was useless against the deadly rain. She clutched his cloak and buried her head in protection. She heard the clang of rocks against the metal; she felt him flinch as a stone hit an old wound. She knew he could not fight so many . . . and as soon as Conaire stumbled and showed weakness, the fear would stop them from tossing stones from afar, and they would descend upon them like wolves. Then, there would be no protection from the knives and swords and spears. Fear inundated her; Conaire was immortal, but she was not. Neither was the helpless child in her womb.

Cursing, Conaire shrugged his cloak off his shoulders and threw it over her. She burrowed in it, trying to muffle the blows of the stones as he broke away from her. She sank to the ground. She heard the neighing of a horse—Aidan's horse—heard the man's cry, the hard thud of a body as it hit the earth. The hail subsided. Through the folds of the cloak she saw her husband wrestling with Aidan, their swords clanging against one another, Conaire driving him back, away from the horse who neighed and reared, skittish so close to the flashing blades. Aidan lunged; Conaire, off balance, threw himself aside, but not soon enough. Blood blossomed on his tunic.

"No!"

She surged from the protection of the cloak, running mindlessly, pushing Aidan, not even seeing the flash of his blade, only knowing that if he thrust again, while Conaire was off balance, Conaire would die—and though he was immortal, she wasn't, and the crowd would kill her and her unborn child—she knew no other thought. She felt the burn of metal graze her side; she felt Conaire tugging her away, tossing her on the ground behind him. She looked down and saw blood on her tunic; but still she felt no pain.

Conaire struggled with the horse's reins in one hand as he fought—his teeth bared, his sword lethal. Aidan was fighting for his life; he knew it, but the crowd cried out behind him, urging him, thirsty for blood, the stone-throwing, for the moment, forgotten. This was single combat between warriors; even in a time of madness, this ritual would be honored.

Conaire screamed something to her; she reacted. She stumbled to her feet, faced the flashing hooves, the white, gnashing teeth of the horse. She'd only ridden a horse once in her life— behind Conaire when he returned with her to the ring-fort. Even then, even then, she had known this was folly, but Conaire would have no part of her fears.

So she ducked and swarmed around the horse, grasping his mane, ducking his foaming mouth, nearly crumpling in two when one of his flashing hooves found a mark in the softness of her side. Beyond the horse, she could still hear Conaire and Aidan fighting. Digging her ragged nails into the horse's back, gritting her teeth, she heaved herself upon him, clinging to his sweat-soaked coat, swinging one leg over his back. She held on with the strength of her thighs, by gripping fistfuls of the stallion's skin.

Below, the rage was upon Conaire. She had never seen him in his battle lust—there was no mercy in his eyes, no hesitation in the mighty slash of his sword. Both men bled, but though Conaire fought with one hand wrapped around the reins, Aidan was the first to stumble.

Conaire lodged the point of his sword in the hollow of Aidan's neck, as the man fell to the ground. "Yield to me."

Aidan spit at him.

"Don't be a fool." The mist parted; briefly, a ray of sunshine flashed off Conaire's blade. "You know my fighting; you know who stands before you."

Aidan lay, mute, his chest heaving with effort, his hazel eyes glittering.

Conaire jerked his chin to Aidan's belt. "Do you love that rod o' kingship so much you'd make me kill you for it, when a hundred thousand kingdoms lay before our feet?"

"I'll not sell my soul for a kingdom." He tilted his head, slightly, toward the silent, hovering mob. "And you'll not win it by tearing that rod from my dead body."

A faint howl of wind riffled the scrubby tufts of grass clinging between the rocks upon the slope, stained black from a spattering of rain. The bellies of low-lying clouds rumbled above. Conaire removed his sword from Aidan's throat, and let the tip trail against the earth. He glared at the crowd. Then he turned and looked at her.

Brigid's heart lurched. Those eyes, once so clear and sure, now clouded with angry confusion. Aidan spoke the truth: A Celtic king was considered the embodiment of his people, responsible not merely for his own conduct as a ruler, but for the fertility of the land and for protecting his tribe against blight and plague of every sort—no unwanted king would rule long. Conaire saw the futility of his fight.

Suddenly he lurched forward. Brigid cried out and lunged for the reins, as Conaire clutched his leg with a grimace and stumbled around to face Aidan, rising from the ground, wielding a bloody sword. Blood seeped into Conaire's tunic and filled the palm of his hand. Conaire swung his sword to parry Aidan's strike, then swung again—this time with fury. Aidan stumbled back with the force of the blow, then lost his balance as Conaire lunged again, and again, until Conaire found flesh, and buried his sword deep into his foster-brother.

The dying man's wail cleared the air and left nothing but its own echo in the silence. With a muffled cry, Conaire drew out his sword; blood washed it and dripped from the tip. He stood over Aidan—whose eyes bulged with the pain—grasping the bloodstained sword until the last frothy gurgle of life bubbled from Aidan's lips.

Brigid shifted on the horse, clutching her injured side, struggling against faintness. The crowd stirred—the scent of life-blood filled the air. She whispered Conaire's name; he lifted his head, dazed, staring at her as if just noticing her presence. A stone flew, and hit her injured side. She lurched, then lost her balance, and tumbled off the horse to the ground.

The taste of grass and grit exploded in her mouth. Shouts and cries rose around her. She was only vaguely aware of a hail of stones bruising her back and thighs—then she felt someone lifting her up, lifting her high—it was Conaire, yelling, fighting, shoving someone aside. She smelled the sour-milk stench of some old hag's breath, saw a mouth with gaping, rotted teeth. Then, somehow, she was upon the horse, her cheek pressed against Conaire's sweat-stained back, her arms wrapped around his waist, and he was swinging his sword, cutting a path through flesh, kicking the steed into life beneath them, until he stretched out toward freedom.

The horse's great, loping strides jarred her bones, but she hardly felt the pain; she was lost in a foggy place, her mind not all her own. All she knew was the smell of Conaire's sweat beneath her cheek, the thunder of his heart in his chest; she heard, in the great distance, the last furious cries of a thwarted mob. They were free, they were free, they were alive.

They rode mindlessly, through deep forest, through sloping valleys, over ridges, following the path of a stream until it merged with Lough Riach. They rode until foam gathered around the horse's mouth, until his great, black sides heaved between their legs. When he would go no farther, Conaire turned him toward the shores of Lough Riach, dismounted, and let him drink his fill.

She was not sure where they were; on some northern shore of the lake. She had a sudden flash of the Sight, of many places like this: unfamiliar, temporary watering holes they would pass from, one to another, until they all seemed the same.

Conaire stood with his back to her. He stared out over the still surface of the water. In his hands he held the bloodstained sword with which he had cut down his foster-brother.

With a mighty heave, he sent the heavy weapon whirling through the air. It spun and twirled, catching the morning's light, before the lake swallowed it.

Brigid knew he would never wield a sword again.

When he returned to her, his eyes were shadowed. He noticed the blood on her tunic and her face, as if for the first time.

"It's nothing," she lied. She had long begun to feel the aches and bruises and cuts; her head throbbed, and the flesh wound on her side burned. To distract him, she nodded to the blood on his tunic. Some of his old wounds had opened.

His voice was hard. "I shall live no matter what wounds they inflict."

She lowered her face. In the course of a day they had become exiles—from all mankind. Brigid knew the feeling well; she had been an exile for half her life. But to Conaire, the loss of a kingship and the loss of Aidan was too fresh a wound to bear . . . especially in the wake of his broken dreams.

His hands curled into her waist, careful not to dig into the slash on her side. "Come down. We are safe here. They'll not look hard for us beyond the borders of Morna. You must be tended to—"

Her sudden cry cut him off. She doubled over, a cramp closing like a fist in her abdomen. She heard him bark her name through the red haze of pain. Something deep, deep inside her tore away. Warm liquid bathed her legs.

"No!" Brigid pressed her thighs together, then flung her head back to scream at the skies. *No, no, not the innocent! Let him live, let him live!* The blood kept coming, the cramping tightened. *"No!"*

She sank to the ground, her sobs lost in the wind. From somewhere in the canopy of oak leaves above came the airy wail of the *bean sí*. With a keening cry of anguish, Brigid railed against the truth.

The *bean sí's* song of days ago had not been for her father, nor for Conaire.

'Twas the death song of her unborn child.

Nine

The rugged cliffs of the Aran Islands crested out of the mists of Galway Bay, their backs curled like stony spines against the fury of the Atlantic Ocean. Heather and bracken and scrawny tufts of grass clung tenaciously to the windswept wilderness of stone, defying the salt spray, the icy fogs, and the gales that frequently clawed at their roots. Froth-crested waves thundered in and out of secret caverns, and the screeches of gulls and cormorants echoed hollowly over the islands, as the birds wheeled over the breakers.

Conaire flexed his stiff fingers over the oars. He eyed the small wedge of sand on the shore behind him, the sole landing point amid the layered teeth of cliffs on the lee side of the middle island. Brigid leaned into the steering oar, her knuckles white with the effort of keeping the prow of the *curragh* facing the roll of the oncoming sea. The boat—nothing more than cow skin stretched over bone—bobbed on the water like a nutshell.

Wave after wave surged underneath them to crash upon the sand. Conaire watched the struggle of the distant waters, counting the time between each wave's crest and furrow, eyeing the froth and swirling foam. After months traveling through the rugged western shore of Erin, he had grown expert at handling these native boats, and at reading this treacherous sea. One wrong move, one wave caught unawares or broadside, and the hungry ocean would suck this fragile vessel into its womb.

He saw his opportunity. Barking a swift order, Conaire

plunged his oars in the water. Before the swell of the last wave had eased beneath them, Brigid twisted the steering oar, and the prow swung around toward the shore. The boat leapt and hurled through the spray. Conaire's shoulders burned as he battled against the tide, straining to propel the boat toward the slip of sand, before the next wave crashed down upon them. As the rib of the vessel crunched the sand, Conaire leapt out, seized the rim, and yanked the *curragh* far away from the surf, as the boggy shore sucked at the soles of his feet.

Brigid dragged a chapped hand through her dripping hair as Conaire lifted her out of the boat. Her swirling green gaze avoided his and instead took in the full of the island. Sea spray soaked black the high thrust of the slate cliffs. Above, a confusion of white-winged birds cawed and screeched at this unexpected invasion. The grays of coming rain shrouded the bay beyond, yet the thinness of the clouds threw a strange, silvery light on the sea and land.

"Och, it's the very edge of the world."

"Aye, 'tis that." He squinted towards the faint purple outline of the Connemara hills, the only sight of the mainland in the swirl and crash of ocean. Any *curragh* which dared to approach this island would be seen long before it neared; and once it arrived, that boat would lay vulnerable, while it waited for the sea to give it leave to land. A man could ask for no better fortress than this rugged island. No better gate than this slip of shore. No better moat than this treacherous northern sea.

"It's fitting," he mused, "that we'd find the end o' the world."

All through Erin, Brigid with her flaming hair and he with his height and breadth were too easily recognized as the witch o' Morna and the king she'd summoned from the dead. The tale had snapped at their heels, growing more and more fantastic, and so they battered about like leaves in a gale, finding no rest, no peace, no sanctuary.

Until now.

Conaire dragged the boat higher on the shore and snugged it into the lee of a boulder. "I'll tell you something for nothing: They won't be driving us away any farther than this."

"All these months," she said, "travelin' around and about, I thought there could never be a more forsaken place than the wilds of Connemara, and now look what we've come to."

His gaze shifted to her upturned face, the long, white arch of her neck, the tightness about her lips. *Aye, my wife, look where my folly has brought you. A place fit for nothing but gulls and seaweed.*

The guilt was a familiar twisting in his innards.

She squinted up at the cliff's height. "Is there not a tree on the whole place?"

He shook his head shortly. To live on this gale-battered island, any living thing had to lie low and cling to the rocks.

"It will take a fine bit of work to get a cow to the top, I'm thinking."

"You'll be getting your cow." He nodded toward a hump of black land across the white-capped sound to their left. "I've seen a herd o' cattle upon the heights o' the north island. No doubt the owners will be glad to trade a few head for the price o' some knives and wool."

She leaned over the edge of the boat to heft up a bulging sack containing all their worldly possessions. "I've no liking for neighbors so close."

" 'Tis a fearful channel which separates the islands. They'll not be visiting."

He might have added, *a flock o' priests live there,* but he said nothing. It was his task, to take worry upon his own shoulders. She'd find out, soon enough, that the most pious of Christians inhabited the largest of the three islands. It was enough that he knew she had no reason to fear. The monks would want nothing to do with them. The Romans had separated themselves from the chaos and comforts of the world—just as they were now forced to do.

Besides, to tell her would require too long an explanation. These past months, words between them were painful, sharp things. They concentrated their thoughts outward, to the world raging around them, and thus avoided the grief and the guilt roiling between them.

"It'll be a fine thing," she muttered, casting the sack upon the sand, "if there's even enough grass between those rocks to feed a calf."

"There's enough to sustain a few head," he argued. "If I must, I'll swim them over to the next island to graze. There's nary a soul upon that island, like to this."

"We'll have to make land, too." She busied herself with hefting logs of peat out of the bottom of the boat. "With seaweed and sand and clay, like the Connemara men do, so we can be planting some barley for ale and porridge—"

"No more o' this." He seized the peat and tossed the pile back into the boat. How it burned in his gut, to hear her talking of bondswomen's tasks, to see her fine, woolen cloak stained with salt and streaked with soil, his *wife*, his queen. "Leave a man's job to a man. Come look about the island."

He gestured her toward the rocky tumble that served as a path to the top of the cliff. With effort, she settled the soggy hem of her cloak over her arm and led the way. He allowed his gaze to linger upon her bowed shoulders, upon the fragile column of neck, revealed as the wind battened back her tangled hair. An aching jab speared through him, like a sword slice through an old and infected wound.

She paused on a small ledge. "Will we be making our house of stones upon this cliff," she asked, "and plugging the holes with seaweed, then?"

"It will be a sturdier house than ever you had in the woods o' Morna."

But there will be no soft oaks' shadows, and no honeysuckle blooming, and no scent o' green summer grass. Aye, he thought. He'd taken all that from her, too.

"There will be no lack of fish, I'm thinking." She eyed the slippery, shell-encrusted rocks which thrust out in ledges toward the sea. "Or ducks. Or limpets or periwinkles or mussels or cockles . . ."

The surf crashed and roared, drowning out her words. He scanned the eastern horizon and felt the cold bite of salty spray on his face. A hooded crow screeched and darted down from its nest on the ridge, and then swept up to dart down again.

She hefted her soggy cloak higher on her arm. "It will take a fine bit of scratching and sweating to make a life here."

"It was you who once said that a bit o' hard work never harmed any man."

"It's a good thing you've had a bit of practice at the thatching, I'm thinking."

His gaze flew to her profile, to the barest shadow of a wistful smile playing about her lips. Soft words, these, yet probing and sore. For a moment, amid the roar of the surf and the shrieking of the seabirds, they shared a bittersweet memory of a sun-lit glade rich with the scent of honeysuckle.

His callused hands curled into fists. "It was a poor enough job I did of it."

She traced patterns in the ledge with her toe. "It'll be a sight to see, the King of Morna hewing stone and cutting peat and wielding a fishing spear."

She dared a fleeting glance, and for a moment he saw his reflection in her eyes. His three-colored cloak hung ragged and worn from so many nights sleeping in it, salt-stained and snagged from leaping in and out of the *curragh*. His neck lay bare of the golden roped torque, for it marked him too clearly a king in any land. A frayed strap of leather had taken the place of his belt of beaten gold.

He turned away swiftly. "Don't you be talking foolishness, woman. I'm a king no more."

Unconsciously, his hand strayed to his hip, naked of the weight of his sword. Again he felt it, that shifting of the world beneath his feet, as if this ledge had cracked from the island and lurched into the sea. Even now, months after he'd tossed the bloody sword into the lake, he walked as if he'd lost a limb. He'd been fed his first solid food on its tip. He'd grown up with the weight of it slung across his hip, or firm in his grip, marking his life by the battles he'd won in one-to-one combat. He'd conquered a kingdom by it. Aye, and this was the end of it: He slew his foster-brother by it, knowing Aidan—or any other mortal— could never best him in one-to-one combat.

"Don't you be telling me I married less than a king." Her cloak snapped as she turned and headed up the rubbled path. "It will take a strong man with a strong back to conquer this island, it will; no less than a king will do."

Brave words these, jutting out into the quagmire of pain swirling between them—but he had no ear for them, for he knew he was a king no more. He was something beyond human, something of another time, another world. He was a man of flesh and bones and blood and something else, something wispy and impossible to grasp, even with his thoughts. He had abandoned more than a shining blade of steel in the north end of Lough Riach that morning after Samhain. He'd abandoned Conaire of Ulster, Champion of the Uí Néill, King of Morna—and still after all his wanderings, he did not know his name. He felt like a boat at sea without oars, at the mercy of the tides and the weather. His hands craved the grip of something, even if it were no more than a stone-pick or a fishing spear.

A gull keened a lonely cry above him. He glanced up the slope to where Brigid climbed, growing more distant with each step.

"Will ye be standin' there all day?" She tossed the words over her shoulder without pause. "Come. You can't climb a cliff by scaling it in your mind."

Conaire grunted up the narrow path which lead to the height of the cliff, tightening the bulk of the basket of seaweed upon his soaking back. Salty ribbons of the damp underwater plants draped over his shoulders like a mantle. With a swipe of his forearm, he wiped the sweat and seawater off his face, then eased his way to where he and Brigid were building their house.

The beehive-shaped dwelling of stone swelled from the earth, nestled in the lee of a small outcropping of rock. As he rounded the pregnant swell, he glimpsed Brigid perched amid fields of drying seaweed, gazing up into the silvery air with a handful of dried seaweed draped over her hand.

Conaire trudged to the smoking peat fire, then ripped apart the rope tied around his waist and let the basket of seaweed thud to the rocky ground. She did not budge from her musings, but remained still, transfixed at something in the sky as her ragged skirt battered her dirty calves.

"It's enough o' working for one day," he said, loud enough to be heard. "Soon it will be dark."

She did not move, not even to acknowledge his words. He trudged through the crackling field of dried seaweed, wiping his salt-sticky hands upon his damp cloak. How pale she looked, her skin as silvery and translucent as the strange light which cast upon this island after the passing of a gale. It was no wonder, with all the hard work they'd done these past weeks, piling the stones one upon the other to make a dwelling fitting for man and strong enough to withstand the forces o' the sea upon this island. And Brigid, workin' as hard as an ox, her bones jutting through her skin and looking fragile enough to break. Working so hard they spoke of nothing but work; and at night they fell upon the rocky earth and instantly into the bonds of sleep, while the abyss yawning between them stretched wider and deeper.

When he reached her side, she nodded toward the sky and murmured a quiet, "Look."

He squinted in the direction of her nod; above, two white swans wheeled in the lonely expanse of sky. They stretched their wide wings and soared beneath a breeze. Beyond, on the horizon, another boiling of gray clouds threatened. "Fey swans, to be flying so calmly about out here, with a storm coming."

"They don't belong here." The wind battered her long braid over her shoulder. "They belong in a cool lake, with calm water and plenty of reeds to hide among."

"Don't you be worrying about them. They'll survive well enough out here, and if they don't, we'll be dining on them soon enough."

She granted him a swift, harsh glance. "We've not come so far from the world that we'll be feasting on swan's meat to survive." She eyed the birds anew. "Do they not remind you of the tale of the Children of Lir?"

His nostrils flared, as if he smelled anew the wood fires of a smoky mead hall, the strum of a harp, the lilting voice of a royal poet, the warm circle of comfortable camaraderie.

This must be what it is like to age, he thought, for memories to cut like blades.

Pebbles scraped against the rocky ground as he swiveled away. "I remember none o' the tales."

"They were turned into swans," she continued, oblivious to the gruffness in his voice, "and condemned to live amid the harsh seas for hundreds of years."

"How fanciful you've become, wife, seeing magic in birds who've done no more than lose their way in the gale."

"They've built a nest, don't you know? On the ledge of one of the caverns." Her features softened in memory. "Aye, I remember the tale now. Condemned, they were, to walk the earth as swans for hundreds of years—exiled from Erin—until a prince of the north married a princess of the south—"

"Will you be telling me," he interrupted, "how you discovered this nest o' theirs?"

Her trance faltered; she discovered a sudden interest in the patch of seaweed at her feet. "I found it as I looked for eggs amid the rocks."

Anger shot through him, hot and fast. "I told you, woman, there will be no prancing about those cliffs—"

"You'll be singing another song, Conaire, when you see the dinner I've made ye."

She swiveled and picked her way through the field of seaweed, before he could seize her arm. He clenched his fists on air. He'd explored those caverns where birds nested upon the ledges; he'd seen rocky outcroppings of stone battered by sun and salt and sea disintegrate and crumble without warning into the yawning mouth of the ocean below, with its jagged granite teeth and swirling froth. He stared at her narrow back, retreating toward the peat fire, and wondered if he'd have to chain her within the *clochán* to protect the fragile mortal soul lodged within those stubborn shoulders.

Then the anger sparking in him found tinder and blazed. For too many weeks this silence had stretched between them; for too many weeks he'd watched her burrow deeper and deeper into a place within herself he could not reach; all while he drifted farther away, his thoughts fixed upon the strangeness of his own existence. Aye, she could hate him for all he had done to her—the loss of the babe, the loss of her freedom, the eternal exile in this barren place, all for his foolish pride—but he would hear the fighting words from her own lips, he would feel her blows upon him, for only then would he know that he had not destroyed her spirit as well as their child that last day in Morna.

She poked at the warm ashes of the peat fire with a sliver of stone, and rolled out a half-dozen birds' eggs onto a matting of seaweed. Her fingers paused as he stopped, feet spread, before her.

"Do you hate me so much, woman, that you'd kill yourself to be rid o' me?"

She clicked her tongue. "Don't be talking foolishness."

"Is it now? With you dancing upon the edge of a cavern for a bit o' food, aye, that looks to me like a woman who wishes for death—"

"You know nothing of it." She rolled a hot stone into a nearby pit of water, sending up a hiss of steam amid the boiling periwinkles. "It's proving to you, I am, that I'm no fainting bit o' thing, like you seem to think."

He scanned the crouch of her thin figure, the hollows of her cheeks, the body denied to him all these weeks. "I've eyes, woman."

She rose swiftly to her feet. Her dress was stained wet and dirty with peat grime where she had knelt. "I can fish as well as you, and gather me food around and about the shore. I can burn seaweed, if I must, for there's not a bit of peat on this island." She gestured to the looming beehive of stone behind them. "Now that the *clochán* is built, I've no more need o' you. I can fend for meself here."

His blood went cold. The horizon tilted. It was madness, she was speaking, for no man could live alone on this island and survive for long. It was madness, she was speaking, for him to leave.

She wants me to leave.

"So you hate me that much then."

"Och, there's no hate in it." She clutched her thin arms and turned away from him, tossing her head so the wind would swipe the braid off her face. "Such foolishness. Hate, hate, what room do I have in me heart for hate, after all that has happened between us?"

"What is it, then?" Indifference. The thought brought a new sense of vertigo. "Can your eyes not bear the sight of one of the *Sídh?*"

She turned upon him, then, and he met that gaze he'd not dared to meet these past weeks, for fear of the accusations he'd see roiling within them; she turned the fullness of those eyes upon him, and he felt the soul-suck he'd always known; and he saw the rich green swirl of forest shadows, dark shadows, rife with grief and mourning and something else, some greater knowledge.

"Such a thing as *that* is not worthy of you. Did you think I would treat you as others have treated me?" Her shoulders shuddered with sudden emotion. "I've known the truth of your birth, Conaire, longer than you . . . and even as I did, I took your seed into my body and gave it succor and life."

Her voice cracked and she turned her face away. The wind scattered pebbles across the earth. The dried seaweed skittered and flapped around their feet.

She bent down and clutched a handful of seaweed, crushing it into a ball in her hands. "I see you sometimes, staring out to the land beyond. Back to Erin."

He shrugged. "I've no liking for unwelcome visitors."

"It's more than that, don't I know." She squinted toward the silhouette of the birds. "You're like those swans, Conaire. You don't belong here."

"This place is fit for nothing but rock and gull."

"It's too small an island. It will be like a cage for ye." She splayed her hand over the stones of the *clochán,* searching for a chink amid the wall to fill with the wadded seaweed. "The mists of Erin still cling to your cloak. You must go back."

"Back? To what?" He snorted in the direction of the dim purple horizon of hills. "I don't belong *there.* I'm denied the place where I belong—the place of my father. And you—"

"This is not about me, I'm after telling ye." She wadded the dried seaweed into the chink, pressing it deep between the stones. "I've been an exile before, I know the way of it."

"Aye," he said, and the words ripped out of him, "and because o' me, you're an exile forevermore."

She dragged her hands down the length of her ragged cloak, leaving two trails of salt and sand. "I was an exile before you came, Conaire, no less than now. Then, me head was full of silly dreams." She raised her chin to the salty breeze. "Now, I know it's my fate to be alone. But you . . . you've left a world behind, a world which needs ye."

"A world which calls me the devil's work—"

"Listen to you, to the bitterness in your voice. On this island, you'll do nothing but grow more bitter by the years. You must go back to Erin, to have your vengeance."

"There will be no more talk o' vengeance, woman—"

"You are still a warrior, a king."

"Am I?" He spread out his arms as if to embrace the whole of the barren island, then whirled into a bow. "Regard the great King of Inishmaan, and his subjects, the bird and the fish—"

"You mock yourself even now, but there'll be no denying your nature."

"My nature." The words fell from his lips like curses. "What nature is that? The liking for blood, the lust for death, the mockery of a battle challenge which I cannot lose?" He turned away and raised his face to the bite of the coming storm. The inside of his lids shone blood-red. There was no use in burdening her with the wretched tides of his own thoughts, for they ebbed and flowed as frequently as any sea. "There will be no more talk o' it. It is you who speaks madness, as if I would leave you in this barren place alone."

As if I could abandon you now, after all I have done to you.

Her feet scraped against the ground. He felt her presence just behind him, as her words fell softly on his ears.

"Have you thought, Conaire, that there may be a reason for your existence?"

He snorted. "Nothing more than the folly of a fairy and a woman by the light of the Samhain fires."

"If it was folly, then surely it would be oft repeated, and there'd be many of you among us."

There was no arguing with her soft logic; he had wondered the same, but the question echoed in his head with no answer. *Why?*

She lay her hand on his arm. "There must be a reason why the gods allowed you on this earth, and denied you access to *Tír na nÓg*. You must go back to Erin and follow your fate."

He glanced down at her. He could smell her, all warmth and woman. "What has the Sight told you, woman?"

Her gaze faltered. "The Sight fails me, in this place, with its winds and barrenness." Her hand slid off his arm. "But I've thought about what you said that day in Morna . . ."

"Too much talkin' and not enough doing that day."

He followed her movements as she wandered apart from him, toying with the knuckles of her fingers, long bereft of the copper rings he'd once given her. Work-hardened and callused, red and raw.

"You could change the way of things, Conaire."

"I tried that once."

"Aye, with the Christians of Morna. But you told me once that fire worship still rages in Ulster; perhaps among your tribesmen you'll find those who believe in you, and then the old ways might return to this land—"

"I'll not be after teaching the dull and closed-minded."

"Och, there ye go, using me own words against me."

"That battle is lost, Brigid. Even if it weren't, it is not mine to fight."

"No? Then whose is it? No one else could fight it as well as you, Conaire of Ulster, Champion of the Uí Néill, King of Morna—"

"These hands," he snapped, "will not touch the hilt of a sword again."

"Then fight with words what you cannot fight with iron."

For a moment he thought about it, about returning to the world and wreaking his vengeance on all who had tormented him, on all who had tormented her, on taking up the sword again and proving himself as invincible as he was—wrestling that high kingship from the hands of the Uí Néill as he'd wanted, and ruling Erin as it should . . . but barely was the thought formed, before he dismissed it. The last burning ember of ambition had been doused with a brother's blood. He was warrior no longer.

That was the heart of it; he knew not who he was anymore.

"My skill was in the sword; and that skill is mine no longer." He slapped open the edges of the seaweed basket and began pulling the harvest out for drying. "You'll not be rid of me, woman. Did you think that I could leave you here on this barren place, alone without the means to survive? It's better you suffer my presence and live, than be without it and die."

"When you win your war with the priests, you can send for me, and there will be no more want for either of us."

He straightened with a growl. Anger welled up inside of him, obscuring the guilt, obscuring the grief. He had lost everything: name, honor, kingship, a son. He would not give her up—he would keep this part of his past.

He tossed the seaweed to the ground and strode to her, dragging her up against his chest. "Nay, lass, you'll not be rid of me so soon."

"I'm thinking of you." Her brows knitted and her gaze darted away. "I'm thinking of your future—"

"When you married me in that glade on Lughnasa, there was

no separating flesh and spirit. You may want a mortal man, but it's me you'll be having."

She jerked in his embrace. "Stop it."

"It's the loss o' the babe that makes you mad." He gripped her more tightly. "I can't bring him back to life, woman, but there could be more, if you willed it—"

"There will be *no* more children from my womb."

The words rang between them. Brigid arched away from him on an anguished cry. It was the Sight speaking, he knew it as well as she.

And it was if some great rift broke open in his heart, and left a ragged, yawning hollow.

"Leave me in peace, Conaire."

A trail of tears gleamed on her cheeks. He cursed himself to the wind, but did not release her. He knew naught of tearful women. He knew naught of comfort, of sympathy, of such things that she might need. By the *Dagdá*. He knew how to lure a woman to his bed, how to please her body, even how to tempt her into marriage—but he knew nothing of a woman's sorrow. Or even of a man's. The frustration added fuel to his fury.

So he pressed her body harder against his, and stared down into her luminous eyes. "What do I want of children? Do you think I would bring another like me, another like you, to suffer in this world?"

He bent to kiss her, but she twisted her head away with a tormented, "No!"

"You deny me, wife?"

"Aye, now and evermore!" She pressed her fists against his unmoving chest, then pounded him. "I want you gone—"

"You are *mine*, woman. I'll not let you go."

Tears welled in her swirling eyes, but did not fall. Words came out then, wrenched from her soul. "Do you think I want to spend the years with you, watching myself grow old and withered in your eyes? Do you think I want to live in a world where I see the light of passion fade in your face, where I see you recoil from me as my hair thins and my skin sags upon my bones—"

"Stop it."

"Och, it's so easy to shake your head and deny it now, while my body still stands strong and straight, but I won't be fair of face and full of form forever—Leave me in peace, Conaire!"

"You'll have an eternity of peace," he snarled, clutching her head and forcing it back. "But for this life, woman, I am bound to stay with you, protect you—and give you what pleasure this life affords."

He found her breast amid the swathed cloth of her tunic; his palm ached for the warm, full feel of her. It had been so long, since before the loss of the babe, since they'd laid down together, for so long both of them had been in too much in pain to touch or hold, even in their hollow grief. Now the passion they'd both suppressed surged to the surface, like a banked fire set free, its flames leaping to the sky.

He tore his lips from hers, drank in the sight of her face, softened by passion. "There will be no more silence between us, woman."

He lifted her bodily against him, reveling in the mesh of skin and limbs. Her body shuddered as he kissed the length of her neck, then below the collar of her tunic, then her arms wound their way around his neck, then her body softened, and he tasted tears in her kiss, salt and surrender, sorrow and sighs.

In her surrender, it was as if the horizon ceased its tilting, it was as if his feet once again felt the solid ground after years at sea. Here was the thing he craved to bring his world to rights, before him all the time, and he not knowing it until now, when he'd almost lost her. What a strange world it had become, for him to be finding his moorings in the embrace of a wisp of a woman.

He cradled her head in his hands.

You're mine, mine, Brigid, all precious things in this world, the best is still mine.

Conaire woke with a start to an empty pallet. He squinted through the dying peat fire and scanned the inside of the smoky *clochán*. He was alone. He frowned and shrugged himself into his cloak. It would be just like the lass, to slip away and cook him some bream and pollack for his morning meal—when all he wanted was to sup upon his wife, as he had done so often these past two days.

He slipped through the low opening and out into the blinding morning sun. Seabirds soared and dipped below the cliff, diving down to the shore below to peck upon the refuse washed up on the sand by the ravages of the recent gale. The rocky bones of the island gleamed like onyx, and sea-rain beaded like dew upon the scruffs of grass. The gale had scoured the hilltop of debris and left everything bare and shining.

He waited, legs apart, for Brigid to return from her morning wanderings. Crisp morning air cleared his lungs of peat smoke. Aye, it was a wild, primitive place, this crag of an island amid the sea. A man could spend a lifetime taming it enough to make it give forth life. It was a humble task, but a worthier cause than most—worthier, perhaps, than any he'd given up.

He nudged the cold, crumbling remains of the cooking fire with his toe, then squinted around the bright horizon. She'd left her seaweed basket inside the *clochán,* and her shell basket, as well. The dew frosting the earth concealed all signs of footsteps. She'd gone down to the shore, he told himself, to search amid the refuse for driftwood and other treasures.

The exercise would do her good, after all the time she'd spent writhing beneath him in the darkness of the *clochán,* while the gale raged outside. The fire in that woman. . . . He'd thought it had gone out for him. Conaire leaned back against the wall of the beehive hut, feeling, as if for the first time, the nip of salt-spray upon his face. The surf murmured against the rocky shore, and a hushed silence lay over the land. The deep place within him that had roiled too long with storms lay quiet now, like a gentle tide that ebbed and flowed with the rhythm of the sun and wind.

The things a man really needed in his life were simple. A solid roof over his head. A hot meal. A fine day. The love of a good woman.

The thought set his feet upon the path down the side of the cliff.

The thinnest veil of haze shrouded the bay, burning off swiftly as the sun rose golden in the east. The mountains of Connemara shimmered violet on the horizon. Below, hooded crows dropped shellfish on the shore rocks to break them, fighting off scavengers to feast on the soft insides.

Amid the shrieks and cawing, their arose a sound unlike any other. Conaire paused on a ledge to listen. The hairs on the nape of his neck prickled to attention.

He searched for the source of the high, plaintive, Otherworldly wailing, half-expecting to see the wraith of some fairy emerge from a crevice, but the sky shone broad and bright and no mist played about his ankles. It came again, that heart-twisting keening, and he glanced up into the silver-white of the sky. To the north, a large shadow wheeled, guarding the fissure to one of the caverns.

It was one of Brigid's swans. Its lament surged through its long neck and into the air, a broken cry of anguish.

Conaire's feet scraped against the rocky drumlin as he headed toward the ravine. The cave was a crack in the solid block of rock which made up the isle of Inishmaan. Sea spray twisted up in tendrils from the foam roaring below, and stretched toward a sliver of sky arching between the cliffsides. Craggy ledges, spattered white with guano, served as perches for sea-birds—but strangely, few birds screeched within the echoing walls.

He heard Brigid's sobbing long before he espied her, kneeling upon a jutting ledge some ways into the cavern. She rocked back and forth, sobs racking her thin body. A thin finger of silver light seeped through the cavern's roof and fell upon the snow-white wings of a swan, laying still before her, its neck bent at an awkward angle.

Something strange and new shifted inside his chest. Never once had he seen her cry so openly, not even all those months ago outside of Morna, when the babe was lost. He had admired her strength and thought no more of it, for too many other issues flooded his thoughts. Yet here she sat, keening wildly, her spirit as battered as the broken swan.

He moved to go to her; his foot scraped an uncertain hold, and a scattering of pebbles rumbled down the cliffside. He stilled and flattened against the slick wall. Foolish lass, he thought with a sudden flash of anger, risking her neck clambering around these uncertain rocks. Aye, she'd grown attached to those swans, fixing upon them all the legends of old, but she was wise enough to know the swans couldn't survive for long in such a place; not even in these caverns was any living thing safe from the ravages of the gale. There was no reason to risk her neck seeing to it.

You're like the swan, Conaire. You don't belong here.

The words floated back to him. Nay, it was *Brigid,* not him, who didn't belong on this forsaken island. It was Brigid whose neck could more easily be broken.

He steadied himself and eased his way along the ledge, then stopped as he glimpsed something wrapped in her arms. Gray feathers peeped out between the edges of the swaddled, yellow wool of her cloak. 'Twas a single cygnet, lifeless in her arms.

Brigid's head fell back in lamentation. He felt a wrenching weakness in the back of his throat.

He'd seen a thousand men wounded in warfare, their faces

twisted in agony from the hacking wounds that drained the life from them, of deep sword thrusts to the belly that left a man gagging on his own blood—or worse, lingering on for days until infections ate the life away. He had thought he had known the face of pain. Until now.

He stood with his hands limp, while her sobs echoed in the cavern and rose up to merge with the mournful dirge of the swan's lonely mate. An unfamiliar weakness shivered through his body and left his knees unstable, his throat parched, his eyes smarting as if from the smoke of a peat fire.

Something bubbled in his chest, a wordless cry, a song of lamentation. He opened his mouth to call, but the sea spray thickened and jutted its tentacles toward him, and a sudden gust of bitter salt-wind blew up from below, sending the song hurling deep into his chest.

A bitterness exploded in his mouth. He looked down upon his open hands, and wondered if he were destined to destroy everything and everyone he touched.

He turned and strode out of the cavern, careless of the grit and rock which sifted away at the plodding of his feet. He stumbled out of the darkness and headed away from the gorge, wiping off the hot smear of stinging liquid dripping from his chin.

And he sneered at his own arrogance, to think his lovemaking could wash away a woman's grief, to think a few pretty words and promises could mend a wound to a woman's soul. There was a place within Brigid he'd never again touch, a place she would forever hide from him. Now, on this crag of an island, he'd married her to his own wretched fate. He was bound to protect a woman whose spirit he'd murdered.

She would have been better off if he had left her lonely and aching in the woods of Morna long, long ago.

At least then she'd still have dreams.

Ten

It was a hard life on Inishmaan. Winters flowed into summers, with little change between the two. But no one came to threaten their sanctuary, and slowly Brigid began to settle upon the island.

Their days took on a rhythm. They rose when the sun peeked over the bay. Their senses grew keen to the saltiness of the wind, the roiling tumult of the water, the strange, silver-white light of the sky, and the mercurial shifts in weather. Brigid tended the fire and gathered food, while Conaire fished and snared ducks and made infrequent journeys to the mainland for peat and fruits of the land. Their sweat watered the stubborn earth, the burn of their muscles kept them warm.

For many seasons, Brigid welcomed the endless scraping and labor for survival. While her back was bent in two as she cleared a stretch of barren land, while her hands were busy piling rocks upon one another in a makeshift fence, while steam ruddied her face as she bent over the cooking fire—then she was too busy and her body too weary to think of the unceasing hollow ache that raged from the center of her womb to the center of her heart.

Only when the surviving swan returned, once, in the spring, searching for his mate while he keened mournfully in the sky, did the ache surge like a bubble in her breast, pushing out a new flood of tears. She had hidden these tears from Conaire, though he must have seen the trails upon her face when she returned to the *clochán* later in the day. She knew he thought she cried for the lost babe, and in part she did—but that was not the whole of it.

How could she explain to him the wordless Knowledge flooding through her? How could she tell him the truth which darkened her days and made nightmares of the evenings, how could she explain to him the magnitude of their loss, when she did not fully understand it herself? Out of the storm of her Sight, she understood only this: There was no more hope.

And so she cried for Conaire.

But just as the wind and the sun and the rain scoured soft the sharpest boulders, time began to dull the edge of the ache. As the seasons passed, there were times when she raised her gaze above the labor of her hands and gazed out to the sea. There were times when she set her gaze upon her husband and found him as brooding and quiet as herself.

How he'd changed. Gone was the laughing, loose-limbed, arrogant warrior she'd come to know in Morna. In his place stood a silent, contemplative man; his body pared down to solid muscle by work and lean rations, his eyes filled with tortured shadows.

A niggling doubt worked its way into her mind. Much good it would do to brood about and mourn for a lifetime, when all the keening and wailing would not bring back what they had lost, nor move Fate a hair's width from its path.

"It's time we got ourselves a cow," she said one day, as they hauled baskets of sand to the height for making land. "You were after promising one, not so long ago."

"Is it a cow you want now?" Conaire heaved the sagging basket of sand over his shoulder and let it thump to the ground. "And we barely keeping body and soul together—"

"We'd have an easier time of it," she argued, "if we had milk and a calf once a year."

"Then it's a bull you'll be wantin', too?"

"What good is one without the other, will ye be telling me that?"

She got her cow, and sometime later, a bull, both bought from the priests who inhabited the next island, in exchange for several boatloads of peat Conaire promised to send them from the mainland. The cow's lowing filled the mornings, as in the old days. She wondered why she hadn't insisted upon the cattle sooner, and she wondered, too, how much else she and Conaire were missing by wasting precious time in silence and painful memory.

"Here," she'd said another day, thrusting a cup of frothy milk in his hand as he returned from delivering another load of peat. "You'll not be tellin' me *that* isn't worth the price of a few boatloads of peat."

He drank the full cup, trails of milk rippling down his chin. Brigid watched the working of his throat, and a familiar yearning arced through her.

"I've boiled you water," she'd said, turning away. "Come, come, strip yourself down. I'll not have you eatin' at me table with such grime upon ye."

While she bathed him within the smoky warmth of the *clochán,* his gaze rested upon her, curious and distant. She'd washed her hair that afternoon, in a pail of rainwater she'd collected overnight, then let it dry with the wind and the sun. It lay loose about her shoulders, the way he'd once liked it. Sunlight streamed through the smoke-hole, and fell warm upon her head.

Then, yet another day, she'd said, "I'm thinkin' we'll be needing some sheep, Conaire."

"Sheep?" He'd clawed another scoop of clay out of the rocks and shook it off his fingers into a basket by his feet. "What will be next, woman? A loom?"

"Aye, but a spindle first." She tilted her head and caught his outraged glare, as she scraped some clay off her own fingers. "Is it the hard work you're complainin' about? Or do you want me to be prancing about for the rest of me life with nothing on but a bit of rag?"

Her skin had grown warm beneath the torn linen of her filthy *léine,* as his gaze burned over her. He'd slapped his hand against the edge of the woven basket and turned back to his work. "You could have waited to ask, woman, 'til I've got the peat out from under my skin."

Finally, on a summer's evening, they sat outside the *clochán* and feasted on a smoky fish chowder she'd made fresh that day. When they were finished, they lolled, warm-bellied, with their backs against the *clochán,* watching the red shimmer of sun sink into the sea.

She dipped a finger into a hole at the knee of her *léine.* "I've been thinking a mite, Conaire."

A ghost of a laugh rippled in his voice. "I've noticed you've been doing a lot o' that lately."

She tugged upon the linen, twisting it around her fingertip. "I'm thinking we can do better than this bowl o' smoke we've been sleeping in."

"Now you've no liking for the *clochán?* "

"It's fine enough, for a dog or a cow. I can't even stand up in the thing, and I'm sick of waking with a night's worth of peat-fire smoke on me face."

"You'd best speak your mind, woman." He shifted his legs. "My bones are already feeling the wear of a good year's work."

She stood up and faced the highest point of the island, a bare sheaf of rock which sloped away on all sides to scrub grass and stone. "That would be a fine place," she murmured, tossing the hair off her shoulder, "to build a home."

She sensed his warmth behind her.

"It would take a mighty fort to keep a house atop that drum-lin," he warned. "A fort made o' stone, and with a strong rocky fence about it to break the battering of wind and gale."

"We could wall off the ground on the lee side of the house," she continued, watching in her mind's eye the rise of the home upon the rosy height, "and fill it with sand and clay and seaweed to make land, and then I'd have a garden."

His hands fell upon her shoulders. "A task like that could take a lifetime, woman."

She closed her eyes to bite back the sting of tears. She thought of the cool silence of the Morna woods, of the way the leaves turned from the translucent green of spring to the coarse thickness of summer to the crackling dry brown of fall; she thought of honeysuckle and foxglove, of a ring of oaks amid the mists . . . of the past.

Then she opened her eyes and stared out over the sea, with the sun bleeding pink and orange and red into the waves, and then to the bare, smooth hillock of Inishmaan. And she felt the heat of her husband, solid and strong behind her—the future.

"What better way to spend a lifetime?" She filled her lungs with sea spray. "It will be our kingdom here. We'll call it—*Dún Conaire.*"

He breathed her name into her ear as his arms banded around her. She twisted in his embrace and faced him, pressing close to his warmth. The sap of life rose in her, hot and eager, filling up the hollowness still lurking in her heart. Och, aye, she thought, as his lips found her temple, her cheek, her neck, *this* wonder is life, and she had been a fool to deny it to herself and to Conaire for so long. All they had left in this world, was this one single moment in time.

"We'll start tomorrow," she whispered, as his lips finally met hers hungrily, again, and yet again. "We've so little time . . . ."

Winters flowed into summers, and their dream took root in the bare rock. Stone by stone, their fort rose, in defiance of the wind and weather. First came a solid house, thatched-roofed, with a floor paved with smooth, flat stones. A rocky, tumbled-down fence wandered around a burgeoning garden. This done, another wall rose, higher, in a great, sweeping ring around the house and garden.

Their days took on a rhythm again—of work and work and still more work, but this time, when the sun began to set, the greatest joy came. For Brigid would see Conaire walking toward her through the open door, his hair lit red by the dying rays of the sun. He'd raise his head and smile beyond his weariness, and he'd clutch her to him, and she'd feel the solid strength of his arms, his body—lean and muscular from hewing and heaving stone over long distances, from wielding a skillful oar on the angry swell of the sea. She would feel the heat of his breath; she would see the light of hungry desire in his eyes; she'd feel the yawning need inside him for something more than their body's joining. And like a reed bending to the force of a gale, she opened herself to him in the dim blue light of dusk, and they became one again—the joyous joining that never lost its glory between them.

The years slipped by unnoticed, for ever there was work to do, grain to sow or harvest, cows to milk, calves to slaughter for winter's meat, snares to lay, periwinkles to collect as she danced carefully among the rocks in the surf . . . But there came a time when the fort was finished, the field rich and fertile, the cows for which they had bartered with the monks healthy and full of milk, and the struggle to survive grew kinder.

Then, they took their well-earned ease. Laughter echoed among the stones of the island, swirling through the mists. They made a crude *fidchell* board from seashells and driftwood, and played in the evenings close to the fire. They found another cavern in the rocks where they could make love under the great, blue white arch of the sky, protected from the wind.

Much time had passed since that fateful Samhain Day. Conaire grew bold and took to intercepting the trading vessels from far-off lands who sailed into the bay, and for the price of fresh fish and water, he would bring back all sorts of exotics. On those days, he would drape her naked form in fine cloth, share some foreign wine, and then dance with her to the music of the wind whistling through the stones.

They were not always alone. During one of Brigid's wanderings on the west side of the island, she saw fairy-foot marks on the cliffs, and she knew then that the *Sidh* had not abandoned them. Occasionally, a certain priest rowed over from the north island, and he would stay a day or two to barter and play *fidchell*. On those days, Brigid would serve the men and keep her eyes lowered; and the priest would compliment Conaire on her modesty. Later, she and Conaire would laugh about it, for the priest was old and wise to the ways of men, and he had seen the Beltaine fires lit upon the height of the island each year, and knew they were pagans, yet he continued to come to the island once or twice a year. He and Conaire would argue gently in the quiet of their home about Christianity and the old religion. Though at first the priest had made Brigid uneasy, she could see the humor and honesty in the man's face; he had seemed to make it his task to convert them, though he tried it with a gentle hand. 'Twas a lonely existence on these isles, and company of any sort was a pleasant diversion; for Conaire's sake, she welcomed this man whose black robes she had once so despised.

The years grew shorter and sped by. The endless battering of the elements smoothed and rounded the stones of their house. Inside, the turf smoke of innumerable fires darkened the walls to a gentle brown. A sprig of ivy which had nestled at the base of the garden wall sprouted, wound its way over the jagged edge, and branched out, until the tiny root blossomed into a great netting of waxy leaves, softening the rock-pile wall like a coating of deep green moss.

The years did not touch Conaire; his body was as unchanged as the great cliffs of Moher Brigid could see on a clear day from the open doorway of the house. He blinded her sometimes, when he appeared in the doorway unexpectedly. His eyes, silver-bright; his hair thick and luxurious and long; his skin as fresh and unlined as when she had first laid eyes upon him in the sacred circle of oaks in Morna. Vitality sparked from his very fingertips, as he picked her up by the waist and whirled her breathless. He was sea and river, earth and sun—ever steady, ever ageless, ever eternal.

But she was fading, growing brittle and dry, like all things of this world. There were days, while she stirred porridge or cut the barley, or when Conaire reached out to help her over some rocks, when she would see her own hands with new eyes. The skin had shriveled and dried upon the bones, so the blue trails of her veins stood out stark against the thin and spotted skin. It was always a shock to see them, fragile and old, in Conaire's broad palm. For though she felt the passing of time in her bones, in her heart and mind and spirit, she, like Conaire, was as young as if she were still dancing among the trees with the *Sídh*.

There came a time when her feet could no longer dance. The familiar path down the side of the cliff became an enemy—a labor which stole her breath and left her joints aching. More and more, Conaire took to gathering food and seaweed along the shore, until Brigid's circle of work spread no farther than the grazing grounds of the cattle, and then, no farther than the crumbling rock fence of their ring-fort.

Then, one year like any other, when the spring gales had washed the world clean, she knew her time had come. The sickness had been eating away at her all winter, and no paste or potion eased her fatigue or stopped the flesh from melting off her bones. Old age only had one cure, and it was final.

Och, but she wanted to live forever on this island, with Conaire by her side, with his smile, his touch, his lovemaking which had grown so tender and so gentle these past years. There were times when she wished she could trade the rest of her days to be, for one single moment, fair-haired and strong-limbed in his arms.

So it was one summer morning when the glimmer of dawn shone through the cracks around the door, when she lay awake among the wolf pelts in their woven-wattle bed, knowing she'd never find the strength to rise from the softness and the warmth again. She heard a song outside the walls; it was Conaire's light, lilting whistle, as he gathered logs of peat to stoke the morning fire. His footsteps approached.

Sunlight bathed the room. " 'Tis a fine, fair day, Brigid." He tumbled an enormous armful of peat against one wall. "The wind's nary a warm breath, and the sea is calm and flat as a silver mirror."

He had once given her a silver mirror, a gift from one of the trading vessels that had passed through the bay. She had never seen the like, and for many years she had used it as she plaited and wound her hair; but the mirror was a cruel reminder of the passage of her days, and now it lay, tarnished, amid a trunk full of other gifts better fit for a younger woman.

Conaire tossed a cut of peat under the hanging cauldron, and poked at it until the flames leapt. She loved him with her fading eyes, all of him, the bright flash of his smile, the swell of his muscles beneath his tunic and the leather that covered his calves. It was ever a mystery to her why he stayed upon this mist-shrouded island, tending to an old crone, when the world spread out before him, begging for the tread of his feet.

How foolish she had been, all those years ago, to try to send Conaire away. Vanity—it was nothing more. How little faith she had had in the strength of his love.

By the gods. She squeezed her eyes shut. She did not want to leave. Not today. Not ever. She wanted to rise from the bed with the grace of a young woman—fair and blond and full of curves, as ever she had wished to be—with her body supple and free of pain, with the strength to take her lover into her open arms.

That was not to be. For the time had come, the time she had dreaded all her life. Not her own death, nay, for that was the way of mortals. . . . She knew there were worse things than dying. One of them was being left behind.

If only . . .

"Is the rain in your bones, *mo shearc?*"

Conaire brushed her white hair out of her face as she blinked her eyes open. Concern shadowed his gray eyes. She had often wondered these past months if he knew that she was dying, or if he pretended not to know for her sake, just as she pretended health for him.

"It's naught but a faint weakness. It will pass with but a little rest."

"You'd think you were a woman of twenty summers, the way you do be tending the fields and climbing down the cliffs."

"Och, would you have me tethered to a bed, Conaire?"

" 'Tis a fine thought, that."

It was a gentle teasing between them, a familiar refrain, for she'd not left the house for many a month. But today she could barely muster a weak smile. He took her wrist in his hand and probed among the bones for her pulse, as she'd taught him. Harnessing what little strength she had, she tugged her arm free.

"Do you remember," she began, tucking her wrist beneath the pelts, "those herbs I steeped for that kind priest, when he was sick with the ague?"

"Aye, I remember everything you taught me o' your witchery."

She attempted a smile, and wished that she had the strength to touch the softness of his hair. "Then boil me some. Perhaps that brew will restore my strength."

The bubbling of water and the scent of boiling herbs soon filled the room. He brought her a wedge of cheese and a cup full of frothy milk. She left the food upon the floor and began to doze.

But when she closed her eyes, she felt a different languor stealing over her; a heavier sleep. She struggled against the fog, fighting to open her eyes, to focus on Conaire's concerned face hovering above her. Brigid sensed of a sudden that they were not alone in the room. The death-crone in her rags hovered in the shadows around the bed.

"Sleep, lass." Conaire's voice seemed to come from very far away. "It's what you need—"

"Nay, nay." She tried to swallow, but her throat was dry and aching. "Is it still light out?"

"It's near midday."

"Take me out, then, to the garden."

He ran a hand over her forehead. "It's best if you rest here—"

"It's the sun I want to feel now, and the sea spray, and I want to see the light of day on your face." She rested her hand upon his arm, so strong and young. "I'll have rest enough before this night is through."

A tremor ran through his body. She had not wanted it to be like this; she had wanted to fall asleep one night by his side, and slip away while his body curled warmly around hers. But a woman could not choose her death, and there was little time left to her, and so much to say, if only she had the strength . . .

Outside, the sun blinded her. She buried her face in his chest. He carried her past the gardens and out the opening in the rock-pile fence. He sat with the wall at his back, settling her on his lap, her head nestled against the nook of his shoulder.

In the shade, she blinked open her eyes and gazed about the bright summer day. Primroses climbed up the rock fence, waving their delicate blooms with the caress of the salty breeze. From somewhere beyond her sight, cows lowed as they feasted on green and stubborn grass. The Connemara mountains shone purple in the distance. The great bay of Galway spread out before them, calm and deep blue, and the rhythmic wash of the tide against the lower cliffs filled the air.

Och, why would it be summer when her end came, such a young time, a reminder of all the summers long past? The cawing of seabirds echoed around them, as the gulls dove in and out of the breakers in search of food. In all her years upon this island, nothing, really, had changed; she and Conaire had eked out a life upon it and made a home, yet it was as wild and untamed and lonely as when they had first stepped foot on the shores.

Her lids weighed upon her eyes; so much she wanted to close them. She glanced up at him and saw that his jaw was tight, the cordons in his throat roped and hard, and that his gaze was fixed on some point far beyond the horizon, to the rim of the world, to a future she could not share.

Her lids drooped. His arms tightened around her. The words rumbled, ripped from his heart.

"Don't go."

Tears surged in her eyes, tears she had not the strength to shed. She would not shed them. She would not leave as her final memory a moment full of sorrow.

The days past began to unfurl in her mind, tumbling one upon the other, like pebbles rolling down a hill. She turned her face towards the sea. "Do you remember," she asked, softly, "the day you brought back that great length of blue linen for me, from the mainland? You worked so hard bringing it up to the fort, with it draped over your shoulder . . . and when you reached the top, the wind tugged it off you and unfurled it like a great sail, and sent it fluttering over the cliff . . ."

He did not smile. His gray gaze probed her face, as palpable as if he traced her brows, her eyes, her nose, her lips, with his fingertips, willing her to stay with him, as once he had done with the fury of his kiss.

She clutched the large metal clasp on her cloak, then traced the amber jewels, the swirling goldsmith's work of the circular brooch she had ever worn near her heart—Conaire's first gift to her. More memories.

"Och, Conaire . . . no woman has ever been so well loved as I."

Something flashed in his eyes. Fear. A moving thing, fear in a warrior's eyes.

"There will be no other, Brigid."

She tried to shake her head, but languor stole over her, draining the last of her strength. It was useless to argue when he had such a voice upon him. He'd learned patience in the unrolling of time, but in this angry rumble was a shadow of the warrior-king, of the man who'd taken what he wanted and never known what it was to be thwarted.

Then, all of a sudden, something else stole over her. She did not know if it were the last gasp of the Sight, or some quivering sprig of hope born of her dying senses, but for a swift, lingering moment, it seemed as if she were young again, as if the wind blew back her long mane of thick hair, as if her heart beat hard and fast in her chest as she filled her lungs with fresh sea air, and she felt Conaire near to her, and happy.

She opened her eyes and the feeling stayed with her, like a great uplifting of the spirit. In the midst of the glory, a voice came to her, and she knew not whether it was memory, or some music from beyond the thinning veils of the worlds. It was her mother's voice—och, that sweet long-forgotten lilt—and the words wafted to her, murmurings of the ways of this world and the other, lessons on the wanderings of souls, how dying was but a transition to another body, another life . . . for though our bodies were mortal, our souls were immortal.

Her heart beat faster. Blood rushed to her face. Och, how she'd forgotten the ways of the Druids with the passing of the years. The words rose to her throat—she'd tell Conaire, surely they'd be together again, surely he'd find her again—but then she hesitated, unwilling to burden him with hope.

Then it was too late, for the blindness descended upon her.

She heard Conaire's swift and angry protest. The salt-sea smell of his cloak filled her head. She heard the sharp cry of a raven, and she knew her time had come.

She spoke, once, Conaire's name.

Above, against the blinding sky, a cormorant soared, its black wings spread. Wheeling, rising . . . wheeling, rising . . .

Eleven

Her passing would be honored like that of a king.

Conaire threw upon the pyre everything within *Dún Conaire:* Spindles, baskets, the bolt of fine blue linen, the bed they'd shared and all its coverings, pails and baskets, and even the loom he'd carved from wood boated over from the mainland. When that was done, he yanked the thatching off the roof with his bare hands, until blood stained the hay. That, too, joined the pyre.

He carried up the cliff the *curragh* he'd built for her, and settled it upon the mound. He climbed up the pyre with her cradled in his arms, and placed her slight form within it. He covered her with a woolen cloak and tucked it tight around the edges.

Gazing upon her face, he thought: May the Christians be right. Let there be peace in death, which we have not in this life.

When the sun set, he touched his lips to hers. Then he climbed down the wreckage of his life, and set the pyre afire.

The flames hesitated, then caught, then caught some more, and then blazed with a violent leap to the sky, shooting sparks at the stars. His throat tightened, for the keening came next, the lamentation, the singing of great deeds, but his ears rang with an inner screeching that could not penetrate the dry walls of his throat. Her greatest deed was staying with the man whose folly had caused her so much anguish; her bravest deed was in surviving so long pretending a joy which could never have touched her broken heart. He watched the flames devour the pyre, basking in the last heat he'd ever feel from his wife.

In the orange glow, he worked his way down the side of the cliff to where his *curragh* waited in the lee of a boulder. The blaze of the fire filled the night, and the crackling drowned out the sound of the sea and wind. Let the priests on the north island think it a pagan rite, he thought. It would make Brigid laugh, to think she'd confounded them to the end.

Conaire stood with one foot in the *curragh,* and the other on the sands of Inishmaan, his head tilted to the pyre, with the heat of tears running down his throat.

Forgive me, my heart.

There would never be another like her, another who would know who and what he was, and understand. There would never be another heart so open, so brave, so full.

Within him, something cracked.

Good night, my love. My life.

Good night.

Part Two

France, 1249 A.D.

Twelve

It was time for the Fair of St. Jean.

Dust clouds billowed up from the roads that riddled the rolling domain of the Count of Champagne. Merchant caravans from all over Europe—and even from the distant East—plodded through the dense forests with armies of archers and pikesmen guarding their flanks. Couriers on swift horses beat tracks into the earth, galloping past castles and monasteries and tilled fields, past carts mired in muddy pools, stopping only to pay tolls on privately held roads and river crossings, before racing on to one common destination.

Every morning the enormous gates of the city of Troyes yawned open, welcoming the weary travelers and all the riches of the world within the safety of the limestone walls.

Conaire plodded silently amid the lumbering caravans. A haze of dust salted his hair and settled deep into the creases of his face. The merchants welcomed him among the donkeys and the carts and the well-mounted men of their guard. It was rumored that this skilled doctor had followed the caravans from as far as the Holy Land, healing broken bones and foot sores and the aches and pains of travelers, making a living of a sort as he followed the annual summer migration toward Troyes. Though he spoke little, ate even less, and asked for no more than safe passage among them, behind their silk-covered carts the merchants whispered among themselves and wondered what a man of medicine with the bearing of a king and the silence of a monk was doing walking the dangerous roads of France, when the weight of his pouch and the fine cloth of his surcoat marked him a man of means.

Their curiosity went unanswered, for whenever they edged a conversation toward his past, he would gaze at them with eyes as flat and emotionless as worn silver coins.

He was a mystery to them, a mystery to men who had voyaged from the sheep-dotted shores of Britain to the glittering Eastern palaces of infidels. Nothing seemed to affect him, not the frigid cold of the Alpine passes, not the sharp pebbles that penetrated the soles of his boots and left him, at one time, smearing bloody footprints along the dusty earth. He refused all offers of donkeys or horses, accepting only gold or silver in payment for his services, continuing to walk like a pilgrim or a beggar. As the merchants neared Troyes, they celebrated and sang and danced, relieved that brigands had not stolen their shimmering silks, their precious pepper and spices, their wagonloads of rich wool cloth; had not struck them through with crude knives and left them bleeding on a road so far from their homes and families—yet their mysterious companion continued to plod along, oblivious to the revelry around him, straight-backed and mute; his feet in this world, his mind lost in another.

Conaire knew what they were thinking. He felt their sharp, curious gazes, but they affected him no more than the buzzing of flies in the hot July sun. Seven hundred years of wandering had a way of dulling a man's senses.

Yet one singular impression had broken through his thoughtless trudging in the past hours of the journey: The sticky sweet fragrance of ripening grapes had ceded to the gritty stench of smoke, the pungent aroma of tanneries, and the acrid odor of human sweat and urine—the signposts of a large city. The greasy scent of wet wool informed him more than any of the merchants' chatter that Troyes lay ahead, Troyes in the height of summer after a rain.

Like a lazy summer bee who'd wandered too far afield, Conaire set his sights upon his next resting place.

He jostled his way through the throng funnelling through the double-leafed iron gate. For the first time in a dozen leagues, he lifted his head from his dirty boots to glance at the city he'd not seen in several centuries. Timber post-and-beam houses still stood cheek by jowl, sagging against each other like tired old dogs. Stalls bowed in front of each house, laden with boots, belts, spoons, pots, and paternosters, surrounded by snapping burghers and garrulous housewives in blinding white wimples. Stray dogs rasped against the pulled wool of his hose, as they snarled and chased each other through the swarm.

Aye, this place will do.

Seeing the merchants distracted, Conaire silently slipped down a shadowed street and melted into the crowd. He'd traveled with those burghers for too long. Something in the country air and the closeness of a shared fire bred a poisonous curiosity; they'd begun to ask too many probing questions, wondering too much about a past he never divulged. There had been too great a stretch between cities.

For in a bold, brash city such as Troyes, glittering with burghers' wealth, stinking of cheese, and stuffed to the rim with transients from all over the world, fighting and screaming and raging in the twisted alleyways—in such a raucous town, a man could live and die—and live again—and no one would know the better of it.

Moreover, no one would care.

Conaire lurched forward as someone barreled into his legs and nearly knocked his knees out from under him. Swift fingers skidded around his waist and tugged on the sacks slung around his hips. Conaire seized a handful of scratchy wool just as the pickpocket wrenched to get away. He heaved the culprit to face him—only to be blasted with breath that stank of rotten fish.

He thrust the creature away. The thief careened into a reeking wet ass who brayed and spat and narrowly missed kicking him senseless. Conaire snorted the stench from his nostrils and stared at the dwarf of a man splayed in the muck. The creature's eyes were small and bright with fury; his cheeks netted with ruddy veins, his beard slick with grease and speckled with a week's worth of crumbs. He wore an ancient, food-bespattered tunic with a kirtle below, and foresleeves cut from a friar's habit.

Conaire scooped up the man's abandoned knife. "You'd do better knockin' a man out with your stench," he sneered as he planted a booted foot on the thief's belly, "than knockin' him down with your body."

"Jesus, Joseph, and Jezebel!" The pickpocket's eyes widened on the knife in Conaire's hand. " 'Tis nothin' but a cur, ye are, to strike at a man in the dirt like a dog."

Conaire's gut wrenched, like the shock of first food after a five-day fast. He'd abandoned the land now called Ireland six hundred years ago. Yet, there was no mistaking the distinctive brogue which garbled this man's French. The rolling lilt of the ancient tongue vibrated through Conaire's head and echoed down through the centuries, rifling memories as a gale would scour the smooth surface of a lake—and sending ripples through waters best left oily and untouched.

"And what are ye doin', beatin' on a poor ol' man like me?" The thief eyed the gathering crowd. "Fie on ye, stranger. Have ye no Christian charity? 'Twas walkin' about, mindin' me own affairs, I was, when ye yanked me around." He surged up, against Conaire's boot. " 'Tis innocent, I am, or may the Good Lord drown me where I lay—"

"Innocent as Lucifer." Conaire jerked his chin toward the leather sack lying clutched in the pickpocket's hands, the same bag the thief had sliced from his waist. He nudged the sack with his foot and a sandglass tumbled out. "You're as bad at thieving as you are at lying—save for it's a doctor you're wanting to be."

"God's Nails!" The Irishman jerked to a sitting position and shamelessly looted through his stolen booty. "Devil a hap'worth is there in this at all but junk—"

"A pity." Conaire tucked the knife in his belt and clanked the alms bag hung from it. "For if 'twas the other you'd taken, what a thundering spree you'd have had this night in Troyes."

The thief squinted up at him, a twinkle of speculation lighting his eye. "Is that a wee bit o' Irish I'm hearing coming out o' your mouth?"

With an angry swipe, Conaire seized his bag. He'd learned the French dialect several centuries ago, but languages changed swiftly over the years, and he had not been here long enough to pick up this new dialect without the hint of his original accent. Swift and perceptive was this dwarf of a man, and it irked Conaire that this common pickpocket had rattled him enough to sniff out such a personal detail so quickly.

"Saints preserve me! It's Irish ye are." The thief revealed a cavern of a mouth gated with blackened teeth. "If I'd be knowin' *that,* sirrah, I'd not've marked ye, not at all, I wouldn't. 'Tis a rare thing to be meetin' an Irishman so far from the blessed Motherland. Meself, I'm a Galway man."

"Save your jabbering." Conaire knotted his bag around his waist, mentally stanching the disturbing echoes of the thief's brogue. "All the Irish in you won't be saving you from an afternoon on the pillory."

"The pillory?" The thief planted his dirty fists on his hips. "Begob, we're brothers, we are."

"I have no brother," he snarled. *Or kin, or countrymen, not in this world.* He curled his hand into the scruff of the thief's tunic and hauled him away from the circle of amused spectators. "And I've no liking for thieves."

"By the rood, 'twas naught but a slip o' me fingers—aye, aye," the thief growled, catching the glare of Conaire's eye, "I see I won't be after foolin' ye, but ye've not lost a Provins penny, ye haven't. You'll be gettin' over it, and I'll be stinkin' o' mush and shyte 'til All Soul's Day, if ye be puttin' me on the pillory."

"It will be an improvement, I'm thinking."

"Go on with ye, ye blatherin' whoreson." The Irishman sputtered in Conaire's wake, propelled by the choking fit of his tunic. "I'll have ye know that I'm worth more than my weight in gold to the man who knows how to appreciate me, I am."

Conaire cast about for a stony church spire. In front of a church he'd find a pillory, and thus be rid of the strange needling of this creature's brogue.

The thief followed his gaze. "You're new in Troyes, aren't ye?"

"I've been here before, I have." *In the reign of Hugh Capet.*

"Then you'll be knowing that the pillory's far on yonder side o' the city."

Conaire shook the creature like a mangy, stray dog. "Do you take me for a fool?"

" 'Tis no lie in it. I know this city like I know the scars on me own hands. I know which taverns water their wine and which whores are free o' the pox, and how to rid a straw mattress of bedbugs. Is it a doctor ye said ye are?" He eyed the fine blue wool of Conaire's surcoat, the scarlet embroidery on the neck and hem, then the dusty, beaten leather of his boots. "Your boots could do with some mending, I'll be thinking. Now I know a cobbler who'll fix them without asking for more than a Provins penny."

Conaire dropped his gaze to the vermin crawling amid the moldy straw twisted around the thief's legs. "If this cobbler's so good, then you'd best be getting some boots of your own."

"I've been a-working on it, you know."

"Aye, so I noticed."

"And what would ye be noticing, but a man tryin' to find a bit to eat among a city o' plenty?" The thief toed a pebble out between the cobblestones. "I'd take a bit o' honest work, if there was any about."

Conaire felt it then; the slightest of tugs, a thin thread of connection seeping up from the Earth to twist gently around his legs. He'd long learned to recognize the seemingly harmless, little pull, for he knew if he allowed it, even for a moment, the thread would thicken and grow as scaly as a serpent—and then shackle him to the creatures of this world with their short, rude, fragile existences and their endless, wracking pain.

He knew better than to ever let that happen again.

Conaire thrust the man away and dug a coin out of his sack. "Take this and be off with you, then."

The thief gaped at the sight of the gold gleaming in the sun. "You'll not be puttin' me on the pillory?"

Conaire shook his head in impatience and jerked his palm at him.

The thief's black eyes glittered on the gold, but he made no attempt to snatch the coin away. His face grew ruddy, his eyes blacker, and he sucked in his lower lip until it looked as if he had swallowed half his bristled chin.

Finally, he shook his head with a jerk. "Nay, nay, ye can't rid yourself o' me so easily, sirrah. I'm no beggar, I'll have ye know. Octavius here can earn his own keep."

Conaire snapped his fingers over the coin, a grumble of anger gathering in his chest at being the mark of the only Irish thief in all of France with a sense of honor. "Be off with you, then. You've no skills that'd serve the likes o' me—"

"Indeed, sirrah, I have." The Irishman snapped his heels together with a muffled thud. "Being Irishmen both, I think it's me duty to see ye settled right. You need someone to walk about the fair and gather your meals, for a good price, ye see, and not let some blaggard steal your coins from ye. You need someone to guide poor, sick souls to your side. Do ye know how many travelers arrive with festering foot sores and skin burnt scaly from the sun, how many Crusaders return from the Holy Lands with exotic ailments and—"

"Enough."

Conaire stifled the urge to slam his palms over his ears to rid his head of the Irish lilt. The creature's wretched accent needled him like long-forgotten fairy music—that was a torment he did not need to hear. It was sleep he needed—the long, innocent sleep of the weary, the dreamless sleep of the innocent—aye, he thought with an inward sneer, wasn't that a fine dream he'd never know. Mayhap he'd settle for just a bed and a moment's uninterrupted rest, for his lids hung as heavy as lead. He scoured the Irishman's face anew. "You wish to be o' service to me?"

"Aye."

"Then lead me to an inn."

"Ye've no place to stay?" His beard crumpled against his chest. "Where did ye think you were coming to? Every room in the city's been taken since Candlemas. A devil a one if there'll be a single empty stable in the whole city—and the innkeepers are charging a king's ransom, they are, just to sleep in the shadow of their doors."

Conaire clinked the coin back into his leather bag and turned on his heel. It had been his experience that almost anything could be found anywhere at anytime, as long as a man was willing to pay the price.

"Now don't be walkin' off, sirrah, I didn't say I couldn't—"

Conaire ignored the sputtering thief cursing his way after him. Sooner or later, the Irishman would find other quarry, and Conaire'd be rid of him. Fortunately, the street roiled with the screaming of a churning mob. Conaire thrust himself into the swarm, away from the thief's cries. An elderly woman jostled at the crowd's head, her hair shorn off, her thin body draped in rough-woven, mud-splattered tunic. A white-robed priest tugged on her tether and sent her stumbling to the ground. Conaire's lips tightened.

Another witch to burn.

He shouldered his way through the mob, thrusting the jeerers aside with more force than necessary. None dared challenge him; aye, his height and size and he supposed the glower on his face sent each man scurrying back into the crowd to taunt instead the old, bound, weak woman stumbling at its head. Cowards always jeered the loudest at another man's burning.

Conaire glanced down a side street and scrutinized the large signs that hung from the storefronts. On the corner he found what he wanted: a hostel with a bright red sign, painted with the silhouette of an enormous, canopied bed.

Octavius belched out of the crowd and stumbled against Conaire's heels. The thief regained his balance and stared at the inn incredulously. "Is it here you're thinking of asking?"

"Aye." Conaire planted a flat hand on the thief's chest. "I'll do better, if I don't have a thief stinking o' fish trailing me in."

Octavius crossed his arms and leaned his shoulder against the doorframe. "I'll just be waitin' here—for the laughter that'll trail ye out."

The innkeeper did laugh, at first. Conaire swiftly cut off his merriment by clanking his purse on the table between them. The familiar gleam of greed lit the innkeeper's eyes. Stammering, he bustled into the back room and returned with a bulky ship of a woman whose face bore the stamp of the Vikings who'd once scoured these lands. Her watery red gaze took in Conaire's gold, clothes, and face with lazy avidity.

Then the bargaining began, like an old dance. People never changed. Faces were nothing more than masks, and the whole of a person's character could be read with one glance into the eyes. Conaire knew, staring into the flat, dun-colored orbs of the innkeeper's wife, that she was already calculating heady profits. But though she couched her offers in vague language, Conaire soon knew that this inn had no bed to offer, and the best he could get from them would be a straw pallet before the kitchen hearth, already crowded with a half-dozen other travelers, and at a price that would curl even a moneylender's hair. Gathering his alms bag, he left the inn to search for another, while Octavius clung like dung to his heels.

After Conaire stormed out of the fourth inn in a row, Octavius swiveled into his path and wagged at him the greasy head of a chicken bone. "Are ye ready to listen to me now, or are ye after asking every innkeeper in Troyes?"

Conaire seized the carcass and sent it flying into the gutter.

"God's Nails," Octavius sputtered, "there was no need to be doin' that—"

"If you've something to tell me, you'd best say it, or next it'll be your bones I throw into the street."

"I've been thinking, I have," Octavius began, hungrily eying the discarded bone, "and I know of a burgher, a man as rich as Midas, with a ring for every finger and enough gold about his neck to put a king to shame. He's in need of a doctor." The little man edged closer. "He's got a young daughter, an odd one, they say, fresh out o' the convent. She's sick near to death, and her father distraught, for he just lost a son, he did, and he's full o' fear o' losing the daughter as well."

Conaire rested an impatient gaze upon the thief, conveying wordlessly how little some burgher's daughter's fate meant to him, when his bones quivered from weariness and his mind wrestled with demons; when in his endless life, he'd witnessed misery beyond any human's imagining.

"Don't ye see, man? The burgher has used every doctor in Troyes and none have been to his liking. You bein' a doctor and all, you could make a fine fee—"

" 'Tis no fee I seek," Conaire snapped, "and I've no stomach to be pandering to some overfed burgher's daughter with a bel-lyache."

"Aye, but this burgher's daughter lives in a five-story house on the Grande Rue." Octavius leaned back against a wall, crossed his arms, and toed one foot across the other. "There's a soft bed in that palace, I'll be thinking, for the doctor who cares well for the lass."

Conaire's eyes narrowed. "How would the likes o' you be knowin' o' the plight of a burgher's daughter?"

"I've ears, I do, and since the strange lass returned here from the convent, she's stirred up more than a mite o' gossip." With an odd, almost triumphant cackle, Octavius jerked away from the wall and danced a jig down the street. "Will ye be comin' then? Or will ye pass on a golden apple dropped in your lap from the skies above?"

Conaire prowled in the anteroom of a rich burgher's post-and-beam home, waiting for the servant who had greeted him to announce his presence to Monsieur Mézières. With each pass, the skirt of his tunic rasped against the bare wooden walls. Octavius pranced around the dark chamber, filling the gloom with cackles of gleeful laughter.

" 'Tis venison, I smell, stewing in its own juices." The thief gorged his lungs with the scent wafting down the stairs. "If ye take your time with your doctoring, you and me might be digging our teeth into a haunch o' that stag afore the day is done."

"In your dreamin' mind."

Conaire planted a foot on the stairs and glared up at the door draped in black serge. He must be crazed with exhaustion to let this dwarf of a thief drag him halfway across Troyes on the slim chance that a wealthy burgher would let a doctor without qualifications tend to his only daughter, and thus give him a bed for the night. This house groaned under the weight of its grief. Beneath the aroma of roasting meat lingered the sickly sweet stench of balsam and funeral ointment, and the air hung thick and still, as if no window nor door had been cracked since the body of the burgher's son had been carried out for burial three weeks ago.

"We'll be gettin' a meal out of it, don't you be worrying." Octavius rubbed the well-worn wool of his tunic. "The burgher's desperate for the likes o' you."

Conaire flinched and resumed his pacing, rolling his shoulders as if he could shake off the fog of human misery. He wanted none o' this clinging creature, none o' the burden of sorrow he felt crushing this house. If he didn't crave the feel of a fine bed beneath his back, he'd be off and think no more of it. "You'll be leavin' here with a full belly," Conaire argued, "but don't be expecting the haunch."

"Leavin'? Nay, nay." Octavius fell into step beside Conaire. "It'll take time to do your healing, no doubt, and you'll be needing a man o' your own, 'tis expected of a fine doctor. Don't let my beard fool ye, for I can shave a man as close and as smooth as a baby's bottomside—"

A crack of light speared down the stairs, and the shadow of a servant fell upon it. "Monsieur Mézières has agreed to see you."

The servant allowed Conaire to pass, but halted Octavius and ordered him to wait below. The servant slammed the door shut on the cursing thief, then ushered Conaire deeper into the dim room.

A haze of wood-smoke permeated the air as thickly as in any ancient Irish mead hall. A single oil lamp suspended by chain from the low ceiling illuminated a wedge of the blue haze, and splashed wavering light over a long trestle table splattered with the leavings of a monstrous meal. Two men presided at the table, one at either end.

Conaire entered the circle of light and thudded his pack to the floor. A derisive laugh burst from the younger of the two men.

"Scraping the dregs, are we, Mézières?" The young man tipped in his high-backed chair and threw one calf over the corner of the table. His sword scraped the floorboards, tracing patterns in the rushes. "Soon you'll be calling in the Jews."

From the other end of the table, Monsieur Mézières cast him a narrow-eyed glare. "If it takes a Saracen, Sir Guichard, then so be it. I will do whatever is necessary to restore my daughter's health."

"Ah, yes, *I* know well that she's your most valuable asset, more precious than a cart full of gold." The man called Sir Guichard slammed his tankard on the table, rattling the scattered dishes. He cast a scornful glance at Conaire's worn, mud-splattered boots, the stubble growing thick and reddish upon his chin. "But even a *burgher's* daughter shouldn't be poked and prodded by every charlatan who wanders into Troyes. Toss this roaming vagabond out on his rump."

The rushes crackled as Conaire swept up his pack and headed for the door, intending to oblige the drunken sot without another word.

"Please forgive my guest, doctor."

Conaire reluctantly paused as Monsieur Mézières's voice rang loud in the room.

"You must understand. Sir Guichard believes I am a foolish old man, casting his gold about like bread crumbs to the birds." His chair scraped upon the floorboards. "Perhaps I am foolish . . . in my desperation."

Desperation. The word reverberated in Conaire's head. *Damn it.* He wanted none of this—none of the muddy quagmire of emotions fluxing in this household. But *she* had taught him too well—the healer in him would not allow him to leave, not yet, not while someone suffered. Not while there was a chance he could atone once more for a former lifetime of killing.

He twisted to face the table. The burgher appraised him with an even, level gaze, as he petted the fur that trimmed his purple surcoat with a hand glittering with jewels.

"If no doctor has yet cured your daughter," Conaire said, cast-

ing a cold glare toward the nobleman, "then there's no foolishness in seeking another."

The burgher unfurled his fingers toward Conaire's dusty gar-
ments. "Should I think you can do any better than the last?"

Conaire's hand tightened on the slung leather of his belt. His
was a skill taught to him by the greatest Irish healer south of
Cruachan, a skill honed in the courts of Visigoth chieftains, on
Viking ships, in the palaces of Saracens, and on more battle-
fields than this man could ever imagine. "There is much medicine," he said tightly, "that can be found outside the boundaries
o' this city."

"You overdo your modesty, charlatan." Sir Guichard sloshed
more wine into his tankard. "Where are the self-deprecating
proclamations of skill? The reluctantly told tales of miracles
done in foreign lands? The stories of wise old Italian teachers?
Come, come, you can bow and scrape better than that, if you
want Mézières's gold."

Conaire eyed the young knight. An aristocrat fallen into hard
times, this. A puffiness softened the lines of his chin and waist,
which would someday sag into fat. A jeweled brooch hung from
the gaping neckline of his surcoat, revealing the frayed, gravy-
stained embroidery of his *cotte* beneath. Conaire wondered why
the burgher suffered such rudeness at his own table, and then
wondered what a nobleman was doing dining with a burgher at
all, then wondered why the hell he was wondering at all.

His only concern was a bed for the night.

"My skill will speak for itself, but there are those who can
speak of it." Conaire repeated the names of the merchants of
Genoa with whom he had journeyed for so many miles. "These
men are here in Troyes. Find them, and they will speak well o'
my skills."

"It's clear," the burgher said drily, "that you lack a doctor's
light-tipped tongue."

"Pretty words won't be after healing the sick."

We've got your authors!

If you seek out the latest historical romances by today's bestselling authors, our new reader's service, KENSINGTON CHOICE, is the club for you.

KENSINGTON CHOICE is the only club where you can find authors like Janelle Taylor, Shannon Drake, Rosanne Bittner, Sylvie Sommerfield, Penelope Neri and Phoebe Conn all in one place...

...and the only service that will deliver their romances direct to your home as soon as they are published—even before they reach the bookstores.

KENSINGTON CHOICE is also the only service that will give you a substantial guaranteed discount off the publisher's prices on every one of those romances.

That's right: Every month, the Editors at Zebra and Pinnacle select four of the newest novels by our bestselling authors and rush them straight to you, even *before they reach the bookstores*. The publisher's prices for these romances range from $4.99 to $5.99—but they are always yours for the guaranteed low price of just *$3.95!*

That means you'll always save over $1.00...often as much as *$2.00*...off the publisher's prices on every new novel you get from KENSINGTON CHOICE!

All books are sent on a 10-day free examination basis, and there is no minimum number of books to buy. (A postage and handling charge of $1.50 is added to each shipment.)

As your introduction to the convenience and value of this new service, we invite you to accept

4 BOOKS FREE

The 4 books, worth up to $23.96, are our welcoming gift. You pay only $1 to help cover postage and handling.

To start your subscription to KENSINGTON CHOICE and receive your introductory package of 4 FREE romances, detach and mail the postpaid card at right *today.*

We have 4 FREE BOOKS for you as your introduction to KENSINGTON CHOICE
To get your FREE BOOKS, worth up to $23.96, mail card below.

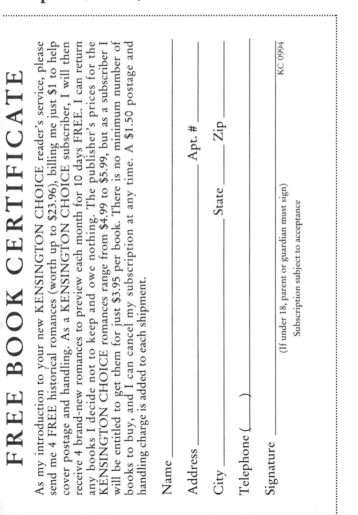

FREE BOOK CERTIFICATE

As my introduction to your new KENSINGTON CHOICE reader's service, please send me 4 FREE historical romances (worth up to $23.96), billing me just $1 to help cover postage and handling. As a KENSINGTON CHOICE subscriber, I will then receive 4 brand-new romances to preview each month for 10 days FREE. I can return any books I decide not to keep and owe nothing. The publisher's prices for the KENSINGTON CHOICE romances range from $4.99 to $5.99, but as a subscriber I will be entitled to get them for just $3.95 per book. There is no minimum number of books to buy, and I can cancel my subscription at any time. A $1.50 postage and handling charge is added to each shipment.

Name _____

Address _____ Apt. # _____

City _____ State _____ Zip _____

Telephone ( ) _____

Signature _____

(If under 18, parent or guardian must sign)

Subscription subject to acceptance

KC 0994

KENSINGTON CHOICE
Reader's Service
120 Brighton Road
P.O.Box 5214
Clifton, NJ 07015-5214

AFFIX
STAMP
HERE

The burgher's fingers stilled upon his cloak. "Your name, doctor."

Conaire resisted the urge to shrug. A name was nothing but an empty label thrust upon a babe before the parents know the pith o' the child. 'Twas best that a grown man choose his own, as he was forced to do, so long ago.

"I am called Conaire MacSidh."

"Mag-*she.*" The burgher's chair scraped upon the rushes. His fine robes moved fluidly around him as he strode to Conaire and scrutinized his features. "You're Irish."

Conaire was wearier than he'd thought, for two ordinary men in one day to see so much of what he kept hidden.

"How cunning of you, MacSidh." Sir Guichard raised his tankard with a flourish and sloshed the spillage off the table with a swipe of his forearm. "But thicken your brogue, charlatan. The burgher's own daughter has more of an Irish lilt than you—and it's been over ten years since Monsieur Mézières rescued her from that savage island."

Irish. Something cold slithered up Conaire's back and twined around his neck. The finger o' the gods was in this, there was no doubt about it. Only they would mock him so by leading him to a place where the Irish buzzed thicker than fleas.

Then he remembered: Soon it would be Lughnasa.

"Come, come, doctor, there's no need to feign ignorance." The nobleman tipped his chair back. "Everyone knows the good burgher's last wife was Irish, and their children grew up on that savage island . . . that is, until the good burgher's *first* wife died—"

"Pray to God," the burgher interrupted brusquely, his blue gaze slicing across the room, "that this Irishman has half the healing skill of my late wife, Sir Guichard. For only then will you find yourself in better straits than you are in now." With a swish of skirts, the burgher headed toward a flight of stairs, eddying angry currents behind him. "Come, Monsieur Mac-Sidh. We shall see if you do honor to your countrymen."

But Conaire stood stiff and deaf to all but his own thoughts.

Aye, old gods o' mine, so you couldn't plant long trails of honeysuckle in the muck o' these alleyways, so you couldn't cast summer sunlight between the leaning faces o' these houses, or raise a cool fairy wind in this stinking air. Two Irish in one day, you give me, damn you, damn you.

Aye, he should have sensed it coming, he should have known, but the road to Troyes had been long, and his senses too dulled to foresee it. The memory of that one life was a scar the gods refused to let heal. Every year it hardened over, thick and scaly, and every Lughnasa the gods found a way to rip it open, so it festered and bled anew.

He clenched his fist around the strap of his bag. *Damn the gods.* He should convert to Christianity and spite them all for their ceaseless mockery. The Christians believed in redemption for their sinners—*his* gods had no mercy: they had cast him into Hell and abandoned him here to burn.

"Doctor MacSidh?"

The burgher halted halfway up the stairs, tapping the railing in impatience. Conaire shifted the weight of his bag and followed. *Mock me, then, if you must, old gods o' mine. I'll fight you, and I'll still fight you, for those amber days are gone, and I'll not suffer through the memory.*

Upstairs, at the end of a short hall, Conaire plunged into a room as hot and humid as Baghdad in July. A great canopied bed loomed in the dimness, shrouded with thick serge. Black cloth muffled the windows. A single tallow candle flickered on a stand by the side of the bed, where an elderly maidservant plucked at her rosary and filled the room with the drone of prayer.

Conaire clanked his doctor's sack upon a bedside table and

cut off the servant's devotions. "Enough o' that. Strip those cloths from the windows."

The coverings tumbled down with a cloud of dust. Thin streams of light sifted through the cracks in the oiled parchment, threading a faint breeze through the stale air. Conaire yanked away the heavy bed curtains. A black cat yowled and sprinted off the bed to dash into the shadows.

He glanced dispassionately at the small, supine figure who lay swathed in wool and fur. His patient was a woman-child who looked as if she'd known barely eighteen winters, with softly rounded features and dark gold hair. Her breath came harsh through white lips.

"She's been like this for weeks." Monsieur Mézières tugged a perfumed linen out of his sleeve and pressed it over his nose. "She collapsed when she heard that her brother had died in a hunting accident. She has lain in that bed restless and half-conscious ever since."

Conaire impassively scanned her features. Death glazed the girl's skin like frost. He searched for her arm beneath the covers, and probed for her weak and irregular pulse. Higher up, by the crook of her elbow, scarlet slashes from recent bleedings mottled her skin. Conaire let her arm drop to the bed. He knew by the limpness of her limbs and the Otherworldly expression on her face, that though she lay weak from leeching and bleeding, her true sickness was not of the body, but of the heart.

He'd seen this form of human misery before.

"I've already lost a son, Doctor MacSidh. She is my only heir." The burgher's voice grew gravelly with edgy anxiety. "Hear me: There is no price—*none*—too dear for her life."

"My price is a bed for a night." Conaire seized the top woolen blanket and yanked it off the girl. "If you can pay that, then I'll be doing what I can for her."

There was a moment of stunned silence, while Conaire ruthlessly yanked cover after cover off the bed.

"A paltry price for a doctor's fee."

"Not," Conaire grunted as he nudged aside the mound of blankets growing on the floor, "compared to the king's ransom the innkeepers o' Troyes are asking for a cold straw pallet."

"You'll have a bed, I'll see to it. But if you heal my daughter, a king's ransom *will* be yours. Think on that as you tend to her." The burgher turned on his heel and headed to the door. "I've not yet met a man whose skills couldn't be sharpened by the promise of gold."

The door clicked shut behind him. Conaire rolled his forearm over his sweat-soaked face, then barked for the maidservant to get rid of the covers he'd jerked off the bed. He planted his hands on his hips and glared at the small, shapely form of the woman laying in it.

Aye, he supposed he could bring this one back to life. Beneath the glaze of her skin, a flush stubbornly ebbed and flowed. She was just at the age when the sap of life surged strongest. It would take little more than rest and broth to drag her back among the living, and then the burgher would have his wish, and Conaire would be done with both o' them.

He'd heal her body, aye, for that was a matter of dispassionate skill, like untangling ship's rigging or caulking a hole in the hull. But her grief, nay, that was her own, and he'd have none o' it, for he'd be gone from this place before the tentacles he'd felt rising from the muck o' Troyes bound him to this house and these people.

She jerked, suddenly, in her sleep. He turned her face toward his. Her skin burned against his fingertips. He'd have to call for the maidservant. He needed a pot of boiling water to mix with yew leaves.

He sat on the bed just as her eyes fluttered open.

Then, time stopped.

Conaire tumbled down, deep, deep down through the centuries, into the whirling colors of a misty forest glade, into the soft ripple of laughter echoing amid the rustle of leaves, into a place where his blood pumped hard in his veins and his heart soared as unfettered as a sparrow gliding on a warm summer breeze.

The air *whooshed* out of his lungs. He clawed his fingers into the linens while his senses reeled in some sightless void, sucked into a vortex of memory as jagged as shards of shattered steel. He knew these eyes like he knew the buck of a stallion beneath him, like he knew the sharp scent of summer's green grass and blooming honeysuckle, like he knew the hills and valleys and growling gray mists of Erin.

Her eyes fluttered closed.

For one burning flash of a moment, Conaire had stared into the eyes of Brigid.

Thirteen

"What's this?" The maidservant clattered the breakfast tray upon a table, then scanned the silent room, her gaze lingering upon the trailing bed linens and the blaze of the July sunshine splashing through the window. "Deirdre Mézières, are ye hiding from me on such a fine, soft morning?"

The tinkling sound of muffled laughter lilted high on the air. The elderly maidservant cocked her ear toward the draperies snuggled against the far bedpost. A hot breeze breathed through the window, and fluttered a pale tatter of linen across the black serge.

"Have ye no sense of fair play, child?" The maidservant waddled toward the bed. A smile slipped across her wizened face, for it was an old game; they'd been playing it near every morn since Deirdre had been weaned from her Ma's breast. "You can see me, lass—but to my aged eyes, you're no more than a will-o'-the-wisp."

The maidservant tugged the draperies. Deirdre's shouted laughter filled the room, as she whirled out of the cloth with a tumble of honey-gold hair.

"Och, Moira, you've no shame, to say such a thing! You've ears like a hound, it's a wonder I can keep the murmuring of me own thoughts from ye." With a flash of bare legs, Deirdre twirled to an abrupt stop and met Moira's glazed eyes, their color long obscured by milky cataracts. "Now, an honest race, perhaps. That would be more sporting of ye—"

"There'll be no more talk of racing and the like." Moira's jowls shook like twin bowls of porridge. " 'Tis daft enough you're being, walkin' about on the cold floor in your naked feet with the sun hardly o'er the horizon, breathin' the chill morning air, and you not a week from knocking at St. Peter's gate."

Deirdre planted her fists on her hips. "Och, give me castanets and a bread basket like a leper, why don't ye?"

"Haven't you got the devil in ye today."

"I'm *not* dead to the world." Deirdre raked up the hem of her shift and darted to the window, then swiped away what remained of the sagging oiled parchment to thrust her upper body into the warm summer sunshine. "I was after thinking my banishment was over, when Papa summoned me here from the convent."

"Listen to ye," Moira chided as she waddled back to the tray laden with food. "Talking of banishment and the like—"

"It's true, Moira. You'll not be telling me these last three months I've been any more than an exile in me own father's house."

"It would not be right for ye to be walkin' about as free as a bird, with this house bowed under the weight o' mourning." Moira sliced a thin wafer out of a hard round of cheese, then waved the knife at her charge. " 'Tis your sickness talking, and you not a week out of your deathbed."

"I'm as strong as a Turk." Deirdre listened hungrily to the sound of *life* drifting over the roof from the street: people thronging about, laughing, gossiping, calling out to one another in languages she did not understand; the yip of dogs, the creak of the common well, the singing cries of the peddlers. "I'll explode like a barrel of tar put to flame, if I don't go out."

She teetered farther out on the ledge, digging her hips into the ridge of the stone sill, trying to cool the hot rush of her blood. Och, here she was, complaining to Moira when it was *she* who had lost her senses, to be prancing about her room like a fey child and yearning for a freedom that could not be. All last night she had tossed and turned, as anxious and fretful as a caged thing, and this morning she'd woken with a fire in her blood, with no sense to it at all. She'd sooner stop the rain from falling, or the wind from blowing, than sit quietly in her shadowy room with her sewing and her lute on a morning such as this.

Something is going to happen. The knowledge had hovered on the edge of her consciousness for days, yet she had not dared to give it more than an instant's thought—until now, when the certainty tingled in her fingertips.

"Look at ye, child, leaning out of the window with the sun streamin' through your shift, showin' all the gifts the good Lord gave ye."

"I'll dress, then." Deirdre tumbled back on her heels, spun into the room, and settled in a pool of white linen in front of her carved wooden chest. She threw open the lid and blindly snatched stockings and a blue tunic shot through with gold threads. "Then to the fair for me—"

"The fair?" Moira pressed the heel of her palm against her forehead. "I've come to the end of me rope, I have. I don't know which saint to pray to anymore." Moira clattered the knife upon the tray and snatched the tunic from Deirdre's hands. She held the cloth close to her face to check it for tears and snags. "The fair's crowd is not for the likes o' you—"

"Will ye be telling me who is, then?" Deirdre plopped down on a stool by the side of the hearth and yanked her shift to her hips, stretching each leg into her stockings. "Too good for the other bourgeois, I am, the only daughter of the richest burgher in Troyes—and not good enough for noblewomen." She stood up and snatched the blue tunic from Moira's hands. While she struggled her arms into it, she gravitated back to the window, like a seal rising to the surface of the sea for air. "I *won't* sit in this room anymore, living always between two worlds." She shimmied the tunic down her legs and jerked her chin toward some hidden street beyond the garden. "Mayhap in that crowd I'll find one of my own, if such a creature exists."

"Child, have ye no sense? They're burning heretics again today at the fair. Two Albigensians brought up from the south, and one little lass accused o' doing the devil's work by preventing the candlemaker's lard from setting."

Deirdre dug her fingers into the gritty surface of the windowsill. Och, she was as crazy as the idiot who cackled at the church door, to think of walking amid the crowd like a normal woman. Moira was right: She'd been told that crusaders milled about, outfitting themselves to join King Louis in the Holy Land; and that the Grand Inquisitor had come, with heathens from Languedoc, to show all of Europe the evil lurking even in its most Christian heart—and what the Church would do with them. Aye, the streets of Troyes was no place for the likes of *her.*

Yet still, a defiance surged in her, fierce and furious; a daring that made her yearn to race in the midst of the fair and taunt the world—anything, *anything* to feel free of shackles, if only for a moment, if only for *this* moment.

"Och, come and dance with me in the garden, then." Deirdre spun away from the windowsill, pried the round of cheese from Moira's grip, and dragged her into the center of the room. "We'll pretend there's an Irish piper, like the one Papa hired for Mama's birthday all those years ago. Do you remember?"

Deirdre herself only vaguely remembered, for it was a happier moment, a joyous instant in her childhood, but her thighs and her arms, her feet and her fingers, the long curve of her back— they all remembered how to dance. While Moira argued and scolded, Deirdre whirled around her and kicked up the hem of her tunic, abandoning herself to the music lilting in her head.

"Och, enough of this!" Deirdre gathered her skirts and darted toward the door. "Come, Moira, to the garden—"

She stumbled to a sudden stop, her skirts snapping around

her legs, as she collided with a solid wall of a man braced in the open portal.

She staggered back and blinked up at the apparition. She had a swift impression of impossibly broad shoulders, of legs braced apart, of an exotic, broad-boned face, stubbled, flanked by unfashionably long hair which hung in shanks, as if he had spent days running his fingers through it, and black, black brows slashed over deep-set eyes—and the rest was a blur, for from old habit she swept her lashes down to veil her own eyes from the stranger.

"What's this?" she demanded breathlessly, yanking her skirts straight. "What are you doing sneaking up on a woman with nary a 'good day to ye'?"

Silence rang in the room, like the deafening aftermath of a clangor of church bells. She drew in a swift, charged breath; it filled her lungs slow and hard, for the brute of a man standing before her seemed to suck the air from the room. She raised her lashes halfway, enough to see fine blue linen straining against the sweep of his heaving chest, enough to see the roped muscles of his forearms, and tight fists at his sides. A flash of memory came to her, of a tattered book one of the novices had hidden under a rock in the convent's garden, of a brutish conqueror coming upon a princess in the woods and carrying her off to some deliciously unspeakable fate.

"Are you deaf as a pot?" The unlaced sleeve of her tunic slipped to her elbow, as she tucked a strand of hair behind her ear. "Why didn't you announce yourself?"

"I was after thinking you might know the sight o' me."

Deirdre blindly grasped the bedpost. His words were snarled, tense, but amid them lilted the warm breath of the Irish. The timbre vibrated through her so intimately, with a strain so hauntingly familiar, that memories flooded through her, of salt-spray tingling on her face, of growling gray mists, of the dense fragrance of blooming heather, of cows lowing on a warm hillside . . . the rush set her knees to weakening. She stifled a yearning to meet this Irishman's gaze—to see the twinkle of her countrymen in his eyes—for the years had taught her well to hide her own gaze from the world.

It had been so long since she'd heard the brogue of her homeland out of anyone's mouth but Moira's. Undoubtedly, 'twas the memory of Mama's lyrical lilt which this man's ragged voice triggered in her heart, she told herself, it was surely no more than that.

"Friend or foe," she retorted, flexing her hand over the hard carved oak, "it's not fitting to burst in on a woman like you did. My life nearly left me body at the sight of ye."

"Aye, but it didn't," he growled, "and you standin' there, as cool as morning, with your wits still about you."

She shrugged. "Wits are a woman's only weapon."

"And yours still as sharp as ever." He strode into her chamber as boldly as a husband. "Was I lured here just to feel the prick o' your tongue?"

"Lured here?" She clutched the bedpost with both hands. "Who are ye? What business have you in my bedroom?"

He clanked a bulky sack upon her bedside table with more force than necessary. "No words o' welcome for me, woman?"

"And why would I be welcoming a stranger into me bedroom, will you be telling me that?" She'd remember a man such as this, even if she'd done nothing more than brush by him in a crowd on the way to Mass. Only a handful of men had made her acquaintance in all her life—priests and kin, all—and none dared to swagger into her chamber as if he owned the room and everything within. "I've never seen the likes of *you* before."

"Child, child, have ye no manners?" Moira stepped forward and patted her chest, her splotchy jowls still shaking from her efforts to ward off Deirdre's dancing. "This is Monsieur Mac-Sidh, the doctor I was after telling ye about."

Deirdre shook her head incredulously. Those rough laborer's

hands . . . surely they couldn't be the ones she remembered, the hands which had grazed her skin so tenderly during her illness. A frisson shimmied up her back, a powerful tremor that had nothing to do with the breeze swirling in through the window. "Och, if he's a doctor, then I'm a queen."

With a impatient jerk, the stranger flung the contents of his sack upon the bed—a sandglass, a series of leather bags, flashing instruments, a small chalice. "Does your majesty wish to hear o' my lengthy education? I know a tale o' misery that would burn your ears with the telling."

Her face was lowered, so all she saw were the scattered implements upon the bed and the blur of his form, but she sensed his fury as she would sense the blistering of the summer sun upon her skin. Och, a snapping brute of a man, he was. She did not understand his rootless, spitting anger—but she would not be cowed by it, nay not Deirdre Mézières! If this man had wanted to do her violence, he'd have done it by now. And she'd have no reason to fear in her own room, in her father's own house. Papa would kill with his own hands anyone who dared to do her harm.

Besides . . . she'd spent a lifetime with her gaze fixed to the ground, and had long learned to read moods by the curl of a finger or the pace of a man's breathing. The fire of fury emanating from this hulking doctor roared in all directions. He raged not at her, but at the whole wide world.

"Hotter than a bog fire, you are," she said, even as he turned away and snarled for Moira to fetch wine, "and for what? It's no wonder I didn't know the look of ye." She only had flickering memories of the doctor, a looming presence who retreated into the shadows whenever she struggled into consciousness. "A week, thereabouts, you've been tending to me, and not until now do I meet ye, and you barging into my bedroom and bristling like a cock."

He slammed a chalice upon the bedside table. "Did you expect a wooing, woman?"

"Och, only in your dreamin' mind. Aye, it's a rare thing for a maiden to share so many nights with a strange man in her bedroom without saying penance for it—"

"Child!"

"—but I expected no more than good manners from ye."

"I won't be simpering and groveling at your feet, like a poor bard at a queen's table."

"All puffed up with pride, are you?"

Her blood raced. It seemed like an eternity since she'd crossed wits with anyone but Moira; even longer since she'd done so with a man—and then only her brother. She thrust herself away from the bedpost and hiked her hands to her hips, daring to run her gaze swiftly over him. He was not a handsome man, with his broad-boned features and his granite scowl, but a vitality crackled around him, like the heat and light and sparks of a raging bonfire.

"Well, I'll have none of your wooing, thank you very much," she continued, thinking, *Och, the devil is in me tongue today.* "If your loving is as blunt as your speech, monsieur, I'm thinking ye'll have no art at all."

"Child!"

He snatched the pitcher of wine from Moira's hands. "Cease your chattering, woman."

"You'd do better ordering a hen to stop her clucking," Moira muttered as she rounded the bed, gathering linens as she went, "than to curb the tongue o' this lass."

"Och, you'd both have me mute. I'll be no simpering little ninny, and not for the likes of a common doctor."

He turned and sloshed some wine into the chalice, stirring it vigorously, his rigid back to her. Such anger, such strange, purposeless fury radiated from him, as if he could barely bank a roar of rage. Suddenly, he slammed his hand flat upon the tabletop. His knuckles grew white with tension . . . yet his fingers trembled.

Trembled.

A hot flush worked its way up her neck. She stared at that strong hand with its quivering fingers, until he snatched the chalice stem and strangled it in his grip. She knew little of men, but she knew the sight of restraint straining at its bonds, and she knew that it was her own presence that had such a violent effect on this blustering brute of a stranger. A tingling surge of heat shot through her veins.

"Drink this." The doctor thrust out the chalice straight-armed and turned the full power of his gaze upon her. "It will keep that thornbush of a tongue in your mouth."

Something in the way he uttered the word *mouth* rang in her ears. Her fingertips strayed to her suddenly tender, throbbing lower lip.

Vanity was a sin. But many times during the lonely years in the convent, she had unwrapped the silvered surface of her mother's mirror and lifted it to the daylight streaming upon her face. She'd parted her lips, examined her teeth—one in the front slightly crooked—then ran a hand down her figure, taking some comfort in knowing she'd been gifted with her mother's fair, fine skin and a lush form—convincing herself that she was a pretty, young woman, if a mite too rounded, bound to turn the head of a fine man someday. But eventually, inevitably, she'd meet her own eyes straight on and wonder what men *saw* in those seemingly ordinary eyes of jade; what was it about her gaze that made men and women so uneasy, that sent priests into secretive fits of self-crossing, that sent servants dodging nervously out of her way?

Then her features receded in the reflection, blurred by hot tears, puckering into the countenance of one of the hideous gargoyles that leered out from over the door of the church. She knew; aye, she knew. There was always a mark: a mole, a wart. A demon could never hide entirely in a woman's heart.

Suddenly, the doctor strode to her side, seized the fingers

tracing her lower lip, and slapped the warm chalice into her palm. "Drink," he ordered as he released her hand, "and be done with it."

He stood before her, waiting. A throbbing heat emanated from his body and engulfed her in a prickling warmth, like the weight of roiling gray thunderclouds on a crackling hot summer day. He smelled of the outside—of rich earth and rain, of sweat and something else, something indefinable, something she'd instinctively call *man*. The restlessness which had boiled in her blood through the morning found an unlikely outlet in their nearness, for now she felt breathless, light-headed . . . vitalized.

She drank the sweet brew swiftly and thrust the empty cup at him. She pressed the back of her hand against her chin to soak up a drop which had slipped out of her lips, when her stomach made an unpleasant lurch. "Is it poison you serve me? It sours in my stomach."

He snatched the chalice from her hand and tossed it heedlessly on the bed, spraying the bare feather mattress with droplets of golden wine. "All sweet things turn as bitter as gall over time."

"Listen to you, talking nonsense. All huffing and ruddy-faced and twisted with fallen pride—"

"Aye, and so I'll stay, for the sight o' you won't make me forget the past."

She blinked, not understanding, wondering if he could truly be in such a rage because she'd not recognized him when he arrived. "Can you not forgive me for not knowing ye, doctor? Or is there another burr in your *braies* that I know naught of?"

"They have you playing games with me, like a kitten with its prey—"

"I'll be thinking," she interrupted, glancing at the bulk of his shoulders, "that there's no woman alive who'd mistake *you* for a wounded mouse."

Och, such meaningless bickering, she did not understand the root of it. It was a rare enough thing, to have such a brawny man in her bedroom, they shouldn't be arguing as if they'd been married fifty years, when they'd only just met. Aye, and she'd done naught but throw hay upon the fire, for she'd spit back at him like a fishwife. A gentle answer quells anger, Mama had taught her, but this man's presence muddled her senses until she hardly knew herself.

"Listen to us, snarling at each other like curs, and over what?" She dared to reach out, to place her hand lightly on that sculpted forearm. "No more of it, then." Her voice grew breathless, for she felt the hot, furious pounding of his pulse beneath her fingertips. "I welcome you, Monsieur MacSidh. I owe you the debt of my life, and for that, you may call me Deirdre."

His fingers wound around her wrist, and strangled it until needles of pain shot up her hand.

"I'll have none o' your flirtation." His breath fell hot on her hair. "This time, lass, I'll not be fulfilling your maiden's fancy."

A flush worked its way up her cheeks. She jerked her hand out of his grip and stepped back, her spine straightening, as an uncertain shame overcame her. "And what will you be meaning by *that?*"

He raised his head and spoke to the rafters of the room. "It means I'm no fresh-faced boy anymore, to be trapped by the sight of a woman's dancing."

The blush burned through to the roots of her hair. Och, the arrogance of him! Deirdre Mézières of Troyes was no giggling little girl, she wasn't, and he was nothing but a brute of a doctor. A traveling doctor, at that, while she was the only daughter—the only *heir*—of one of the richest burghers in Troyes. "Is that what you're thinking now? That I danced for the likes of *you?*"

"I know you better than you know yourself."

"Moira!" She turned away, to hide the evidence of her shame. Moira straightened from a pile of dirty linens. "Do you hear this? He thinks I danced for *him!*" Cat's fur rasped against her ankles, and Deirdre swept up her pet, hugging him close to her side. "I'll have you know that a *burgher's* daughter can dance when she pleases. I danced for myself and the glory of the morning, not for some brutish stranger who doesn't have the manners to knock upon a lady's door—"

"He's brought ye from the jaws of death, child," Moira scolded. "Don't be complainin' about his ways."

"How do we know he's a doctor?" She glared at her maidservant as he strode back to the bed and began clanking implements back into his pack. "He doesn't have the look of one. And it's an odd doctor, who slinks away like a thief whenever his patient awakens."

"You've no need o' me. You are cured from what ailed you." The doctor scoured a silver spoon with the rough weave of the sack. "A blind man could see you no longer grieve your brother's passing."

Her fingers froze in the cat's fur. He'd pierced her heart as deftly as a knight slipping his broadsword through a crack in an opponent's armor. Pain flooded through her. Jean-Jacques had been dead barely a month, but she'd been grieving for much, much longer, and she had no more tears left to shed.

She dumped the cat back into the rushes and strode to the light and air pouring through the window. "So you have a cure for grief?" She swallowed a hard lump lodged in her throat. "Faith, you must talk to Papa. You could make a fortune in these sorry days for such a potion—"

"Forgive the poor, wee lass her lightheartedness, doctor," Moira interrupted, as she tugged a new linen over the mattress. "It's her nature to be as bright as a summer day. 'Tis not callousness, no, 'tis a blindness to sorrow. She's had so very much of it since her mother died—"

"Moira, have you no stockings to mend?" Deirdre seized a belt of tiny bells laying upon the chest. "Surely you have linens to soak or—"

"I'm defending ye, lass." She piled the pillows upon the bed with a *thwack*. "A stranger would think you're an unnatural sister, to be so lighthearted while the funeral lamp still shines o'er your brother's grave—"

"I'll not wear my heart on my lips, when I'll be grieving until the end of my days." She clasped the belt about her hips, then tilted her chin at the doctor, staring at his hard, square chin through the veiling of her lashes. "You've not cured me at all, *doctor*. Have you no other potion to give me now?"

"Time."

He spat the word. Then, to her surprise, he laughed—a short, ugly laugh, dripping with bitterness and totally without humor.

"What? You'll not prescribe me milk of pulverized almonds or barley waters sprayed with oil of roses?" She paced to the table littered with perfume bottles and the breakfast tray and seized her prayer book, slapping it into the cup of her palm. "You'll not fill my ears with talk of melancholic humors and hectic fevers and the passing of stars? You'll not even play the pretense?"

"The stars care *not* what happens on the earth below. And of the two of us, it's only you who may be playing the pretense still." In two steps he was by her side, his voice harsh as gravel. "I'll have no more o' it. Look at me, woman."

"Och, are your senses as blunt as your speech?" She jerked, but he seized her arm and held her fast. Something proud within her swelled and straightened. The doctor spoke as a man who could command armies, not as a healer. But she was no footarcher to answer his whims. "I'm no maidservant to be ordered about—"

"You don't know the pith of a person 'til you look him in the eye—look into mine. I'll not ask again."

A dangerous whisper, spoken in hot breath above her ear. A breeze gusted suddenly through the window and the light dimmed, as if a raincloud passed across the sun.

"It's my father who pays your fee." Her fingers tightened over her prayer book and the frisson of danger rushed in her blood. "I will *not* be commanded."

He seized her chin and thrust her face up; the cup of his hand lay hard on her throat. Her breath faltered. How callused his fingers, how hot his grip—she stubbornly set her gaze upon the dent in his bristled chin; the mercilessly sculpted jaw. Vaguely, she wondered what Moira was doing; surely she saw how he dared to touch her, but Deirdre heard the maidservant's quiet humming as she worked around the bed.

"You tease and shift your eyes about," he growled, "but I will see them, and you will see mine, and we both will see if we can be rid of the mischief the gods have wrought."

She heard none of his words. The recklessness which had simmered in her blood since morning finally boiled over. Aye, a touch of madness possessed her, to think of doing such a thing. But it would be no less than he deserved, mauling a helpless woman like this. She'd make him hurl back quicker than a man struck by an arrow.

She raised her lashes up, up, past the bristle of his chin, beyond the tight, white lips, up, until their gazes locked, and then she stared with defiance, throwing her gaze at him like a spear.

But something jolted her from within, like the strong kick of a full-term babe within the womb. White-hot lightning arced between them. The clear, silvery depths of his eyes were as familiar to her as prayer. She felt she would have known this man anywhere, though in life she'd never laid eyes upon him before.

Strange. *Foolish.*

They stared at one another in some timeless void, snared, motionless. His eyes blazed at her like fire-tortured steel, fluxing with emotions she could not all name—a roiling mixture of the shock and denial she always saw in men's eyes—but there was more . . . a raging, volcanic, angry emotion she could not identify, for she'd never known an anguished fury like this, and she was a virgin to the ebb and flow of a man's gaze. Looking at this man was like teetering on the edge of a cliff and staring down at the storm-tossed sea, jagged with violent eddies and swirling whirlpools. Yes, that was what she remembered, the turbulent gray Irish sea of her childhood, with wind-whipped waves beckoning beyond the breakers, with gulls wheeling above, cawing mournful cries.

Then Deirdre's breath rushed back into her lungs with the sharpness of a hundred thousand knives. She probed his gaze and defied him wordlessly to hold her own still; and he did, as no Christian had ever dared. A seed of fluttering wonder blossomed in her heart, for among the passions raging in his eyes, not one among them was fear.

With a groan, he released her chin and seized her arms. He pulled her up close, close enough to feel the angry heat of his breath on her face, close enough to see the bristles on her cheek and chin, close enough to see the gold sparks in his silver eyes. He smelled of sunlight and sweat and, strangely, like steel, like chain-mail links warmed by the sun—oddly familiar, this scent, for it sent a sharp and sudden ache spearing through her, and for one brief moment she ached for the touch of his lips so sharply, that her body crumpled with the hollow yearning.

Her senses reeled; the air around them churned furiously. Her limbs quavered, at the mercy of these violent, invisible currents, at the mercy of his fierce, direct gaze. He deepened his search into her gaze, probing, questioning, and she felt the force of his examination as if his broad, callused hands raked over her bare skin—*Och,* what was this? What was happening to her? She welcomed the tautness of his strong hands on her arms, for her legs were no longer capable of holding her full weight. Och, had any man ever looked into a woman so intimately? She felt as if he saw through all the ugliness and evil shining through her eyes into the part of her soul, buried deep, deep within, that was still good, that was still pure, the part that defied all who called her evil.

Then she knew that *this* was the reason she'd been wrapped as taut as wool upon a spindle these past days: Here was a man who did not stumble back at the sight of her "devil's eyes"— she'd never known there'd be such a creature. Now she filled her lungs with the man-smell of him, gorged her sight upon his height and breadth, and felt her heart flutter on wings as light as air that for once, *for once,* God had smiled upon her.

He shook her, suddenly, hard. "Damn you, woman."

Confusion rippled through her senses. This was not the soft voice of a lover, these were not a lover's gentle murmurings— this was not a lover's nail-tight grip upon her arms.

"Damn your *eyes.*"

Words rumbled in her throat, but her tongue lay too stiff to murmur them. *Not you, nay, not you, doctor—you can look into my eyes without flinching—surely you among men can see past the horror to the goodness buried inside—*

"Aye, woman, your secrets throb in those eyes—I know them better than you yourself know them."

Ice seeped through her veins, chilling the vestiges of her euphoria. Raw fury blasted from him, but did nothing to thaw her growing fear. The moment of hope which had risen in her heart shattered like ill-made glass. What a fool she had been, letting herself believe that *any* man could see more than there was to see; the madness racing in her blood had weakened her defenses, and blinded her to the danger. Now another fear stirred in her, dark and terrifying: Perhaps this doctor had been sent to determine the truth—to seek out the worm of Lucifer in the heart of a young girl.

And destroy it.

"I know this." He thrust her against his hard chest, closer than she'd ever been to a man, closer than she'd ever been to another human. "You dreamt of your brother's death while he still lived—aye, aye, there's no use shaking your head, I know 'twas that which sent you to your sickbed. Tell me this now: Did you dream of me, woman, before my coming?"

Later, much later, when she relived this moment over and over in her mind until the fabric of the memory frayed and thinned, she wondered what fount of self-possession had kept her from sliding into a trembling heap onto the floor. Was it the firmness of his hands on her arms? Or was it, as she suspected, the stark terror of being so baldly found out which forced her to keep her wits about her?

At the moment, she did not think; she couldn't, for it seemed that the bells of Easter morning rang in her ears. He couldn't know—he *couldn't* know. She blinked at him, and it was as if the world around her spun and slowed, and in the second her eyes closed, something cold bit into the back of her neck and sucked her into the horror of memory. Against the veined inside of her lids, she saw it all again; the fire-lit room, the monotonous chanting from the shadows, the frankincense burning her nostrils, strange hands clawing the flesh of her wrists.

But that was memory, nothing but memory, of a time long, long ago, when she'd been too young to know better than to tell everyone of her dream of Mama's death, the first of many dreams she spent her life praying to stop.

And is it my fault that God gave me these dreams which show me what will come to pass? And is it my fault I cannot stop them? Would I willingly call upon me the sight of my mother's death, the sight of my brother's death?

She crushed her terror into a tiny ball and crammed it in that secret place in her heart; terror would make her panic, terror would make her rash. She could not be rash, for *this* time, she was a woman, full grown, not a child in the thrall of a demon. This time, all her father's gold, power, and influence couldn't keep her from a witch's fate. This time, Inquisitors roamed France searching for women like her, searching for fodder for their pyres. For she'd been taught from her mother's dying day that her dreams were the devil's work, and when she allowed them, she became the devil's handmaiden.

When the devil gets his foot on a woman's neck, she never lifts her head again.

No! No—she'd been purged of evil for eight long years. So thought her confessor. So thought the world. So thought even Moira, the person closest to her, the woman Deirdre tried hardest to fool, and daily thanked God for the blinding powers of love.

No charlatan of a doctor could pry the truth from her lips. Not after all these years of practiced deception. Not after being tied to the rood screen at church.

Not after the exorcism.

But he was still glaring at her, his sword-sharp eyes slicing away the hard shell of pretense she'd spent years building around her, mocking all her bravado. Who was this man, what power did he hold, to strip off her skin and muscle right down to her naked bones? She could not hide from that piercing gray gaze, anymore than she could hide from the burning vault of the open sky.

Hot tears blurred her vision. Terror gave her strength. She pushed out of his grip, her nails snagging upon his tunic. She stumbled back in sudden freedom. From the corner of her eye, she noticed Moira suddenly rising from behind the bed, where she'd been tucking the linen beneath the mattress, ignorant of all that had passed between her and the doctor.

Deirdre mustered all her courage in that single moment, every last ounce of strength in her body, and straightened her spine to face the doctor in defiance.

"The portals are narrow in this house, *doctor.*" She swiveled with a swirl of cloak and strode toward the shadowed hall. "See to it that your swelled head doesn't get stuck in the door."

Once under the cover of darkness, she raced down the hall. Her booted feet scraped on the old floorboards. She hurled herself down the back stairs and lurched against the garden door, banging it open to the light and air even as panic blinded her.

She stumbled through the garden, her feet slipping over the dew-cooled grass, her heart setting the pace of her mindless flight. She grasped her skirts in her hands, hiking them up only to scratch and muddy her stockings. She heard no footsteps crashing behind her, yet she raced as if chased by a demon, clinging to the dark, chill edges of the path, a sister to the shadows, but even then the sunlight sought her out—not even here could she hide from the truth and the light.

The thunder of her heart pounded in her ears, as she reached the moss-laden stones that formed the far end of the small garden, then pressed her cheek against the cool, gritty wall. The stones rasped against her skin, as she sank to her knees in the musty corner along with last year's crackling leaves.

Then, without a whisper of notice, a cloud passed over her eyes. *No!*

She cried out as she curled her hands into fists. She struggled against the gray vapor that blurred the edges of her vision. She thrashed her head back and forth—*No! No!*—this evil within her emerged only when her strength ebbed, and now, now with all the fight drained out of her, she was helpless against the whirling smoke which gathered and thickened until the black haze cut off the brilliance of the midsummer day.

She pierced her palms with her fingernails, but the pain faded beneath the smothering silence.

The vision came, writhing like a serpent. The earthy scent of moss-drenched moisture billowed from the gray haze. Tall, silvery forms shimmered through the fog, moving more and more slowly until they stilled and solidified into the shapes of mighty trees. This grove *lived,* for it had a warmth and a welcome she fought against, even in the mute silence of her thralldom. Blue green light filtered eerily through the vaulted verdure to cast an uncertain glow upon her bare skin. Somewhere close, fire crackled high and hot. Above, in the star-studded skies, an unearthly moon-sun burned metallic and white-hot.

And one part of her thought, *This place is Hades,* even as another part of her thought, *This is where I belong.*

One of the trees swelled, then birthed a shadow which unfolded into the silhouette of a man. The creature approached. She felt the stretch of her arms as she welcomed him . . . and then the vision shifted, changed, for the creature embraced her and there was nothing but warmth in his arms, a sigh, a homecoming. He wore a dark cloak which shimmered with gold crescents—a pagan thing which he shed effortlessly. The heat of his breath fanned her cheek, redolent of rain and dew, and his large hands rasped on her bare skin—*Oh* . . . she arched beneath the caress of a human hand which sent heavenly sensations rushing through her limbs . . . the fire flared, higher and hotter, her skin burned with it. She felt herself sucked into the vision, yearning to open herself to this creature of her dreams, and let him ease the growing ache in her body, this lonely void in her soul. And she sensed all around them the bated breath of hundreds of unseen creatures, watching, watching and waiting . . .

Then the scene dissolved into mist, and like every other time, she fought to stay with the creature who filled her heart. She wanted to look upon the face of her lover, to finally capture in her memory the beloved features that always swirled in darkness. She struggled to probe through the veils that kept this last bit of knowledge from her . . . but inevitably the shadowy images receded, lost to her.

The smoke obscuring her vision thinned to filmy whorls, and then dissipated altogether. She found herself propped against the garden wall, staring up at a single filmy stretch of white cloud in a stark blue sky. Hating herself for her weakness, hating herself for her fate. And more, hating herself for yearning for that fate— something no Christian woman should dare contemplate: the dark, forbidden merging of her body with some creature of that other world.

Hot tears streaked her face. All her life she had battled to stop these visions. She'd prayed until her knees froze to the church floor, but she might as well have been praying to wood and stone, for all the answer she got. She'd not called this upon herself; she'd never blinded babes in the womb or stopped a cow from milking or summoned hail down into the fields; she'd never do such a thing, even if she knew the way of it. Now, they'd finally discovered her again. Now the Church would have no choice but to do again what it had tried to do all those years ago and failed: Purge the demon from her body and hurl it from this world.

She fumbled with the laces of her sleeves, jerking them tight to her wrist, and then trying, in vain, to tie them into knots, all the while watching the garden door, waiting for *them* to come and take her away.

It was over now, she told herself; all those years of struggle, of subterfuge—it was all over. There'd be no more lonely isolation, no more silent mockery, no more pain.

She waited, silently trembling in the shadows, and wondered if the flames she had perceived in the distance of her vision were the burning stakes of her own witch's pyre.

Fourteen

It was over.

Conaire curled his hand around the neck of a pitcher of wine, and tilted it blindly upon the cluttered table. He strained his ears until he could hear her frantic footfall in the hall no more, his body still bruised with the imprint of hers.

It was over now, all over. He'd guessed right thinking that no one knew she had the power of the Sight. She'd done well hiding it all these years, though he was sure she'd had little choice. Such a gift as that wouldn't be understood in this time and this place, and the consequences of being marked the devil's hand-maiden in Christian Europe were fierce: Torture, to elicit a confession. Then death, by fire.

Now she looked upon him as if he held the torch.

He slammed the pitcher upon the table harder than he intended. Aye, he was the warrior still, wielding a different sword, but cutting with it as carelessly and as brutally as ever he did in *that* life. She hated him now, he'd done a fine job o' that. There was no doubt he'd crushed whatever fragile lover's dreams she may have harbored—she'd dream o' him no more.

Good.

That was as he wanted it; that was for the best.

He strode out of her bedchamber, shouldering by the waddling maidservant so roughly that the plates on her tray rattled. He plunged into the dark hallway and swiped the air with his hand, as he passed through the faint fragrance of honeysuckle *she* had trailed behind her when she'd flounced out of the chamber and out of his life.

He stormed into the room he'd been sleepless in for too many nights, the stale refuse of last night's bread crackling beneath his boots. A path in the rushes trailed from Octavius's empty pallet to a lump lodged like a fattened tick in the pile of furs on Conaire's bed.

Conaire spied one of his old boots amid the chaotic debris, swept it up and hurled at the lump. With an outraged howl, Octavius jerked out of his nest.

"Pack." Conaire kicked aside a dirty pair of *braies*. "We're leaving this place before the terce bells."

He slammed the door on the Irishman's incredulous sputtering and strode toward the stairs. Aye, soon he'd be rid of that worthless sluggard, as well as everything and everyone else in this house. He'd not known why he suffered that lazy thief, except that the creature was tenacious, and Conaire had too much whirling through his mind to focus upon him. But no more; nay, no more. *She* was healthy, so his duty was done in this wretched place.

Damn the gods. For seven hundred years he'd battled the wisps and mists of their making, and now they mocked his efforts by leading him to *her,* reborn in the very image of her long-dead wishes, as innocent as a child of all that had passed before, and ignorant of how every gesture, every glance, every word from her lips, skewered him to the bone.

He halted in the gloom of the hallway and crushed his brow with the butt of his fisted hands. Even now, a thousand crazed whispered voices whirled in his head, stirring up a thick bog of emotions he thought had long solidified. *She is here again, she is mine, I can live again.* How many hours had he tossed and turned in the black of night thinking of the possibilities, *feeling* as he had not felt in centuries, letting that whole first life unfurl before him—

Aye, remembering. His fists sank deep into the valley of his eyes. He remembered too well. Memory was why he'd leave this place today; memory was why he'd leave her in peace. She would remain here, to live a better life, to live a simpler life, without fear, anguish, loneliness—without him. And in the end it would be *he* who would laugh at the gods.

He uncurled his stiff, white knuckles and walked heavily down the stairs. He knew he could have forty, fifty, even sixty years with her, if he willed it. Sixty years: A lifetime for most men. A blink of an eye to him.

In the end, she would still die in his arms.

In the solar of the main floor, the shutters gaped open, drawing off the stench of sour wine. The boards of the trestle tables lay in a hurried, clattered heap against the wall. A rat, gnawing on something discovered amid the rushes, darted off, and slithered through a crack in the warped corner plank of a large cupboard.

Sir Guichard lolled in a seat by the hearth, swinging one leg over the arm of the chair. He glanced up sullenly as Conaire turned off the stairs.

"Voilà, Mézières." The nobleman's voice dripped with scorn. "Here comes the man who raised your golden goose from the dead."

Monsieur Mézières peered around the carved back of his chair, then rose swiftly to approach Conaire in a cloud of orange scent. "Ah, Monsieur MacSidh, I've been waiting for you." Freshly shaven, his blunt-cut, silvery-white hair shimmering with care, the burgher grasped Conaire by the arms. "Forgive my absence these past days; the fair is a harsh taskmaster."

Conaire stiffened in the man's embrace. The burgher's palms felt hot, and they quivered with unnatural excitement. "It was your daughter I came to heal."

"And that you've done well, by the sound of laughter coming from her room this morning—"

"I'll be leaving this day." He jerked out of the burgher's grip. "My work here is done—"

"Please, *please,* doctor, I know you're the impatient sort, but I'll not be denied." The burgher raised a single finger to silence him. "We've a fee to discuss, and it will be a generous one, but this is neither the time nor the place."

The burgher clapped twice, the fur-trimmed edge of his scarlet tunic flapping. A servant bustled into the room with a pitcher of wine and three gem-studded chalices.

The burgher's face crinkled into a smile as he reached for the chalices. "First, doctor, we three must celebrate."

Conaire's jaw stiffened. Through the cocked window wafted the babble of the crowd, a stew of fetid scents, the bustle of anonymity—the empty anonymity of *freedom*—while he stood still and chafing, listening to the servant gurgle wine into three chalices, bound by the strictures of polite society.

The burgher handed Conaire a chalice. "To your patient's brilliant health, doctor." He raised his own. "For my daughter's happiness." He held out the third chalice to Sir Guichard, while a slow, tight grin slipped over his face.

"And to your future wife, Sir Guichard."

At that moment, the bishop's cathedral clanged the hour of terce. The bells reverberated through Troyes, joined by another chiming, augmented by the bells of a third church, then a fourth, the cacophony clattering through the city until the vibrations penetrated the very pith of the house's timbers and seeped into the marrow of Conaire's bones, until he felt as if a hundred thousand clappers crashed on the inside of his throbbing skull. He clenched his jaw as the clamor gonged with chaotic abandon, until bell by bell, peal by peal, the din thinned until nothing remained but distant echoes and an ear-numbing hum in the air. Conaire stood with his eyes fixed open, telling himself he'd only imagined what he'd heard before the ringing of the bells. 'Twas no more than a twinge of madness, a sort of vertigo which gripped him whenever churchbells rang, those bells which had long driven all magic from the world.

"A fine omen, this." Monsieur Mézières glittered with pride sharper than any of the cut jewels on his fingers. "I wanted you to be one of the first to hear the news, doctor, for if it weren't for your skill, this day would never have come. The arrangements were completed just this morning. Sir Guichard has honored my daughter by consenting to take her as his wife."

"Consent?" Sir Guichard barked a humorless laugh. "I consented to keep my fine family name out of debtor's prison." The nobleman swung his knee still farther over the arm of his chair. His tunic gaped; one of the ties of his stockings hung undone, revealing a fleshy strip of hairy upper thigh. "Even the noblest fields need a little manure now and again."

Conaire's hand stole to his hip, but the leather he clutched caved under his grip—it was the battered skin of his doctor's bag, not the worn hilt of his sword. *That* was nothing but a faded memory, as was, until this moment, the powerful, primitive urge to wield the killing steel.

"To Deirdre's health." The burgher hefted his chalice, his smile triumphant and unwavering. "And to a rich and fertile marriage."

The chalice burned in Conaire's palm. This is what he wanted, he told himself. This was for the best. For all the nobleman's blustering, Sir Guichard would make a better husband than ever *he* could—the nobleman could give her children, the nobleman would grow old with her—and he damned himself for even thinking of the possibility.

He choked off the surge of possessive fury and raised his thoughts to the Otherworld.

Play another tune upon your willow-reeds, old gods o' mine. I've danced to your music before, and my soul died from the sweetness of it. I shan't dance to it again.

Nay, never again.

The cold rim of the chalice bit Conaire's lips. His throat fluxed as he forced himself to swallow. The wine seethed like acid in his belly.

Then she entered the room from the kitchens with a blast of hot air, her saffron cloak billowing around her skirts, her golden hair tangled and wild, the chimes of her belt jarring. Conaire gripped the chalice harder to brace himself for the blow, for she was the gods' most potent weapon, the spearhead lodged in the beating muscle of his heart.

She stopped abruptly as she noticed the three of them with golden chalices gleaming in their hands. She blanched as she caught sight of him, then knotted her hands together, and swept her gaze to the floor.

Tendons stood out stiff in her neck. "You summoned me, Papa?"

"Welcome, daughter." Monsieur Mézières spread his arms wide, begging an embrace. "I have news for you, the most joyous of tidings."

There was a pause, infinitesimal, but Conaire knew the way of his own wife's face, aye. He saw the emotions flood through her; terror, uncertainty, the fear of oncoming doom, emotions *he'd* forced her to feel. In the working of her brow, he watched thoughts race through her head—tumbling upon one another— and then he saw the dawning realization that he'd not told her father the truth, not yet, or her father would not be talking of *anything* joyous. She did not look at him, but he sensed with every fiber of his being her confused, hesitant rush of relief, like a hanged man granted an unexpected stay just as the rope scraped his collarbone.

The spearhead twisted; Conaire mentally seized the shaft and stilled it.

She kneaded her hands together. "Joyous tidings?"

"Yes, child." The burgher raised one brow, then smiled down

like a benign benefactor upon a leering Sir Guichard. "The most joyous news a young woman could hear."

· The color which had only just rushed back into her cheeks ebbed out again. She glanced in confusion toward the kitchen door, then back to the floorboards. "M . . . Moira just came rushing down after me clucking like a hen who has lost her chicks, and babbling on about the rumors . . ." She swallowed drily, disbelieving. *"Tell* me she was after teasing me. Och, tell me it's not true, Papa!"

Monsieur Mézières deliberately planted his cup on the hovering servant's tray, then folded his hands before him in a gesture of exaggerated patience. Sir Guichard rose and snatched the half-full cup, then dropped back into his chair to suck greedily upon the rim.

"It's true, isn't it?" She drew in a deep, shaking breath. "Is that why this creature has been turning up for dinner every night, like a hair in the soup?"

"Daughter," the burgher began, as if she'd not said a word, "Sir Guichard has generously consented to take you as his wife."

She gathered her wits like so many scattered pins. Aye, she'd always had the quickest and sharpest of wits; Conaire watched in mute and pained silence as she pit them against the world.

"Nay, I *won't* be his wife." She clutched her prayer book to her chest, as Sir Guichard wrestled up a resounding belch reeking strongly of sour wine and onions. "I won't marry him—I'd sooner be after marrying a *worm.*"

The nobleman's derisive laughter bubbled into his chalice. "It's no worm you're getting, my beloved, have faith in that."

"And will you be telling me what use you have for a wife?" She whirled in a blur of skirts toward the nobleman, the bells of her belt jarring discordantly. "I've heard all about you, Sir Guichard, and not a bit of good in it. Haven't you enough mistresses to fill every bed in King Louis's castle?"

"Daughter!" Monsieur Mézières's fingers unraveled. "Show some respect for his title."

"Title? *Title?* Och, I'll be thinking the moneylenders of Troyes know a few names for him, since they see so much of his tail—"

Sir Guichard surged up from the chair, bumping it back three paces with the force of his rising.

"She's a child," the burgher interrupted, before the nobleman found his sluggish wit, "and speaks without thinking."

"She'd best speak now, then," Sir Guichard growled, "for there'll be none of this when she's my wife."

Conaire raked ragged fingernails into his hand. *Wife.* His palm ached for the weight of a sword; his knife burned where it nestled against his calf.

Heed me, gods . . . Play not your music. I'll not dance.

I won't.

"To think I imagined you a timid thing these past months." Sir Guichard thrust his cup out blindly toward the servant to be topped. "So modest, casting your eyes away whenever I saw you in the garden."

She snapped her skirts and headed toward the window. "I don't give a peascod what you think."

"You will. For now I see a bit of a savage in you, and I'm looking forward to the taming."

Deirdre clutched her heart. "Papa, do you hear him? Surely France hath no greater lecher—"

"Daughter, there is much you don't understand about a man and wife."

"Bother her not with details." Sir Guichard gaze followed the streak of sunlight buttering the length of her curves. "I'll begin her education on our wedding night."

"Do be blathering on, my lord." She flexed her hand over the sweat-stained palm print on the spine of her prayer book. "The emptier the drum, the louder the noise, and your rattling's near to deafening me."

"Enough!" Monsieur Mézières's eye twitched with the force of his uncharacteristic outburst. "You are distressed now, daughter, and know not what you say."

"Och, Papa . . ." Deirdre swept to his side and gripped his forearm—her eyes, as always, downcast. "I know why you've done this, I do. It's no secret that his father borrowed a fortune from you to fund his way into the Crusade. But I'm thinking there are other ways—"

"Silence, child." The burgher clamped his hand hard over hers. *"Obey* me!"

Silence stretched taut in the room like the warp threads of a loom. Conaire gripped the edge of a chair, the carved wood digging deep impressions into his palm. The room tilted, warped, as if he hovered high in one of the corners and peered through a thick pool of water. Urgency squeezed his vitals like a vice. He had to get out—leave—*run.*

He swiveled and silently headed toward the stairs.

"I should have known this announcement would come too soon after Jean-Jacques's passing," the burgher said, "Because of that, I will forgive you your insolence."

"Forgive me? Insolence?" Her voice vibrated with surprise. "But—"

"Don't leave, doctor."

Conaire paused on the first stair, his fingers white against the wall.

"I must apologize to both of you," the burgher continued, nodding to Sir Guichard and himself, "for my daughter's sharp and over-quick tongue. Her mother was the only one who had any control over her, and the convent seems to have forgotten to teach her even the simplest of commandments—Honor thy father."

Deirdre dipped her head, and her hair cascaded across her face.

"There, there, my child." The burgher stiffly patted her head. "The banns will be read this Sunday. Perhaps I should have waited before making the arrangements, but I'm an old man, and have lost patience with the years. In the passage of time, you will see that I have arranged a match without equal for you."

Aye, 'twill be a far better match than she can even imagine. A muscle flexed in Conaire's cheek. A marriage which will give her peace, of a sort, a marriage where she will not wither away, shamed beneath the gaze of a man forever young. He gazed up, into the shadows of the stairwell, the urgency choking him.

Run.

"Och, enough of your teasing, Papa." Confusion quavered in Deirdre's voice. "Surely, you'll not be marrying me off so soon, when we've only had a few months together?"

"You foolish girl." Sir Guichard's sneering, scornful voice cut through the tension. "Do you think a father's love is stronger than a burgher's ambition?"

Beyond the shadows of the stairwell, Conaire saw a ribbon of light streaming from under the door to his room, he noticed the shadow passing by it: Octavius, no doubt, furiously packing his things—but his feet would not move. For out of the corner of his eye, he witnessed a metamorphosis.

His heart throbbed—a hard, heavy beating, like the stirring of a creature long lost in winter sleep—for he saw her, aye, *Deirdre,* painfully innocent, youthfully curious and eager, sheltered, isolated—he saw the anger rise in her and straighten her shoulders and peel away the chrysalis of her innocent youth, and reveal something he did not want to see; something that thrust his heart into his throat, for as sure as he stood living, the sunlight glinted reddish amid her honey-gold hair, and her chin tilted at that half-cocked, defiant angle, and her lashes raised— for she dared to brazenly meet the nobleman's gaze—and even across the room Conaire felt the blast of anger which had blazed off the cocoon to reveal the pith of the woman beneath.

Brigid.

"By Christ." Sir Guichard stumbled back, tripped upon the leg of his chair, and grasped its back to steady himself. His florid complexion paled, then flared with mottled color. "By Christ!"

Her body quaked, suddenly. Terror blossomed in her widening eyes, swamping the fury. Her lashes dropped, her shoulders collapsed in upon herself, and in the span of a moment, she'd burrowed back within a thick cocoon of fear.

"You told me nothing of *that*," the nobleman snarled, pointing straight-armed at her. "Not before you had me roped to this betrothal. Is she a devil's child?"

"Calm yourself, Sir Guichard." Monsieur Mézières moved out from beneath Deirdre's hand. "Your imagination is getting the best of you."

Damn foolish lass, Conaire thought, staring at such a sot as that—she knew better, she *knew* better, for a man saw the truth of his own soul when he looked into the eyes of a woman with the Sight, and Sir Guichard's soul was as black as tar. She'd get herself roasted for her foolishness; then Conaire realized that she felt she had nothing to lose: She was convinced she was damned already.

Because of *him.*

Damn the gods. Damn them. They'd trapped him into it. Fate's tenacious vines climbed up his body, sliced across his throat. *Have you nothing better to do than play peg-games with our lives?* He would have none of it—none of it—he'd not dance to their music—and the thought echoed in his mind as she raised her lashes again for no more than a fleeting moment, this time to probe the shadows near the stairs and then seize his gaze.

Once in his travels through the Far East, Conaire had tried to scale the snow-laden slope of a mountain whose jagged peaks pierced the clouds. Halfway up, a deafening crack like a thousand thunderbolts had knocked him to his knees. He had clawed the snow, searching for a grip, but the world buckled beneath him and he plunged into the ice-turned-powder, flailing and kicking as he spun down, down, weightless down the slope, while all the world dissolved into a suffocating, dizzy, white brightness.

"Listen to me, woman," Sir Guichard continued angrily, "think not to unman *me* with your witchery, or I'll have you before the bishop—"

"A marriage, Monsieur Mézèires, is out o' the question."

The words fell from Conaire's lips without thought, without planning.

"Not even you can restrain your tongue today." Monsieur Mézières threw his hands into the air. "Explain that outrageous remark immediately, doctor."

His tongue moved even as his mind screamed for it to stop. "She's not well."

"You speak foolishness." The burgher wagged his finger at his daughter. "Look at her—*Listen* to her."

Conaire could not look at her, with the faint sunlight playing amid her hair and a breeze toying with the hem of her cloak. She bowed her head, like one convicted and about to receive sentence. "You mistake the first flush o' health for health itself."

"I believe my eyes and my ears. She's well past ready for a wedding." The burgher's feet scraped against the thickly scattered rushes as he paced with uncharacteristic anxiety. "I am an old man. I want grandsons to carry on after me."

Conaire felt her gaze suddenly upon him, hot, curious, questioning . . . torn between terror and hope. He hardened his heart against it. "Heed me well, Mézières: No strong sons were ever born of a weak woman's womb."

The arrow found its mark. The burgher stilled. He narrowed his eyes and met Conaire's gaze from across the room, holding it for a long time.

"Papa," she began, "it's true that I feel poorly—"

"Silence." The burgher paced toward Conaire, then stopped in front of him, his tight nostrils flaring. "You told me yourself that your work here was done."

"She doesn't need me to convalesce."

"A convalescence? Is that all she needs?"

"Tie her to the rood screen and shave a cross into her head," the nobleman slurred, glancing uneasily at his intended bride. "That will cure her."

"Stop babbling, Sir Guichard, really—you sound like a superstitious peasant." The burgher plucked at the fur on the shoulder of his surcoat, still eyeing Conaire. "You have a manor house in the countryside, Sir Guichard, your ancestral home."

"What of it?"

"I cannot leave Troyes during the fair, but your mother lives there, and she has a reputation as a good, pious woman. She will be a ideal chaperone for a short convalescence." The burgher did not turn to see the nobleman's shrug and grunt of assent, still riveting Conaire with his gaze. "And you, doctor? Do you enjoy the fresh air of the countryside?"

"No." The word bellowed out of him. "I'll be no wetnurse to the lass—"

"I insist." The burgher's cloud of orange scent quavered like a threat. "Think of it as a compliment to your skill. Since only *you* can see she's still ailing, only *you* can tell me when she's well." The burgher swiveled away. "Now, Sir Guichard, you must see to it that your mother is forewarned . . ."

Conaire stood as still as stone, while the burgher barked for servants and made arrangements for the voyage. Deirdre, dismissed with her father's fierce reprimands smarting in her ears, lowered her head and fled toward the stairs. As she passed Conaire, she blindly brushed her fingers against his wrist. 'Twas a fleeting touch, no more than a brush of their skins . . . no heavier than a twined bracelet of foxglove blossoms.

Suddenly, through the open window, high, high above the raucous clamor of the fair, Conaire heard the drift of a reedy melody. It was a mocking music, a taunting air . . . the Otherworldly lilt of a fairy wind blowing through willow reeds.

Fifteen

"Come, come, my little pet." Deirdre twitched a thread in front of a sleek black cat crouched at her feet, teasing him with a bouncing ball of wool. "It's no secret that you're choking with impatience."

The cat's muscles bunched. With a flick of her wrist, Deirdre made the wool jump. The cat leapt back, uncertain, its back arched and its black eyes bright and wary. Then it crouched belly down in the dew-laden grass, ears perked, watching.

She flickered the bit of wool over his head. "Don't you want it, *maoineach,* my precious?"

The cat shot up on its hind legs and cuffed it. He tumbled on his back, then twisted his sleek body to all fours to bound up again in pursuit of the elusive ball. Deirdre twirled in a little circle around him, her laughter riding on the gentle summer breeze.

"Silly little cat." She dipped down and scratched the pet behind its pointed ears. "Since you were a wee, wounded little kitten, we've been playing this game. A body'd think you'd have the sense to know by now that it's not a mouse."

Her fingers stilled in the creature's glossy pelt. The sun slanted down through a break in the greenery, to pool in the little clearing she'd discovered in the midst of the Clunel garden. Though the gentle rays warmed her hair, a cold prickling seized the back of her neck.

She glanced up and saw him—*him*—striding through the

shadows of the manor house. Her breath caught, for by some trick of sunlight and early morning dew, gold glistened around his neck and arms, like the jewelry of some barbaric warrior. But then the harshness of daylight poured over him, and dissolved the illusion.

Och, it was no wonder she was seeing things, with her mind churning over and over these past days until there wasn't a single thought left whole in her head. And all a-cause of *him,* who'd accused her of the worst witchery, then said no more of it. Aye, not another word, though he'd had opportunity enough during the few terse conversations they'd had in the past days. And atop it all, here they were, in Champagne—all because he'd chosen to interfere in her father's wishes and save her from a hasty marriage to a drunken brute.

For her. Only for her. And she couldn't on her life figure out the why of it.

She rose to greet him. Her heart tripped a little as he approached, for he wore no surcoat; only the thinnest of linen tunics. A length of blue cloth was slung over his shoulder, tugging aside the neckline of his tunic to reveal the strong jut of his collarbone.

She smoothed her hands over her yellow linen surcoat. "Good morning to ye, doctor. A fine, soft morning it is."

He stopped suddenly and blinked, as if the sun blinded him. He cast his gaze around the clearing. "Where's Octavius?"

She cocked a brow at him. "I'm doing very well, thank you."

He gestured towards the thickening woods. "Does he think to escape me in this forest, the lazy sluggard?"

She tossed the ball of wool into the sewing basket by her feet, only to have the basket tip when her cat lunged at it. As foolish as her own pet, she was, expecting anything but rudeness from this brute of a man. All her kind words would be wasted on him when he was in such a fit.

"Och, you've the sun in your eyes." She swiveled down into

a pool of yellow skirts. "There's been nary a soul through this garden since early morn."

"None o' your mischief, woman."

"Och, still so quick to turn to temper, are ye?" She snatched the altar cloth she'd been embroidering and dropped it on her lap. "I'd have seen him if he'd been here, for unlike his master, Octavius is not one to pass by without a 'good day to ye.' "

Without another word he strode on deeper into the weed-choked garden. She glared after his broad back until the lush green woods swallowed him in shadow. Och, impossible, he was, like a ball of needles, there was no reasoning with a man like that, and to think she'd set out to win him over on this fine, glorious morning. She'd done everything she could to seem inviting, even spreading her cloak upon the ground like a carpet of buttercups. She'd even worn the matching butter-yellow surcoat and her belt of silver bells; and she'd knotted a few into the unbound length of her hair.

She glanced up moments later when she heard his boots crackling through the grass.

"In league with my servant, are you, woman?" He slung the length of blue cloth over his other shoulder. A sweatstain marked a trail down his chest, where the wool had lain. "He'll find himself picking pockets on the streets o' Troyes again."

"I don't doubt you'll beat him sure when you find him, but he's not hiding behind me skirts, I'll tell you that."

"The creature just disappeared into the air, then?"

"If Moira were here," she retorted, pouring a length of thread through the altar cloth, "she'd whisper it was the little people making mischief with ye."

With an angry grunt, he turned and thrashed through the weeds, then halted abruptly to glare at her. "Where is your maidservant?"

"Moira was summoned back to Troyes this morning." She

jabbed the linen anew. "Papa has guests in the house, and he needs her more than I."

A slight heat worked up her neck. She had come to this manor house expecting a fleet of servants and a house with enough room to sleep them all, not this sagging, crooked little building no better than a peasant's hovel, with no hostess but a disgruntled noblewoman, and certainly not a single servant idle enough to play watchman when she was alone with the doctor. Yet when Moira received the summons this morning, Deirdre had allowed her to leave—thus leaving herself, for all intents, completely unchaperoned.

Just as she'd secretly wished.

"Come." He held out his hand and curled his fingers regally. "You'll not be sitting here, with ruffians abounding through these woods."

She clucked her tongue. "Aren't you a thundercloud on a glorious day?"

"Two days ago a merchant caravan leaving Troyes was set upon by thieves, less than a half-day's ride up the very road which passes by this house. Two o' the men were killed."

She'd heard the story. Set upon at twilight, as they passed through the dense woods, so it was told. Disemboweled and left bleeding by the side of the road. She'd heard a thousand stories like it all through her youth, tales of wolves and monsters and wicked men, stories to keep her firm abed after the light was doused.

She believed not a word of it.

"For a convent-bred lass," he growled, "you've no sense at all. This is no place for a woman alone."

"I've you, doctor, you're chaperone enough, with you spitting and snarling like you slept on a bed of nails." She wrinkled her nose at the manor house. "And I've no liking to be trapped in that musty old hovel, with Madame de Clunel peering out from behind her door, as if I were a rat to be chased out by the cats. I'll be staying here, thank you very much."

His words came out as an angry growl. "Still as stubborn as ever."

"I would not spend a glorious day like this in the finest castle in Champagne." She swept her embroidery aside and rose to her feet with a jangle. "And what is it that's got your *braies* all twisted this morning?" Her gaze fell upon the swath of dark blue wool. Before he could stop her, she snatched it off his shoulder. "Was this for your servant, perhaps?"

He reached for it, lightning-quick, but got nothing but a fistful of air.

She snapped out the cloth and found a tear near the seam. "Is this the problem, then? You surprise me, doctor. With all your travels, I'd think you'd know how to wield a needle and thread as well as any wife."

"It's none o' your affair."

"Is it your pride, then? No pinpricks will be found on the fingers of Doctor MacSidh? Well, I'll do it for you. My fingers can sew better than any man's."

"I've no need o' your services—"

"I'm thinking you do, since you've lost sight of your man." She settled down in her skirts and shooed the cat away, then poked in her basket for thread to match the cloth. "It will take me but a moment—"

"So the heiress of Mézières will set to mending the tunic of a *common* doctor."

"Och, listen to you, shamelessly twisting me own words." She pinched out a length of thread, turning her face away so he could not see the flush of shame on her cheeks. It had been arrogant of her, to mention their differences so, the other day in her room. But he *had* taunted her into it. "Can you not forgive a lass for a slip of the tongue, while she's in a temper?"

"It was the truth you spoke. I've no liking to take crumbs from the queen's table."

"Och, listen to you, all puffed up with pride." She jabbed the needle into the cloth and dropped it on her lap. "If you'll not be accepting a simple act of kindness, then you'll pay for me work."

"I'll find my man before I bargain with you, woman."

"I'm not going to bargain with you like a common fishwife. My price is your company. For the length of time it takes for me to sew the tunic."

She could not tell if it were the trick of sunlight passing through the dappling of the canopy of leaves, or if his face grew mottled at the thought.

Och, this doctor could spit and snarl all he liked—she wasn't done with him, not yet, nay not in the least. It was looking to be a long stay in the countryside, and it'd been too much time since she'd heard of what passed at the Provins fair, or at the court in Paris while King Louis was on his Crusade, or in all the other places that had felt the tread of this man's feet. If nothing else, she'd suck dry the last bit of this doctor's knowledge of the world, and to the devil with all his blustering.

Besides . . . after what he did in Troyes, she knew she had naught to fear from him, even if he did stand staring at her right now, as puckered as if he'd drunk a bowl of four-day-old milk.

"Is it such a labor," she asked, jabbing the cloth, "whiling away a morning in me company?"

"I've no tongue for meaningless pleasantries."

"Don't I know that well enough?" She pooled the thread through the first stitch. "Well, then, you're a brawny sort, doctor. I'm sure we can be after finding some use for you here. Would you rather set to the thatching? The house needs it, I'm thinking. Poor work, this thatching. It won't even keep out the sun—"

"I won't do your bidding, woman, not this time."

Anger, volcanic and barely contained. It rumbled amid the

rustling leaves, in the swift, hot gust of wind which riffled the hem of her gown. But she knew that his anger was just that; hot air and no substance.

"Och, 'tis true, then. Honest sweat won't be found on the brow of Doctor MacSidh, it won't. Very well, then, you must stay, though it's a meager price indeed for me labors." She slanted him a glance. "Even a surly brute of a doctor is preferable for company than the few sullen peasants who run this house."

He stood stiff and awkward on the edge of the clearing, all strained muscles and tight fists, like a mighty buck ready to fight, but poised nonetheless for flight. She sensed his gaze upon the spread of a brilliant yellow blanket, at the tipped sewing basket by her side, the cat wrestling with a frayed ball of wool, resting with growing intensity on the game board carefully laid out in the middle of the blanket.

She tipped her head toward the chipped wooden pieces as she made another stitch. "I found it in a chest at the end of my bed. Worse for wear, like most of this wretched manor house, but all the pieces are there. Do you play chess?"

His hands, she noticed, had curled into fists.

"Chess."

"Aye. Surely a man of your learning knows the lay of the board.

He jerked away, toward the manor house. "I know the way of it."

"It's been many a moon since my brother and I played. My palms have been itching for someone to challenge—"

"Find another to play your games."

Her hands fell in exasperation upon her lap. "Is there no softening to you, doctor? What must a woman do to cool your spitting anger?"

"Leave me be."

"Very well." She picked up the tunic again and set to piercing the wool with another stitch. "We shall divide up the manor house, then. Shall you take the left side of the main room, and me the right? Or shall you eat your meals under the eaves where you sleep, on a pile of hay, whilst I'll stay within my stuffy old room with the broken shutters—"

"Have you not done with the tunic yet?"

"Three stitches I've done! A watched pot never boils, it doesn't." Not that he'd been watching her; he'd done everything in his power not to lay eyes upon her since he entered the clearing. He prowled a circle of grass flat, like a creature trampling his bed for the night. His head swiveled constantly toward the manor house, once or twice turning angrily into the depths of the woods. But his gaze skittered over her, swift and careless.

She winced as the needle pierced her skin. "It will be a long stay in the country," she muttered, examining the bead of blood oozing from her fingertip, "with none but surly peasants and a boorish doctor to keep me company."

"You'll be gone by Lughnasa—and so will I."

She jerked at the word *Lughnasa,* for it brought with it the memory of a warm summer day with bees lazily swirling in the air, of distant sea-salt spray and the hum of Irish sunlight. Ten years, it had been . . . She, Mama, and Jean-Jacques used to pick bilberries in the woods on Lughnasa, surreptitiously eating them until the juice stained their teeth and ran sticky down their chins. And there were fires deep in the forest at night that the priests frowned upon, and Mama would not let her attend for her youth—though Mama herself would slip away when she thought Deirdre was sleeping, ambling home in the dawn with brambles in her hair and the flush of sunrise on her cheek . . .

Och, had it been ten years since she'd breathed the sweet air of Ireland?

Deirdre absently sucked the drop of blood off her finger and pressed the wound against her saffron cloak. "It's been so long since I've celebrated Lughnasa, that I no longer know the roll of the Irish year. When is it now?"

"Four days."

"Four!" She seized the needle anew. "So quick to be rid of me, are ye? It's a wonder you insisted on a convalescence at all."

"It's a question I ask o' myself each morn, when you mock me with your own health."

She jabbed the needle through the cloth and yanked the thread through. Och, truth be known, there was no understanding a man's mind. Aye, she'd little practice in the ways of men and women within the confines of the convent, except what she'd overheard between the girls and their friends' brothers in the common room on occasional afternoons, but certainly she wasn't so daft as to mistake her own eyes! It was this doctor, not herself, who'd insisted upon this convalescence—and at no profit to himself. Yet here he stood before her, gruffly denying there was anything more to his actions two days ago, when she knew well enough there was.

Bluster, she reminded herself; it was all bluster. She remembered too well the look in his eyes after Sir Guichard's words, when the doctor had come to her defense and lied to save her from a hasty marriage—all while knowing the pith of her. No man risked the good will of his patron without reason. And now, alone with her, he covered his awkwardness with bluster and gruffness.

"Whatever the reason," she said, "I thank ye for it. Papa will change his mind about the marriage for sure, when he comes and sees the great estate of the Lord of Clunel, and knows for truth the worth of the title."

He braced one hand against an oak and spoke toward the woods beyond the perimeter of the garden. "Sir Guichard will make a fine husband."

She did not bother to stifle her snort of disbelief.

"He's bitter," he insisted. "He'll come to his senses with age."

"All the world couldn't make a racehorse of an ass." She tossed her hair with a jingle of bells. "I'll not marry that sot. When the right man comes, I'll marry *him.*"

He pushed himself away from the tree. "Don't be living in dreams, woman."

The word writhed in the silence between them, as she made the last stitch in the tunic with a trembling hand.

"There. I've done with it." She snapped out the tunic as she rose swiftly to her feet. "Better than what that strange little servant of yours can do, I'll be thinking, though he's had enough practice, by the look of his own rags." She gathered the cloth over her arm and approached him, her feet light on the spongy carpet of grass. "It will be a small thanks," she said, thrusting it at him, "for all that you've done for me."

He snatched the tunic and tossed it over his shoulder without a glance. "Your father pays my fee; I need no thanks for doctoring."

"Och, you've a head made of stone." She reached out to smooth the blue wool; he twisted away and left her hand suspended between them. "You know that's not of what I spoke."

She raised her gaze to his face, to the square, sculpted jaw, to the angry tucker of a muscle in his stubbled cheek. Then, with a deep, indrawn breath, she dared what she'd done once before: she raised her gaze higher, until their eyes locked.

A tingling rush filled her blood. Aye, he knew of what she spoke, there was no doubt about it. The fury emanated from him again, that unexplainable rage. He stomped away only to stomp back and glare at her so close, she felt the heat of his breath on her head. Yet, despite the angry trembling of his muscles, the piercing heat of his gaze, she felt no fear before him. Somehow, *somehow* she knew now what she'd known all along: He would not hurt her. Somehow she knew, staring into those turbulent gray eyes, that what he fought was himself.

"Did you think," he snarled, flexing his hands to grasp her

shoulders, only to curl them into fists by his sides instead, "that I would send an innocent to the pyres for the 'crime' of being born with the gift of Sight?"

Gift of Sight. She took a deep, trembling breath spiced with the scent of man and anger. *So it has a name.* No man nor woman had ever called her visions a gift. She had never dared think of them as anything but curses.

Nay, that was not entirely true . . . She vaguely remembered a time, when she was young, when she thought everyone had these foggy midday dreams, and she'd thought nothing more of it—a time in Ireland, before Papa had come to take her, Jean-Jacques, and Mama away. Aye, it wasn't until the exorcism that she'd thought otherwise . . . then, she'd spent her days fighting the visions away, only to have them come to her, stronger and more vivid, in her sleep. That she could never stop, though she'd prayed until her throat was raw, to any saint who'd listen.

Och, and here stood a man who called her visions a gift, not a curse; here stood a man who *understood.* She curled her hand around his knotted forearm, as tears surged in her eyes. Words she had never dared to speak bubbled in her throat, like a swollen river threatening to lurch over its banks.

"You can't change your nature, woman, no matter what foolishness the ignorant tell you." He snatched his forearm from beneath her grip so swiftly that her nails scraped deep into his skin. "So don't be after trying. And don't be starin' at me with those calf's-eyes o' yours—I've told you nothing but a bit o' common sense."

He swaggered away from her, yanked off his belt, and stretched into his tunic, all the while rolling his shoulders as if he, too, felt the bonds growing between them, as if he wanted no more than to shake them off and escape.

Bluster, she thought. *All bluster.*

"You can argue all you want, Conaire. Aye, aye, I know your Christian name, I heard Octavius speak it." She followed him, relentlessly, stopping to stand only inches from him, close enough for her breath to ripple the soft cloth of his tunic, close enough to see the emotions warring in his eyes.

"I'm thinking," she whispered, the air suddenly hot and thin between them, "that despite all his roaring, the lion has the heart of a lamb."

Why? Why? Why?

Conaire heaved the axe over his head and hurled it down upon a log teetering on a stump. With a resounding crack, the thick wood snapped in two. The sections hurtled apart, only to skid through a rug of wood chips and sawdust until they clattered to a halt. Octavius stumbled through the slippery refuse to retrieve and stack the firewood, cursing and racing out of range as Conaire ruthlessly set another log upright upon the stump.

Why? Why? Why?

The sky echoed the crack of the wood with a growling roar of thunder. Conaire paused long enough to blindly fist the tunic he'd long torn off his sweaty back. He swiped his dripping face with the stained wool, to sop up the salty rivulets of sweat stinging his eyes. Then he threw the garment *she'd* mended this morning back across the growing pile of wood.

Damn foolish woman, staring at him as if he were her only hope of redemption, staring at him with a face glowing with hope—damn it—with *hope,* when he could give her none— when there was none.

Crack.

He yanked the blade out of the deep furrow in the stump. His head had grown as soft as porridge in this place. Even now, the cinnamon scent of fresh-cut oak inflamed his senses, rippling memories he'd thought long dead. All of it—the strong perfume of old woods; the slant of light through summer leaves; the buzz of summer insects—the sounds, smells, tastes, and textures of these wretched woods intoxicated him more thoroughly than any opiate he'd ever come across in the Far East.

Give him the stinking anonymity of a city—any city—over *this*.

He seized the rough bark of another segment of oak, and planted it on the wide, level stump. He'd ordered the woodcutter off to his cottage hours ago, when the storm had been nothing but a ribbon of tartness on the wind and a few reedy gray clouds; yet still Conaire chopped, though the pile had long topped the edge of the thatch. He needed to sweat off the fire in his blood.

For the first time in more years than he cared to count, his blood coursed swift and demanding through his veins; his palms tingled for the feel of a woman's flesh; a heaviness settled in his loins just at the thought o' her. That's what was defeating him the most—the basic desire for the touch of human flesh, for the touch of *her* flesh—the passion of having her again, of feeling her throbbing and warm and human beneath him. To lay with her again—

Crack.

A sputtering of raindrops sizzled in the clearing, darkening circles upon the layer of fresh wood chips. The scent o' this place, the clean wind . . . it softened him, opened his mind to possibilities. Too often, damn the gods, even *now,* he found himself wondering if a few decades of loving might be worth seven hundred more years of agony—

No.

Madness, those thoughts . . . worthless little dreams that would twist into nightmares in the blink of an eye. What did it matter now, if he thought he could bear the pain? His life was not the only life which would be destroyed. Now, he had to think of *her* welfare.

He had to save *her.*

For he'd seen the signs tumbling upon one another, the parallels that could not be simply coincidence. Aye, every moment that passed drew him deeper and deeper into that other life.

Deirdre was the daughter of her father's second wife—as was Brigid. Deirdre's mother died young—as did Brigid's. Both had a brother who died, and his death was the event which led Conaire to each. The parallels continued: A banishment—one into the woods, the other into a convent . . . a father's reconciliation after the loss of his heir . . . their isolation here in the woods . . . the coming of Lughnasa . . . chess—aye, even that wretched mockery of *fidchell.*

Conaire slammed another log upon the stump and hurled his axe through it. Lightning sliced open the sky and limned the world silver. Rain sluiced down the long-dried riverbed of his face. The wood split to the crack of thunder, and the two halves hurled in opposite directions.

Do you take pleasure, gods, in watching a man's soul bleed? Do you take pleasure in grinding a woman's spirit to its nub?

He would not do it to her, he *could not* let her relive the betrayal, the loss, the wrenching agony of that lonely existence all over again.

For it was all the same, it would all *be* the same, from the first innocent, flirtatious laugh to the last agonizing blow . . . every wretched moment relived, the good and the bad.

History was repeating itself.

Crack.

Why? Why? Why?

Deirdre threaded the fine strand of linen through her pinched fingers, then licked the tip. Her wrist cracked with stiffness and cold, as she tugged the strand taut through a flashing silver needle. She shrugged deeper into her cloak and squinted over her work.

She snuggled her toes up to the very edge of the fire crackling in the smoke-blackened fireplace, but no matter how close she came, she could not dispel the chill, musty damp that permeated her bones, and instead was forced to breathe in lungfuls of soot from a chimney which had undoubtedly not felt the bristles of a sweep's broom in a generation.

She jerked in her seat as one of the servants clattered the dirty dishes off the warped trestle tables. She glared at the sullen peasant, who ignored her as she none-so-gently replaced the mismatched plates upon the split planks of the cupboard, dodging the dented pots scattered about the floor to collect the rainwater pitter-patting from the ceiling.

At some point in time, the Clunel manor house must have been a fine residence for the noble family, with its broad-beamed hall and large fireplace, but that time had long passed. Now, no wall hangings hid the great dark stains that marred the walls where water had done its damage over the years. The trestle table upon which they ate—with bent tin implements—was bare of cloth and riddled with childish carvings, and she had spent her first night curled up on the rushes wrapped in her own cloak, while a reticent, grumbling servant doused the lumpy mattress with a pungent ointment to kill the fleas that infested the straw.

In this cauldron of mustiness she'd been imprisoned for three days, while rain poured from the skies of Champagne. She paced endlessly across the floor, snapped at the lazy servants, and flayed several with the sharp edge of her tongue, contemplated doing the same to the oft-infirm Lady Clunel who had yet to descend from her room to introduce herself formally, and considered returning in indignity to Troyes.

But she did nothing.

For every nerve in her body thrummed with a buzzing anticipation. Uncertain excitement shimmered in the air, tremors vibrated in the earth beneath her feet. The very air she breathed sizzled through her blood and set her skin tingling. Everything had changed since those moments with Conaire in the clearing of the garden—*everything*.

Heat swelled like the tide within her to burn the tips of her

ears. She glanced from beneath her lashes at him sitting on the
floor on the opposite side of the hearth, his face limned by the
firelight, seemingly oblivious to the activity around him, his
nose deep in a battered book he'd retrieved from his pack. He
claimed that only the distaste of the soggy wet pallet waiting for
him under the eaves of the upper floor kept him here in the main
room. For three days he'd been as sullen, distant, and brooding
as a monk.

But he'd turned not a single page since dinner.

She lowered her head over her work and set her mind back
to the sewing. Foolish, she was, wanting what couldn't be. It
was dangerous to trust him. He *knew.* He held her life in his
hands. He still could be after destroying her, despite his kindness, despite the look of utter despair which had flashed in his
eyes that day in the garden, before he'd turned away and marched
back to the manor house. She might be doing nothing more than
weavin' girlish fancies out of hope and desperation.

Yet every time their gazes met, her bones softened like beeswax left in the midsummer sun. Och, he had no right to stare
through her with those clear gray eyes, intense and raging with
some emotion she did not fully understand—some emotion
which found a mate deep within her heart. He had no right to
send her senses spinning wildly out of control. He made her
yearn for things she never dared to hope for—a man who would
understand her, a place she could truly call home.

And so she fluxed, constantly, between hope and terror.

"Och, I've had enough of this." She swept a cloud of sheer
fabric off her lap and dumped it into the sewing basket at her
feet. "I'll go blind if I do another stitch, I will. I'll have no more
of it."

Octavius, Conaire's manservant, started from where he
snoozed on a rare spot on the floor whose rushes were still dry.

"Have we nothing better to do here, than go mad listening to
the rain?" She rose from her seat, and clutched her mantle tight

around her as she paced before the fire. "Juggle for me, Octavius. Or dance, as you did yesterday."

"On a half bowl o' soup and a bit o' hare meat?" Octavius eased himself up. "I've no strength in me, lass, to be bouncing about, and me limbs are fair sore from yesterday's work."

"Aye, and well they should be," Conaire interjected, "for jumping up and down like a man crazed, and all for the fancy of a maiden."

"Listen to you! 'Tis ye who should be seein' to the lady's needs, not I." Octavius winked at her and jerked his bristled chin at him. "Now there's a man who could crush the rushes with his footwork, if he set his mind to it."

"Och, in your dreamin' mind." She plucked at the threads of her cloak, as she sidled Conaire a glance. "He has no likin' for dancing, don't I know that well enough."

His gaze flickered over the edge of the book, hot and intense and utterly unreadable.

"Chess, then," she suggested. She snapped her fingers toward the stairs. "Aye, the set is worse for wear, but you told me, Doctor MacSidh, that you knew the way of it—"

"I've no patience for the game."

"Just a ray of sunshine, you are, Conaire, breakin' through the clouds." She whirled to Octavius and raised a brow. "Well, Octavius? Will ye take up the challenge?"

"Nay, lass, I know naught o' those fancy peg-games. Now if you had a pair o' dice . . ."

"No singing and no dancing and no games." She threw up her hands in exasperation. "I may as well be sittin' in me cell in the convent."

Conaire scraped over a page in the ringing silence.

"If ye please, lass," Octavius said, "for the price of a bit o' your string, I could be after telling ye a story."

"Ah, a story then!" She swept her cloak off her shoulders in a flash of yellow, and fell back into her seat. She rifled through the cloud of fabric and found thread and scissors. "It's a sad day," she said, snipping a length of white thread, "when a servant must do the work of his master."

The scrape of another page punctuated her words.

Octavius took the string and settled before the fire, brushing away the rushes to sit one leg cocked and one leg curled under him. Resting his elbow on his knee, he dug the dirty butt of his hand into his temple and contemplated the rafters. "I've a hundred thousand tales whirlin' in me mind. Have ye any one favorite you wish to hear, lass?"

She remembered a time, long ago, when she and Jean-Jacques used to sit by the fire in their hamlet in Ireland, listening to the crackle of the wood, while Mama told a tale as she rocked and busied her fingers with sewing.

"Make it an old Irish story, Octavius. It's been a lifetime since I've heard one."

"Now, doesn't that do not a bit o' good? Is there any other kind o' tale, lass, but an Irish tale? None as proud and fine, I wager." Pinching the ends of the thread between his fingers, he slipped the length of it between his blackened teeth. His bright eyes flared. "Ahhhh. I've a tale for you." He yanked the thread out of his mouth. "I'll tell ye of your namesake. Deirdre. Deirdre o' the Sorrows and the three sons of Usnagh."

Octavius slipped the thread between his teeth again and mouthed it as he began.

"This happened a fine bit o' time ago, more time than a man can count. There was a king in Ireland, whose wife was heavy with child. Pagans, they were, as were all the men o' the day. So they called in a Druid to lay his hands upon the woman's belly to tell about the child within, though it seems to me a strange way to go about the thing. The Druid had no liking for what he saw, there was no mistakin' that." Octavius leaned forward into the light of the fire, his eyes wide. "A girl, he told them, a girl so fine that no other so beautiful had ever walked the earth. And on account o' her, all the rivers of Ireland would run red with blood."

At Octavius's hushed words, the servants ceased their clattering of plates. They hovered near the door which led to the kitchen, ears cocked. A silence hushed over the room, but for the pattering of seeping rainwater and the occasional crackle of the fire. Octavius, oddly still, his eyes fixed on the hearth, idly wound the thread Deirdre had given him around his fingers.

"Let there be no mistaking, many men called for the babe to be killed the moment she was born—which didn't happen, of course, for then there'd be no story. The wife pleaded so piteously, you see, that they called upon the greatest king in all the land for advice—King MacNessa was his name." Octavius straightened up to glare at Conaire. "Aren't ye goin' to listen, man? There's a lesson in here for you."

Conaire scowled wordlessly and turned another page.

"Well, then, that king I was after tellin' ye about, he was a sly and greedy one. He said he'd become the girl's guardian, and he'd marry the lass when she came of age, which wasn't much of a burden, I'm thinking, with she being promised to be the fairest woman in all of Ireland. It's a bargain I think you'd not take too well to, would ye, Conaire? Aye, but you're listening, don't I know, with one ear half-cocked.

"So the babe was born in the course o' time, and sent off to be raised far from the world. And, oh, lass," Octavius breathed, squinting an eye at her, "as she grew, she became near as fair as ye."

"Och, Octavius, you won't get any more wine in your cup by talkin' that way to me."

"But it's the truth, lass! Fair beyond words, she was, but lonely, oh so lonely in the place where she was forced to live. She knew no one but her devoted maidservant, and it goes without sayin' that she ached for more, being a strong and lusty girl.

"Now Deirdre had a meddler of a maidservant, she did, who

loved her, but was the cause of all the trouble, truth be told. She knew a man she thought Deirdre would want, a bold, young warrior in the king's court. An Ulsterman."

Out of the corner of her eye, Deirdre saw Conaire drop his book upon his lap.

"With a bit o' work, the maidservant arranged that the two should meet in the woods near where Deirdre lived; and there's no doubt 'twas love at first sight.

"Now Naoise—the young Ulsterman—knew that the king was powerful and jealous, so he packed up and took Deirdre to Scotland, where the wrath of the king could not touch them; but the king was a proud sort, full o' himself, and no ocean would come between him and his vengeance. He sent a messenger to Naoise, and promised him the world, no less—a full pardon for Naoise's crimes, can ye believe it? Not even an afternoon on the pillory for him.

"But Deirdre had a rare and wonderful gift, as sure as skill in spinning or weaving or telling tales. The night before the king's messenger arrived in Scotland, Deirdre dreamed of Naoise's death. The next day, she begged her lover not to accept the king's pardon, for she knew 'twas the vilest treachery."

The hairs on the nape of her neck rose. Deirdre glanced at Conaire, but he did not even look her way. Strangely animated, he leaned forward, his gaze fierce upon Octavius.

"But 'tis sure no one paid any attention to the lass, calling it the devil's work, or whatnot. Naoise pined for his blessed Ireland, and he'd not give up the fool's gold offered him a-cause of a woman's dream. And 'tis sure that as soon as he stepped upon Irish soil, he was captured and put to death." Octavius sucked anew upon the thread. " 'Tis said that Deirdre, weeping, had to be dragged off her lover's dead body."

A log tumbled from the andiron and crashed into the flames with a shower of sparks. With the flaring came an odd glow; a silvery light, like she'd never seen from burning wood. But it was as if she had no strength to turn her head and look into the mouth of the fireplace and see what caused such an unusual gleam. She thought she must be growing drowsy, for a sifting haze fell over her sight, and the rest of the room receded into shadow. Octavius's voice echoed, as if he spoke beneath a great arching dome, rather than in the squat, broad-beamed hall of the Clunel manor house.

"Ye see," Octavius continued, "the king had his prize, but now she was called Deirdre of the Sorrows, for she spent her time a-wailing and a-keening o'er the death of her one true love. It did not take long before the king could bear it no longer, and he sent her away. That very day, she dashed herself headlong from her chariot and died."

Odd, Deirdre thought. There seemed to be something sparkling around Octavius's grease-splattered beard, and the same sparkling flashed about his head and feet.

"Don't leave it at that," she said, shaking her head to try to rid herself of the foggy lethargy. " 'Twas a happy ending to the tale when me Ma told it."

"Aye, of a sort."

Octavius stretched out the thread between his two fingers, and raised it for all to see.

"Out of Deirdre's grave grew a great yew tree. The branches twined and spread across the wide countryside," he said, winding one end toward the other, "until they found the branches of another yew, which had grown from the grave of Naoise." He raised the opposite end of the string. "The branches meshed and entwined like two hands coming together, and in the end Naoise and Deirdre were one."

Octavius rolled the string between his fingers.

"For 'twas the way of the ancient Irish: Though a body dies, a soul does not. Souls are reborn again, and again, and each lifetime a soul seeks out those it loves, forever searching, like the branches of the yew tree, for its mate." He snapped out the string, tied end to end in a perfect circle. "There is no rest for a weary soul, until the circle is complete."

Conaire's book clattered off his lap. He towered to his full height. By some trick of the shadow, his hair looked as black as pitch, his skin as pale as sun-bleached linen, with two spots of color burning high on his cheekbones. He glared at Octavius, who smiled with mischief.

"I'll have a word with you, Octavius." Conaire strode out of the room. "Upstairs."

Octavius tucked the string away. He rolled with a jaunty little bounce to his feet, and the strange gleaming scattered away.

Octavius winked at her with a grin. "Seems I'm after getting a bit of a talkin'-to."

Then he pranced up the stairs, his laughter trailing after him.

Sixteen

"Where's Octavius?"

Deirdre whirled with a start. Sunlight flashed on the shimmering circlet across her brow, the only tether to her golden waterfall of hair.

"Must you do that?" Her scarlet surcoat, trimmed with gold braid, stretched taut across her breasts as she lifted her hands to her hips. "Can you not even manage a 'good day to ye,' before you go frightening a lass out of her wits?"

"Are you hiding him again then?" Conaire scanned the ill-fitted masonry of the manor house, then the weed-choked garden, anywhere to avoid looking at the blinding light of her in the Lughnasa morning. "The cook said you'd found him."

"Aye, he was here not a moment ago, but it's glad I am he smelled your anger and went on his way."

Conaire clamped down on his rage. Did he expect the creature to do his bidding? Nay, not now, never now, that Conaire knew the truth. Now the mischievous imp would scurry about and hide from him, taunt him from afar and leave nothing but mocking laughter in his wake.

"He'll not be groveling at your feet." She hefted a basket nestled in the weeds into the crook of her elbow. "It's a wonder he's not off to find another master, after the beating ye gave him last night—"

"Is that the story he's spreading?"

"I expected better of you, Conaire, than to strike a poor unfortunate for doing nothing more than telling a story, pagan though it was."

"And I expected better of you, woman, to believe the tales of a lying thief."

"With his word against yours, 'tis his I'll be believing, with you always so full o' spit and fury."

Conaire suppressed a growl of anger as he swiveled in frustration, the tough spines of weeds crackling beneath his feet. He should have seized the creature by the neck when the chance was upon him, instead of waiting upstairs in the eaves for nothing but bodiless footsteps and secret tittering. Now, there was no knowing *why.*

And he'd not stand here any longer, so close to the pull and tug of *her.*

"I'm off to the woods, Conaire. If I'm not back by sundown, send a man to fetch me."

His attention shifted with fierce suddenness to Deirdre's swaying back, as she headed toward the far edge of the garden. "And what do you think you're doing, woman?"

"I told you clear enough."

"And what makes you think," he growled, following her since she made no attempt to slow her pace, "you can go off wandering alone in the forest like a fool?"

"And who in this place would dare to stop me? You, Conaire?" She waved a hand in the air, her words drifting back more softly as she retreated. "This could be *my* land some day, and I've a fancy to see the vineyards I'm told grow just beyond—"

"You're more likely to see one o' the poachers who steal the Clunel deer, or a pack o' ruffians workin' their way through the wilds to the Fair o' St. Jean."

He skidded to a stop as she glanced at him over her shoulder, all rosy-cheeked from the kiss o' the sun, all flying hair and knowing eyes. Her gaze impacted upon him like a blow to the chest. She looked more and more like Brigid each day, though her appearance had changed not one bit.

"Is it worried about me, ye are?"

He shook the thoughts from his head. "Your father would skin me alive, if you came to harm."

"Then, if you value your skin," she argued, stepping over a trough in the garden's stone fence which had long crumbled to the ground, "you'd best stay close to me skirts."

She dipped into the shadows, the fading crackle of litter beneath her feet and a vague humming wafting back to mock him as he stood amid the weeds.

Blasted woman. He'd forgotten the bold way she'd state something, then go about it with a never-you-mind. The fool lass had a better sense o' self-preservation seven centuries ago. The influence o' the cloisters, no doubt, leaving her full o' stubbornness, with not a wit o' common sense. And now he stood, knowing he had no choice than to go after her, wondering if he'd grown soft with the years, to follow her smallest whim and lope after her like a pup—or, more fitting, like a lamb to slaughter.

Not today.

Today was Lughnasa, and she could go to her devil. He glared at the leaves swaying from her passing, until they creaked to a stop. Her humming faded into the rustle of the wind. A gust rose behind him, and lay his tunic flat against his back. He stood still as stone, resisting, even as something unwound within him and furled deep into those woods, toward the woman prancing alone under the great arch of the trees.

No rest for the weary soul until the circle is complete.

Damn Octavius and his wretched riddles. Damn himself for paying heed to them, for reading into them whatever he wished. And damn himself for standing here, letting the Lughnasa tides lap over him, heating his blood until they boiled the reason from his mind.

Lead the horse to the well, if you must, he sneered at the sky. The trick is in making him drink.

He bent beneath the overhang of a twisted branch. The cool salt-sweet womb of the woods closed over him. Honeysuckle and rainwater swirled rich, and a buzzing began around his ears—a familiar swarming that raised not a bit o' dust.

His feet stumbled upon the path. A splash of sunshine buttered the way, at the end of which he glimpsed a flash of her white undertunic as she kicked fleet-footed up a winding path. An edgy breeze gusted from the earth, and tugged and plucked at his clothes. High in the oaks the leaves rustled with life, and saplings nodded at him like wizened old men.

Time lost meaning in this rustling world of deep green shadows and gauzy light. A branch nodded against his thigh and he thought it his sword, as much a part of him as the heavy torque lying upon his throat, and the bold sweep of his *brat* slapping against his calves. Youth rushed through his blood and bones, the hard pumping of heart and lungs, the recklessness and the folly—a memory made real in this time of timelessness, new and old, full of mystery and full of knowledge.

The land began to slope upward. Clear fingers of hazy light poured down between the massive oak trees, and faded to a dusting of amber. Beyond, her shadow darted between the trees, quick and sure.

He found her standing atop the hill, on a smooth stretch of rock, warm under the full blaze of the sky. The gently sloping lands of Champagne rolled out to the horizon. Silver threads of river wound around patches of deep forest, plots of golden grain, and paler stretches of low-lying vineyard. Chalky gray houses pitted the countryside, and here and there the ochre spires of rural churches pierced the treetops.

"Och, 'twould be a fine place for a Lughnasa fire." She unhooked the basket from her elbow. "Don't you think so, Conaire?"

He suppressed his humorless snort. How predictable the gods, how lacking in imagination. "And you'd have me cut wood for your pyre, wouldn't you, woman?"

"Och, far be it for you to dirty your hands with a common man's work."

"A week away from the eye o' your confessor, and you turn pagan already."

"It was a fancy, no more." She strode to the shade of a tree and dropped the basket beneath it. "In any case, you've nothing but your ire to do the cuttin', though I've no doubt it's hot and sharp enough to slice wood."

"I'd do better using your tongue."

Something rustled on the edge of the forest. Nearby, a dull gleam caught his eye. He tore away the woodbine twisting between a yew and an oak sapling sprouting out of the same mound of earth. Clods of sod flew as he hefted up a rusted axe.

A gleam lit her eyes. "Och, a gift from the little people."

He stretched his fingers over the warm grip. "Is that more pagan nonsense I hear comin' from your mouth?"

"It's not pagan, it's not." She jerked her cloak off her shoulders and snapped it out. "The little people are angels, don't ye know."

"Angels."

She straightened the sweep of yellow cloth over the shady grass. Conaire willed himself to ignore the curving sweep of back and hip as she stretched to each corner.

"You've no business fillin' the word with so much scowling. It's the truth. Moira was after tellin' me, not so long ago, and she's as good a Christian as you'd find." She plumped a hip down on the cloth and began unloading the basket. "When Satan sinned, so the story goes, the angels divided up among themselves—between those who stood with him, and those who stood with God. But there were some who wanted nothin' to do with the battle, and so they stayed out of it. When Lucifer was tossed from Heaven with his minions, those angels had a punishment of their own: they were banished to the Earth. Of course, they were told on the Last Day they might be pardoned . . . but until then, they live among us to do their good, or their mischief, more often than not."

"Then we won't be disappointing them." He wrestled off his surcoat and threw it in a blue heap upon the ground, anger flaring within him. "Today, I'll give them a pyre to mock all o' Christendom."

He grasped the heavy-headed axe and heaved it around, hacking the blade into the wood, once, twice, thrice, until the oak snapped and thudded to the ground. *Is this what you want then, old gods o' mine? A tribute to forgotten deities, in a place that mocks your existence? Mayhap that is why you keep me here, on this earth; one last o' the faithful to do your bidding. One last o' the faithful to mock.*

The yew crashed to the earth, and golden light flooded deep into the forest. He tucked the saplings one under each arm and headed to the height of the rock, raking the earth behind him with their crowns. He tossed the wood across the open plain. As he snapped off bough after bough, slivers of wood flew and embedded themselves in his clothes, his skin, his hair. He bound the branches into bundles with their own stripped bark.

He felt her gaze upon him, wide-eyed, as he worked; he sensed her stillness. Power surged through his sweat-soaked body and pumped liquid force into his burning muscles. *Did you think me an old man, wife? Did you think time would rob the marrow from my bones?*

He tossed the bound branches aside and set to the other tree with fury. When it was denuded of boughs, he searched for the axe he'd tossed carelessly aside.

She thrust a flagon in his path. Her gaze flitted down to—and then swiftly up from—his chest running dark with sweat.

"It's hard work," she murmured, "tearing a tree limb from limb."

Grasping the flagon by the neck, he uptipped it and swilled

his fill of golden wine. Cool rivulets ran down his neck and drenched the sweat-dampened linen of his tunic.

"The nuns at the convent," she began, "oft punished me for my wretched tongue. Always taunting them, I was, always vexing them. One of them said that the devil lived at its root." She licked her lips. "I hope," she murmured, her gaze sliding to the carnage of the trees splattered over the hilltop, "that it wasn't me on your mind, when you set to this task with such fury."

A breeze slipped a tendril of white-gold hair across her mouth. She brushed it aside absently, her lashes dark against her stained cheeks.

The ice inside him cracked.

There was no explaining this. It was his rage against the gods which kept him snarling and angry; he harbored no hate for her—nay, nay, 'twas *love* for her that kept him here when he knew he should be far away; 'twas love for her that kept him from reaching out and tilting up her chin, from touching those lips—soft and full—and drowning in the salt-warmth of her kiss.

"Lass . . ." He strangled the neck of the flagon in his fist. "I'll not be after doing you any harm."

Her shoulders lifted and fell in an exaggerated sigh; she pressed her hand against her breast. " 'Tis glad I am o' that, Conaire MacSidh. For a doctor, you're a brawny sort. For a moment me mind was full of imaginings; that ye were a black-hearted knight, posing as a doctor to have your way with foolish young women."

He handed her the flagon, then reached down and hefted up the axe.

"Nay, Conaire."

Her soft, white hand fell upon his arm. How small her hand, how tender the flesh, how hot her touch.

"Leave it be now. Come into the shade." Her hand slipped off. She gathered her skirts and headed toward the blanket of her cloak. "It's sure I've food and wine enough for two . . . if you've the stomach to share it with me."

They ate in silence as they sat upon the sun-warmed wool, with thrushes warbling in the bushes and late summer bees buzzing idle swirls in the air. Deirdre broke off a piece of bread from a loaf still warm from the oven, and lazily chewed it as she watched Conaire from beneath lowered lashes.

She worked down the rising tide of a flush. Och, it was foolish she was, acting like a twittering, young girl, and all because he lay stretched out, his elbow sunk into the ground, draped in nothing but his undertunic. Sweaty and gritty, too, and smelling like heat and salt and something else disturbing and primitive.

It was glad, she was, that he lay so still and quiet. It was a fine change from the creature she'd watched moments ago, hacking away at the trees, his teeth bared, and sweat dripping off his face and splattering on the hot stony earth. Why hadn't she noticed before those bulging muscles, or the fine, brawny stretch of his shoulders, or the leanness of his waist? Worthy of a knight's mail, he was, and young enough to catch any lass's eye. Why hadn't she noticed before that not a gray hair streaked his head, that only the faintest fanning of lines edged his disturbing gray eyes? Others in the manor house, and in Troyes, as well, deferred to him like a man of much age. Yet laying as he was at his ease at the edge of her cloak, the collar of his tunic pulled to reveal a strong stretch of collarbone, he was a man at his youthful prime. She wondered why she and everyone else perceived him as a man older, wizened, grizzled, and battered more than a bit by the roll of time.

Around them danced a breeze, which kissed their cheeks with coolness. She felt it slip through her, whirling up strange, new emotions in the still places in her heart. She placed before him a bowl of new berries with sweet clotted cream. He ate the wild fruit slowly, sparsely, without comment. Aye, 'twas that which gave him the air of a worldly man. He savored his pleasures, instead of gobbling them up before they were well tasted.

It was that, and the secrets swimming behind those murky gray eyes.

She followed the drift of his gaze o'er the rolling land of Champagne. In one of the distant, ochre spires, a church bell began to ring, joined by still another, a calling of the faithful to Mass.

A memory came to her like a whisper.

"In Ireland," she began, softly, as the chimes shimmered through the air, "Mama, meself, and me brother used to live a bit away from the village, beyond a sliver of forest between the river and the sea." She waited for him to comment, and when he said nothing, she hesitantly continued, the memory unfurling in her mind. "On Sunday mornings, me brother and I used to race through the woods on our way to church—for we were always late, we were—and the bells used to toll from afar and ring through the air like living things . . ." She breathed deeply, filling her lungs with the fragrance of heather. "On a fine, soft day like this, Conaire, does it not remind ye of Ireland?"

He snorted as he plucked a sliver of wood off his tunic and tossed it into the grass. "And what part of Ireland would you be thinking of, woman? All I remember of that place are gales and cold and rain."

"Aye," she conceded, "we'd our share of storms, livin' by the sea. But they made the glorious days all the more fine, don't you know."

"Spoken like a child who never had to keep the wood dry for a long night's fire."

"Och, you'd have made a fine priest." She slapped the rest of the bread onto a square of cloth, folding it firm even as she tucked the amber memory away. "In the brightest day you'd stand in the shadows and call it gloomy."

He shifted his weight uncomfortably upon his elbow, avoiding her eye. "Did you expect fair words from me, woman?"

She did not know what to expect from him; he'd been so brooding and silent these past days, but hope had begun to conquer her terror nonetheless.

"It's a long road that has no turning, Conaire."

"You should know by now that I'm a crusty, old man, not fit company for a young lass."

"Don't be saying that; you're not an old man."

She felt the heat of a blush rising to her cheek. Och, but 'twas true. He'd not taken a blade to his face this morn; a sprinkling of dark bristle prickled on his jaw and shadowed his upper lip. Sweat glistened on his brow, and flecks of bark and tiny slivers of wood speckled his smooth skin. Even his clear gray eyes held the burning light of a man with no thought of the grave.

"And if you were, what difference would that make?" She tucked the bread back in the basket and tugged out a square board wedged in the bottom. "Mama was fond of telling me to take the old dog for the hard road, and leave the pup on the path."

He glanced at the checkered board she tossed carelessly between them, then raised a brow as she clanked another bundle of cloth atop it.

"Was it the little people you were planning to play that with," he asked, "when you packed it in your basket this morn?"

The heat of her cheeks intensified. She'd not meant to take out the chessboard so blithely, but he'd put her in such a state, that she'd paid no mind to what she was doing. Now he'd know for sure that she'd had every intention of luring him out here, into the Lughnasa sun, away from the wretched shadows of that hovel of a manor house where he'd brooded for so many days, away from the perked ears of curious servants, away to a place where she could murmur the secrets of her heart, if she dared to trust him.

"You shouldn't mock the little people so, it's angry you'll make them." Defiantly, she tugged open the knot and upturned the cloth to let the chipped wooden pieces scatter over the board. "There's no telling what sort of mischief they'll think up on such a day as today."

"I've got a fair, fine idea of it."

"And why would I be after thinking *you'd* play me a game of chess," she argued, setting up the wobbly pieces, "when you've refused my request twice already, with no more than—"

"I'll challenge you, lass."

"—a never-you-mind." She knocked over a piece with her knuckle. "What did you say?"

"You heard me." He rolled up and braced himself with one hand splayed flat upon her cloak. A shock of auburn hair fell over his forehead, a stark contrast against the searing brightness of his silver eyes. "I'll not avoid your challenge any longer."

She noticed the dark hairs sprayed across his firm forearm, the deep hollow of his collarbone, aware only of the wild recklessness of his gaze, which cut her through to the quick. He loomed, suddenly dangerous and sure, leaning forward over the board. Words melted in her throat. She vowed she'd never understand the ebb and flow of his moods—for moments ago he was as distant as the churches in the valley, and now his attention focused upon her like a ray of light she'd once seen burn a smoking hole through a fallen leaf, after passing through a pair of spectacles abandoned in the cloister's garden.

"Och, aren't you a strange one, changing your mind like the wind."

"State your color, lass, before the wind shifts to the north."

She reached across the blanket and clutched a handful of stones laying amid the grass. Her tunic shifted over the limb. The recklessness invaded her as well, for she did nothing to set the cloth aright. "This set is worse for wear, you'll be noticing, like everything else in the house of Clunel. You'll have to use a stone for one of your bishops; and I'll use two more for my castles, for I have none."

And so in silence they played chess, as the tree stretched its boughs above them to guard them from the burning sun. They sat so still that two blackbirds, burrowed deep within the leaves, dared to lilt their full lay, apparently ignorant, Deirdre thought, of the charged currents fluxing between the man and woman sitting upon the cloak below them.

How deep the shadowed hollow of his throat, how long and firm the stretch of his collarbone . . . A lass could hang a lifetime of worries upon those shoulders, and not see them bow from the weight of it.

How large his hands. Broad-palmed, strong-fingered. Scars nicked small, white lines across their backs. Yet how well he used them, like a lute-player, plucking what he needed from amid the bristled pieces on the small board and moving with quick, sparse gestures to the new spot, without the clumsy tremors she'd expect from a man with such callused, worker's hands.

She imagined those hands would rasp against her skin, like the brush of a cat's tongue.

A light breeze swept over the hill, carrying with it the faintest perfume of heather, but no relief from the simmering of her blood. She picked up the flagon of wine to take a sip, surprised to find it heavy, when surely she and Conaire had already drank the most of it.

She tried to concentrate on the board. She was an indifferent player, for though she had learned the way of it in her youth, the game was frowned upon within the halls of the cloisters—for amid the better classes, it was the custom to play it for wagers. Only in the months before Jean-Jacques's death, those few precious months they'd shared together in Troyes, had she redis-covered the joy of it. Now, with Conaire breathing over her, small rivulets of sweat running down his neck and deeper, below the gaping neckline of his tunic to places no lass had any business imagining, the fate of the wooden kings and queens on the board between them held little meaning.

It was little comfort that Conaire seemed distracted, as well. For his interest was over his shoulder, to the quicken rimming the open slope of the hill, to the sway of a low bough brushing against the feathery spray of a fern, and she wondered with a spurt of shame if she were just imagining the rivers of trembling sensation flowing between them, or if they were the amorous imaginings of a girl left too long in the cloisters.

She reached into the woven basket and took out a piece of fruit, biting into it without tasting it, just to settle the roiling of her belly. Only after the thing was half-eaten did she realize it was a ripe, red apple—and she wondered at the curious thing, when she'd not remembered packing it, when she was sure not a single apple tree in all of Champagne had yet dropped its fruit.

She looked up to make a mention of it to Conaire, but his face was averted again, to the shivering tremble of a bush on the rim of the woods, making a mockery of all her fluttering.

"Checkmate." She moved a bishop across the board, knocked over Conaire's king, then seized it in triumph. "Still looking for ruffians, Conaire? Och, you would have done better to keep your mind on the game."

He blinked at her, his gaze murky like the gathering of clouds before a storm. His pegs were scattered all over, the ones she'd captured lying upon the cloak at her knees.

"Was it your pride, Conaire, which kept ye from playing the game before now?" She softened her voice. "If I'd known ye were so new at it, I would have taught ye a trick or two."

He swiped at the board and sent the pieces scattering across the grass. " 'Tis naught but a game."

Och, the quickness of a man's temper! Must it always be this way, a woman tiptoeing with tender feet around a man and his bruised pride? " 'Twas a game nonetheless," she argued, "and there'll be a wager to fulfill from it."

"There was," he growled, jerking to his feet, "no wager."

"Then I've the right to set it, I do, and you've the right to call another game."

"And whose rules are these you're spouting?"

" 'Tis the way of it, it has always been the way we've played."

"I'll finish your pyre, woman," he said, marching to the scattered bundles of wood, "and we'll be done with it."

"I'll not waste my win on a pyre," she called after him, as she brushed the pieces off her lap and rose to her feet, "when I've a task that'll take every last bit of your might."

"What, then?" He wrestled the bundles of wood into the shape of a pyre even as he spoke. "Would ye set me to the thatching, woman? Or better, the same trials as the sons o' Tureen?"

"Nay."

She paused on the edge of the shadows, the sparse grass warm beneath the soft leather of her shoes. She ran a damp thumb over the blue and white painted face of the battered king in her hand, as the dappled light shimmered o'er the ground between them. Recklessness seized her and flooded her with courage.

When she looked up, he was standing at his full height in the blazing sunshine, his hands tense at his sides.

Waiting.

She closed her hand over the captured king. "The price, Conaire . . . is a kiss."

Seventeen

Once, in his early wanderings, Conaire had stumbled upon a Scottish village destroyed by sea raiders, the skeletons of the thatched ruins still smoldering in the morning fog. Whilst he searched for survivors among the dead, he stumbled upon a Norseman's abandoned weapon. 'Twas a twisting spear, its shaft coiled about with cord, so that it spiraled in flight and skewered the iron point swift into its target. The warrior in him admired the weapon, even as the healer in him despised it.

Such a thing as this would bolt through the air with a hiss and a whirr, audible only when it was too late.

"Is that all you want, woman?" The words passed through his throat like gravel. "Just a kiss?"

A breeze riffled her hair over her shoulder. "A man of your age should know the way of it, I'm thinking."

Aye, aye, he knew the way of it; aye, he couldn't thrust the thought of it from his mind, nor the memory, for both assaulted him now as he stood with the sun beating hot upon his head, whilst the woman he'd lain with more times than a man could count stood in the cool shadows with a beckoning shine in her eyes.

He'd seen that gleam a hundred thousand times across the space of a room, behind the sweep of lashes, above the curve of a knowing smile; amidst the scent of sleep and sex beneath a hot cocoon of furs. His blood rushed to his loins at the hint of it, and the gates he'd kept so long closed in his mind burst open under the flood o' memories; the flash of a naked limb, the tumble of her blazing hair upon the green grass; the softening of her spine in surrender; the sweet grimace of her features as he joined his hot flesh to hers—tight, deep—the cries in her throat, the taste of her throbbing pulse upon his tongue—

And her laughter, aye, her sweet, throaty laughter when it was all done and over, and he lay upon her heaving like a horse run too hard, and her soft arms slipped around him and held him close, and the dampness of their bodies merged them into one flesh again; and then the playful teasing, the touching of nose to cheek, the nip of teeth on shoulder, soon dimming to the soft talk o' the day, to the sharing of their worlds.

Even in the days of her frailty, they'd shared that last joining. He jerked where he stood, for deep within keened the loon-cry of his soul, silent to all but his ears, for though in the years past he'd slaked his human lust between a maid's legs when the base hunger was upon him, never again had he shared with any creature the soft talk o' the day.

They had plans then, first of building a grand *ráth* upon the height of the hill, and calling it *Dún Conaire*. Then of making land to grow barley, for bread, for ale; and fashioning straw hives for bees, for collecting honey, and maybe making mead. Even at the end, they'd been planning to buy another bull and put the old one to rest, and give him a new herd o' cows.

He'd not made a single plan in seven centuries after the day she died, not a single decision truly of his own making, letting his whims and his moods drive him, and the four winds buffet him to the corners of the Earth.

Now they had swept him here, face-to-face with his own fate, then held their breath and waited.

Her smile had dimmed. She gripped something still in her hands. A faint breeze swept over the hilltop, flattening the grass and laying hard against his back.

"Will ye be having me think that you've no intention of paying your wager, Conaire?" A tremor of angry shame shook her words. "That Doctor MacSidh is not a man of honor?"

Her eyes widened as he approached, aye, and that's how he knew he approached, for 'twas not his will that set his feet upon the sunny path that lay between them; 'twas something stronger, something deeper than his own self. The cool shade dappled over him.

She dropped something upon the ground, but made no effort to retrieve it. She arched her neck, her gaze fixed upon his as he stopped before her. He felt the pull and suck of it, the roaring in his ears as she drew his soul in and turned it inside out.

Why had he not noticed before the faintest spray of freckles across the bridge of her nose, tapering onto her cheeks? The red gleamed in her tumbling locks of gold, aye, reflected off the golden circlet resting upon her brow. And what was that which lay upon her throat? A tiny mole, dark and distinct against the cream of her young skin—that was new, and yet it was *her*.

He lay his finger upon it. His knuckles grazed the line of her throat. The heat of her skin burned beneath his hand, the blood pumped swift beneath her skin. He heard her sharp intake of breath. Her breasts, unbound beneath the tunic and surcoat, gently rose and fell as she struggled for air grown suddenly thin between them.

In the distance, the sound of plucked lyres drifted high on the air. It was the same music which had vexed him throughout the chess game, the hollow echoes of revelry in the Otherworld; fairy music mingling with tiny voices raised in shouts and laughter, the stamping of dancing feet and the slosh of liquid as the *Sidh* sipped honeysuckle nectar from cups made of foxglove blossoms.

He ignored it—even as he ignored the furtive breeze which gusted and swirled around his ankles. The rush of his blood blocked his ears from all else but the woman before him, her sweet breath soughing between her wet lips, the feel of her flesh beneath his fingers, the sway of her figure. He rasped the back of his hand up her throat, and rested it in the warm nook of jaw and chin. She turned her face into his knuckles, like a kitten.

The sunlight pouring through the leaves dimmed, bathing her skin in a pale luminescence. How dewy her skin, how unmarked by the passage of time, how unscarred by worry and work and pain. How baldly her hope cried out in her eyes; innocent and eager. How it beckoned to him, reached for him, drew him closer toward her, until he felt the brush of her surcoat against his legs.

He turned his hand over and engulfed her cheek. He resisted the siren's call of those lips, engorged now, full and pillowy. The fragrance of her rising warm from her skin made him teeter on the edge of drunkenness—it was too much, the full feast before him; the silk of her hair, the sweet memory of the taste of her temple. He wanted to nibble each delicacy, count the hairs upon her head, bury his face in her throat and breathe the scent of her rising from every hollow, until he knew the full o' her with his eyes closed, as he already did, as he already did.

A strange shimmering shadow fell across the hilltop. The leaves above them rustled with the wind's furtive agitation. Conaire worked his hand beyond her cheek, into the temptation of the warmth of her hair, behind the curve of her ear. A strangled noise came from her throat and her heavy lids dipped over her eyes, as she swayed into him, her hands flat upon his chest.

So it was a kiss you wanted, lass, a simple kiss; nothing but a trifle of an embrace on a summer's day. How innocent, not to understand the power of a single kiss, the power that left her leaning upon him, her eyes closed in the heavy languor of yearning, the power that clamped him to the spot like a vice.

And he curled his fingers deep in her hair, remembering a day upon Inishmaan when a gale roared outside the *clochán,* and they'd loved by the glowing heat of a peat fire, her hair wrapped around his wrists in playful silken bondage.

And he remembered another time, when he'd run through her

hair a comb made from the antlers of a king stag, when it was still long but as white as snow, and she'd not the strength to plait it as she pleased, and he not the skill, and so he'd combed it for long hours while she dozed upon the furs.

She blinked her eyes open, slowly, a soft confusion lurking within the depths, a wordless question.

He could not answer, for the aching dryness of his throat, for the lump of lead lodged heavy in his chest.

So they stood for a timeless moment, staring at one another across the chasm of two worlds, knowing it could be closed with but a kiss.

A strange silence rang over the hilltop. A hazy twilight bleached the colors from the world around them. Something in the shifting of the dappled light caught her attention, dragging her focus suddenly away from the tension that stretched between them. Her eyes widened as she looked around to the hazy gray veil closing in on them, to the living greenery melting away to a ghastly leaden hue, and then up to the pewter cloudless sky. In the trees nearby, a flock of birds burst into squawking, and with a flutter of wings took sudden flight.

She made a soft cry of fear. Her fingers curled into his chest, as she moved instinctively closer. His free arm moved of its own accord, drawing her body within the circle of his protection, drawing the full warmth of her against the ache in his chest.

"Conaire . . ." She shivered with more than the embrace, with more than the lift of her hair by the wind, suddenly chill. "Something . . . something is happening . . ."

Aye, something was happening. Something he'd battled against, something he knew was folly, yet something he'd not had the strength of will to escape from—something he'd taunted in the arrogant thought that he could fight it—the gods, his fate, the power of the love o' this woman. Now she stood in the circle of his embrace, her head beneath his chin, with the wind tangling their tunics. The rage of a passion long-suppressed surged against the bonds of reason, until a webbing of a hundred thousand fissures spread through his resolve.

"The sky . . ." She tugged on his cloak. "What is this, that happens around us?"

It's the world turning over again, wife, and here we stand in the sweetest part, and me, fool that I am, knowin' better . . . and still standing mute as a dog.

"It's the passing of the moon across the face of the sun," he heard himself murmur. He bit down on the words, *There is nothing to fear.*

For what followed hard upon the sweetness was betrayal, exile, death. Eternal loneliness.

Captured in the soughing winds of the magic flux, Conaire felt the thought tear apart and flutter into the four winds.

"I have dreamed this." She traced something upon his chest, and stared at a peppering of narrow crescents of sunlight, which sprayed over them from through the leaves above. Then she blinked up at the sky, at the sliver of sun, which hung now like a two-day-old moon in a spangled purple sky. "I've dreamed of this very day."

He sensed the shifting of the veils, the rush of the Otherworldly breeze between the thinning doors, the sparkling of the *Sídh* as they raced about, set free to roam the Earth in the midst of day. She turned her eyes to him, full of wonder, and full of knowledge—unsure no more.

"Aye, woman." His palm burned against her flesh. "I've dreamed of it, too, a long, long time ago."

A dark hand closed over the world.

"Kiss me, Conaire."

High in the sky pinpricks of light flickered around the black disk of the moon-sun, poised, as if time were momentarily arrested, then extinguishing, one by one, until the last stubborn bead winked and died. And in that moment of darkness, streams of pure, translucent, pearly white furled out from the black sun—

the white of fairy's wings, the misty foam of their phosphorescent trail upon the still indigo waters of a midnight lake.

He looked down upon her in the time between the times, and he saw the face of Brigid.

A heaviness seeped through him. He'd felt such a languor once before, on the limestone plains of Ireland after four days of ceaseless fighting against the Leinstermen.

Seven hundred years of waiting.

His head dipped toward hers. He felt the rush of her breath against his lips.

Even an immortal could not struggle forever.

She had waited forever while the world around them shifted into darkness, studying the inscrutable emotions fluxing across his face, wishing she could plunge into his heart and read all the secrets and ease away all the anguish . . . and now, now as he made his decision and lowered his head, all the impressions jumbled atop of one another. The long raking of his hand through her hair, dragging her head back and tilting her lips up to meet his; hot, ragged breath billowing against her cheek, fragrant still of wine; the sudden gripping of his fingers against her back, the rasp of his bristled chin against her cheek—

The dream had prepared her for the hot, metallic moon burning in the twilight sky; for the ghostly silence and the eerie blue-green light swirling around them—even the unearthly look of Conaire's face—but no wisp of a vision could prepare her for the first touch of human flesh against quivering human flesh.

A weakness flooded over her from the press of his mouth; a languor which penetrated her bones like a hot stream of honey. Firm, his lips; sure upon her own, but they moved with the ease of thorough possession, suckling each ridge, nipping deep into the corners of her mouth. She did not know how to shape her mouth beneath his; she did not know how to move. She angled her lips to his, but he drew back, away, to suckle on another curve, to draw between his own lips the fullness of one of hers. Then his lips slid beyond, to the hollow of her cheek, then higher, over the tilt of her cheekbone, and she felt an urge to cry out with the frustration of ignorance—to cry out for more, for all of his kiss.

But words eluded her, even the thought came and went like the flare of a meteor across the sky, for as his mouth roved across her temple, into her hair, she lost all sense of time and place and sank heavier into his chest, surrendering to the sensations roiling within her, surrendering to the mastery of Conaire.

The vision had been but a pale mockery of this. The memory of the dream melted and drifted away from her, like the softening of the sharp, midsummer shadows in the moments before the moon had eclipsed the sun. By some reflex she balled Conaire's tunic in her fists. This time, she vowed, his face would not melt into the darkness; this time, the fog would not come between them and separate them again.

He discovered the curve of her ear, the sweep of valley within, the lobe below. With a sweet grimace of sensation, she turned her head aside only to feel the brush of his hot breath against her throat, and then the trace of his tongue along her jaw.

Rising from the sweep of the softly rolling countryside, church bells tolled, a dim clangor ringing through the silence of the midday twilight. By some trick of the dusky silence and her muddled senses, they seemed to peal like tiny chimes all around her—like the bells she'd once heard on a Christmas carriage, jingling with joy into the night.

She tried to speak her heart—och, how the words fluxed and surged within her! She loved him, she'd waited for this moment forever, she _missed_ him—nay, there was no sense to that, for how could she miss a man she'd only begun to know? Her mind was all a-muddle with the slow, sure burn of his kisses—and before she could even murmur his name, he hushed her with his own lips.

Then there it was again, the warm, fluid weakness that seeped through the pith of her bones, stronger now; a trembling weakness that softened her knees and urged her to slip her arms over his shoulders, around his neck, before she melted into a puddle at his feet. Then, just when she thought she couldn't bear the sweetness any longer, he slanted his face and parted his lips, and she tasted the first hot breath of his passion.

She'd not heard of such a thing; she'd not dreamed of it; and in her surprised stillness he coaxed her into parting her own lips, so their breath mingled between them. He tasted of wine and the lingering tartness of wild berries, and of something else elusive and strong; eagerness, need. Craving the flavor, she parted her lips further, and found herself welcoming, with a racing heart, the intimate brush of his tongue.

Och, the mysteries of this man, the mysteries of this loving! She'd not felt the like in all her life, yet, at his gentle probing, at the unexpected, unknown intimacy, some primitive sensibility roused within her, stretching and uncoiling as if from a long slumber.

His arms hardened around her, strong and sure, holding her within the warmth of his embrace. *I'm safe here, safe with this man.* No one could harm her, no one would dare; here she was wanted, needed, loved.

A stark, lucid happiness flushed through her. She thrust her hands through his thick, sun-warmed hair and cradled his head, drawing him so close that her nose dug deep into his bristled cheek, that their mouths locked in this heady joining. All those years of fervent prayer . . . Her anguished pleas had been answered after all. Here stood the man of her dreams, a man who would love her, accept her, and bring such a joy as this into the lonely hollow of her life.

Their lips separated as he hefted her up against him. Her circlet, knocked askew by his loving, tumbled off her brow and chimed to the ground. Her hair cascaded over them; blindly, she kissed his brow and burrowed her cheek in his hair—how soft, how fragrant—only vaguely aware that he was carrying her somewhere, sensing only the roll of his gait, the strength of his arms around her. The furrowed bark of a tree pressed against her spine, as he leaned her down upon its slant. Her head fell back; he took the curve of her chin into his mouth, and then, the arch of her throat.

In the sky above, a sudden explosion of light burst around the black disk of the moon. Sunshine flooded down through a break in the canopy of leaves, bathing her face in renewed warmth. Birds chartered in sudden unison in the forest beyond, and the buzz of insects rose from the earth, as if for the dawning of day.

She knew she should be frightened of all that occurred around her; she should be racing to the churches whose bells pealed in panic, still, in this midday daybreak—but the thought was distant and wavering, inundated by the strong flood of new emotions waking in her. She'd existed too long in darkness insensate; now passion slipped around the gloom, like the blazing flood of new light pouring upon the Earth.

Sunrise. Rebirth.

Her scarlet surcoat slipped easily off her shoulders and pooled over her leather girdle. She shrugged her arms out of it without a thought, as his kisses burned a path over her collarbone and into the hollow of her shoulder. His fingers tugged the cloth between her breasts, loosening the laces of her tunic until the neckline sagged and slipped to her elbow, and one bare shoulder lay exposed to the air.

His cheek rasped against hers as he breathed ragged words into her ear. "Is that enough of a kiss for you, woman?"

He loomed over her. His tunic gaped, and she caught a glimpse of flat, rippling belly, of naked chest sprayed with hair. Golden sparks lit his gray eyes; eyes of smoke—hot and dangerous.

His fingers traced a path from her cheek to her throat, and then lower. "If you had any sense in you, you'd be putting up a fight."

"Och, Conaire," she said through a sigh of frustration, as his fingers hesitated at the curve of her breast, "is it true then, that an Irishman isn't at peace unless he's fighting?"

He balled the cloth of her tunic in one fist and tugged. "Did they not warn you o' temptation in that convent, woman?"

Aye, she thought, herein lies the pith o' the man; even as his breath drew harsh between his lips, even as a sheen of sweat glimmered on his skin, even as the primitive nature of the man roared for release with the woman who leaned back beneath him, soft and willing, he checked his lusts for the sake of her.

"Aye, they spoke of temptation." With a soft shrug of her shoulder, she let the tunic shimmy to her waist. She slipped her arms out of the sleeves and framed his face in her hands. "But if I were to fight temptation the way you fight me, Conaire, I'd be a saint."

She kissed him, swiftly, out of boldness and also to hide her flushed face, tingling with heat. Never in her life had she bared so much skin to the sky, to the gaze of a man. Her breasts felt heavy, engorged, aching, and so sensitive that she detected the spotted warmth of dappled sunshine, and the lick of a warm breath of wind.

He growled something under his breath, then bent his arms and lowered his weight onto her body, imperceptibly, so first all she felt with a shivering gasp was the rasp of damp linen against the tips of her breasts—the tug and pull of the threads as he shifted side to side, teasing her with the grate of fine, warm cloth against her nipples, until they puckered into tight little knots of exquisite sensation. All the while kissing, tasting, savoring the planes and angles of her face, her neck, her throat, with merciless, maddening rigor.

The warm, thick languor which had invaded her limbs began

to simmer. She *wanted,* though she knew not for what; she yearned for a greater intimacy. She arched her back, but he pulled away and denied her the harsh contact she craved. Her fingers dug into the balls of his arms and she tried in vain to pull him closer, to stop the maddening gentle rasp, to bring relief to the ache coiling deep within her, but her nails did nothing but grate his sleeves, he stood so tense and immobile, a hair's breadth away from her flesh.

When she thought she could bear it no longer, he made a strangled sound deep in his throat, then with the full of his weight, pinned her against the incline of the tree.

She felt the bite of the bark against her back, but paid it little heed: for this is what she craved—the heat of his body flush against hers, the ragged sawing of his breath against her ear, an urgency in his kiss—a crack in his control. The rough palm of his hand closed over her breast.

She broke away from his lips, for the air between them grew thin and rare, and she heaved to take more in, only finding the motion thrust her breast deeper into his hand; deeper into the callused, demanding warmth. He splayed his fingers, filled his grasp.

Sensation blended into sensation, each sweeter, more exquisite than the next: the curl of his fingernails into her skin, the pinch of his palm, the lightness as he lifted her breast into his grip, as he rolled his fingers over the peak of her nipple; och, 'twas possession, this, and it sent her senses reeling into a bright oblivion. She knew not herself, she knew not the throes which possessed her body; but she was no longer the innocent girl straight from the convent, swathed in her wimples and veils, lowering her gaze from all who glanced—nay, she barely knew this creature emerging from some deep place within herself, arching and moaning against Conaire as he worked his magic over her flesh, sensing in some deep, instinctive place that this would be called lust; this would be called sin; and knowing in a even deeper place that it wasn't, not between her and Conaire, not between them.

For this was their wedding day, aye. Today he would cleave to her—and only now, as he thrust his thigh between her legs and she felt the hard length of something pressed against her loins, did she vaguely grasp the meaning of the words—today, Lughnasa, on this open hilltop under the wonders of the sky, he would take what a wife gives her husband, and all they lacked were a few words spoken over them upon holy ground.

Och, but this was holy ground now, for what they shared was surely of the spirit as well as the flesh—for her soul above all craved the nameless joining to come—never to be lonely again, never to be one—and that was all she thought of as his fingers rasped over her breast, and tugged with urgency upon the buckle of her girdle, lost under the drape of her tunic and surcoat.

Her spirit soared into the air like a sparrow riding a filet of wind. For a moment, she imagined she was looking down upon the two of them, entwined together against the tilt of the tree trunk. She sensed a strange familiarity in the clouds smeared across the sky; in the play of light and shadow o'er Conaire's wide back; and she knew with sudden, stark clarity that this night was planned by some higher power—had she not foreseen it? And she wondered whether her gift, as Conaire had once called it, had finally given her wisdom, or whether this day, this act, was simply elemental; if she sensed no more than man claiming woman, a ritual as ageless as time, as simple as the rain falling, as necessary as air and water—or some greater joining.

The weighty thought slipped from her mind like water through open fingers, for with a wrench he tossed her girdle to the earth and her tunic rustled down, and all her senses plunged back into the turmoil of her yearning flesh. Her tunic draped around her loins, hiding nothing from his gaze, held there only by the press of her hips against the tree.

He loomed over her, blocking out the world. A shock of hair

shaded his brow, but could not dim the golden sparks in his silver eyes, burning hotter than any Lughnasa fire. Impatience thrummed from the taut muscles of his body, but leashed, ever leashed. He had intense eyes, like a lion she'd once seen on fair day, pacing in its cage at the end of its tether.

How she wanted to snap that leash; how she wanted him un-bound, free, following the dictates of his heart. Words trembled on her lips—*Love me, Conaire*—but before they were spoken, he pressed his face against her throat, then he slid down her body, rubbing his stubbled chin through the valley between her breasts, and still lower, his lips tracing a damp trail on the razed skin straight through to the indentation of her belly, his hands gripping her sides, then her hips, then lower, and the force of need spiraled down deep into her womb.

Without thought, she parted her thighs at his gentle insistence, felt the warmth of his breath and then—

Oh.

Sparks flashed through her and set her body to quivering—her heart racing, racing, racing in her breast. She felt the sudden moist warmth of her loins, the heavy dissolving into a boneless heap so only his hands held her up; his hands, and the relentless craving for more of this kiss.

The world tilted; she spun in a weightless place. She knew not what she did anymore. Strong ridges of bark pressed against her cheek, her palms dug deep into his shoulders. She opened wider; she felt him deeper within her, probing and stroking, a deep, hot, intimate kiss, and though her eyes were closed, she winced at the blinding lights racing toward her—flooding over her with sharp heat and brilliance—and she squeezed her eyes shut tight, as they hit her and exploded her senses.

For a long time she leaned blind, her breath rasping through her throat. Conaire rose and wrapped himself around her, his strong arms giving her support, where she would have fallen without thought into the soft arms of the Earth, his cheek against her hair, her nose in the hollow of his throat. She clung to him, tears pricking her blinded eyes, while her heart trilled a hymn of thanks to the bright, blinding blue sky.

Only when she sensed the tilting of the horizon; only when she felt wool brush against her back, did she realize that the loving was not yet finished.

He was drunk—more drunk than he'd ever been in the early days, with Aidan in the mead halls after a day o' hard fighting, when life still pumped through their veins; and they'd toasted their survival with honey-mead, and in delirium drowned out the sight o' their brothers-in-arms dying on the battlefield.

Aye, he was drunk, and it wasn't upon the wine sloshing in the skin he brusquely brushed away as he lay her down upon the bolt o' yellow cloak. He was drunk on the taste o' her; on the nectar he'd sucked from the flower which now lay open and hot and ready and gleaming for him.

He thought he was done with this mindless passion—with the urgency that gripped a man's vitals and propelled him beyond all reason—he was a man of nearly eight centuries; he knew every nuance o' mating there was to know—but the scent o' this woman sent him reeling; he who'd learned long ago to control hunger, thirst, pain—all feeling—all the agonies and all the pleasures of humanity—and with one urgent moan from the base of her throat; with one arch of her back, the feeling snapped its claws into him and dragged him into a whirlpool of need.

He let it seize him. For in this moment the grass beneath the golden cascade of her hair blazed greener, its crushed scent sharp on the air; the sunlight sharper, hotter; the scent o' wildflowers clinging desperately to the edges of the rock fragrant like honeysuckle. Life pumped in his blood as it hadn't for seven centuries. He stripped the last of the clothes from her limbs and followed them with his own; and they lay under the arch of the sky naked to the world, the rod of his humanity throbbing for her.

He brushed her hair off her forehead; she lay heavy-lidded, soft and yielding, her cheeks flushed and her lips still engorged from their kissing. 'Twas time now, while her body lay numb from the pleasures of moments ago—when her body hummed moist and willing.

His hunger overcame him; this pleasure, he could savor no longer.

At the first touch, her eyes fluttered open; clouded but still swirling with deep knowledge, still fluxing and flowing and drawing in a man's soul. She welcomed him, languidly shifting beneath him to accommodate his size, flexing her hands up his arms to rest upon his shoulders, a smile lurking about her lips—a smile of knowledge, a smile of wonder, a smile of the discovery of consummate pleasure.

He pressed deeper, finding the hot, welcoming fold, demanding entrance and feeling with a groan the slightest resistance—a tightness which clamped around him—a tightness he eased through with slow, gentle thrusts, which wiped the smile from her face and replaced it with that grimace of pleasure he knew so well—and he told himself he must be patient, her body was new at this again, but there was no tethering a passion unleashed—so he drove deeper, waited, then moved with tiny thrusts a bit deeper, letting her accommodate to him, while her tightness sheathed him a little more, drove him farther into madness.

"Och, Conaire—" her voice, broken, hoarse, anguished, "—Conaire, *mo rún*—"

In the end, it was that, those words of Irish whispered in the hoarse voice of her passion, that broke the last chain, for they echoed through his memory. He buried himself to the hilt, lifting her off the ground with the force of the thrust. But her cry was not of pain, no, he'd heard this loving cry a hundred thousand times; and even as he thrust again he felt her throb around him, seized in the flux of another climax before he'd barely begun the stroking.

He let it flood over him; and he knew nothing then but the smell of her hair, the soft sounds of surprise, as instinct moved their loins against one another. He buried his face in the wash of her hair, and in the mindless roar of his body's release he dared to let a seed of hope find a resting place in his heart; he dared, for the brief moment of madness, to dream.

The hope lingered on long after, as they lay entwined in the shade, dozing in the half-sleep of lovers—in the protection of the soft, hushed silence of the woods.

Eighteen

He should be used to waiting.

The wall sweated against Conaire's back as he lolled on his damp pallet of hay, listening to the servants on the floor below squawking like hens, as they bickered with one another over who should lay upon the driest place in front of the dying hearth flames.

His gaze strayed the familiar path to the second of two doors in the hall. A dim glow seeped up from the stairs and cast the portal in scarlet, revealing a crevice of blackness where the door stood slightly ajar, beckoning to him.

He dug the butt of his palm into the crinkling old hay and shifted his weight beneath his cloak. The stink of burning tallow billowing from the candle at his feet did nothing to cut through the mildew thickening the air. Rainwater from the afternoon's summer storm oozed through the roof, and rhythmically dripped into fissures in the rotting floorboards.

Conaire found himself thinking of the Inquisitors of Toulouse, who used several forms of water torture to extract confessions from accused heretics—and wondering if they'd taken the idea from the ways of his own gods.

There was naught he could do about the endless *drip-drip* carving a sore in his brain, not yet, not while the Clunel servants quarreled among themselves at the bottom o' the stairs. For if they saw him sneaking into Deirdre's room in the middle of the night, there'd be no stopping the sprouting of the rumor which would reach its tentacles to Toulouse, to Deirdre's father, to the end of this brief idyll.

He'd not felt this urgency since he was a young man, thinking death lurked at the end of every battle, and ignorant o' the glut o' time he had on his hands. He wished upon the servants all the curses of old, if they did not settle to their pallets soon. For time was dripping away. He and she had so little of it left, before everything turned sour.

The quarrels settled into grumbling resolution. The voices gave way to the rustle of cloth, the scrape of a buckle across the hearthstones, an occasional murmur. A door opened and closed, followed by the footsteps of someone who'd lingered too long in the privy. The nub of Conaire's candle sputtered with a faint draft of wind, flickering his looming shadow high upon the slope of the eaves. A moth descended from the darkness and flirted with the flame.

Silence, but for the thrashing of the moth as it flitted close to the flame, then shot away, blinded, to career into the low slope of the eaves. Conaire waited, straining his ears for movement below, his gaze drawn inexorably to the crack of the door. Rainwater suddenly dripped from a new seepage in the eaves, and the candle sizzled and sputtered out, plunging the hall into darkness. The moth reeled into the inky night.

Conaire's damp cloak slipped to the pallet as he eased up and made his way toward the heavy wooden door, along a quagmire of creaks and squeals that he'd well-mapped in the night and day since Lughnasa. One part of him rebelled against the secrecy of sneaking around like a man thrice-wed seeking his bondswoman's bed, when it was his *wife's* bed he sought this night. But this is what he'd come to: If this secrecy could win him one day more, an afternoon—an hour—before this flickering exquisite moment drowned in bitterness—then he'd suffer the silent disgrace.

The door swung open beneath his hand. She stood in the

middle of the room like a chatelaine awaiting an expected guest, draped in a shift of something sheer and white which frothed around her feet. Clear blue starlight poured through the open window behind her, and cast her face in shadow.

But with one glance at the set o' that chin, he knew that she was in a state.

"Och, so here you are, Conaire, finally blessing me with your company."

He eased the door closed behind him. "Do you want the Lady of Clunel and every servant in the house to be listening at the door, lass?"

"It might be to me own good, I'm thinking," she argued, whispering none the less, "to call someone to protect me from a rogue such as ye."

Aye, a snit she was in, that was sure; his gaze fell upon the swift rise and fall of her breasts beneath the shift, as translucent as a high summer cloud. Yesterday, upon the hilltop, she'd been eager for more loving than he was willing to give, knowing as he did more about the state o' her own body than she did herself. Now, 'twas clear that the night and the day he'd left her alone had sharpened the lass's impatience—and her pique. A heaviness filled his loins. She'd be an eager thing this night—and he no longer had to hold back for delicacy's sake.

A wolf of a smile stretched his lips. The motion felt strange, awkward, as if the muscles of his face had atrophied from lack of use all these centuries.

He crossed the room in two steps and reached out for her. "So you missed me, lass—"

"Do ye think this to be the way of it, then?" She skittered back, leaving him with nothing but a handful of her shift. "You coming here to me bed, whenever the mood's upon ye?"

"Aye." He clamped his fist on the cloth and tugged her closer. "Have faith, the mood'll be upon me often, woman."

"Och, listen to ye!" She batted the cloth between them until he set it free. "A night and a day I've waited for ye, and not a wink from ye, not a thing—"

"Would you have me groping at you, with the servants about?"

"You can whisper, can't ye, Conaire? Faith, I think your fingers can write."

He shrugged a shoulder and lunged for her anew. "I thought ye'd want none o' me, after yesterday."

"None of ye?" She slapped his hand away. "Och, when I've thought of nothing else—"

She swirled around in a froth of white, hiding her face from his view. She paced to the window, then away, toward the bed, her gown floating behind her, jerked along by her fists curled in the cloth. He watched, as one would watch water simmering into a boil, waiting for the bubbles to burst through the surface.

Finally, she stopped her restless wandering and turned to him with fury. "Was yesterday nothing more for ye then, Conaire, but an idyll on a summer's afternoon?"

His nostrils flared with the memory of the fragrance of crushed grass, of the feel of her lying supple beneath him on a warm hillside. "Don't be talking nonsense."

"Nonsense, is it? With ye sneakin' about like a thief in the night, and during the day not daring to meet me eye—"

"You think too much," he growled, "buildin' yourself up into a fit o'er naught but your own imaginings."

"Is that all it is, then? Well, I'll not let go of it, Conaire." She crossed her arms beneath her breasts, and he watched with growing frustration the way they surged beneath the neckline of the shift. "I'll not let ye wiggle out between the tree and the bark."

"What do you want from me, woman?"

"I'll have the truth from you: Are you just biding your time before you move on to another conquest?"

He curled his hands in frustration. She wanted words, aye, as all young women want words o' tenderness and love, words that never came easily to his lips. "If I'm not a rogue, I'll tell you what I'm thinking, and if I am, I'll tell you what you wish; and since you don't know which I am, the words'll mean nothing."

" 'Tis not words I want, do you think I'm a fool? 'Tis action that makes the man."

"Then here: The truth of it is this." Before she could whirl away anew, he seized her hand and fit it over his swelling loins. "Is that enough proof for you?"

She yanked her hand away. " 'Tis no more than any stallion could do around a mare in heat."

"Well put," he argued, his gaze raking her veiled nakedness, "for by the looks o' you, you wouldn't protest if I set to you."

She grasped frothy handfuls of the sheath and yanked it in a defiant swirl. The twilight flooding through the window cast its sheer light through the fabric, revealing the curve of her hip, the shadowed juncture of her thighs.

When did she lose the modesty, when did she take on the mantle Brigid had always borne, a sure pride in her nakedness?

She shook fistfuls of the cloth at him. "This belonged to me mother, Conaire. It was part of her trousseau when she married me Da."

"It's a fine thing," he growled, "but I'd be liking it better if it were tossed across the floor."

"Me mother," she continued, ignoring his words, "was no more innocent than I by the time she got about to wearing this; she'd given birth to me and Jean-Jacques long before she could marry our father." She thrust the cloth away. "I thought it was fitting I wear it now, since the same might happen to me, if ye don't go about making an honest woman out of me soon."

A breeze heavy with the scent of rain shimmered through the pale blue light of the night pouring through the window, and whirled tendrils of her hair as light as fairy wings.

So that was the pith o' this. He should have known, aye, he should have expected that in the cold sober morning after the blind fury of their passion, her convent-training would emerge again, and she'd be wondering about the sin of it all.

And at first he thought—*no, no I'll not marry her again*—it would be a mockery of their first wedding, but then he wondered what difference it would all make, to have a priest mutter some words o'er their heads under the arch of a church, when in his world, the thing was already done—she was already his wife. The Christian ceremony might give her comfort in the days to come, so that she might look back upon this brief, intense affair with sweetness—at least he'd seen fit to marry her, she'd think; at least she'd not imagined he cared.

"And why," he asked, as he brushed past her to lean upon the windowsill, "would you be after wanting an old man like me?"

"Listen to you, talking nonsense. It's better to be an old man's darling than a young man's slave."

The deep blue twilight poured in through the window and cast her face, finally, in full light. And in that moment, as she lifted her gaze to his, he saw the hope lurking in the depths of her swirling eyes. Something in his chest slid heavily away. He'd seen that look before, he'd felt the same breath-stealing blow in the middle of his gut. The lass had lived in cages since she was barely a woman—first in a convent, and now trapped by her own gift in a world that dubbed it evil. And as in the days of yore, in her blissful ignorance, she had hung upon him all her hopes for freedom, all her hopes for happiness.

He found himself holding out his open palm. "I'll marry you, lass."

"Och, well!" She swallowed down a cry. "Will you now? 'Tis glad I am the words didn't break ye."

And more of this, more defiance, when he'd meant what he'd said out of love, not pity, and she'd not know the difference. "Enough o' your barking—"

"You make it sound like such a burden, Conaire, that I'm thinking never-you-mind."

"Married or not," he growled, dropping his outstretched hand, "I'll love you just the same."

She stopped before words rose to her tongue, and set her gaze upon him. Her chin lost its stubborn set under the onslaught of a soft glow which illuminated her skin from within, under the rush of a tremulous smile. Conaire glanced away, out to the milky smear of stars across the sky, then he rose swiftly to his feet and thrust out his hand anew.

"Are you going to waste away the night with sputter and drivel, woman?"

"Nay, not no more, never no more, Conaire, *mo rún.*"

Her gown trailed out behind her as she launched into his arms. She covered his face in kisses—the embrace of the eager, the untutored, full o' passion but vague in direction. He grasped her waist, searched for her lips, but she would not stay still—she swayed and slipped and wriggled against him like a Saracen dancer, inflaming his already well-swollen loins, and burning him with frustration at the smooth, translucent stuff of her gown which slipped like water through his fingers, but clung stubbornly to her body.

Finally, he seized her head and stopped the madness and kissed her—hard—to obliterate from his mind those eyes full of hope. Anger burned in him, anger at saying words which should never have been said, at admitting something he'd never wanted to acknowledge, and so he determined to turn it into passion, to dull the numb pain which throbbed in his chest.

He'd forgotten with the years the eagerness of a young, passionate body—his and hers both—the relentless driving to the consummation. Yesterday he had savored the feast; today he treated it like a final meal before battle. By the purring sound of her surrender as he tossed her down upon the bed, she did not mind that he near to tore her shift from her flesh; she did not mind that this time, he did not linger o'er the curves and hollows of her body, but spread her legs and thrust himself into

her the moment he'd disentangled the wretched gossamer web-
bings in which she'd swathed herself. That, she minded no more,
for her body arched against him with a frisson of pleasure.

And he watched her face as he thrust in her, again and again,
thinking; *Be the rogue, be the deceiver, destroy any lingering
hopes that this will last,* and the thought fueled his rough lovemaking. For their Fates were set on a course to agony, and he
was determined to change them. Aye, they'd love now, they'd
have this brief moment, but then it would be over—he'd see to
it. It was better to sever the love swiftly, than let it turn rancid
before his eyes.

He'd cut off the limb to save the life. *Her* life, for his was
long destroyed.

When the loving was spent, he lay heavily upon her, a cool
breeze chilling the sweat on his body. Her arms curled around
his neck, and rested there as she pressed her lips against his
shoulder.

He squeezed his eyes shut against the splay of her hair and
felt the anger ebb. *There is still some time left, aye, a few more
stolen moments,* and he determined to think only of the present.

She shifted beneath him. "Och, it will be a fine thing to have
such a big body as yours by me side in the winter, Conaire, but
now you're near to cookin' me."

He slipped off her. The bluish starlight did not quite reach the
bed, so all he saw of her face was a gleam of a smile and a
twinkle of eye before he lay back, and she sought the comfortable fit of his shoulder.

They lay in silence, and he felt the languid urge to sleep shudder through him; but he wanted none o' that, not now, not when
the best was upon him.

He spoke into the darkness. "What are you thinkin' of, lass?"

"Hmm?" Sleepily, she shifted her shoulders against his side.
"Och, trifles."

He caught at the splayed hand she ran over his chest. " 'Tis that I want to hear."

"What would ye be wanting with a young woman's foolishness?"

That's what he wanted most of all. *Tell me o' spindles and wool, o' the toughness o' the meat at dinner, o' the grayness o' the open sky as you peered between the parchment o' the window, o' the little things that make up the roll of a life.*

"It's a strange one you are, Conaire." She rose up, folded her arms on his chest, and planted her chin on her hands. "Me head is full of nothing but fancies now. But you . . ." She traced his hair off his brow. "You've a head full of mysteries."

Her face was too close; her lips gleamed in temptation. He felt his loins react in a way better suited to a younger man. "I am what you see."

"Nay," she said, drawing away, "you'll not be putting me off now, Conaire, now that we're to be married. I don't even know of your family."

"I've none."

"None? Och, you must have somebody back in Ireland—"

"They're all long dead." He wanted none of this; there was too much he still hid from her; too much she had no need to know. They would only have weeks, mayhap a month: he would not speak of the past, for that would only bring up questions of who and what he really was.

"Och, you're fibbing. Every man has kin."

"Does it bother you, lass," he snapped, "to be marrying a man o' no name?"

"Don't be talkin' foolishness."

"Then we both have heads full o' foolishness, and I'd rather be listening to yours."

"Och, I suppose the best way to get an Irishman to refuse to do something is by ordering it. For now I'll let you thrash away like a fish set loose, Conaire, but I'll be knowin' the full of it before we're married." She slipped down upon his shoulder again. "Now, if you want to know the truth, I was dreamin' of the lovely swath of blue silk put aside for me wedding dress, and I was thinkin' of the surcoat I'll make of it . . ."

Her voice lilted in the darkness. He let it lull him into half-slumber, he let it ebb away the uneasiness, the frustration, until his thoughts drifted out of his grasp.

The smoke of peat fires drifted through the window; he heard the distant roar of the sea breaking upon the cliffs. Then a breeze tart with the passing of rain sighed into the room, carrying with it the faintest tinkling of fairy bells.

He opened his eyes to see the gleam of the sweating roof above them, and a strange, blinking swirl of lights which faded as soon as he glimpsed them. The sound of the sea was no more than moisture pattering down into the softness of the corner, and a slow and gentle tapping lost amid the rustling of the linen as, beneath it, she idly ran her foot up and down the length of his calf as she spoke. The smell of peat fires, nothing but his imagination and the mischief of the *Sídh*.

In the darkness, he let them weave their magic—he gave himself over to it. For now. Only for now.

She fell silent; he glanced down to find her gaze intent upon him.

"What were you thinking, Conaire? Just now? You'd such a look upon your face."

He lay his head back down upon the pillow, and found the truth on his lips. "I was thinking of Inishmaan."

She rolled the name on her tongue; savoring it like a mystery, like a dream.

" 'Twas my home in Ireland."

Then under the cover of darkness he spoke of the land; of the rocky spine o' cliffs braced against the gales of the Atlantic, of the silver-white light which suffused the place like a great veil of mist; of the fish so plentiful one could grasp an armful by reachin' into the sea; of the clear blue bay; of the sunshine glittering gold on the water; and as he spoke, the taste of salt filled his mouth; the scent of seaweed left drying upon the sand filled his head; and his skin flushed as if the chill ocean wind braced his figure.

"We must go there," she whispered, as his words lapsed into silence, "after we are married."

"Aye." He tightened his grip around her back, gripped by a strange urge to stand upon that barren rock again. "Aye, we'll go there."

And he let himself believe, aye, as he looked into those eyes, he let himself plan that they'd return there and live out the length of their lives. But then he grasped one of her hands and lifted it to his lips to kiss the smooth, white skin, and knew with sudden certainty that she'd never survive on Aran. These soft, white hands had seen no more pain than pinpricks from her embroidery needle. Only weeds survived in such a place as Inishmaan, not fragile spring flowers.

He shut out the darkness edging into his thoughts, and told himself that it could be; he deluded himself into thinking that it would be.

"When, Conaire?"

Impatience vibrated through her, the impatience of the young and the eager.

"Soon," he murmured, rubbing his lips in her hair, letting his senses fill with the scent o' her. "Soon."

"No, no, we must plan." She pushed away and sat up suddenly, rippling the dreamy mist around his senses. "We must set a date for the wedding."

"Tomorrow." He reached for her and dragged her down upon him, his lips in her throat. "Aye, tomorrow . . ."

She laughed—the throaty, confident laugh of Brigid—as he set to tasting the curve of her shoulder. Then she gently pushed him away again, so she could meet his eyes.

"Have you not listened to a word I've said, Conaire? I've a wedding tunic to make, and unless you set the fairies to it, it'll not be done for weeks."

He caught a handful of the gossamer shift, tangled beneath their limbs, and lifted it for her view. "I'd marry you in this before I wait so long."

"And have the guests see what should be kept only for me own husband's eyes?"

The darkness seeped into his senses like a gray fog into the light o' day.

"Nay, I think not, *mo rún,*" she continued, oblivious to his sudden stillness. "I've a liking to be married near Michaelmas. It's not so far away, and it will make Papa happy not to waste the leavings of the wedding feast."

A chill shot through him; a premonition. He tried to shake it off. "Lass," he said, drawing her close, "we'd best find the village priest and have done with it."

"The village priest? Och, Conaire!" She pushed him away and sat back. "You're jesting. I'm no loose-skirted milkmaid to sneak off to a friar to be wed."

The fog thickened; the bright light of his dreams dimmed. *Not yet,* he thought. *Not yet.*

"Have you forgotten," he said, "that you're already betrothed?"

"Och, the Sire de Clunel?" Her hand fluttered white in the air, sweeping away all the complications of the contract her father had already signed with Sir Guichard. "Papa will take one look at the great Clunel manor house, and he'll have no more to do with him. Besides . . ." She drifted down upon him, all softness and warmth, "Papa will do whatever pleases me, Conaire, he loves me so."

He grasped her face and looked deep into those eyes. She was so sure of herself, so sure of her father's love, and he wondered again if history must always repeat itself.

His grip tightened on her face No, no—he wanted more time,

more time before it all crumbled. *Damn you, gods, you gave me three months in that last life, will you give me no more than three days in this?* He'd thought he'd never want more time— he'd enough time—he thought he'd never think it, but here he was with her face in his hands and he hated the swift run of time—he wanted to reach out and stop it—just for this moment, just for an eternity—to hold her like this, skin against skin, heart against heart—yet the water dripping in the corner quickened, *tip-tapping* away, and he felt the moment slip through his fingers when he'd barely set his grip upon it.

And the anger came back, forcefully, and with it an ache ripped into a chasm in his heart, and a determination to steal what fruit the Fates would give him. For now, for now.

"So be it." He dragged his arms down her back, and pressed her hips into his loins. "I'll send a message to your father tomorrow, and I'll hear no more of it."

He kissed her, deep and hard, to wash the taste of the lie off his tongue.

Nineteen

Deirdre rushed fleet-footed through the overgrown garden. Grass slapped her bare ankles, soaked her thin slippers, and yielded spongy and soft beneath her pace. She paused near an opening in the crumbled, piled-rock fence, then whirled to gaze past the gape of her hood, through the curling mists, to the sodden little manor house, with its lolling roof of thatch and skewed shutters. Then, with the faintest of chimes, she launched a silver bell into the crushed grass of her path.

"Come, Conaire," she whispered, "a race amid the forests of Champagne may shake the brooding out of ye."

She plunged into the cool gray shadows of the woods with a soft, private laugh. Her cloak billowed behind her like the morning fog. The mist eddied as she skimmed along the familiar path, avoiding the slick surface of protruding rocks and the moss-edged pools of rainwater scattered in the hollows. Gauzy light streamed down from breaks in the forest canopy, and illuminated the thin froth of mist flooding the ground.

She paused and launched another chime over her shoulder. She tucked her basket securely in the crook of her elbow, hefted her hem high above her knees, and darted deeper into the wood. Her unbound hair clung in tendrils to her face and shoulders. She let it fly wildly around her face as her hood tumbled off. She felt like a child again, racing through the woods of Ireland with Jean-Jacques chasing her in jest. Raindrops trickled off the hollow palms of leaves and cascaded to the litter, pattering around her like a thousand tiny footfalls amid the verdure, urging her faster, faster, urging her away from the thorny bushes and the outstretched branches of thin bare saplings which plucked and tugged upon the hem of her billowing cloak like tiny children's fingers, so much so that she imagined the Little People raced alongside her and tripped upon her cloak.

But when she thrust herself against the furrowed bark of an oak and turned to lay her back against it, her breath hoarse in her chest, there was nothing behind her but stillness; the flutter of a leaf to the ground, the splatter of rainwater from a high bough; the crackle of grass arching back after being crushed by the force of her flight.

She thrust her forearm over her eyes and smiled at her own foolish fancies. Och, she was acting like a fey child, racing about before the sun topped the horizon, alone, no less, amid the dangers of the woods—but she couldn't stop herself anymore than she could stop the wind from blowing—a madness lived in her now, a delirious joy which gleefully destroyed all reason and set her spirit soaring above the clouds.

She blinked her eyes open and peered with sudden intensity toward the still greenery of her passing. Though nothing moved amid the thick trunks, though a single bird sang fearlessly in the boughs above her, an uncertain prickle of foreknowledge tickled the nape of her neck.

She sucked in a slow, deep breath and opened her mind and heart to the hazy image. She had vowed to fight it no longer; Conaire had deemed her unusual power a gift, and so she'd determined to stop fearing what she could not change.

The vision wavered, flirted with her, then suddenly crystallized. *Conaire,* she thought with a trill of excitement. *Conaire has discovered the first bell.*

He wore his blue surcoat, the one she mended that first afternoon in the garden. In her mind's eye, she saw him crouch to retrieve the small, silver bell from where it glittered amid the grass. He stared at it impassively and turned it in his hand. Suddenly, he swallowed the bell in his grip. He hung his head and pressed his white-knuckled fist against his heart.

She stood mute as the vision wavered, then drowned in whorls of gray mist, and when the blindness cleared, she found herself standing, bereft, her arms outstretched toward the distant manor house.

Och, Conaire, mo rún, her heart whispered. *Do you think ye can hide your anguish from me?*

She wasn't blind to the shadows in Conaire's eyes, nay, not even her delirium could blind her to those. At first, she'd thought it was her betrothal to Sir Guichard which troubled him so. Conaire had no kin: he would not understand the bond of love which held her and her father's hearts so tightly together—a bond of love more powerful than any wretched little document. But each time she broached the subject, he snarled, dismissed her explanations, and spoke of other matters.

And so she had set to curing him of his gloom. Two days ago she'd spotted a group of *jongleurs* on the road, retreating from the thinning Fair of Troyes, and, despite the grumbling of the servants, she called out to the minstrels and invited them into the manor house to play for their supper. After a repast of stale bread, and a soup clogged with more leeks and onions than ham, the *jongleurs* cleared the room and did handsprings, juggled flaming sticks in the air, performed sleight-of-hand, then sang to the music of a pear-shaped lute. She, who'd only heard such music wafting over the roof of her house in Troyes, turned bright and excited eyes onto Conaire . . . only to find him as straight-backed and impassive as ever.

"Och, Conaire." She had scowled up at him where he stood beside her chair. "It won't break you to bend a bit."

"I would have you alone in this house," he had murmured, in a pitch only she could hear, "and you go and fill it with people."

It was a demanding lover she had welcomed into her bed that

night. Long after the loving was done, he'd held her as if she would dissolve into the air and leave him nothing but an armful of mist.

It was in the cool blue of the following morning when a strange wisdom descended upon her. Her heart ached with his, for whatever torment he suffered, but it was folly to force the truth from him. They were new to this passion, still caught in the rushing waters of the first flood. Surely, it would not always be like this, so all-consuming, so intense. Whatever tortured him lay deep in the past, that much she knew, for he snapped like an angry hound whenever she asked about his wanderings. She was not after thinking he'd share the full of himself with her now, even in the closest moments of their loving. An apple wouldn't fall until it was ripe.

Aye, and marriage was forever, the holiest of sacraments. She'd work until the white threaded through her hair if she must, just to see an easy smile crack his features.

So she pushed away from the tree and swept down the path, scattering the bells thinly behind her. Today, she'd planned a different sort of diversion, more to his liking, she suspected. Tossing one of the last bells over her shoulder, she veered off the beaten furrow and plunged into the verdure, lured by the sound of a stream trickling over a bed of well-worn stones. There, on a bank, atop a grassy knoll buttered by the first rays of dawn, she settled her heavy basket.

Some time later, she heard the clanking of the gathered bells. She plunged a needle into the froth of the shift he'd torn that second night of loving, and set it aside. "Och, Conaire, as slow as a woman ten moons gone with child, you are. I was after thinking of breakin' the fact by meself, before the noon hour descended upon us."

She turned her gaze upon him. He strode through the shadows, his cloak tossed over his shoulders. The dappled morning light shimmered over him. By some trick of the light, golden swirls and vines edged his cloak, and a thick brassy band circled his neck and arms, but then he stepped into the clearing and the illusion melted beneath the onslaught of the sunshine.

He tossed the bells to her side with a clatter, and loomed over her. "It's lucky you are, woman, that I caught sight o' you as you entered the forest this morning."

She frowned up at him, wondering if he always woke as if he'd slept upon a bed of nails.

"Have you nothing to say? Who was going to tell me you went racing through the woods alone?"

"Och, listen to you, blatherin' already. Octavius was going to tell you, I told him so."

"You saw that thief?"

"Aye, as plain as day, sitting outside the back door of the manor house mendin' his boot with a never-you-mind." She dragged the basket upon her lap. "And don't you go telling me he doesn't know the full of it, with you steppin' over him each time you come to me room, and him with his eyes all a gleamin' when he looked up at me—"

"He scurries to his hole when I'm about."

"And it's no wonder, with you spittin' and foamin' at the mouth at the mention of his name." She unfolded the cloth, and the fragrant steam of fresh-made bread wafted up from the basket. "Sit down. Mayhap some barley cakes and a little honey will sweeten that foul disposition of yours."

His nostrils flared as the fragrance reached him, and his beetle-black brows drew together. "Will ye be telling me the little people were after leavin' you that?"

"I made the barley cakes with me own hands, thank you very much." She rifled through the cloth for a knife, and then peeled the cloth off a pot of honey. "I thought you'd be after liking a little taste of Ireland on such a fine, soft day."

He lowered his big body somewhat reluctantly to the pool of her cloak, and took the barley cake spread with honey that she

handed him. She spread another for herself in silence, thinkin'
she'd wait until his belly was full and warm before she broached
another subject; there was nothing like a full stomach to stop a
dog from barking.

She gripped the flagon of wine she'd brought, and didn't it
taste like the hazel-mead Ma used to make? And as she bit into
the barley cake, didn't the honey taste like heather honey? But
she remained mute, for she'd long grown accustomed to such
odd illusions, in Conaire's presence, in these enchanted woods.

As he ate, he leaned upon his hand, then sagged down into
the bulk of his arm. When she finished her barley cake, she
licked her fingers free of honey.

He seized her wrist and tugged her toward him. She braced
her other hand against his chest. He met her gaze, then sucked
her thumb deep into his mouth.

A frisson of excitement shook her to her toes.

"I'm thinking," he said, after he'd licked her thumb free, "that
you brought me out here for more than a taste o' bread and
honey, woman."

She lay braced against the broad width of his chest, his breath
hot with promise on her cheek, his lips firm on her thumb again,
his eyes burning with silver fire. Liquid heat surged through her
veins, softened her bones; a feeling now deliciously intense,
exquisitely familiar.

"Aye," she murmured, melting against him, "I did that, *mo rún.*"

She almost yielded. The tips of her breasts brushed his chest,
then flattened against the resistance; her head tilted, her lips
parted to accommodate his mouth, and his hand raked over her
back to curl in her hair.

Then she remembered all the times he'd forced her to wait,
when he'd lingered with exquisite care over every stretch of skin,
when he'd feather-stroked and teased and made long love so
languid, that she wanted to scream from the tight, relentless ache,

and then she pulled back, slipped down to her hip, and let the cool morning light pour between them.

"Aye, I brought you out here for a reason, Conaire." She fumbled with shaking hands through the basket, then pressed a square of painted wood against his chest. "We've a score to settle, we two."

He scowled down at the chessboard.

"For wagers," she added, turning her flushed face away to search for the pieces bundled in cloth. "There'll be no more mistake about that. The last time, I set the wager without a word to you, so this time we'll do the same: Let the winner decide the price of losing."

He traced the edge of the board with his thumb. "Anything, woman?"

She let the word linger on the sweet, cool air.

He shifted up on his hand and lifted one black brow. "It's a dangerous weapon you put in me hands."

"Every sword has two edges." She swiped a lock of hair off her shoulder. "Are you willing to risk the weapon turned upon yourself?"

He seized the bundle of pieces from her hand and let them fall on the board, then set to the game with intensity. As the morning progressed, the first rays of dawn intensified into the bright white light of day, dissipated the last whorls of morning mist, and deepened the shadows of the surrounding woods. Birds, roused from slumber, chirped raucously and flittered from bough to bough.

Conaire played with a cleverness he'd not shown the one other time, on Lughnasa. She played to win, but when he finally seized her beleaguered king, she welcomed the end of the game with a trill of excited anticipation.

"Och, a fine roll of luck." She let the cloth of her tunic fall over her shoulder, as she leaned toward him with a growing smile. "You'll be wanting a prize now, no doubt."

"Aye."

"Speak," she whispered, her eyes drifting closed, "and it will be yours."

When his kiss didn't come, she blinked her eyes opened. A long tube of dried grass stuck out of his mouth. He chewed it to the other side. A strange expression spread over his face, an expression unlike one she'd ever seen before.

She frowned and settled back on her hip. "Are you going to state your wager, or just sit there and gnash away like a cow?"

"Bilberries."

He spoke around the stem of the straw, and at first she was sure she'd misheard him. "Did you say bilberries?"

"Aye."

"What are ye blatherin' about?"

He pulled the straw out of his mouth and waved it toward her basket. "The food you brought would hardly sustain an ant, woman. I'll not last 'til dinner on a bit o' bread and a spoonful o' honey. Somewhere in these woods there must be bilberries ripe and ready to eat."

He planted the straw back between his teeth. Deirdre raised her hands to her hips, anticipation uncurling into indignation. "Am I hearing you right, Conaire? Did you just ask me to go about and pick berries?"

"There's not a thing wrong with your ears, I'm thinking."

"Nay, not a thing, but it's your wits I'm worried about." She tugged loose her skirts with short little jerks and smoothed the wrinkles over her knees. "Can't you think of a worthier wager than sendin' me into the thistles?"

"Is the daughter of a burgher of Troyes too proud for a bit o' honest labor?"

Her spine stiffened. Och, she had brought him out to the banks of this stream for lover's games, and here he was wastin' his wagers on setting her to slave's work. And what did he know of it, what did he know of the before-time, when she lived with her

Ma on the edge of the village? She was not always the pampered heiress he thought she was, nay. Now, as she stared at him in outrage, she recognized that odd gleam in his eyes. It was mischief he was after.

Crumpled linen spilled to the ground as she swept up the basket and marched toward the trees. Och, she'd get him his wretched berries, may he choke on the whole lot of them. She'd be givin' him a taste of his own medicine, when the tables were turned about.

She plunged into the thicket and purposely wove a path beneath low-slung branches, knowing without turning around that Conaire was forced to bob and weave to make his way after her. In Ireland she used to find the bilberries in the bogs, but she did not know these woods well, and thus did not know a place where a bilberry bush thrived. Instinctively she headed through the thickets toward the stonier grounds and poorer soils.

She came upon one near the edge of a meadow, a ways farther upstream. Without a word she set to picking the small blue black berries from the shrub, and tossing them in the basket nestled in the crook of her arm.

He lay his hand on her shoulder when the basket was a quarter full. "It's a fair fine gatherer you are, lass. There's plenty and more for the two of us to share—"

"Och, not near enough, Conaire! 'Tis true, that man makes love on the fullness of his stomach. I'll not have ye faintin' away for lack of sustenance—"

"Have no fear o' that."

He pulled her around flat into his chest, and she glared up at him, at the firm line of his lips, at his eyes gleaming with wickedness. She spread her hands away from him, her fingertips running blue with the juice of the berries, the basket swinging upon her elbow.

"You've a fit on you, woman, but I wager I can kiss it out o' you—"

"Och, be off with you, you scheming deceiver." She pushed out of his embrace, leaving sticky blue handprints on his tunic. "Do you think I can be bought like a laundress on fair day? You had your chance to taste me kisses." She thrust the basket at him. "You chose bilberries."

She set back through the woods, retracing the path to the grassy knoll, a smug smile spread across her face. He wasn't quite stomping behind her, but 'twas near enough; she sensed that if he were so lucky as to win the next game, they'd finally get what they'd both been yearning for since the first rays of dawn, and there'd be no more mischief.

The stream widened and curved through the thinning fencing of trees. Conaire curled his hand around her arm as a low chanting sounded through the woods.

They stopped in the shadow of a thick oak. On the other side of the stream, a procession emerged from behind a copse of trees and headed toward the edge of the stream. A clergyman in white robes led the way, with several black-robed monks in his wake. A clump of peasants followed a respectful distance behind.

Deirdre made the sign of the cross. The procession halted at the banks of the stream. The familiar, rhythmic cadence of Latin flowed over the trickling waters as a ceremony commenced, and the clergyman—a Dominican friar, by the looks of his robes—flicked droplets of holy water across the current.

Conaire's fingers tightened on her arm. "What's he doing, out here in the open—the one in the white robes?"

"He's blessin' the stream, don't you know." She sidled him a glance. "If you'd gone to Mass the other day, you'd have heard that he was after coming here, to ask for God's blessing on the fields and the like."

They watched in silence, still in the wood, as the simple ceremony was completed and the clergymen filed off, back whence they came. The peasants came forward then, and in the spot where the friar had stood they lay their gifts; a bag of grain, a tureen of milk, something wrapped in cloth, all the riches of the poor.

Conaire spoke upon a humorless, strangled laugh. "Leaving gifts to appease an angry god."

"Och, don't you be scorning such a thing." A shiver quivered up her spine. "You sound like the nobility of the convent, mockin' the ways of the common people. They're giving the full of their hands, and the full of their hearts, and who's to say it's not for the good?"

He gave her a queer look.

"Now come." She plunged anew into the thicket. "You owe me another game, Conaire."

It was a quiet man who sat across her when they returned to the grassy knoll. He played with less intensity, yet she still found herself scurrying across the board, usually chased by one or more of his men. This was not how she'd imagined spending the afternoon, bent in two over a chessboard, and snagging her tunic upon bilberry shrubs. She grew impatient over the slow pace of the game, and especially over Conaire's brooding silence—a silence she'd hoped to break, at least a little, and now it lay as thick as a pilgrim's shroud.

Finally, he snatched her king and rolled it in the palm of his hand.

She squinted at him suspiciously. "On Lughnasa, you played with all the skill of a child. Is it a fool you're making of me, Conaire?"

"Nay." He flung the king upon the board. "I'm thinking it's you who's making the fool o' me."

Och, there'd be no sweet lovemaking upon the grass today, not with such a fog upon him. "Do you think I'm losing on purpose? Why would I be wantin' another slave's duty?" She jerked to her feet and waved her hand toward the stream. "Is it a fish you'll have me catch now, Conaire? I can do that, too, you know, better than I can find bilberries."

Bunching her skirts in one hand, she set to searching the edge of the clearing. Och, the day wasn't going at all as she'd planned; she was walking beside herself, she was. And now, here she stood searching for a pointed branch and thinkin' of crawling out on the stones of the creek as in the old days, and searching for the silver flash of dinner beneath the murky waters.

Ah! And there it was, a fishing spear, as straight as a hunter's arrow, and as sharp as if she'd spent a morning honing the point.

She swept it up and shook it at him. "The Little People are sharing in your mischief today."

Wordlessly she trudged to the bank of the stream. Dropping the spear at her side, she swept up the length of her skirts and jerked them into a knot at her hip. Och, surely he'd say something now, surely he'd stop her; did the sight of her legs—bare clear up to her hip—do nothin' to the man? But the silence behind her stretched, and so she sullenly retrieved the spear and plunged into the shock of the icy water. The clear, swift current crept up her ankles, then to her calves, as she nimbly stepped from stone to stone into the middle of the creek.

She stilled and bent her knees in the slightest of crouches, the spear upraised. The scattered bits of her reflection reconverged, wavered, and then softly rocked upon the rippling water as she focused on the pebbled riverbed.

She thought of Jean-Jacques and the old days, when they would stand in the brackish water of the wide creek which fed the sea, feeling the salt dry tight upon their legs, searching for the telltale ripple of the water, while the linings of their bellies rasped hollow and hungry, and laughing at the growling none the less. Her heart cried out for Jean now—how she wished he were here, in his proud manhood, so she could ask him about the strange ways of men.

She choked back a sudden sob. She could not fish with tears blurring her eyesight; she could not have done with this mockery of a lover's morning.

The sun beat upon her hair. A fly buzzed close to her ear, retreated, then circled again. A drop of perspiration ran slowly from her temple to her cheek.

Her reflection shattered as she plunged the spear into the stream, then jerked the weapon back up with a spray of clear droplets. A fish arched its last upon the splintered wooden point.

She tossed it, spear and all, upon the bank as she splattered to the shore. "There's some magic to that blessing after all, I'm thinking."

He stood up from his seat on the knoll. "There wasn't a bit o' magic in that, lass."

"Och, so now you know." She jerked free the knotted length of her skirts, and let the cloth fall over her damp legs. "Aye, I can spot a bush of bilberries from ten paces, and aye, I can spear a fish. I can even milk a cow, don't you know, and do a bit of spinning. Life was not easy for two bastard children, livin' with a tainted woman on the edge of a village."

His shadow fell over her. She met his gaze brazenly—but her boldness fled as she saw the strange look upon his face. Those eyes of gray which always seemed as sharp as a silver blade, or as hard as stone, now glowed as soft and welcoming as the billowing smoke of a hearth fire.

She raised her hand and hesitantly traced his mouth, almost not daring to believe what she saw lingering upon it; for surely, 'twas the faintest shadow of a smile which curled the corners of his lips. Aye, it was here, the smile she'd not expected to see on his face for half a lifetime, yet the ghost of it hovered, and it did not matter that it was a bittersweet smile, full of sympathy and regret.

He curled his fingers over her hand. "You'll never have to scrape for a living, lass. You'll never feel the bite of want again."

"I would willingly return to that life, if just for one moment," she insisted, "I could be as happy now as I was then."

His grip on her fingers faltered. That strange, glorious feeling surged between them again, as it did whenever they stood so close together. She knew it was love—for such a river of emotion flowing between a man and a woman could be nothing else. And though even now she felt him yielding to the currents, still in his eyes she saw a wariness of this strong magic over which neither he nor she had any control.

"You never gave me a chance," he murmured, lowering his lips to her temple, "to state my wager."

Wordlessly she drew his hand down and placed it over her breast.

They made love like two peasants on a tryst in the furrow of a field; pillowed on the soft grass with the scent of the rich earth swirling around them, rolling about careless of their soiled and rumpled clothing, careless about everything but the urgent need to feel the sunshine on their skin, and the heat of their joined bodies, and all with their eyes wide open, so they could gaze upon one another.

When the loving was over, they lay on their backs, Deirdre's head cocked on Conaire's chest, watching the float of the clouds through the jagged break in the greenery above. At Deirdre's gentle urging, Conaire spoke of his travels. He told her tales of a place where it never rained, where mountainous dunes of sand spread from horizon to horizon, and burned through the soles of the thickest shoes. He spoke of a far northern land where all winter it was night, and all summer it was day. He spoke of the Cathay people who believed the soul was immortal, like Christians, except in a different sense. They believe that upon the death of a man, his soul enters into another body and, depending on how he has acted during his life, his future state becomes better or worse than his last.

He ran his fingers through her hair and told her more; of people who willingly scarred their skin with designs; of dogs that pulled sledges across endless snow; of a land where the cattle were sacred; of widows who threw themselves upon the pyres of their dead husbands; of men who turned over their womenfolk to every strange guest; of naked dancing girls dedicated to the service of gods in Hindu shrines.

"Och, it's talking you are," she blurted, finally, at this last, and tallest tale. "I'll not believe a word of it, I won't."

When the sun finally ascended to the treetops, they both roused from their lazy slumber and set their clothes to rights. The Clunel servants would soon be expecting them for the midday meal. Conaire lingered over Deirdre's hair, plucking the twigs and leaves out of it and combing it through with his fingers. Then they strolled leisurely through the high straight trees toward the manor house.

Just outside the Clunel garden, they stumbled upon Octavius snoozing in the shadow of an oak. He snored openmouthed, drool oozing into his beard, with his hood pulled down over his eyes.

Conaire stiffened to a stop.

She squeezed Conaire's arm and strode toward the little man before Conaire could wake him with an angry roar. She'd grown fond of the dirty little creature during these weeks in the country. A spritely thing, full of humor, he was. She'd do what she could to protect him from Conaire's unreasonable wrath.

She bent into the shadows and gently nudged him. He snorted and turned his face away. She nudged him hard enough to topple him off his precarious perch. He sputtered and spit into sudden wakefulness.

"Saints alive, can a man not get a bit o' sleep on a summer's afternoon?" He struggled with his hood until he managed to pull it off and glare at the offender. "Never a bit o' sleep for the weary, is there—Lass! Ah, never you mind, I did not know it was ye!"

Deirdre realized with a sudden start that she was meeting Octavius's beetle-black eyes—she was out of practice casting her gaze away, after so much time alone with Conaire—but before she could lower her lashes, she noticed that Octavius looked her straight in the eye, and did not flinch away.

"I've been waitin' here for the two o' ye for half the day, whilst ye were about traipsing through the woods with a never-you-mind. How's a man supposed to find ye in such a place, will ye be after telling me that?"

Deirdre's neck began to prickle. "Who is it, Octavius? Who has arrived?"

"Your father, lass. Come to check on your welfare."

Her hand flew to her unbound hair. "Papa!"

"Aye." Octavius cast a sly look toward Conaire, standing as still as a stone. "And I'll tell ye something for nothing; woe be the man who has to face him, for he's hotter than a bog fire."

Twenty

Conaire stood rooted to the earth, as Deirdre nervously brushed at the snags and soil upon her tunic and queried Octavius about the details of her father's arrival.

He clenched his hands into fists to prevent himself from lunging at the creature and choking the life out of him. He had not laid eyes upon the wretch since the night Octavius told the story of Deirdre and the three sons of Usnagh. With the passing of the days, Conaire had near forgotten about him, he'd near forgotten about the thunderclouds lurking just beyond the horizon of these sunny days; he'd wanted to forget everything but the moments, one after another, and he'd succeeded.

Here, time had stopped, rolled backwards, and there were moments, like today, when his heart felt young again.

Now here *he* was, leapin' out into their path like a wolf in a children's tale. Just when Conaire's mind was at its softest, just when his will had frayed down to nothing, there that wretch stood, answering all o' Deirdre's questions, his beady eyes set upon him, twinkling as if this were naught but a peg-game, with a slow grin spreading above his beard.

"It's a fine time," Conaire snarled, surprising Deirdre into silence, "to be showin' me your face, Octavius."

The wretch discovered a patch of his lower back that needed scratching, and set to it with vigor. "What more would ye have me do, man? I've been following ye like a shadow long enough, don't ye know."

"Coming and going as you please."

"As if it were that easy!" He squinted one-eyed at Conaire and scowled. "Are ye blind, man? Deaf, dumb? What d'ye think I'm doing here, if not to make it easier to come and go as ye please?"

"What are the two of ye blatherin' about?" Deirdre glared at each of them. "Me father's here, and fit to be tied, I'm thinking. It'll not do a bit of good to stand out here talking nonsense."

Octavius threw his hands in the air. "I'll be off, lass, to leave the two o' ye alone."

Conaire took a step toward Octavius "You'll not be getting away, Octavius, not this time."

The little man ignored him and trudged through the shadows toward the manor house. "I can only interfere in the ways o' the world so much, the rest is in your hands." He waved a single dirty finger high in the air. "Ye'd find that out yourself, if ye stop gnashing and fightin' against what should be."

What should be. Conaire stared after the wretch, his mind full of *what should be;* of the lonely screech o' gulls wheeling above the plugged stones of a smoky *clochán,* of the bare rock scraping the flesh from his fingertips as he wrestled a harvest from bits o' clay and sand, of back-breaking loads o' peat heaved up the steep slick cliff and burning with a heatless flame, choking him with soot. *What should be.* Thirty, forty, perhaps fifty years with his woman, caged anew on a barren rock of an island, watching the work wear her down, watching the light in her eyes slowly dim, watching her die in his arms.

Yet the thought had not yet faded from his mind, when he yearned with sudden intensity for the taste of salt-spray on his tongue, for the music of the seabirds cawing o'er the breakers, for the bob of a *curragh* beneath his feet, for the feel of honest weariness in his bones, for the chance to build again on the island he'd abandoned forever.

And more than this: He wanted those thirty, forty, or fifty

years. He wanted the glut of moments, one after another, a whole new lifetime of seconds tumbling upon one another. By the gods . . . he *wanted* to be there again. He wanted to catch her last wheezing breath against his body, knowing all the same that he'd suffer more the second time around.

"Come." She lay her hand soft on his arm. "I love me father, but he has all the patience of a babe, and it would not bode well for us, if we set him into more of a fit."

She'd pulled her hood on. He could see the tracks of her fingers through the hair at her brow. A thin, pink scratch traced the curve of her flushed cheek. Bits of leaves and soil clung to her throat and streaked across her tunic. What a mussed, little fairy-sprite, he thought, fresh from her dew-laden bed, clear-eyed, soft-lipped. What a fragile creature, and how innocent of the world.

Her fingers slipped off his arm as his silence lengthened. "Am I to think you've changed your mind, Conaire? That you'll not be wanting to marry me after all?"

He shouldn't. His mind said leave her be; she'd find a husband, a family, a life without hardship, and she'd know in the end the comfort of growing old with her husband and her children. But his guts screamed the louder—*she is mine, she will always be my wild heart.* And he knew then what he had known in some deep part of himself since the moment he first saw her blink open her eyes—what he had denied to himself every day since: He did not have the strength to walk away.

Weariness seeped into his spine. He'd spent a lifetime fighting Fate. Now, in the end, all his struggles were for naught, for he could no longer resist succumbing to it. He'd finally been defeated, in the only battle he'd ever fought which had meant anything. He was, truly, a warrior no more.

"Sweet Mother Mary, what's wrong, Conaire?"

Anxiety whirled in her eyes of forest-green. The pale crease between her brows grew taut. *My love. You, too, will be a victim of my weakness.*

With the thought came a spurt of defiance, one last struggling gasp of strength. *Sweet Mother Mary.* Aye, aye. 'Twas a wonder he'd not thought of this before. One last secret hung between them, the deepest, the most fantastic, the one that defied all she'd been brought up to believe. He'd sling that last weapon at her like a pebble at the fates.

Since he could not walk away from her, he would give her one last chance to walk away from him.

He brushed off her hood, then settled his hands firmly on her shoulders. "You must make me a promise, lass."

"Och, all I've heard lately is promises, but when the time comes to fulfill them, you linger like a man in the shadow of the hanging tree."

"Do you love me, woman?"

The question silenced her ire. "Do you doubt me? Och, and I thought it was as plain as the nose on me face—"

"Do you trust me?"

She searched his face, puzzled. The light around them dimmed as a cloud passed across the face of the sun. A cow lowed somewhere in the distance. On the road beyond the manor house, a farmer shouted and snapped his whip over a lazy ox's back.

"Aye." She grasped his forearms. "With me own life, I trust ye."

"Good. Then listen." He rapidly calculated how much time it would take for him to travel to the coast and back, to make the necessary arrangements. "This is the promise you will make me: Three months hence, you will meet me on the hill where we first lay together."

"What foolishness is this?" She pushed away from him. "We'll be long married by then, and there'll be no more need to be sneaking about like thieves in the night—"

"Woman—hear me out."

She spun away from him and turned her back.

"There is a day called Samhain," he continued, "the first day of your November. On its eve we shall meet in that place."

"I know of the day—it's All Hallow's E'en." She crossed her arms. "And why would ye have me traipsing about the woods on the day when the souls of the dead fly free, will ye be telling me that?"

He started. Such was the way of the ancient Celts. Had the Christians absorbed that belief, too, or had she just learned it through some folklore still surviving among the people of Ireland?

"Are you goin' to marry me, Conaire? Or these past weeks have I just been giving you the rope, so you can stand at me back while it's hanging me?"

He heard the tears behind the defiant words. He thrust an arm around her waist and yanked her against the length of his body.

"I'm off to ask your father—did you really expect anything less?"

She turned her face into the swell of his arm.

"You must trust me. Fate has many surprises, and not all o' them are good."

"Och, it's the betrothal you fear. You don't understand, me father loves me—"

"It's not that." Her words struck daggers in his heart, for he knew the pain of the betrayal to come—the first of her many agonies. "The future is uncertain, woman, and we must prepare for the worst."

"I would have seen it." She jerked her head up and peered at him with her swirling eyes. "Have you forgotten? I've the gift of foresight."

She spoke the words with pride, and be thought, *if nothing else, I have gifted her with courage.*

"Your power is uncertain, when it comes to your own fate."

"But—"

"Argue with me no more." He felt time slipping away like the last grains in a sandglass. "Just promise me: No matter what happens this day, or in the days to come, no matter what you see or hear or feel, you will come to the hill where we first laid together, on Samhain's Eve."

"On me mother's grave, I swear it."

On her words he grasped her face and kissed her lips, and her eyes, and her temple, and filled his head with the scent of her hair, his palms with the feel of her skin, her breast, her yearning, and he stole a few more moments, just one more, and yet another, knowing in his heart they may be his last.

And so it was, when they heard a man's voice raised in the garden just beyond the woods. Deirdre broke away from Conaire, flushed and panting, whispering "Papa! It's Papa!" even as she raked her hair back and fumbled with her slipped neckline and tumbled hood. She gasped when she glimpsed a flash of black through the trees, and an elderly woman dressed in common robes waddled into the woods.

"Moira!"

Deirdre skirted the trees which separated them and launched herself upon the old woman's bosom.

"Lass, lass," Moira exclaimed, patting her charge's bare head. "What are ye doing idling here, with your own father near to pacin' a furrow in the ground a-waiting for ye?"

"Och, we're coming, Moira." She hugged her maidservant more tightly. "Octavius didn't tell me you had arrived, too; he'd not said a word!"

"Easy, child, me bones are brittle and like to snap, if ye squeeze me any harder. Now let me get a look at ye." She disentangled herself from Deirdre's arms, then pressed her hands to her own bosom. "By the saints, look at ye, all bubblin' with life, with your face as bright as the sunshine. Aye, Doctor, have ye any of that medicine for me?"

Conaire said nothing, his thoughts in the Clunel garden and the upcoming confrontation.

"What's this?" The maidservant peered more closely at her charge, then lifted up a tress slipping around the hem of her cloak. "Lass! Are ye walkin' about with your hair flying as free as a milkmaid? And what's this?" Moira plucked at something clinging to Deirdre's tunic, then squinted at the full dishevelment of her clothing. Her jowls began to shake like twin bowls of porridge. "Look at ye! Ye'd think ye were a child of ten summers who'd spent the afternoon in the bog—not a fine burgher's grown daughter. Come, come, ye can't be after greetin' your father a-looking like that, child."

Deirdre hung back as the maidservant turned away with a flutter of robes. "Och, there's more important things to do than change me clothing." Deirdre strolled to his side, and lay her hand on his arm. "I'm staying with Conaire—"

"No."

He covered her hand to ease the harshness of the word. She would have enough pain in the months—maybe years—to come. He would spare her this.

"Go with Moira," he said, more gently, all the while memorizing the lines of her face. "Your father and I must speak alone."

"I'm not going to hide away like a—"

"Join us afterward. For the celebration."

How easy the lie rolled off his tongue, and how easily she swallowed it. Her lips curled into a smile.

"Me dowry is twenty thousand *livres,* it is. Don't let me Da cheat you out of a bit of it, Conaire, for he's the kind that'll pinch a sou until it squeals."

With a flash of bare ankles, Deirdre set off around the edge of the garden, along a narrow path that led to the front of the house.

Moira lingered behind and turned her unfocused milky gaze

upon him. "Monsieur Mézières is waitin' for *ye* in the garden, doctor."

Something wrenched in the back of his throat. "Look after her well."

The skin crinkled around her near-sightless eyes as she hefted her skirts and waddled, elbows wide, in Deirdre's path. "And isn't that what I've been doin' all along, don't ye know?"

Conaire found the burgher pacing in an open square of the garden, crackling under his feet the bleached weeds long baked brittle by the white-hot sun. His scarlet cloak embroidered in gold lay carelessly tossed across an old stone bench. Waves of scorching heat rose from the paving stones, lost amid a netting of weeds.

The burgher ground to a halt as he caught sight of Conaire approaching him through the shadows. He dug his thumb beneath his jewel-studded belt. "Ah! You've finally chosen to bless me with your presence."

A barely perceptible nod was Conaire's only greeting.

"I am not the type of man who takes kindly to be made to wait for underlings."

Conaire bent over and swept up a stick, hiding the ruddy fury rising to his face. There had been a time, a dozen lifetimes ago, when he had faced her father as a *king*.

"Have you no excuses?" The burgher's blunt-cut hair swung with anger. "I expect some light and oily words to ease a patron's anger—or have you lost your tongue entirely?"

"This is not Troyes." Conaire leaned a shoulder against a tree, and used the stick to flick off a clod of mud clinging to his heel. "You come unexpected, Mézières.

The burgher's chest inflated in affront. "Did I hear you correctly?"

Conaire glared at the man who'd put a sudden end to his brief happiness, and banked the fury rising like the tide in his heart.

Anger would not help him now: he must be calm and deliberate; he must taunt this cool-headed burgher beyond control.

"A note," Conaire drawled, "announcing your arrival would have been adequate, I'm thinking."

"A note?" The words came out hoarse, sputtered, as if he could draw into his swelling chest not a mite more air. *"You* are lecturing me on etiquette? *You,* who came to me dirty and unkempt off the streets of Troyes? *You,* who in three weeks has not once sent a single word to me about my own daughter's welfare?"

Conaire slung the stick into the woods. "Why should I be after sending you something that you never asked for?"

"Do they serve up audacity with the porridge here?"

"Nay. Common sense." Conaire swaggered into the light, then stood, wide-legged, crossing his arms across his chest. "Why should I spend three *deniers* sending you a message about the health of your investment, when you can damned well afford to make the trip here and see her for yourself?"

The burgher's blue eyes narrowed to slits. Color flooded out of his face, then rushed back in, leaving only his lips white between mottled cheeks.

"Ah, yes," Conaire added, with a bold little bow of his head, "your daughter is doing quite well."

The heat rising from the weed-edged paving stones shimmered between them. The shrill buzz of summer insects swelled; held; then ebbed away. The burgher's blue eyes simmered with pale blue flames.

"I'll assume," the burgher began, trailing his fingers over the embroidered stripe running down the center of his surcoat, "that all the weeks you've spent in this rotting hovel, amid the surly peasants of this uncivilized countryside, is the sole reason for your insolence." The burgher's gaze roamed over Conaire's dirty and snagged clothing. "You obviously know no better, but a Mézières will not suffer such conditions as this—and no daughter of mine will be left unchaperoned and unattended in any woman's house, be she noble or not. Because of the indignities you have undoubtedly been forced to suffer in my employ, I will overlook your behavior."

What a master of masks, this burgher was. How easily the man could set aside an affront, if he wanted more from a person; how easily he could ignore the truth, in favor of what he willed the truth to be. Witness Sir Guichard's dissipation. Deirdre's defiance of the betrothal. Conaire's own insolence. All, he ignored, for they went against his wishes. 'Twas no wonder the burgher had grown rich. He possessed all the ice-blooded cunning of the merchants of the East.

Aye, well Conaire'd give him a truth he could not ignore.

"Where is my daughter?" The burgher spread a hand glittering with rings toward the sagging house behind them. "Has she, like the mistress of this mockery of a noble house, deigned not to greet a mere burgher? Or is she just keeping me waiting, like the insolent doctor I hired to treat her?"

"I sent her away."

One finely combed brow arched.

"Don't fear." A slow, humorless grin spread across Conaire's lips. "She's safe in the manor house. We need to talk, you and I."

"There is only one thing we must discuss." The burgher squared off before Conaire and clasped his hands behind his back. "Deirdre has had her weeks in the country. I trust she is strong enough for a wedding."

"Aye, she's ready indeed."

The burgher nodded sharply, satisfied. Conaire strolled toward the stone bench. Something in his swagger caught the burgher's attention and set his speculative gaze back upon him, upon the wide, thrown-back shoulders, upon the ease of his pace, the fluidity of his muscles.

"It does not compliment a man of your age," the burgher scowled, "to be strutting about like a cock."

"Aye, but now I feel like a man ten years younger."

Conaire took a seat and crossed his leg over his other knee. He eyed the burgher's belt, the sagging alms purse, the decorative sheath of a dagger, and the protruding gold hilt—aye, a delicate little thing, that, but it would do the job. Then Conaire threw his arm across the back of the bench, so his tunic stretched tight across his body.

And as Conaire intended, the burgher's gaze fell to the blue streaks, the handprints Deirdre had left upon Conaire's chest after picking bilberries.

"Always into something, your daughter is." He allowed himself a rogue of a smile. "Which is why she's off dressing more properly for the greeting."

Just beyond the clearing, a dead branch snapped off a high bough and crashed to the ground below. The crack upset a flock of birds nestled amid the leaves, and launched them screeching in every direction.

Conaire twisted the burgher's discarded cloak around his dirty hand. A long time coming, this moment o' confrontation. Over seven hundred years in the making. Aye, revenge was a sweet, savory dish—especially when he thought never to partake of it—and now it lay before him, steaming its fragrance into his face. A dead man couldn't resist taking a bite. Conaire glanced over his shoulder, toward the manor house. Deirdre was not near; and the way was clear between here and the manor house. What will be done will be done, and it mattered not if he took his fill o' this sweet vengeance in the by-and-by. What he said to the burgher was immaterial, as long as, in the end, the deed was done.

For then, the burgher would tell her whatever he wanted her to believe, and Deirdre would have to decide in her heart who was the liar: her father or her lover.

"Don't you know there's something about this wild, uncivilized countryside you hate so much, Mézières." Conaire idly brushed off some nettles sticking to his boot. Silence lay as heavy as lead between them. "Such a place brings out the most primitive urges in men and women, and that's the way it should be, I'm thinking."

The burgher stood as mute as one of the deep forest's ancient oaks, his pupils constricted to pinpricks, the thinnest sheen of sweat beginning to bead on his forehead, his fingers curled around a gold chain draped around his neck.

"Men construct too many buildings to worship in," Conaire mused, taking more than a measure of wicked enjoyment in the burgher's swelling shock, thinking, *This is for Deirdre, too, for what you'll do to her in the weeks to come.* "We should be doing our worshipping with each other in the open air, like the Irish at Samhain, and there should be no more talk about it. You being a man, with a bit of a past of your own, you'll know what I'm talking about."

Conaire shifted his shoulders and let his hand, dirty with nettles, fall again upon the scarlet cloth of the burgher's cloak. "Just so you won't be thinking I'm an utter rogue, I fought against this thing between us, for I was after thinking I was too old for this sort o' thing. But your daughter is a woman o' great charm and great beauty." He gestured vaguely to the shaggy old oaks, to the blue white sky. "We being all but alone out here, well, it's no surprise that nature took its course."

The burgher swiveled with the crunch of gravel and showed Conaire his back. The hem of his robes trembled in suppressed fury. His fingernails, shaped into perfect rosy crescents, dug deep into his sleeves.

"Am I to understand," the burgher said in a tightly controlled voice, "that you have taken my daughter's innocence?"

Innocence. What an exalted thing that was, as if leaving a woman in a cloud of ignorance was the best way to send her into a world where skill amid the linens could smooth the roughest o' marriages. Wasn't it like a burgher o' these times to name the first flowering into womanhood in such a way?

"I think of it more as giving the lass a bit o' knowledge and experience."

That is for the agony you will cause her in this life, and twice for the agony you have caused her in the other.

The hem of the burgher's robes rippled anew, the silver embroidery flashing in the white-hot sun. A dog barked, somewhere beyond in the next holding. Monsieur Mézières eased his hands down to his elbows, then grasped his wrist behind his back. He began a slow, deliberate pacing.

"Congratulations, *Doctor* MacSidh." His throat flexed as if he struggled to pull out the words. "Your deception was flawless, your treachery, unimagined. This ruse should earn you a good, long time in Hell."

For a flash of a moment, Conaire reluctantly admired the burgher's control. Another father might have raged the moment he'd understood, he might have attacked him blind with fury, or called men to do it for him, but this burgher assessed the situation and the cost, as if he were bargaining for dangerous wares on the back streets of Baghdad, as if he were a king on whose smallest decision hung the fate of thousands.

But Conaire needed emotion—he needed blind, outraged fury, and he felt a needle of irritation that he'd thrown his biggest spear—the seduction of the man's daughter—and found his foe still standing.

"I'm sure you're well informed about the consequences of your actions, should I bring you before the courts of high justice in Troyes. The count of Champagne is an acquaintance of mine; he owes me a large sum of money. I could accuse you of rape and see you hanged."

Conaire couldn't wait that long—nor would he put Deirdre through the shame of a long trial and the misery of the sight of his death. "Aye, I suppose money could twist justice, if you were that set on having away with me."

"You're quite adept at this, aren't you, MacSidh?" The burgher continued as if he were talking to himself. "I suppose you know already that I will do everything in my power to prevent a scandal which would sully my name—and my daughter's prospects."

And have you thought once about your daughter's wants, your daughter's needs, your daughter's heart? Nay, that would be askin' too much o' the cold-blooded burgher.

The burgher ceased his pacing and set his icy gaze upon him. "How much do you want?"

Conaire stanched the disgust threatening to curl his lip, and brushed some soot off his sleeve with exaggerated calm. "I don't know what you're talkin' about."

"Let's have done with it. How much will it take for you to crawl back into the hole you slithered out of? How much? Hmm? Five thousand *livres?*"

The metallic taste of acid seeped into his mouth. "A man would have to be daft to take five thousand *livres* when the lass has a dowry o' twenty thousand plus whatever—"

"Twenty thousand, then."

A merchant, indeed, thinking everything has a price, too foolish to know there are things on this earth so precious they cannot be gauged by the weight o' gold.

The cordons in the burgher's neck stiffened as the silence stretched. "Thirty thousand, MacSidh."

Acrid fumes filled his head, and a bitterness burned in his belly. Conaire wondered for how much the burgher would sell his own flesh and blood. Impatience seized him, as it had not seized him in centuries; impatience at the games people play; the old, tired steps they danced around one another, which always ended in the same place. He wanted this over, and it looked as if the burgher lacked the courage to have done with it here, the courage to have done with it himself.

"Fifty thousand *livres*."

"I'm not in the market to be bought." Conaire rose to his full height, realizing even as he did it that he'd do his cause worse by threatening the old man with his size; so he turned his back to him and snarled the words over his shoulder. "Unlike you, Mézières, I value her more than for money."

"Eighty thousand—"

"Enough."

The burgher raised his arched brows, then swiveled, and leaned his hip against the arm of the stone bench. He tapped one fingernail against a rusted iron rivet.

Tap tap tap tap.

"You are too old to be in love." The tapping ceased. "Is she with child?"

He started to sneer, instinctively, for wasn't that the bane of his endless lifetime, that though he'd brought a thousand babies into this world, never a one had he sired—when suddenly the sneer froze upon his face.

There had been a child, once—his and Brigid's child—conceived by the shadows of the Lughnasa fires, amid the wonders of the eclipse, in the same way that he and Deirdre had been frolicking these past weeks; and he began to wonder if fate was fickle, or if that bit o' history, too, was to be repeated, was already ripe in Deirdre's womb.

The air thinned in his lungs and black spots exploded in his sight. *A babe, a babe. A child o' my own loins.* He grasped the gritty stone back of the bench. A bit o' happiness sown in these days of enchantment . . . mayhap to be harvested by Beltaine Day.

He'd forgotten the good of that life, in the midst of the agony that followed, and before the thought left his mind he found himself pressing back the black clouds of remembrance, the knowledge of the loss of that long-ago babe. Surely, that tragedy was not the roll o' fate. That was his own foolishness, his own unbound arrogance. If he'd not gone back to the *ráth* to face the people o' Morna, if he'd listened to Brigid's wise words, they'd have both lived, and aye, mayhap the babe would have lived, and there'd have been no loneliness on Inishmaan.

What was it that Octavius had said? *I can only interfere in the ways o' the world so much. The rest is in your hands.*

A steely courage flooded back into his limbs. He knew the roll o' fate; he knew what was to come. He'd use that knowledge to protect his wife and his child, to give all three of them one more chance at life.

"Alas, not yet," Conaire responded, turning to face the burgher with a grin spreading across his face. "But it's not from the lack of trying, I'm thinking. If it's grandchildren you'll be wanting, you'll get them, let there be no doubt o' that—"

"One hundred thousand *livres,* MacSidh. Not a *denier* more."

Conaire laughed—a short laugh full with more glee than he'd felt in a long time. He knew what this greedy burgher wanted; the old wretch was still struggling for a noble title, as Brigid's father had been struggling to retrieve his crown. The motives were still the same, and perhaps the souls themselves—that knowledge was beyond him—but he would use what he *did* know to change the roll o' fate. In the end, it would be the burgher's rapacious greed for the one thing which he could not buy, which would undo him.

"You won't be rid o' me so easily, Mézières. We're to be family, for I'm after marrying the lass."

Aye, the arrow hit its mark, for the burgher stood up stiff from his perch on the arm of the bench and swept his cloak off its back.

"What makes you think I will allow such a union?"

"Because I want it. Moreover, because your daughter wants it." He laughed again, mocking him. "But I see by the sneer on your face that that doesn't make a bit o' difference to you. It wasn't my idea, bringing this to you, but your daughter loves you. She knows no better."

The burgher's face mottled. "I won't permit it."

Conaire managed an easy shrug. "There are ways o' having it done without a father's permission."

"You'll get no dowry." The burgher cut the air with the edge of his stiff hand. "I'll cast her out."

Aye, and it won't be the first time you denied your kin. "Do you not understand, Mézières? Your money means *nothing* to me. I've made my way well enough without it all these years. It's your daughter I want, as my wife, now and forevermore." Conaire swaggered to the burgher's side, close enough to smell the sticky orange perfume wafting up from his skin. "You have a choice: approve o' the match and be content, or disapprove and lose a daughter—and a future."

Mézières turned upon him, his red-rimmed eyes burning like embers within twin holes in a dead husk of a charred tree. Aye, aye, no more ice flowed in those veins.

"You touch my only daughter," he warned in a harsh, restrained voice, "and I'll have your throat slit in the night by men who do it for sport."

"She's *mine,* Mézières." Conaire laughed again, a mocking sound, then brushed a finger over the embroidery of the burgher's neckline, taunting, teasing. "And you don't have the courage to bloody your hands."

Then Conaire deliberately turned his back. He sensed the moment the burgher's trembling fingers curled around the gold hilt of his dagger, he sensed the moment the burgher's rage overflowed, and the fury spilled over into the primitive, bestial violence latent in all men. Conaire spread his shoulder blades, relaxed his muscles, and waited for the blow—

Cold steel ripped through skin and muscle and bone and soft, yielding organs. He jerked forward against the force, thinking—

The burgher's aim was true—for Conaire knew enough about death to sense it in the swift draining of his blood, and the shiver of the oncoming chill. Pain, delayed, seared through him, and he squeezed his eyes shut against it; no matter how many times he died, always, there was this mind-numbing agony before the blind, dark silence; and he was determined to die without a sound, so as not to alert Deirdre to witness it.

He fell like a rock; the hot paving stones seared his cheek. He squinted up against the white blaze of sun. The burgher loomed over him, a grimace distorting his features as he yanked the dagger out of Conaire's back, then methodically wiped the blood on his scarlet cloak.

"A pity," the burgher drawled, snapping the dagger back into its sheath, "about the roving bandits in these savage woods. One never knows when they will strike."

Twenty-one

The last rays of the setting sun gleamed over the rolling hill-sides of Champagne, painting the billowing edges of the eastern clouds blood red. A scouring wind flattened the long wild grasses which clogged the pathway from the manor house to the muddy road, unleashing a stinging spray which hissed upon the hot earth. A single rickety cart waited atilt on the ridged road, hitched to a bowed-backed mare. The Clunel servants huddled in the lee of the manor house, pressed against the sweating stones to avoid the dripping thatch overhang.

Deirdre stood apart from the others. The wind wrestled with the sodden weight of her cloak, until it wrenched the wool from her white-knuckled grip. The folds battered her legs. The capricious gusts slapped her hair across her face.

She let the damp tresses blind her. She needed no eyes to see, for the scene unrolling before her was naught but a strange, vivid nightmare. For though the wind howled o'er the land, and bolts of silvered lightning threatened in the east, Deirdre stood as still and straight as an ancient oak. From the moment she first laid eyes upon Conaire's pale, waxen skin, she'd become an observer, detached, silent within some calm place inside herself. 'Twas naught but an illusion, those lifeless gray eyes, the stiff iciness of his bloodied limbs. Conaire couldn't be dead.

She felt the threatening rumble of oncoming tears, distant, but as violent as the coming thunderstorm.

The thin leading edge of the high clouds fogged over the

western sunset, casting the world in pewter. Octavius rounded the corner of the manor house, leading a makeshift bier. Four white-robed clergymen with their hoods pulled far over their faces gripped the bier upon their shoulders, and walked solemnly past the servants to take the path to the cart. The women wailed at the passing of the swathed corpse.

Anger rumbled up from deep within her, and she stood gripped by the urge to race toward those screaming women and rake their faces with her nails, pummel them until they ceased their wretched moaning, for Conaire was not dead—Conaire was not dead. 'Twas naught but sleep that kept him silent and still upon the bier.

But she stood motionless, her fingernails biting into her flesh, as the bier approached, as the strange, white-robed men shuffled by her on silent feet, staring up at Conaire muffled in the linens and thinking—*Untie him, he cannot breathe. He shall catch his death of chill and dampness.* While a small voice whispered in her ear—*You've gone mad. You've gone mad.*

For she'd seen him with her own eyes. She'd seen Conaire's stiff body turned over in the bloodied weeds, his face pale even in the buttery sunlight. She'd fallen upon him and shook him and kissed his cold blue lips, and strained her ears to hear his heart torn and still.

And even as she was torn from his body, she wondered why she hadn't felt the slice of steel through her own flesh, why she hadn't tossed and turned for months in an agony of knowledge. For the wretched gift which Conaire had taught her to accept had never before failed to torment her with oncoming tragedy, not with Mama, not with Jean-Jacques—it would not fail her with the man who was spirit of her own spirit, the heart of her own heart.

Now she stood with thin spray blinding her, watching the clergymen slide Conaire's stiff body upon the cart, thinking, *I've gone mad. I've gone mad.*

Then she gagged upon the cloying scent of orange which suddenly inundated her.

Her father's hand fell upon her shoulder. "It's a woeful day, my dearest Deirdre."

She pressed her hand against her nose and mouth. The weight of her father's grip seemed to press her into the ground. Through her flying hair, she watched the white-robed men tie Conaire firmly upon the cart, then cover him with an oiled sheet to protect him from the splattering rain. The black bellies of the approaching clouds skimmed the tips of the trees.

"Weep." Her father curled his fingers into her shoulder. "Weep as a woman should. As a wife would."

Och, wasn't it kind of her father to say such a thing, to grant her the dignity of that word, when he'd come to her only this afternoon full of stern scolding, and then, hard upon it, haughtily granted promises of reluctant concessions. For the love of her, he'd said, he would see to it that her betrothal to Sir Guy was broken, and her marriage to Conaire arranged, and at the time her heart had trilled with wonder at having a father so generous, so openhearted.

Now suspicion twisted within her and thrashed like a demon. Her father had come to her after his talk with Conaire with skin pink from scrubbing, his hair damp and clinging to his nape. He'd had a quick, jerky way to his walk, and smelled oddly—a sweet, yet rancid stench, like the rotting of fresh vegetation. She hated herself for the sinful seed germinating in her heart. She hated herself for doubting the last of her kin, her flesh and blood, her only family.

Honor thy father.

The world was turned upside down, and nothing remained as it once was.

"Come." He urged her to turn toward him, toward the portal of the manor house, as the rain spattered harder at their feet. "There's no more to be done here, Deirdre."

Aye, and you were quick to cede the making of the arrange-
ments to Octavius, Father, quick to cede the responsibility of
seeing the man who would have been your son-in-law well buried.

"You must think of your future," he continued, relentlessly.
"You'll catch your death of cold here—"

His words ended on a gasp, for she turned to him and let the
wind scour her hair from her face, and met his gaze with her
own, thinking—*Leave me be, leave me be.* But she did it without
thinking, for she'd forgotten the potency of her piercing gaze in
the weeks she'd spent in Conaire's company. At the sight of her
eyes, her father's face washed gray.

She jerked her shoulder from beneath her father's grip and
stumbled toward the road, as Octavius climbed upon the cart
and gathered the reins. Above, black clouds rumbled and hissed
a thicker rain. Her skirts dragged upon the weeded path as she
raced toward the cart, which jerked forward, then set upon the
road.

She clutched the rough stone pillar which marked the open
gateway, trembling, hot tears mixing with the rain pelting her
cheeks. She did not run beyond the boundary of the manor
house. Something bound her here, at the limits of her world,
while her heart stretched out to the white-robed figures walking
beside the cart and retreating into the gray mists of twilight, of
rain and storm.

Moira suddenly stood behind her, a calm presence amid the
madness swirling in her head.

"Octavius will see him well settled, child, ye've no need to
be worrying."

Deirdre sank to her knees at the gateway. The gritty texture
of the damp stone pillar scraped her cheek. Slivers of the chipped
stone dug into her knees. The driving rain obscured all but the
briefest flash of white robes, and the rumbling thunder drowned
the creak of the battered wheels.

Lightning flashed and silvered the cart, before plunging it all into grayness again.

Behind her, Moira began to moan.

"Stop it," Deirdre snapped as she met her maidservant's cloudy eyes. "I'll have no keening in Conaire's wake."

" 'Tis not keening." Moira's eyes glowed strangely opalescent in the misty twilight. " 'Tis a lullaby, and I sing it for both of ye."

"Go back to the manor house, Moira, there's no use in both of us drownin' in the rain."

"Och, child." Moira reached down and ran gentle fingers through Deirdre's hair. "Ye must believe."

Believe.

Deirdre sat in the muddy portal until the storm swallowed up the cart, then she sat some more, while thunder cracked and lightning arched across the sky, staring at the silver curtain of rain through which he'd disappeared. Waiting for something, and she knew not what.

A seed of hope settled in the fissures of her heart.

Believe.

The first chill howl of winter wailed through Troyes. Deirdre perched on a stool by the hearth of her bedroom, listening to the gusts winnow through the cracks of the oiled parchment stretched across her window. Her wrist cracked with stiffness and cold, as she jabbed her silver needle into the woolen hem of the cloak draped across her lap. Glancing through her lashes toward the door, she slipped her hand into her alms bag, lying casually open on the floor beside the stool. She palmed another dirty silver *denier* from it, then tucked the coin into the hem of her cloak before stitching the tiny pocket shut.

Slicing the thread with her teeth, she hefted up the thick, blue gray wool and passed a critical hand over the ripple of pockets running the length of the hem. Och, but for a bit of heaviness in the drape, not a man would know that the accumulated change of ten years of frippery purchases were secreted away in this common cloak. There was a bit of the burgher Mézières in her, after all.

God willing, thrift would be the only trait she would ever inherit from her father.

She crushed the cloak in her lap, then busied herself with setting her sewing basket to rights. Even as she did it, she wondered what she was after thinking, fussing with a jumble of threads and ribbon as if they could distract her from the pain spearing like a hundred thousand knives in her heart. Then, as if to taunt her, she felt the wincing pierce of silver, and glared down at a bead of blood swelling from her fingertip.

The door suddenly squealed open. Moira backed into the room, her arms bowed under a teetering pile of linens. Deirdre pressed the wound in the folds of the linen cloak.

"Och, you're here, Moira. Not a moment to spare, I'm thinking." Deirdre stood up, carefully draped the woolen cloak over the stool, and reached for the clink of her alms purse. "Put those linens aside, it's nigh terce and Mass will be starting soon."

Moira tumbled the heap upon the stripped bed. "Listen to ye, child, so full of impatience, and me workin' me fingers to the bone. You know well enough that we'll have time to make Mass, if we leave when we hear the bells—"

"I've no liking to battle the crowds just to get inside the church." Deirdre tied the fringed silk purse to her girdle and adjusted the sag. "Today every sinner in Troyes will be out worshiping, praying for forgiveness."

"You'd think 'twas Easter, the way you do be going on and carrying about; not all Christians are as pious as you, child. There'll be plenty o' room for all in that cathedral, even if it is All Hallow's E'en."

Aye, All Hollow's E'en. Deirdre clutched the cloak and squeezed gently, feeling the ribbon of coins running through it.

She'd been waiting for this day forever, counting the hours through Michaelmas and the interminable weeks of the harvest, planning, scheming, preparing. The preparations kept the loneliness at bay. Aye, loneliness, in a house where she was rarely alone, a house full of the whispers of servants who feared to meet her gaze, and the silent, angry impotence of a father whose wishes she contrived to delay. But now, finally, the spicy scent of baking soul-cakes wafted up from the kitchens below. Now, the wood was piled high by the hearth. Even in this pious place, a long night's fire would burn to keep evil from entering the house.

For it was All Hallow's E'en. The night of the Dead, when the ghosts of the departed revisit the earth.

A frisson shook through her, a muddled mixture of fear and anticipation.

It was time.

"Truth be known, it warms me heart," Moira said, sliding the hem of the top linen between her fingers, "to see ye so full o' faith these past months."

Deirdre's cheeks grew warm. Aye, she supposed she appeared pious to most people, racing to the church at every opportunity to find some solace in prayer. They didn't know she prayed for a selfish miracle: For her dead lover to rise from the grave.

She draped the cloak over her arm and spied her prayer book on the bedside table. "I'm no hypocrite of a Christian," she argued, tipping up the book and balancing it on the wood, "to worship only on the holiest of days."

"Aye, 'tis true, ye've prayed to enough saints to prove that." The maidservant snapped out one of the linens and let the cloth billow down evenly over the feather mattress. Her blue white eyes crinkled at Deirdre over the cloud of linen. "And there's something special about this day, I'm thinking, to have ye jumpin' about so anxious to go to church. Is it because it's the old Samhain's Eve, child?"

Deirdre thumped her prayer book down on the table. The flush rushed to tingle the tips of her ears. "It's just another name for the holy day, Moira, it's the same no matter what name you call it."

Dried rushes scraped beneath her feet as she headed briskly to the window. There was no time for weakness, not now. Moira spoke without thinking—she *couldn't* know, it was impossible for anyone to know Deirdre's plans—impossible.

Deirdre dug her fingers under the taut parchment and let the slap of the chill breeze cool the flush of her cheeks. Och, how she yearned for the feel of the cold wind on her body, how she yearned for the splatter of rain on her skin. She'd never known freedom before Champagne, and now, here in Troyes, back in this coffin of a room, she felt suffocated, stifled.

Today, *today* that would end. Today she would join the world of the living.

"Look at ye, so flushed, child," Moira continued without a breath, "are ye sure there's naught else you'd want to do besides standing in a cold, drafty church on a day such as today? I'm thinkin' God'll forgive ye for missin' a single Mass, if ye've something else in mind today, a walk in the country, perhaps—"

"What greater thing than to worship God?" She hated this deception she was forced to play, just to be free for a moment, long enough to seize her life back. "And what's this talk about missing Mass? Is that why you idled in the kitchens so long this morning, thinking we'd miss the bells, and I'd not bother about dragging you out to Mass?"

"Dragging me out to Mass? Child, ye should know me better, nothing does me heart more good than to stand next to ye and sing to the heavens." Moira straightened from her tucking with an indignant jiggle of jowls. "And what's this talk about idling in the kitchens? I'll have ye know that 'twas your father I was talkin' to, before I came up here."

Moira's words checked Deirdre's anger, and sent icy filets through her blood.

"Aye, lass. Do ye think even an old woman has a moment of peace in this house? Nay, your father asked me about your health again, all the while with me standin' there with linens topplin' out of me arms."

Aye, he would, she thought, her lips tightening. She could imagine him pacing the length and breadth of the main room, his arms behind his back, his wrist fisted in his other hand, while Sir Guichard taunted and laughed and guzzled more of her father's finest wines. She could imagine her father mentally counting the clinking drain of his *sous,* secretly cursing her for "ailing," all the while gently inquiring Moira about her state.

What did you say to my father, Moira? Did you tell him I was weak, listless, still in mourning, not sick enough for a doctor, but too fragile to marry, as I overheard you telling him that first day back in Troyes, when he wanted—again—already—without a single word to me—to set a date for the wedding with Sir Guy?

Did you lie to him, again, Moira, for me?

"Now think, child, what your father be after thinkin' of me, after all me talk of your weakness," Moira continued, stretching across the mattress and dragging back another linen, "to see ye up and about so early in the morning, and racin' off long before Mass?"

Deirdre forced down the panic rising to her throat and swept her cloak around her shoulders, its weighted length billowing out stiffly. "He'll think I'm getting better."

"Then ye'll have yourself married to that wretched drunkard of a nobleman before dinner."

Aye, there was no doubt about that: Her father would have his way, despite all of Moira's clever deceptions. He'd marry her off to that dissolute mockery of a nobleman, and do it with a grin splittin' his face—except for one small detail. Deirdre would *never* consent to marry the Sire de Clunel.

No prediction of the future, that. Her future loomed murky and uncertain, for her capricious gift of Sight failed her in these turbulent months, battered by the flux of too many conflicting emotions. But the distortion which had warped her perceptions for a lifetime had dissipated on the long trip back to Troyes, nearly three months ago, when she had gazed upon her father lounging across from her in the silk-draped litter, and seen him for who he truly was: A heartless man bent on ambition at any cost.

It was a cruel twist of fate, really. Where once she had been blind, now she could see. And where once she could see, now she was utterly blind.

In the end, she decided that since her destiny lay untold, she'd take it into her own hands.

"It doesn't matter anymore, Moira." She strode to the bedside table and fitted her palm over the sweat stain on the spine of her prayer book. "I will pray at Mass that my father will find wisdom enough to set Sir Guichard out on his rump."

Sweeping around the bed, Deirdre grabbed her kneeling pillow and hooked it under her arm. In a rustle of skirts, Moira backed up and blocked the portal. "I think it does matter to ye, lass. It matters very much—or ye'd not be up and so anxious to be about this day."

Those eyes of blue-white probed deeper, and saw more, Deirdre suspected, than most women of healthy sight. But in the face of that all-knowing gaze, Deirdre only tilted her chin higher. "I'm going to church now, Moira."

"Aye, 'tis plain by the look in your eye," Moira grumbled, "that I'll not have any peace until you're there."

"Nay, you won't." Determination set her shoulders, straight. "Are you going with me, or must I go by meself?"

"Of course, I'm going with ye! But I'll not have ye make a liar out of me, child." Moira snatched the prayer book and the pillow out of Deirdre's grip. "A veil and a wimple you'll wear, and you'll walk hangin' on to me arm every step of the way, do ye hear me?"

Cold autumn air blasted them when they left the town house some time later, blessed with having just missed the burgher on his way to church. Despite the bite of cold, the Grande Rue swarmed with people. In a few days, the second yearly fair—the fair of St. Rémi—would begin, and already the full length of the wide avenue clattered with the ruckus of banging hammers as the merchants set up their stalls. Deirdre eyed a clump of tattered men loitering on the far corner. She curled her gloved hands over the handwarmer Moira insisted she take, thinking that the hollow metal sphere which cocooned a few warm coals would make a fine weapon, if she found she needed one.

Without a backward glance at her father's house, Deirdre plunged into the stream of humanity just as the church bells of terce began to clang. A schoolboy with close-cropped hair squealed and barreled by her, swatting at anyone who got in his way with his hand-copied, Latin grammar book. A pastry peddler cried his wares in vain above the clangor of the church bells, and Deirdre's pace faltered as the spicy scent of hot apples and buttery dough wafted over her.

The cathedral loomed up at the end of the street, shooting its limestone spires to the sky and casting a sharp, looming shadow over the crowd. Deirdre tugged Moira out of the flow, toward a poulterer's shop on the south side. Geese, tied firmly to the apron of the stall, honked and gabbled at the church bells. Chickens and ducks, their legs trussed, floundered about on the ground around them.

"What are ye doing, child? The bells are near done—"

"Fetch me one of those pastries before church." Deirdre tucked the handwarmer under her elbow and dug one-handed into her alms purse. "They smell like a bit of heaven itself."

Moira shook her head until her cheeks jiggled over the edge of her wimple. "First you're jabberin' on about gettin' to Mass early, now you're stopping me while the bells still ring to have a bite o' pastry—"

"I'll go mad if I don't have one." She pressed a few *deniers* into Moira's hand. "Get one for yourself, too, now go on."

Moira squinted blindly into the crowd, bobbing back and forth amid the flailing fowl, trying to pick out the shape of the peddler's cart with her dim, foggy sight.

Deirdre nudged her into the fray. "You can't buy a pastry by paying for it in your mind."

"By God, what I do for ye, ye contrary child!"

Then she was off, waddling through the crowd, wielding her elbows to knock a path clear to the pastry peddler. When Deirdre was sure her maidservant's bleary eyesight could not distinguish between Deirdre's gray cloak and the limestones of the house behind her, Deirdre murmured a silent apology to the faithful attendant of her youth, then whirled away and plunged into the dim shadows of a narrow alleyway.

She barreled through the crowd. Her foot skidded through something slick and warm. She braced one hand against a wall sticky with drainage, until she regained her balance. The hand-warmer burned against her breast as she hefted it, and the weight of her cloak, above the cluttered gutter and veered toward the wide Rue Moyenne, and from there, through yet another alleyway canopied by sagging, old houses, twisting her way farther and farther from her father's house with her heart pounding, like a man running for his life to escape the hanging tree.

She halted in frustration at the Trévois canal as two young boys herded a stream of squealing pigs over the narrow bridge to pastures outside the city walls. She pressed back in the eaves' shadows. She tugged her wimple free and pressed it over her nose to block out the rancid stench of the sluggish canal water.

In an alley nearby, men barked in harsh voices above the clattering of dice. Her gaze darted back whence she came, searching for Moira, or worse—for her father's men. The weight of the coins pulled the cloak down hard on her shoulders. The trip through the city seemed farther on foot than it had looked in the litter, when she had returned from the Clunel manor house. But she did not turn back. She did not want to turn back. She had a promise to keep to a dead man.

Nay. The word came hard upon the thought. *Nay nay nay nay nay nay.* She squeezed her eyes shut and let her head fall back against the wall, fighting off the whirlwind of her mind. Och, she would not grapple with it again—no, not again, not anymore. For three months she'd battled the ravens that pecked and clawed at her mind, as if it were a dead and rotting carcass—ripping apart all she'd thought she'd known, bloodying memories, devouring all she had believed in since birth—and now she felt as if her mind bore bloody jagged furrows where all that knowledge used to be, empty gaping places aching to be filled—with truth, aye, with truth.

But what was truth? Aye, there lay the pith of it. No matter how much she wrestled with the murmurings of her senses and those of her heart, she could never reconcile the two. Conaire was dead—Conaire *could not be* dead. She could not grieve, she could not rejoice. All through the long, lonely months, she wondered over and over if she'd finally gone mad, if she'd end up in one of those wretched places where the insane were kept chained naked to the wall, until they died of cold and hunger and neglect and the torments of their own minds. For today, today, the day she'd been waiting for, though she moved coldly and deliberately through the stages of her plan, still her heart raced in her breast as it did the first time she'd met Conaire, with that breathless excitement that set her blood coursing wildly through her veins, and every fiber of her being sang that Conaire was *alive.*

If she were wrong . . . Deirdre clutched the handwarmer to her heart. If she were wrong, then the world was not as it should be, and this one day would be her last moment of hope, before she allowed her spirit to burrow deep into a quiet place inside herself for the rest of her life, while her shell of a body went through the motions of living.

Even as the thought passed through her mind, she knew it was a lie. She plunged onward when the bridge cleared of swine, and followed the pungent stench in the direction of the Rue de la Grande-Tannerie, the putrid odor that her oversensitive nose would not let her ignore. Therein lay the reason why she *must* care, why she *must* continue to live. For alive or dead, Conaire gifted her with a bit of himself, a life growing warm in her womb.

Her hand strayed over her belly, still firm and flat, as her goatskin slippers brushed silently over the bridge. *Och, I'll take ye to Ireland somehow, child of mine. I'll show ye me Ma's house on the edge of the woods and the sea. We'll see how far the honeysuckle has trailed through the thatch these ten years, and we'll find our shelter beneath that old roof.*

She imagined with a quivering trill of excitement that she could feel the first flutter of movement under her palm.

She turned a corner and the stench put a quick stop to her whirling thoughts. The tanneries stood side by side here, and the street reeked with fresh blood and dung and rotting carcasses. Men swarmed outside each shop, scraping freshly stripped hides and strewing bits of excess flesh into the streets already full of rotting raw meat. Flies swarmed in black clouds around steaming bowls of poultry and pigeon dung, which groups of men vigorously rubbed into the hides, all while laughing raucously and making crude gestures with hands leathered to the shade of oak bark.

She rushed through the street, holding her breath until black spots exploded in her eyes. Finally succumbing, she stumbled against a wall and drew in deep, gasping breaths through the fabric of her wimple, battling down a wave of nausea until she could hold her breath again. Then she stumbled farther on, to the blessed cold slap of wind funnelling through the Tannery Gate—the gateway out of Troyes, the beginning of the road to the Clunel manor house.

She wiped her clammy brow with her veil and hurried around the wide, cobbled clearing to avoid the farmer's carts lumbering through the gate. Against the wall a boy dozed, his donkey standing, head bowed, by his side.

Deirdre stopped in her tracks and blinked her eyes clear. The knee-cocked pose of that "boy" stirred a vague memory, a memory which crystallized as her gaze fell upon the flea-ridden straw strapped around his legs.

Sensing her presence, Octavius peeled his hood up over one eye. A blackened grin split his grease-splattered beard.

Incredulous, she seized one gnarled, work-hardened hand, seizing her only link to those amber days in the countryside. "Octavius, och, Octavius!"

"Ah, lass, ye remember me, ye do." He pushed his hood off. His black eyes twinkled with mischief. "Could it be 'twas me ye were after yearning for all this time, and not that strapping, foul-tempered buck of a doctor?"

Och, she couldn't believe her eyes. A shaky laugh escaped her lips. She bit it short to stanch the sob which followed. She drank in the sight of him, the rosy cheeks pushed out by the wide, blackened grin, the stains streaking his tunic, down to the last crumb speckled in his beard, searching for some bit of Conaire on him, wondering if he'd saved something of her love—a cloak, a belt, a bit of embroidery from his tunic—before he saw him buried—

Och, it was foolishness she was thinking. Conaire was not in the ground, cold and still.

"We'd best be off." Octavius struggled to his feet and jerked his donkey alert. " 'Tis a fair walk to the manor house, and the sky's been threatening rain all morn."

"Manor house?" Deirdre swallowed the end of the word.

"Aye." The grin turned wicked and Octavius capped it with a wink. "Your father should be screamin' like a horse fresh gelded by now."

Her breath hitched in her throat. *How could he know?* "What are ye jabbering about?"

"Don't be worrying, lass, the doctor told me all about the promise ye made him. Me, I knew ye'd be here; no doubt about that, I told him."

The overcast sky rumbled and splattered a few cold droplets onto the paving stones. Octavius squinted up at the clouds, then darted about, checking the fit of the donkey's bit, smoothing the blanket over the creature's back, adjusting the weight of the lumpy packages draped on either side; while the uneasy crease between Deirdre's brows deepened.

How could Octavius know what she and Conaire had whispered to each other in the woods, only hours before Conaire's death? Octavius had never mentioned that he'd seen him before his death, he'd not mentioned anything of the sort.

"Well, lass?" Octavius slapped the donkey's matted coat. "Are ye going to mount, or just stand about counting the lepers?"

Deirdre wedged her foot in Octavius's cupped hands and heaved her weight onto the beast's back. "Och, there's a fine bit of explaining you've to do, Octavius—"

"Praise be to God, praise be!"

Deirdre's breath caught in her throat. Moira barreled out of a narrow alleyway and raced blindly across the gateway clearing, her black robes flowing out behind her, her arms outstretched. The donkey bucked beneath Deirdre as she stiffened. Deirdre clawed for the reins, but Octavius held them tight in his fist until the donkey stilled.

In that brief moment she noticed three things: Moira ran alone; Moira's blind eyes were fixed upon them from all the way across the clearing; and Octavius waited for the elderly, red-faced servant, sporting a wicked grin.

Moira launched herself against Deirdre's legs. "Child, child, I thought I'd lost ye for good, I did. What are ye thinkin', racin' off without me, wanderin' around with thieves and brigands—"

"Stop it, Moira, your jabbering will bring the guards down upon us."

Deirdre hardly recognized her voice, but the swift and sudden terror that she might be caught and hauled back to the prison of her room left her no patience for tender words.

"I'm off to the Clunel lands, and I'll not hear a word," Deirdre interjected before Moira could speak the volumes shivering in her jowls. "It's a promise I made."

"Have ye no faith in me, lass?" Those translucent eyes of blue-white pierced her. "It's a promise ye made, and we'll be seeing it done. All this talk about goin' off to Mass . . . Did ye think you were after fooling me? I knew you had somethin' cookin' in your head. Have I failed ye once yet, in all this time?"

Deirdre felt a spurt of guilt. Aye, 'twas true, she should have trusted Moira. Though they never spoke of it, Deirdre knew Moira understood what caused Deirdre's early-morning nausea, her fatigue, the loss of her monthlies—and still the faithful servant protected her. Och, she'd been so busy wrestling with her own soul, that she'd had no room left in her heart for trust. Moira, Moira, it had always been Moira, even in the dark days after Deirdre's mother had died, there had always been Moira's cool white hands, Moira's lilting song, Moira's steadfast love. Moira had always been a bulwark against the world outside—keeping all Deirdre's secrets safe and hidden—keeping *her* safe and hidden.

The words tumbled out of her in a rush of love and trust. "If you'll be knowing the truth, I'm not going back, Moira."

The maidservant grinned, a wide, yellow-toothed smile that crinkled her flesh and put an odd sparkle in her opalescent eyes. "I didn't think so, lass."

What a strange couple they would be, traveling about the countryside; a young pregnant girl and a blind old woman. At least now, she'd not have to worry about birthing the child alone.

"You, it is!" Without another word, Moira turned to a grinning Octavius and planted meaty hands on her hips. "I should have

known *you'd* have a hand in this, and not a word to me o' the details! A fine way to see the job done."

"It's no fault o' mine that the lass held her tongue around ye—"

"And would it have broken a bone for ye to come and tell me yourself, instead of havin' me worrying to death and waiting and waiting—"

Their argument dissolved into meaningless bickering, and Deirdre glanced from one to another in mild surprise, not knowing they'd passed more than simple pleasantries in the past.

"Come, both of you," Deirdre said, finally. She jerked the reins of the donkey from Octavius's hands and gestured to the gaping gate. "If you're both coming, then so be it. There'll be time enough to argue on the road to Clunel."

The rutted road cut through city pastures swarming with cattle, sheep, and pigs. Beyond, the hillocks and swells dotted with thatched-roofed houses ceded to forests of beech and oak, pitted here and there with great fields stripped of grain and gleaming flaxen with chaff, and vineyards long harvested and chopped back for the winter. Huddled in her cloak, Deirdre dozed atop the lumbering donkey as the handwarmer clutched against her belly cooled. The sky growled above like a wary hound.

For lunch, Octavius pilfered a tunicfull of late-harvest apples from an orchard of trees whose bare, twisted boughs thrust stark against the white-gray sky. Deirdre crisped into the skin. A spray of juice dribbled over her chin. She washed the cold, tangy flesh down with sips of clear, icy water gleaned from a roadside stream. The simple meal soothed her troubled stomach and infused her limbs with new strength.

Sunset slipped under the haze of clouds and glazed the land amber, when the group finally neared the Clunel manor house. Deirdre slid off the weary donkey. Her knees gave way as she hit the hard dirt; she gripped the donkey's matted coat until she regained her balance. She peered down the road to the stingy curl of smoke rising from the leaning chimney, and battled with the wind for possession of a strand of hair which had come loose from her veil.

Without a word to her companions, she tucked her hand-warmer into one of the donkey's bags, then plunged into the forest, feeling oddly bereft, unsettled. The sunset and the change of season had stolen her bright summer woods. No more did lush greenery burst from the ground and drip from the boughs overhead; no more did brilliant stalks of flowers trim the base of trees. The thin, dry remnants of leaves rattled in the breeze, tore loose, then spun down from the boughs to join the crinkling carpet of their kin.

Somehow, she nosed her way closer to her destination, recognizing a gnarled tree here, a cluster of stones there, the ribbon of the tumbled-down fence that marked the edge of the Clunel garden. Fingers of sallow light winnowed through the bare straight trunks of oaks. Vaguely, she wondered how she was ever going to find her way out of the forest in the dark of night—and realized she'd be sleeping on the hillside, awash in the grief and memories which even now threatened in her dry throat.

Her hood tumbled down. She tore off her veil and fingered free the wound plaits, leaving a glittering trail of silver hairpins, remembering, with a catch in her breath, a long-lost trail of silver bells.

Urgency tightened into a fist in her innards. She raced over the ground, careless of the shadowed gullies beneath her feet. Moira and Octavius followed silently behind; she heard the patter of their feet, swift and hard upon hers. A mist began to curl up from the roots of trees, kissing her cheeks with its wet chill, cooling the heat of her unexpected tears.

It was torment, this, she told herself, for all that would greet her at the end of this reckless race was an empty place that had once echoed with laughter and overflowed with love—a parched and dry riverbed where once there flowed a raging stream. She had thought she would be strong enough to see it once again, but with each step her icy sheen of control melted a little more, a little more. She clutched saplings, using them to pull herself up the slope to the bare, open hill. Her breath hitched hot and dusty in her throat as memories inundated her, and something else as well—a coiling anticipation.

A soft sound filtered down from the height of a hill—the gentle whinny of a horse.

Och, a saner woman would at least falter in her pace upon hearing the sound of another's presence, in woods rumored to be rife with poachers and thieves. A saner woman would usher Octavius up ahead, to see who invaded the sanctity of the place where she and Conaire had first loved. But a saner woman would not be racin' about like a fey child at the twilight of All Hallow's E'en, on a promise made to a man whose heart had long stopped beating.

Feeble rays of amber light misted over her face. She told herself it was the flickering of the cool sunlight that drew her through the thinning fencing of trees. She told herself it was the glow of memory that lured her back to the site where she had first come alive. In the end, she stopped rationalizing and simply followed the yearning of her soul.

The horse loomed into sight. The mighty beast pawed the exposed rock, snorted twin streams of mist upon the chill air. His black head turned her way with a flicker of ears.

A few paces beyond the horse, a man stood with his back to her, the embroidered edge of his scarlet cloak billowing with the first breath of the evening breeze. The last ember of sun blazed on the horizon, and streaked his hair with flame.

She stumbled to a stop and choked a branch of a yew sapling with her fist. The man turned his head slightly, so she could see the amber light glazing the three-quarter profile of his face. A brother, she thought. A twin.

Then he turned fully and fixed her with that tortured gaze of silver.

Conaire.

Her heart thumped to a heavy stop.

Conaire.

Twenty-two

There she stood poised on the edge of the clearing, like some fairy-sylph clinging to the safety of the woods, her hair tangled and cascading down her back, her reedy, graceful beauty striking him like a blow to the gut and wrenching the air from his lungs. The chill wind had painted her cheeks with streaks of rose, but as their gaze remained locked and the still moments passed, the living color ebbed away and her skin frosted.

He wrenched his gaze away from the sight of her, his cloak snapping behind him. He crossed his arms and showed her his profile, his chin scraping his chest.

She kept her promise. He tamped down the hope welling inside him, then crushed the fierce urge to cross the distance that separated them and drag her frozen form into his arms. Too many times in the life before, he'd bent her to his wishes by the sheer force of his size and the overbearing arrogance of his will—this time she would make the choice on her own.

He slumped down to the hard rock and placed his elbow on a bent knee, kneading his brow as he tried to find a way to explain something he still did not understand. Below, the blue mist of twilight hazed across the rolling land, pierced only by the crossed steeples of silent, scattered churches.

Conaire dragged his hand down his stubbled face and gazed off to places far beyond the horizon. "There's an ancient Irish tale I would tell you, lass," he began softly, so as not to jerk her out of her frozen shock. "Perhaps you know of it, perhaps your mother once told it to you."

He did not turn, but every sense was trained upon the slip of a girl hovering tense by the edge of the clearing.

"A long, long time ago, in an age when the men of your God had only begun to spread the word in Ireland, there was a woman named Sabia, who was a powerful pagan priestess in the lands of Ulster." He draped his arm across his knee and let his hand dangle. His gaze followed the flight of a sparrow sweeping home to its nest before the darkness descended. "At the Samhain fires one year, she conceived a child. 'Twas rumored that the child's father was one of the *Sídh*—the ones you know as the Little People."

Vaguely, Conaire sensed the growing change in the world around them; the softening, salt-sweet breath of the wind; the mist creeping through the trees and unfurling fingers of fog toward the sky; an odd tilting of the dim, distant horizon; the hushed whisper of creatures rustling in the wood's deepening shadows, as if roused from sleep. His horse shook its head and pranced a few steps, trying in vain to snort the smell of the Otherworld from his nostrils.

"Sabia died birthing a son, taking the secret of his true parentage with her." He could not keep the scorn from seeping into his voice. "The boy grew to be a mighty warrior, invincible in battle, and determined to win himself a kingdom of his own.

"He got his kingdom, in the full roll o' time. But by the clever treachery of his enemies, he was killed." The heel of his boot scraped against the stones as he sank his knee to the ground. "On the morning after the funeral, he rose from the dead."

Her soft gasp cut through the clearing and through his heart. He swept one hand over the pitted surface of the rock. A sliver of stone sliced his callused skin. He stared down at the dark blood welling from his palm, at the hand of a beast, a creature of another world.

"He stood then as shocked as you are now, lass, struggling with a world turned all a-tilt." He closed his hand tight over the cut. "But you see, there was a woman. Aye, a woman unlike any other, a woman with fairy blood running in her veins. A woman," he added, hoarsely, "who was no less than the other half of his soul."

Swiveling on the knuckles of his closed fist, he rose to his feet and paced across the open clearing, letting the Samhain wind batter his cloak about his legs—not daring to glance in her direction, a damned coward, unwilling to witness the revulsion and terror in her eyes.

"She told him that the rumors which had haunted him all his life were true. He was half-human, half-fairy." He shrugged, then let his arms fall heavily against his sides. "Like his father o' the *Sídh,* he was immortal."

The words heaved to his throat. "The thing simply *was,* she told him, as the Earth was, the sea and the air and the grass, and there was no more reason for his existence as there was for why the moon waxes and wanes, or why the stars move across the night sky, and she told me I should just—"

Her strangled cry alerted him to his slip. His pace faltered to a stop. The wind blew clear through his bones, chilling him deep to the marrow. Something cracked and broke away inside him.

"I should just accept it," he continued, his words harsh and rough, but not loud enough to drown out the crash of her footsteps through the dried carpet of old fallen boughs—aye, he heard *that* above the shattering of his heart—"and so I lived, and lived, watchin' all I cared about wither and die, and roamin' the world for centuries after like a man half-dead, until—" a desperation coiled in his chest, ripping free words he'd vowed not to say "—until I lay my gaze upon the ailing form of a woman-child, and saw in her eyes the soul of the wife I had lost, my fairy-bride, the only woman who would accept me for what I was, the only woman I would ever love—"

He swiveled to glare at where she had stood, expecting to see nothing but the flutter of her robes in the distance, the flash of her golden hair in the twilight grown inky and thick; and instead found her standing within arm's reach, her face shimmering with tears.

A dustless wind sifted up from the fissures in the ground and eddied around her, toyed with the hood of her cloak and buffeted a long golden tress over her shoulder, before the directionless little gust suddenly shifted and breathed across his face, misting him with the scent of honeysuckle.

"Don't you be standin' there still as a stone," she scolded in a ragged voice. "Kiss me, Conaire, prove to me you're no apparition born of me twisted mind."

Her words rang in his ears, and his senses shook like the trembling of a bell after being struck by an iron clapper.

"Did ye hear me, Conaire?" Her chin quivered. "Or am I just talkin' to the air?"

Her breath caught in her throat, as he seized her by the arms and dragged her against him. "No apparition, this." His gaze fell upon her parted lips. "Apparitions don't breathe. Apparitions can't do *this*."

He captured her mouth, felt the shock of the contact ripple through her body and reverberate back through his own. *Lass, lass, lass, mo shearc.* He dragged his arms around her body and thrust her small form tight against his—so she could not fight, so she could not escape—and he reveled in the feel of the yielding crush of her breasts and the supple give of her spine. He plundered her mouth, stole her breath, ran his tongue along the soft flesh of her full lower lip, feasted on the forbidden fruit, all the while knowing this was his last taste.

But in the midst of the violent kiss, she wriggled her arms from where they wedged against his chest, and wound them tight around his neck. Gasping for air, she broke the contact of their lips and rubbed her face into his shoulder.

By the gods. He fisted a handful of her tangled hair to still her head. *She believes.*

She believes.

In that moment of surrender, it seemed that something amid the heavens and the earth readjusted, like a cart wheel gone wobbly finally bumping into place. It happened so swiftly amid the haze of passion, that Conaire wondered if he had imagined the subtle movement of the sky, the almost indiscernible change in the pitch of the wind's whistle.

"It's a fine dance ye've led me, all these months," she mumbled against the soft wool of his cloak. "Did you think me heart wouldn't know you still walked about, livin' and breathin'?"

"Aye, but would you listen to it? And would you believe what I am—"

"I don't give a peascod why or how you are here, Conaire MacSidh." She tilted her head back to meet his gaze. "As long as you take me with you, wherever you go."

Something buckled in his chest. He squeezed his fairy-bride tight to stop the heaving surge of emotion shuddering through him, and tilted his face back to the flat, slate sky.

"It's a hard life you choose, woman," he said, harshly, to stanch the swell of a unmanly wetness in his eyes. "There's no oil lamps on Inishmaan."

"Firelight is warm and bright enough. And you can't see the soot on the walls by it."

He tugged her head back by the fistful of hair and sealed her lips with his own, hiding from her the single tear which squeezed out of one eye and trailed hot liquid over his cheek. Damned, foolish lass. Didn't know the first thing she was doing, didn't know what she was saying, didn't know how every word sliced away more and more of the dead wood which encased the battered, ever-beating remnants of his heart. He swallowed her low and eager moan, and then slid his lips down to the throbbing pulse at her throat. Damn the woman, she made his head soft.

She made him want things he had no business wanting; she made him dream again.

But it was nothing but loving he had on his mind as he snapped the ties of his cloak and threw it across the ground—there'd be enough time later to talk more o' this, to tell her the full of the tale. But as he softened one knee to press her down with him, a flicker of movement on the edge of the clearing caught his eye.

There stood Octavius, leaning against an oak with a grin splitting his face.

Conaire gripped Deirdre's sagging weight until she regained her footing. She followed his angry glare and saw what put a sudden stop to their passion.

"Aren't you a fine one," Conaire snapped, "hidin' when you're needed, and showin' your face when you're least wanted."

The imp's grin shifted into a scowl. "Is that all the thanks I get for what I've done for ye?"

The old anger flared up in him. What had Octavius and his kind ever done for him, but play peg-games with his life, and the life of the woman in his arms? Octavius thought it nothing more than wicked mischief, Conaire supposed, slipping in and out of Conaire's life at the creature's own whim, while a hundred thousand questions burned in Conaire's brain. Octavius and his kind thought it no more than mischief to put him—and Deirdre—through the same agony they'd suffered in the last life.

For even as he held her close against him, his body vibrating with need like the plucked string of a taut-strung lyre, his heart raw and open, he knew the end o' this story. It was as inevitable as the setting of the sun. He would have thirty, forty, perhaps fifty years with her. He would watch the light in her eyes dim.

And while he still lived, she would die in his arms.

"You want *thanks?*" Conaire hurled the words at the creature. A sudden gust rattled the last of the autumn leaves. " 'Tis a curse I would put on you, if I knew the way of it, as vengeance for the curse your kind put on me."

"Don't be like that, did ye think we were after tormentin' ye like this? Ye didn't give us any choice, don't ye see?"

"Go back to your hole, Octavius." He wanted no more of him, not now, 'twas a waste of precious moments, and his body screamed for release with the woman in his arms. "Tell whoever sent you here to keep the door open the next time I come knockin'." Aye, that damned silvered door to the Otherworld always bolted against him, between him and her. "Then maybe we'll talk about thanks."

"Listen to the both of ye."

The soft voice rose in the clearing, lilting and disembodied. A rustling revealed the faint outline of a woman amid the trees. Moira's wide and sightless eyes glowed like opals in the gloom.

Moira made a sound like the clucking of a tongue. " 'Twas a wonder to me that they sent *ye* to do the job, Octavius, when ye can't even find your own shoes."

Octavius waved a dirty hand their way. "I'll have ye know they led me on a merry dance, these two. It's a fine piece o' work I've done, if I say so!"

"It's not enough that it's done. We've a lifetime o' pain and anger to soothe, and not much more time to do it in."

Darkness spread its hand across the land, but on the hill where they all stood, under the rumble of the clouded sky, a phosphorescent glow shimmered and intensified in the air. Conaire drew Deirdre into his embrace, as she hissed a shaky breath through her teeth.

"Moira?"

"Child." The word rolled out of Moira's mouth holding all the softness of a mother's tongue. "I'll be off now, 'tis sure ye've no more need of me. It's glad I am of that, for all that I'll miss ye."

The wind whirled and whispered, like the brush of silken

veils. The gusts pricked their exposed faces with a hundred thousand drizzled tingles. The Otherworld loomed close.

"This is a world of choices, Conaire," Moira said. "Human choices, over which no creature of this world or t'other has any real power."

A feeble ringing sounded on the air, a haunting melody which ebbed and flowed. Deirdre gazed around her, confusion pulling her brows together. She searched the darkness beyond the eerie silver glow for the source of it, until her gaze finally fixed on the woman she'd known since birth, but had never known at all.

"Ye've power enough," Conaire growled, waving to the shifting world around them as he took Deirdre deeper into his embrace, "to be here now."

"It's by your graces we stand here. Aye." Moira's head bobbed heavily at Conaire's wordless denial. "Did ye not suspect that 'twas you who kept the worlds together, all these years, just by living?"

Something cold breathed against the back of his neck. "I've had a bellyful o' riddles—"

"I know it's been a heavy load ye've carried, Conaire, all along not even knowing you were carrying it." Moira raised one white finger. "Now listen."

The mists swirled close around her form, obscuring all but the glowing eyes, and the soft, strangely hushed voice. The tenuous music intensified, until he could distinguish the beat of drums and the hollow whine of reed pipes. It was ancient fairy music, siphoning through the veils to lilt on earthly air.

"Your mother," Moira began, "made a brave choice when she dared to conceive a child of the *Sidh*, at a time when we were all fading fast from the Earth. What fairy blood *did* flow in some human veins was, by then, diluted nearly to naught. So the only way to bind the worlds, don't ye see, was to forge a fresh strong bond of spirit and flesh."

Conaire felt Deirdre's sudden quivering, felt her gaze hard

upon him. He would not look away from the creature called Moira, lest she fade into the mists and leave him with another seven centuries of wondering.

"Your mother paid a price for her choice. She had to abandon you, alone in a world which scorned our existence. In that moment, she lay the burden of keepin' the worlds together on your shoulders."

"It would all have come to a fine end," Octavius interjected from his lair in the shadow of an oak, "but 'twas your own arrogance which led ye away from the path we'd laid—contrary, snarling creatures you humans are, always fightin' what should be, and not listenin' to your wiser halves—"

"And you," Conaire growled, "took your time tellin' me this—"

"Time, what is time? A moment in our world is a century in yours—"

"Enough." Moira's voice was nothing but a breath of wind now, her image merging with the murky shadows beyond the opalescent glow, the light of her eyes fading, even as Conaire scented the faint perfume of Otherworldly smoke-fires.

"Care well for that babe in the lass's womb, Conaire," came the reedy thread of Moira's faltering voice. "She's your only hope. And ours."

"Aye, good night, and I should say good riddance to ye, for all your fumin' and yellin', but ye've done good in the end, I suppose." Octavius jerked his hood over his head, then winked at Deirdre, a sudden grin splitting his face. "Mayhap we'll be racin' one o' these mornings, lass."

Then the music stopped, as if an iron door had slammed shut in a mead hall.

Conaire stared where Octavius and Moira had been. Nothing remained but a faint silver glow limning the ring of trees, and an elusive, high laughter fading into the whine of the wind.

Epilogue

It was a fine, soft day on Inishmaan.

The springtime sun blazed through the hazy sheeting of ocean clouds to shimmer upon the black cliffs with a pure, luminous warmth. Galway Bay, almost too blue to look at, licked the graveled shore with a thin glaze of froth. Crazed by the scent of freshly caught mackerel, a flock of gulls screeched and cawed as they whirled in a cirrus of wings above the small fleet of *curraghs* bobbing just beyond the surf.

Deirdre stood with the other wives of Inishmaan. Dried salt and sea spray ribboned her arms from an afternoon collecting seaweed, which she would use to make land upon the barren rock of *Dún Conaire,* high atop the cliffs. She shifted the weight of the dripping basket on her hip, then shaded her eyes against the flash of the ocean.

Och, 'twas no surprise to find Conaire in the thick of it all, standing at his full, mighty height at the bow of the lead *curragh,* riding the dips and swells with his knees, while he peered out to the roll of the oncoming waves.

"*D'ár m'anam.*" Red Sean's saucy young wife leaned toward Deirdre with a wink. "By me soul, don't *you* have a man of a race that never owned a coward."

Deirdre grinned and met the woman's dancing gaze, then sank the weight of her basket into the gritty sand. Over two years Deirdre had lived here, and she'd come to believe that there wasn't a woman breathin' on the whole island who could see past the tip of her nose. Not once since Deirdre had stepped on these shores had any of the hardy natives staggered back in revulsion at her gaze. They were all as blind as bats, for sure. Blinded by the ocean spray which vaulted ceaselessly over the western spine of cliffs, or the milky mists which swathed the island half the year until she thought it floated upon a cloud. Or the squinting, she reminded herself, as she squeezed one eye shut against the beaming shimmer of the bay.

A squealing blur dashed by her, launching a spray of pebbles with each fleet-footed step. With a swiftness born of instinct, Deirdre lunged, seized a handful of blue wool, and hauled her squirming daughter up onto her hip.

"Is it being hit by a *curragh* you're after, Aileen? Or drowning in the sea?"

Aileen squirmed in Deirdre's embrace. While Deirdre worked, the toddler had scoured the shore for "treasures" with the other village children. Now she flailed two fistfuls of shiny rocks toward the sea.

"Daidí, Daidí!"

"Aye, 'tis your Da makin' a spectacle of himself out there." Deirdre brushed at the sea spray beading on her daughter's flushed cheeks. "But ye'll wait here, safe and dry, with the rest of us, *a stóirín.*"

Aileen stilled as the *curragh* suddenly surged upon a wave's crest. Conaire plunged the oars into the foaming water and pulled back so hard that his muscles strained against the sleeves of his tunic. Another wave loomed up behind him, surging high and fast, but before the first whiskers of foam frothed the peak, the prow of the *curragh* scraped the shore. Conaire gripped the rim, leapt out, and dragged the boat out of harm's way.

Only then did Deirdre release the breath she had not realized she'd been holding.

The shore rang with masculine voices, with the slap of sea-leathered hands against muscled backs, as one by one the other boats scraped upon the shore. Conaire helped the men unload the *curraghs* of fish and tackle. His sharp, shared laughter cut through the roar of the waves.

Aileen flexed and struggled in Deirdre's embrace like a fish battering on the shore.

"Och, be off with ye, then," Deirdre exclaimed, patting her daughter's behind as the child darted off. Deirdre watched with a warmth glowing in her chest, as Conaire seized his screaming daughter in mid-run and whirled her through the air. Then Deirdre hefted up the basket of seaweed and searched for a place to lodge it for safekeeping.

Conaire was home, it was Beltaine Day; there'd be no more work today.

A shadow fell over her as she tucked the basket securely behind a cradle of boulders nestled close to the cliff.

"Shirking your duties, woman? There's a price to pay for not greeting your man proper."

She squinted up at him. His tunic draped open, showing the hard plates of a chest gleaming with sea spray. His grin rivaled the blaze of the sky above. Aileen sat easily upon his shoulders, her arms flailing as she stretched up recklessly and tried to reach the gulls swooping across the shore.

Deirdre raised herself onto her toes and kissed Conaire's salty lips, then whispered, "I'm not so sure I don't want to pay that price, *mo rún.*"

"Listen to you talking." He lowered his head and stole another kiss. "A convent-bred lass. In front of your daughter, no less."

"Och, the fairies did not leave that babe under the ivy, Conaire."

The corners of his eyes crinkled as he laughed—a deep, rumbling sound full of night-time promises. His teeth flashed white against skin grown leathery from sea and sun and weather. A lock of hair battered across his face. Tenderly, she grasped it, then raked it through her fingers as she pushed it aside. Sunlight shimmered on a fine silver strand threading through the lock.

She let his hair slip through her fingers, as she trailed her hand lovingly down his chest. Och, 'twas a small price to pay, this worry that needled her every time he raced out into the open sea in the fragile shell of a *curragh*. He was strong, clever, more experienced in riding this moody ocean than all the natives of Aran. 'Twas human, she supposed, to wish the man she loved with all her heart to be immortal . . . again.

"Horsie, *Daidí!*" Aileen pummeled her father's chest with rapid little feet. "Play that game! Play that game!"

"Aye, I suppose I'll have no peace until I do."

Deirdre met Conaire's glowing eyes, the pale gray of the calm morning bay, and all her selfish thoughts melted away.

It was foolish, she was, wishing for such a thing. The mantle had been passed on now, as it should have been all those centuries ago, if all had gone well. Deirdre understood that now, as she understood many things she never had before. Conaire had no more need of his fairy gift. As Aileen grew bigger and stronger, it ebbed away from him, and now she knew that he was as mortal as herself. Her daughter, that red-topped, squealing bundle of joy babbling now on her husband's shoulders as they headed to the height of the cliff, was the next link in the chain, the strongest bond between this world and the other.

"Have ye no fish for me?" Deirdre asked, linking her arm with his and breathing deeply of the scent of sea and hot air and man clinging to his tunic. "I'd had a yearning to make a stew of bream and pollack tonight."

"Red Sean's seeing to it." Conaire rolled his shoulders, and the ride sent Aileen into a new fit of squeals. "He'll have our share of the catch cut, scaled, and sitting by our door by tomorrow morn."

"Don't ye be tellin' me that, you're fibbing." She playfully slapped his forearm. "Red Sean, coming to *Dún Conaire?* I don't believe it."

"It was his offer. Payment, he said, for settin' his son's leg last week, after he tumbled off the fishing ledge."

As the path grew steep, Deirdre grasped her woolen skirts and lifted the hem above her ankles. Within the tiny row of *clocháns* that edged the cliff, it was common talk that the ancient ruins upon the hill were inhabited by fairies. When she and Conaire had first arrived, the villagers had warned them away from building within the windworn, rambling circle of tumbling stones. They'd seen fairy footmarks upon the cliff, they'd told them, and strange, airless gusts of wind swept the place—but Conaire was adamant. *Dún Conaire* was home.

She'd known it was her home, too, the moment she had laid eyes upon the majestic height, safe, guarded, strong.

"I don't know if I'm liking this," she mused, frowning. "Isn't Red Sean afraid the fairies will be doing him mischief?"

"Don't you want your fish, lass?"

"Aye, aye, but first it's Red Sean, and then it's Red Sean's wife who'll come a-visiting, and soon the old widdy Pegeen will be dropping by on her Connemara pony." She slanted her husband a glance. "I've grown to like our privacy up there on the height."

Conaire halted abruptly and swept one arm around her waist, thrusting her hard against the full, hot length of his body. He bent his head to kiss her, but a tiny, cowskin-covered foot got in the way.

"Down!" Aileen battered Conaire's head with her hands as she caught sight of two of the village children with baskets full of slivers of mackerel. "Let Aileen down!"

Conaire hauled his daughter off his shoulders. With a flash of feet she was at the little boys' sides, thrusting her hands into the baskets.

"Cruel wench," Conaire growled, thrusting Deirdre up against him anew, "to speak to me o' such things when you know the little lass won't drop off to sleep until the moon is nigh over-head."

Laughter bubbled up deep in her throat, but he put a quick stop to it. His damp woolen tunic smelled of brine and open air. His kiss tasted of honey-mead and passion.

Aileen wiggled her way between her parents and twinkled up at them with her father's gray eyes, bright, innocent and reborn. Deirdre and Conaire broke apart to the giggles of children and the rich, knowing laughter of a cluster of islanders, who'd caught up with them upon the path.

"I see who got the best catch o' the day," one of the men remarked.

"Aye, and well-hooked he is, I'm thinking."

"Do ye now?" came a woman's voice. "I'm thinkin' *she* caught the biggest fish o' the lot."

Shouldn't ye both be saving that for the Beltaine fire?"

"Only you, Patch Pegeen, would save it for Beltaine," Conaire retorted, a sly smile tilting his lips, *"We've* a Beltaine fire around our hearth every night o' the year."

In the midst of the roar of laughter, a priest strode out of a patch of Celtic crosses sunk into the soft earth of an ancient pagan burial ground, just at the height of the path. His black robes battered his legs as he approached the crowd with a swift, lusty gait.

The priest's blue eyes twinkled as he fixed his gaze on Con-aire. "Was that pagan nonsense I heard coming from your mouth, Conaire MacSidh?"

Humor laced the priest's voice, and his face crinkled into a smile he didn't have to hunt for.

"Now don't you be askin' me husband such a question, Fa-ther." Deirdre hefted Aileen upon her hip and wiped the child's face free of dirt. "I'll not have the two of you off talkin' and debatin' nonsense over a skin of honey-mead tonight, I won't."

With a wink, the priest said, "Now there's a good lass, keepin' her man home and out o' mischief."

Then the priest was gone with a wave of his hand, striding at full speed down to the shore to meet the *curragh* which would take him back to the north island before the sun dipped into the sea, before the Beltaine fires flared scarlet in the night.

With Aileen dancing a weaving trail before them, Deirdre and Conaire climbed to the top of the path with the villagers. One by one, the families disappeared into the beehive huts which ribboned their way parallel to the edge of the cliff. The low silhouette of *Dún Conaire* beckoned beyond, at the height of the stony rise.

Arms around one another, Conaire and Deirdre paused at the edge of the rock-pile fence. Primroses clung to the stones and waved gently in the briny ocean breeze. Cows lowed in the field as they feasted on green and stubborn grass. Across the bay, the Connemara mountains rose purple from the deep blue water, and the rhythmic wash of the tide against the cliffs lulled them with soft music.

Aileen raced through a opening in the fence, giggling and twirling in happy delirium. Och, a fairy-child, she was, there was no doubt about it. Deirdre wondered when the lass would show the full of her fairy blood; if it would come upon her in secret, or if it would, like Deirdre's own gift, wait until the brink of womanhood before it manifested.

Conaire's gaze followed his daughter's antics. "Full o' life, that one."

"Aye, she dances like the wind."

Suddenly, rising from a crack in the stones beneath their feet, a frantic little gust whirled, salt-sweet, humid, and carrying not a bit o' dust.

Deirdre and Conaire shared a secret smile as the gust veered off toward their daughter, who squealed and whirled with it.

"It's good to know," Deirdre murmured, "that there's still some magic in the world."

Conaire drew her back against him and combed his fingers through her hair. From the mainland, a whole fleet of hookers rose into the sky and headed toward the west for a night's fishing in the deep water. The ocean breeze shifted and grew cool.

She stirred in his arms. "I've got a pot of stirabout warming o'er the peat, and fresh buttermilk cooling in the house." She trailed a finger down his stubbled cheek. "You must have a powerful hunger, Conaire."

"Aye, I do."

He growled the words in such a way that there was no mistaking his true meaning.

"Och," she grinned, pushing him gently, "can't you get your mind off your dangle for a moment?"

"Nay, not a single moment."

She headed away with a tingling in her womb and the promise of a kiss on her mind, but he seized her hand before she'd taken two steps.

"Stay here for a moment." He drew her close, not with his hands, but with the soft warmth of his eyes, the color of the sea on a misty morning. "We still have time yet."

Deirdre sank into the warmth of his embrace. Aileen raced with the breeze, her laughter as free as the bubbling of a stream. Above, the silhouette of two swans passed across the sun. The birds soared and dipped and twirled, weightless with the wind beneath their wings.

Deirdre and Conaire stood for a long time, sharing the soft talk of the day.

Glossary

Irish is a Celtic language, closely related to Scots Gaelic and Manx, and more distantly related to Cornish, Welsh, and Breton. Even among the *Gaeltacht,* the regions of Ulster, Connacht, and Munster where Irish is still spoken, there exists at least four distinct dialects. For this glossary, I used "official" standardized spelling and pronunciation wherever possible. In the case of Irish words not in common use today, I used the rules of pronunciation of the West Munster dialect, which is considered to be, phonetically, the simplest.

A stór = (pronounced "ah store") My treasure, my darling (for children *a stóirín*).

Bean sí = (pronounced "BAN shee") Fairy woman.

Beltaine = (pronounced "BAL teen") The Celtic May Day festival. This feast is connected with the promotion of fertility, and encouraged the growth of both cattle and crops.

Bóaire = (pronounced "BOW arah") A cattleman, the highest grade of freeman in ancient Celtic society.

Brandub = (pronounced "BRAND oob") A board game mentioned in ancient Irish literature which may have involved gaming pieces and dice.

Brat = (pronounced "brat") A woolen, four-cornered cloak worn by the ancient Irish, wrapped several times around the wearer and fastened at the breast with a pin or brooch.

Cailleach = (pronounced "KALL yuckh") A witch.

Clochán = (pronounced "CLO ckhan") A kind of drystone beehive hut found in the rocky districts of western Ireland.

Cú Chulainn = (pronounced "coo KHULL in") The legendary hero in the Red Branch cycle of ancient Irish tales, who is the personification of a Gaelic warrior's virtues: courageous, honest, bold in war.

Curragh = (pronounced "CURR ockh") Primitive canoes covered with hide and propelled with oars or sails.

Dagdá = (pronounced "DY dah") The "good god," or the father god in Celtic mythology, generally considered the highest of all the pagan Irish gods.

Daidí = (pronounced "daddy") Daddy.

D'ár m'anam = (pronounced "DAR man um") By my soul.

Dochloíte = (pronounced "do CKHLEE cha") Indominitable, invincible.

Dún = (pronounced "doon") An earthen ring-fort or fortified residence, usually circular or oval, enclosed by one or more earthen banks and ditches. "Ring-forts" are known by a number of different names. *Dún* implies a site of some prestige.

Fad saol agat = (pronounced "fad seal UG ut") Long life to you.

Feis = (pronounced "fesh") A fair.

Fidchell = (pronounced "Fi ckhal") A battle game played upon a board, which is often mentioned in ancient Irish literature. Similar to chess.

Imbolc = (pronounced "IM bulk") The Celtic festival on February 1st which coincides with the lactation of the ewes, also St. Brigid's Day.

Léine = (pronounced "LAY nya") A linen tunic reaching to the knee or calf, worn by both men and women in ancient Ireland.

Liss = (pronounced "leash") The open space within the enclosure of a ring-fort.

Lúgh = (pronounced "loo") Often known as Lúgh of the long arm, this god possessed a magic spear that flashed fire and roared aloud. The festival of Lughnasa was thought to be held in his honor.

Lughnasa = (pronounced "LOO nass ah") The Celtic Midsummer festival, often considered a harvest festival, and the most joyous of the four major Celtic feasts. The feast itself took place on August 1st.

Maoineach = (pronounced "ME nyackh") Precious, beloved.

Mo rún = (pronounced "ma roon") My darling.

Mo shearc = (pronounced "ma hark") My love, my beloved.

Ráth = (pronounced "rah") The grass-grown earthworks and isolated farmsteads where the land-holding class of Early Christian Ireland dwelt. These earthen enclosures are more commonly known as ring-forts.

Rí = (pronounced "ree") A king. *Rí Ruirech* is an over-king.

Samhain = (pronounced "SOW in") The Celtic New Year, the time between the season of light and the season of dark. Here, the Otherworld became visible to mankind, and all the forces of the supernatural were set loose upon the human world. It was celebrated on November 1st, as well as the night before. It is known to us today as Halloween.

Sídh = (pronounced "shee") The beings of the Otherworld; fairies; also the ancient burial mounds of Ireland, where the people of the Otherworld are said to live.

Tír na nÓg = (pronounced "CHEER na nohg") The Land of Youth, the Otherworld, i.e., the Celtic counterpart of the Christian heaven.

Tuath = (pronounced "TOO a") Tribe, or district where the tribe resides.

Please turn the page for an
exciting sneak preview of
Lisa Ann Verge's next historical romance
Heaven In His Arms
to be published by
Zebra Books in
April 1995

Prologue

Paris, July 1670

This was her only chance.

Genevieve Lalande clutched a bundle close to her chest. She straightened against the wall and merged her silhouette with the shadows. The dampness of the stone seeped through her thin woolen dress and chilled her skin, already clammy from fear and anticipation. She dug her fingers into the bundle. She had come this far. All that was left was to pass the guard at the end of the hallway, and she would be *free*.

The distraction had already begun. A slip of a girl emerged from one of the doorways which pocked the hall. With a flash of white legs, the sylph raced toward the dozing female guard and seized her arm. The guard started from her nap and stared at the wild-haired creature with glazed eyes. The young girl, a deaf-mute, pointed frantically toward her room. Cursing, the stocky woman hefted herself out of her seat, grasped a sputtering candle, and lumbered after the thin wraith.

As the guard disappeared into the chamber, Genevieve launched herself through the hall, her bare feet swift and soundless, her gaze fixed on the dull gleam of the high oak doors, one of the last remaining barriers to freedom. She would only have a few moments before the guard realized that the young woman's unspoken fears were imaginary—the crazed ravings of a simpleton, the sleep-befogged guard would think—and then the old laywoman would shrug them off and return to her dozing.

The brass handle chilled Genevieve's hand. She eased the door open to prevent the hinges from squeaking. When it was cracked enough, she slipped through and edged it shut behind her.

She leaned for a moment against the outside wall, sucking in the humid night air as she waited for her heart to stop pounding in her ears. She listened for pursuers, while a breeze filtered around the building and cooled her skin. Shifting her bundle, she murmured a prayer of eternal gratitude to the deaf-mute who had aided her in her plans. Then, she put it behind her. She had no time to waste—she was already late. If she didn't hurry, her second accomplice would lose courage and destroy all their well-made plans.

Peering around the corner of the building, she scanned the enormous courtyard of the Salpêtrière. The night was clear but moonless. Bits of smooth, flat gravel scattered the meager starlight, making the courtyard glitter as if it were covered with frost. There was no sign of her accomplice, but she didn't expect to find her waiting like a lost child in the middle of the open courtyard. She glanced at the debris scattered at the opposite end, where the church of St. Louis was being built between the two long buildings of the Salpêtrière. There was no better place to hide and wait but among the hewn stones, the piled earth, and the skeletal wooden scaffolding on the site. There, she was sure she'd find her accomplice.

She turned the corner and clung to the walls, as she worked her way toward the site. Sharp chips of gravel bit into the callused pads of her feet. A night breeze swept through the open courtyard, heavy with the ripe stench of rotting refuse which rose from the nearby Seine river. She glanced up at the rows of windows in the opposite building, which winked at her like a thousand eyes, then stumbled and bit back a curse as she kicked an abandoned pick. The tool clattered loudly on the gravel. Her bare toe smarted. She squeezed her eyes shut until the pain passed. Then she limped on until she reached the shadows of the scaffolding.

She shifted the weight of the bundle to her other arm. She waited, tensely, for someone to emerge from the darkness. Her accomplice must have heard her stumbling in the dark; the clatter of the pick against the gravel had been loud enough to wake the dead. As the minutes passed and no one emerged, she picked her way through the debris to search for her. She followed the curve of the church, whose wooden dome was just beginning to take shape high above the masonry. She circled each pile of stones and peered around the tumbled stacks of wood and earth.

Marie Suzanne Duplessis was not there.

Genevieve clutched a support of the wooden scaffolding. A splinter pierced her skin. Marie should have been here by now. The last note Genevieve had sent her was specific—tonight was the night they were to meet in this courtyard to complete the plans they had made over the last three weeks. She and Marie had been passing notes back and forth through the same system without fail for too long for there to be a sudden mix-up.

Somewhere in Paris, beyond the walls of the institution, church bells rang. Genevieve counted each discordant resonance and scanned the courtyard. *Come, Marie. Come.* She hugged her bundle more tightly, stepped over a pile of wood, and edged along the shadows of the construction. She startled a bevy of sleeping birds into an anxious fluttering of wings. A slow stream of silt filtered down from the higher scaffolding, dusting her shoulder. The sleeping birds settled, and she continued her careful course to the other side of the unfinished church.

Amid the fading clangor of the church bells, a figure emerged from one of the buildings. Genevieve pressed back against the masonry. If one of the guards saw her, all would be lost. But as she watched the figure emerge into the courtyard, she knew it was no guard. It was a woman, a young woman by the quick pace of her walk, an anxious woman by the way her head pivoted back and forth, by the way her hands darted out of her cloak and curled into its neckline. As the woman headed toward the debris around the church, Genevieve knew it could be no one but Marie.

Genevieve intercepted her near a pile of bricks.

"Marie."

The young woman stopped short and pulled back the edge of her scarf, revealing a pale, drawn face. She peered in Genevieve's direction as she stepped into the starlight.

"You are Genevieve?"

"Oui. Come into the shadows."

Genevieve scrutinized the woman as she approached. She had never seen her so close before today. She noticed with relief that they were of the same height. Of all characteristics, height would have been the most difficult to disguise.

"Thank God you are here—I feared you would leave." Marie loosened her headrail and snagged the scarf off her hair. "The *gouvernante* on my floor would not fall asleep, and I was forced to check three doors before I found one unlocked."

Refined speech, Genevieve thought, shifting her bundle under one arm. Well, she could mimic that well enough. "You need not have feared. I would have stayed until dawn."

Marie peered at her face in the darkness. "I have never seen you before."

"Nor I you." Genevieve didn't bother to explain that she was housed in a separate building, isolated from women like Marie. Marie was a *bijoux,* a jewel of the Salpêtrière, an orphaned daughter of the petty nobility, pampered and educated and protected from those like herself. "There are hundreds of other women in the Salpêtrière."

"You write with such a fine hand," Marie murmured, glancing at Genevieve's common, russet wool skirts, "that I thought you might be one of the noblewomen."

Genevieve's lips tightened. In another time, in another world, she might have been worthy to be a *bijoux*. But that was long ago and best left forgotten. She gestured to Marie's skirts. "Is that what you planned to wear tomorrow?"

"Yes." Marie parted her cloak to show a glimpse of a dark blue traveling dress. "I've packed a small case and left it by my bed. In it, you'll find what you need to disguise yourself, several other dresses, and a few gold *louis*. This is all I can give you for what you are doing for me."

"You should have kept the money," Genevieve argued. Such foolish, innocent generosity. "You'll need it more than I will."

"I couldn't. I owe you a debt greater than gold." Marie twisted her headrail in her hands. "You do know what you're doing, don't you? I couldn't live with myself—no matter how happy I'd be to escape my fate—if I misled you."

Genevieve dumped her bundle on a pile of bricks. *"I'm* the one who suggested this plan."

"I'm going to be sent away," Marie continued, ignoring Genevieve's words. "King Louis the Fourteenth himself has dowered me. He has paid my passage to some horrible place called *Québec*—" her breath hitched in her throat. "He intends to marry me off to some coarse, rough-handed settler—"

"I know you're a King's girl." Genevieve snatched the mangled headrail from the other girl's hands, then shook it out to judge its fit. Every year since Genevieve had arrived in the Salpêtrière, dozens of girls of all social classes had been dowered by the King and sent off to the Caribbean islands or to the northern settlements of New France, to marry and settle in the colonies. "I chose you *because* you're being sent away from this place."

"Haven't you heard the rumors? Don't you know anything about . . . *Québec?*" Marie's smooth white hands, bereft of the headrail, knotted and twisted and pulled at each other. "The forests are filled with red-skinned savages. The winters are long and frigid, and there's so much snow that it tops the rooftops." Her voice wavered. "And the voyage—over the sea— halfway across the world, in storms and sickness—"

Genevieve expertly snapped the headrail smooth. "Have you changed your mind?"

"Oh, no, no!" Marie clutched her hands to her breast. "It's just . . . Why are you doing this? Why would you take my place and go to that dreadful colony, and leave all this behind?"

Genevieve glared at the two long buildings of the Salpêtrière and thought, *I'd rather sell my soul to Lucifer than spend another year in this wretched place.*

She bit her tongue to repress the retort. Marie wouldn't understand. She and Marie both lived in this charity house, but they lived in entirely different worlds. Marie lived in the Salpêtrière of King Louis the Fourteenth; the charity house that succored aging servants with no pensions, old married couples of good birth, and the younger daughters of impoverished petty nobility; the charity house was staffed with religious women and headed by a benign Mother Superior. Genevieve lived in a place ruled by brutal guards, a place peopled by orphans and waifs and beggars and whores taken forcefully off the streets of Paris. Since the day she herself was captured, three years ago, she found no charity in this house—only an eternity of hunger and drudgery.

A hundred times, as she scrubbed and rung and batted linens by the Seine, she had considered escaping by racing toward the nearby gates of Paris and losing her pursuers in the maze of streets she knew so well. But she knew what awaited her in those streets—she knew too well. Nothing had changed. She was the same girl the police had seized from the courtyards of Paris all those years ago, except that she was three years older, and wise enough to know the fate of a nineteen-year-old left alone without means in the streets of Paris.

And now, this Marie Suzanne Duplessis offered an escape far,

far better. Marie offered her a new life—*her* life. But Genevieve knew that trying to explain her reasons to this *bijoux* would be like trying to teach a blind man to see. Marie had never tasted a stolen apple. She had never raced through the streets of Paris after cutting a nobleman's purse, fearing hunger more than the threat of capture and punishment by whipping. Marie would never understand the forces of utter desperation.

"I'm . . . I'm surprised Mother Superior didn't recommend you to the King himself," Marie continued when Genevieve did not answer. "I've been told she's having difficulty finding enough girls of . . . of modest birth to fill the King's ship to Québec."

"I'll make a better marriage disguised as a Duplessis than as a Lalande," Genevieve argued, folding the headrail and laying it upon her bundle. "Because of your birth, you'll be put aside for the wealthiest men in the colony."

"I see." Marie cast her gaze down. "I didn't think of that."

You wouldn't, would you? You with your good birth and your sheltered upbringing and your ignorance of the harshness of the world. Genevieve wondered if she'd have grown up with the same wide-eyed innocence, if the world had been kinder, all those years ago.

"But, of course, it makes perfect sense. How very sage of you." Marie's hands fluttered white in the starlight, and she released a nervous laugh. "I almost didn't dare believe . . . When I found your first note among my laundered shifts, I was sure someone was playing a trick on me. *None* of the girls want to go to this dreadful place. The halls echo with their sobbing, as if tomorrow they'll all be executed in the square."

Fools. Fools who don't know their own good fortune. "You will do this, then?"

"Yes. *Yes.*" Her face lit with joy. "I received a note this morning. François is waiting for me, just inside the gates of Paris."

So that was his name, Genevieve thought, the name of the

French Musketeer Marie loved enough to risk everything to marry—even the displeasure of the King. Genevieve dearly hoped, for this woman's sake, that he wasn't like the strutting, shifty-eyed Musketeers *she* had known in her younger days. In their blue coats and gold or silver braid, they had terrorized the city, taking whatever women pleased them and pulling their swords at the slightest provocation.

"Then we mustn't delay any longer." Genevieve nodded to Marie's cloak. "Take off your clothes."

The young woman started. "Here?"

"Quickly."

Marie glanced up at the skeletal scaffolding of the church and crossed herself. "What am I to wear? I can't escape in your clothing."

Genevieve waved at her bundle. "You'll wear the clothing of a *gouvernante*—a black wool skirt, a white coif, and a black mantle. Dressed as a governess, you can leave the Salpêtrière without being stopped."

"Where did you get it?"

"Hurry."

Genevieve unlaced her bodice, tugged it off, then slipped out of her coarse, russet wool skirt. The night was warm and balmy, and the breeze toyed with her tattered shift as she stuffed her old clothes beneath a pile of bricks. She scrutinized the girl more closely, as Marie fumbled with her laces. Marie's tresses were long and chestnut-colored. Genevieve's own hair was a mass of copper, a gift, her mother once told her, from the father Genevieve had never known. Marie's skin was smooth, while Genevieve had a sprinkling of freckles across her nose. Problems, she thought, but nothing that couldn't be overcome by brushing the roots of her hair with a lead comb, covering the rest of it with an ample headrail, and patting her face thick with powder.

"Tell me about your family." Genevieve snatched Marie's bodice and thrust her arms through the sleeves. "I'll need to know their names, ages, and everything you can tell me about them."

As Marie struggled out of her skirt and petticoat and reached for the bundle of clothing, she told Genevieve about her past. Her mother had died in childbirth when Marie was only a few years old. Later, impoverished by the civil wars of the Fronde which had flared through France, she and her father had lived on the charity of distant relatives until her father died, leaving Marie to the mercy of an unscrupulous second cousin. He refused to dower her, or pay to put her in a convent, so she was sent to the Salpêtrière. Genevieve dispassionately noted all the names and dates, as she slipped on Marie's discarded petticoat and skirt. She would need to know as much as she could remember—the rest she would have to make up as she went along.

But her mind wandered from Marie's hushed, trembling monologue, as Genevieve ran her hands over the brushed broadcloth of the blue traveling dress. It had been a long time since she had worn clothes so fine, and the feel of the soft cloth against her skin brought a rush of memories of a better time . . . She closed them off. The past was the past; it was the future that mattered now.

Genevieve set her mind to fitting into Marie's bodice. Marie was small boned, but despite the meager rations of the Salpêtrière, Genevieve was generously formed. It took both of their efforts to lace the tightly boned bodice closed over Genevieve's bosom.

"There's another girl in the building who will be going with you tomorrow," Marie said as she secured the last knot. "Her name is Cecile."

"She knows, yes?"

"Yes. She will await you tonight and take you to my bed."

"Good." Genevieve smoothed her fingers down her boned form, then arranged the crumpled headrail over her hair. She twirled before Marie. "Well?"

"You've the carriage of a noblewoman." Marie plucked at her plain black robes, hesitating. Her voice quivered with hushed bewilderment. Perhaps . . . perhaps this shall all work out as you planned."

It will, Marie Suzanne Duplessis. I swear on all that you hold holy, it will.

"You'll be leaving at dawn tomorrow for Le Havre," Marie continued. "Cecile will help shield you from Mother Superior as you board the carriage."

"Mother Superior will never notice. I'll be crying like an onion seller into my—your—handkerchief. Will we be traveling in a public carriage?"

"Oh, no!" A fluttering, white hand emerged from the black sleeve to rest on her throat. "It will be sent by the King, of course."

"Who else will be in it?"

"Some guards will ride outside to see that we are protected, until we reach the ship. You know there will be other girls following from the Salpêtrière?"

"Yes."

"What if someone recognizes you?"

Genevieve leaned over to force her feet into Marie's boots. "None of the women who live in my section of the Salpêtrière were chosen. Once I'm out of Paris, I don't have to worry about being recognized."

Marie hesitated. She slipped her foot nervously in and out of Genevieve's common, wooden shoes.

"There's no need for you to wait any longer." Genevieve glanced up from where she struggled to lace Marie's tiny boots over her much larger feet. "Go. Your Musketeer is waiting."

Marie turned on one heel, then, as Genevieve straightened, she suddenly whirled and embraced her, swift and hard. "If I could give you a bag of gold, I would," Marie said fervently, seizing Genevieve's hand. "I will never forget you for the sacrifice you've made for me—Oh!"

Genevieve pulled her hand from Marie's grasp—but it was too late.

Marie stumbled back and covered her mouth. Genevieve met her shocked gaze squarely. What did the girl expect? Did she really expect another *bijoux?* Or one of the poor orphans who crowded the halls of the Salpêtrière? Would any of those women be so bold as to switch places with a King's girl?

No.

"So now you understand how I could send notes back and forth to you, and how I stole the clothing you wear, and why no other King's girl would recognize me." Genevieve watched Marie's face in the darkness. "Obviously, I'll need gloves. Even in Quebec, I imagine, no one will believe that a *bijoux* has the hands of a washerwoman."

Marie backed away, then whirled and raced swiftly toward the arched entrance that led out of the Salpêtrière. Genevieve tilted her chin and stared sightlessly at the place where she had been. Genevieve had been right, these three weeks, to hide her true identity from that daughter of the petty nobility. Marie would never have agreed to this desperate scheme, if she had known the truth.

In the Salpêtrière, it was common knowledge that the only women who washed the linens lived in *La Correction.* The section of the institution reserved for wayward women . . . and common whores.

Genevieve pulled her headrail over her hair and strode toward Marie's building. *Let her believe what she will.* God willing, Genevieve would never lay eyes on the real Marie Suzanne Duplessis again.

One

Quebec, August 1670

"I'm here."

André Lefebvre slammed open the door to his agent's office, and splattered wet moccasin prints on the polished floorboards. He tossed his balled linen shirt on an imported rosewood desk, spraying Philippe Martineau with grit and river water.

André glared at his old friend. Philippe leaned back in the creaking, wooden chair and blindly wiped the grit from his blue silk coat and silver buttons. His gaze swept over André's nudity, broken only by the flap of a breechcloth, and rested with distaste on the water sluicing down his legs and darkening the rug.

"For a week I've been trying to get you in here." A froth of lace spilled over Philippe's hand, as he rolled his fingers toward a chair on the other side of his desk. "I'm pleased you finally saw fit to grace me with your presence."

"I'm not staying long enough to sit," André argued, as he paced across the rare Turkish carpet. "What the hell do you want from me, summoning me like a lackey in the middle of the day?"

"That's when most men conduct business," Philippe mused wryly. "In the middle of the day."

"I was doing well enough," André growled, slamming his hands on Philippe's desk, "conducting my *own* business before your boy interrupted—"

"Business?" Philippe's cold blue eyes remained level under

the slow arch of one brow. "Splashing at the river's edge like a boy—is that what you call business?"

"It was a canoe race—and it's a hundred times better than *this*." André swiped his shirt off the desk, sweeping some papers to the floor with it. "Because of that race, Tiny has agreed to sign on with me."

"Tiny Griffin?" Philippe cocked a brow higher. "That burly woods-runner?"

"Oui. The best steersman in Quebec, joining me on this crazed voyage of mine. Not a bad day's work, eh, partner?" André tossed his shirt to the floor and waved a hand over his agent's strewn desk. "Now, just collect the papers and tell me where to sign, so I can get back to *my* work."

André turned and strode toward the window. He banged open the shutters, flooding the room with bright July sunlight. Philippe's warehouse wedged up against the sheer rock face of the cliff of Quebec, and gazed strategically over the cul-de-sac where the boats unloaded goods from the French ships anchored in the St. Lawrence River. The crowd which had watched the race still lingered on the lip of shore, a motley clutch of Ottawa Indians, bearded woods-runners, and a few Frenchmen pecking around like tamed peacocks set out in the wild.

André shook his head, like a great shaggy dog, spewing river water across the room, not giving a damn that he was splattering Philippe's precious gleaming furniture and exotic Turkish rug with river-bottom silt. Serves the peacock right for sending a boy to drag him away from the river. André had explained the division of labor from the moment he and Philippe had become partners in this upcoming fur-trading voyage: They would do what they both did best—Philippe would take care of paper and politics; André would hire the men, outfit the canoes, and make the voyage.

Make the voyage . . . yes, make the voyage. André raked his fingers through his shaggy hair and shook it wild. His heart still

pumped wildly from the race. His arms ached, and the burn
between his shoulder blades had only just begun to cool. He
flexed his arms in circles to unravel the kinks from his muscles.
Damn reckless fool he had been, daring Tiny to a race when
Tiny was only a month back from a season in the woods—work-
hardened, strong—while André had just returned from France,
doing nothing more arduous than pacing in the antechambers
of courtrooms. And the race had been but from one side of the
St. Lawrence to the other; easy currents, open water. Three years
away from Quebec had made him soft; he only had a few weeks
to toughen up before the voyage began. For then, he would lead
an expedition fifteen hundred miles into the interior; over mountainous portages, through the most ferocious of whitewater . . .
into uncharted territory.

He'd had three years to dream of *that*.

"My dear André, we could more easily discuss this matter if
you weren't gazing out the window like a schoolboy dreaming
over his lessons."

"I'm paying you to take care of things, not to discuss them
with me." In the midst of the St. Lawrence, a ship unfurled its
limp, salt-stained sails like a portly priest undressing, to set an-
chor in the midst of the river. "Another ship is in." André cocked
an elbow on the sill. "Shouldn't you be out there, cataloguing
your wealth or whatever you do when you're not suffocating on
your own perfume?"

"It can wait." A drawer squealed as Philippe pulled it open.
He thumped a wrapped package onto the desk. "Unfortunately,
this conversation of ours can be avoided no longer."

André sucked in the clean river air, then snorted out the stench
of cleanliness and order. *Hell and damnation.* Business, always
business. Would he ever be free of it?

He leaned back against the sill, his hands dangling on either
side of him. Philippe had removed his blond wig, and his sweaty,
close-cropped hair stuck up awkwardly all over his head.

Philippe sliced an end off a carrot of tobacco. Then, with all the stoic majesty of an Indian chief presiding over a circle of his men, he tapped the tightly packed leaves into his pipe, lit them with a spark of flint against steel, then hollowed his cheeks as he drew in the first smoke.

It was an old ritual, an *Indian* ritual, anachronistic in this low-raftered room with all its oiled and gleaming French furniture. It was a peek at the old Philippe André remembered with fondness. But the sight made him edgy, as did the smile Philippe cast his way. The movement pulled the skin around the mottled scar which ran jagged from Philippe's temple, through the edge of his thin, wax-tipped mustache, and faded into the tuft of blond beard in the center of his chin. It gave him a rakish, devil-may-care air, in sharp contrast to his fripperies.

But André knew the man too well to be fooled by that easy grin. He'd fought too many Iroquois skirmishes with Philippe, spent too much time in the woods hunting and fighting and struggling to survive. André noticed the tense crimp of muscles which edged one of Philippe's cool blue eyes as he sucked on the pipe, and he knew his old friend was bracing himself for something.

What could it be now, André thought, striding across the room to snatch up his damp shirt and rub it across his stubbled face. What the hell could it be now? Hadn't he had enough trouble wheedling his own inheritance from the courts in France? Hadn't he spent three years fighting for what was his, by right, all the while itching, itching, to be back home, here, in Quebec?

Philippe extended the pipe. André frowned at the face of the fox carved in the bowl—Philippe's totem, from the old days, before Philippe's marriage. André considered refusing it. He belonged out on the shore right now, seeking out the fur traders just in from the west, plying them with good French brandy and sucking dry the last bit of their knowledge: the lay of the western land, the fierceness of the rivers, the distribution of the Indian tribes. It was *Philippe's* duty to make arrangements with the fur-trading company, get a trading license, to take care of all the minutia he wanted nothing to do with. And he suspected he didn't want to hear whatever it was that Philippe had to say.

"No brandy for me?" André flipped his shirt over his shoulder and seized the pipe. "You have a look upon you as if I'll need it."

"Brandy? *Moi?* In the middle of the day?" His petticoat breeches rustled as he rose from his chair and opened a small cabinet in the corner. He clinked a bottle of amber liquid on the marble top. "I'm a married man with three children," he said, setting out two glasses, "a respected member of the community."

André seized the back of the chair, jerked it around, and straddled it as he exhaled a blue stream of smoke. "And Marietta will have your head."

Marietta was Philippe's hot-blooded Italian wife, who, even five months gone with child, brooked no nonsense from the husband she'd only half-tamed. Philippe's grin turned rakish again as he poured. *"Oui,* she probably will." He handed one glass to André and raised his own. "To old friends, *mon vieux ami."*

"Salut."

The amber fire burned down the back of his throat and lit his belly with warmth. André clinked down the empty glass, savoring the hot taste. He would miss only two things when he finally left civilization: Brandy and a Frenchwoman's scent.

"Three years in France did you no good, my old friend." Philippe nodded at André's smoke-ripened, deerskin breechcloth, the damp moccasins, and finally at the Indian medicine bag slung around his neck. "Already, the old ways creep up on you."

"Thank Christ." André snorted at Philippe, in his blue silk coat, shiny silver buttons, and froths of lace at neck and wrists.

"One more day in waistcoat and petticoat breeches, and I would have sprouted breasts."

"*Oui,* well . . ." Philippe gave a purely Gallic shrug. His chair squeaked as he settled back into it, cradling his half-empty cup of brandy. "One must change with the times. Life is not the same as it was three years ago."

"*You're* the one wearing a skirt, not I. And this—" André scowled and gestured to Philippe's desk. "How can you stand this vomit of paper?" He'd lose his mind scribbling over a desk all day. Already the sickly perfume of wood oil and soap permeating this room threatened to make him sneeze. But Philippe seemed to thrive in it. When the two of them had left the local militia to go their separate ways after the war with the Iroquois, Philippe had just begun his business in a makeshift siding-and-rubble hut, and had a wife, a child, and another on the way. He'd done well in such a risky business, as an agent for small fur traders, it showed in the office's carved paneling, the tinkling of the chandelier above the desk, the rich smell of oil and leather emanating from a shelf full of books. Philippe always had a good sense of the blowing of the political winds, whether they be Indian or French.

Which was why, André reminded himself, as the brandy essence rushed through his blood, he had hired his old friend to tackle that labyrinth *for* him.

He narrowed his gaze on his agent. Philippe twisted the glass in his hand, around and around, spilling drops of brandy on his pale fingers.

Something was wrong. Very, very wrong.

André clattered the pipe into its clay holder, splattering red embers out of the bowl. "Out with it, Philippe."

"Really, André, carrying on a civil conversation with you these days is like teasing a hungry bear." Philippe finished his brandy in one gulp and placed the glass on the table with two fingers, then tapped at the embers until they sizzled out. "I was getting to it. I spoke of great changes these past years, but I didn't mean in us, I meant here, in Quebec."

André rolled his eyes and snapped his shirt off his shoulder. "Spare me one of your speeches."

Philippe managed a tilted smile that looked more like a grimace. "You were never very interested in politics."

"Politics." André chafed his hair vigorously with his shirt. "If it's the peace with the Iroquois, or the English fur-trading in Hudson Bay you want to discuss, then I'll stay and have another brandy."

"It's not politics, really. It's more a matter of philosophy—"

André snapped his shirt out with a *wack* and stood up, banging his chair out of the way. He leaned deep over Philippe's desk, close enough to smell his perfume over the curling tobacco smoke. "What the *hell* is going on? Have you lost your edge, Philippe, in this black-aired room? Why did you drag me here?"

Philippe tugged a piece of parchment from under André's hand, then laid it on the edge of the table as he took the pipe. "I had hoped you'd discover this yourself this past week, and spare me the unpleasantness."

André looked at the thing as if it were a piece of rotten meat. "I hired you so I would never have to look at another piece of paper again."

"You've had your head buried in too many warehouses and ships' holds since you returned. If you had taken a moment out of spending that inheritance of yours, you'd have seen this notice posted all over the city—and I wouldn't have had to send four shop boys to summon you."

André knocked the paper off the table and sent it skimming to the floor. "I've got better things to do than read petty ordinances."

"It contains strict orders from the King's minister." Philippe hooked his lip over the end of the pipe. "And it concerns restrictions placed upon men seeking trading licenses."

"Of course it does." A breeze flooded the room, rattling the other papers on Philippe's desk like autumn leaves and sending the crystal drops on the chandelier chiming. "When in the history of this damned settlement *hasn't* the government tried to suck the life out of the fur trade? Jesus, Philippe, just take care of it. I've had a bellyful of bureaucracy in France—"

"It's not that simple."

"Anything is simple with money." He wrestled into his shirt and yanked the hem over his rippled belly. "Do whatever you have to do. Offer the king's minister a percentage of the furs—"

"The king's minister won't be bribed."

"Then bribe," André growled, frustration thickening his words, "his administrators."

"Don't you think that was the first thing I tried?" He raised the pipe to stanch André's words. "I'm not one of the best agents in Quebec for nothing. But you see, this is not a matter of money. As I started to tell you, it's a matter of philosophy."

André kicked the chair, though it was not in his way. He crossed the width of the room in four wide strides to glare out the window at the bustling street. The first *barque* had landed on the lip of shore, and the crowd buzzed like a hive of bees around the bounty unloaded from the new French ship.

He should be there, haggling over provisions for his trip into the interior. He was suffocating in this low-raftered room—he was suffocating under Philippe's gloom. Philippe didn't understand—André would have *no more trouble* with this voyage, he'd waited too long to see it done. He'd traveled the familiar route to the west a thousand times in his mind, during his self-imposed exile in France. Right now, he wanted nothing more than to be waist-deep in the rapids of the Ottawa River, portaging around a violent set of falls, or paddling across silvery Lake Nipissing, closer and closer to Georgian Bay. It had been three years since he last journeyed into the wilderness, and the soles of his feet itched for his well-worn moccasins and the feel of the rocky path. To live with the roof as his sky, to live forever roaming, to live with a commitment to no one but himself. He was so close he could taste gritty Indian *sagamité* in the scent of wood-smoke.

Nothing, *nothing* more could prevent him from fulfilling the dream he had harbored since he had first set foot as a boy in the North American wilderness: A dream of traveling farther west into the unexplored forest than any white man had gone.

Certainly no petty government ordinance.

"When you lived here last, André," Philippe began, despite André's rigid back, despite his attention to the goings-on outside the window, "the philosophy was to suck the lifeblood from this country—take the beaver pelts from the west, search for minerals and whatever. And so every autumn the strongest men flooded into the woods, and every spring we returned as wild and disruptive as brandy-soaked Indians. But now the King doesn't want us leaving every winter. He wants to settle Quebec. As the English and the Dutch have settled their lands in this New World—with farmers, blacksmiths, tanners—"

"What has this got to do with me? With the voyage?"

"You must fulfill the requirements of the ordinance to trade furs. It's that simple." Philippe tugged on the edge of his lace cravat and took sudden interest in the brass edging of his inkwell. "The requirement is simply, really, and won't cost you much . . . You must . . ." He cleared his throat. "Marry."

André knees loosened, abruptly and instinctively, for it seemed as if the floor bucked beneath him, like a birch bark canoe riding the swells of whitewater, and it kept bucking and rolling and the room rocked around him, and only his latent skill in riding the swells kept him upright, glaring steadily at Philippe like the only steady point on the twisting horizon.

"More King's girls are coming to Quebec." Philippe raised a finger from its delicate brushing of the inkwell to point toward the window. "There's undoubtedly a whole new batch in that ship just coming in. The ordinance requires all single men in the colony to marry within a fortnight of their arrival, or else . . ." He rolled one shoulder. "Else they'll refuse you a hunting, fishing, or, more relevantly, a trading license."

"The bureaucrats of Quebec can't enforce *that,* and you know it. It's like condemning all of the settlement to starve."

"They *can* enforce it—and they will. I told you this place has changed."

"Not that much."

The skin of his palms cracked as he curled his hands into fists. *Not here, not here.* He'd just returned from Louis the Fourteenth's France. The monarchy was like a great, choking, parasitic vine—it could not have found a way to reach across the Atlantic to strangle this new world.

"If you refuse, I can do nothing for you."

"Is this *you* talking, Philippe, the man who fought the Iroquois with me in '66? You've been behind that desk too long. The stale air of civilization is curdling your brain. They want money, as all greedy bureaucrats do." André speared the air westward, pointing toward someplace well beyond the walls. "There's a bay out there, a bay where a dozen Indian tribes travel to fish and trade each spring—you and I have both heard the talk. You know there's no better place to build a permanent fur-trading post."

"You don't have to convince me." He shifted in his seat. "I've a hefty bag of gold invested in you."

Yes, in that, and in more than that, Philippe—in the dream. For this single trading post will only be a base for further exploration into the uncharted western forests. It would be the first of many posts, stretching farther and farther west until I reached the elusive China Sea.

But best of all, I will live like a Caesar of the wilderness, a king of my own domain, and there would be no one to tell me otherwise—no commitments, no obligations, no ties, no one left behind . . . definitely no wife.

"He's going to fill Quebec with abandoned wives, and the forest with cuckolded husbands." André crossed the room and planted his hands flat on the desk. "Get me out of this."

Philippe tapped the pipe onto the desk, loosening the last blackened coals. Then he looked up, and memory passed between them.

"It's not the same world." Philippe set the pipe down, leaned back, and folded his hands across his swelling middle. "We are at peace with the Iroquois now."

A cloud passed across the face of the sun, casting the room in darkness. Shadows dripped from the corners of the room, and the rafters loomed low and dark—Christ, he was in a box, suffocating in here—he tugged the neck of his wide-opened shirt until the sound of a tear filled the room. *It makes no difference.* André knew that now. Peace or no peace, he'd not have a wife in the settlements.

Then, a thought came to him. He laughed—a dark, humorless sound. A twisted grin stretched tight over his teeth.

"By God, the last time I saw a look like that," Philippe murmured warily, "you were facing two Iroquois warriors who took a liking to the color of your hair."

"We *are* at peace with the Iroquois, aren't we?" He slapped his hands on the desk. "I can go into their country now. I can trade furs with the English at Fort Orange. They'll give me twice the price that the French will, and they won't charge me tax—"

"That's smuggling." Philippe's fingers stilled on the bowl of the pipe. "That's *treason.*"

André snorted. "Is this the same man who traded brandy with the Ottawas despite the threat of excommunication?"

"Treason can get you *hanged.*"

"Only if I'm caught."

"Think, André. For once use your head and not your impulses." Philippe tapped the ash out of his pipe on the side of the desk, already pocked with dents. "Smuggling to the English the amount of furs you intended to collect is unreasonable—impossible. And what of the string of trading posts, hmm? If you refuse this edict, that dream of yours will crumble before the foundation has even been set— By God, where are you going?"

André slammed open the door without a pause. He had to get away from these walls, this roof—he needed a good long suck of brandy. "Find a way out, Philippe. I won't marry."

No, no, *no*, he thought, as he plunged out into the muddy street. He wouldn't marry.

Never, ever again.

Genevieve gripped the weathered railing of the ship's prow as the vessel sailed deeper into the channel of the St. Lawrence River. On the northern coast, a pewter wall of rock heaved up from the lip of the river, its rough surface pitted with gnarled spruce trees and streaked with scrawny tufts of grass, which clung along the sheltered clefts of the naked stone. On the southern shore, luxuriant, blue green forests bristled to the very edge of the horizon, seeping the fragrance of pine sap and moist, mulchy earth into the air.

Genevieve tightened her one-handed grip on her mantle as the chill September wind whistled through her bones. Out of the corner of her eye, she glimpsed a flap of a gray habit—one of the Ursulines who'd accompanied them across the sea. Lurking in the shadows and watching me, no doubt, Genevieve thought, suppressing a shiver. Eager to drag me down to that death-hold with the other girls and stuff noxious ointments in me, and make me cough my life into a dirty linen.

No, no. Not me. She pressed her belly against the railing, for support, she told herself—the river rocked differently than the open sea, but her legs had not yet learned the movement, that's why her head was swimming so much, that's why nausea heaved in her throat. She couldn't show one flicker of weakness now, not when the fulfillment of her dreams loomed just beyond the next shimmering curve. She'd suffered the long, hard voyage; she'd not succumbed to the shipboard fever which had claimed a dozen girls' lives, and even now lingered, below, in the stinking ship's hold. She'd survived, yes, again, she'd survived.

Hot exhilaration rushed through her blood, ebbing away the wind's chill. A hoarse giggle escaped her raw throat. It was over—she had *won*. With stiff, shaking fingers, she tore off the headrail which enveloped her head and let a gust buffet the cloth to the sky. The wind yanked at her loosely bound hair, tugging it free to rise weightless in a cloud around her face, sweeping clear the black clouds of memory.

Genevieve Lalande did not perch here, watching the cold blue sky of this new world melt into an evening gold. The shadow called Genevieve had died at Le Havre. Now, now, she was Marie Suzanne Duplessis—now, she would have a roof above her head instead of the sky, now she would have a house to call her own, a place to settle—to set down deep roots in this fertile place. A shaky laugh rippled out as no more than a breath. *Oui,* a husband, too, she'd never imagined that in her lifetime. And a family. Someone to love who'd be all her own—children to raise in a civilized place.

Oui, civilized. Her gaze drank in the whole of the country, the endless forests not yet tamed by plow or sickle, the deep silence broken only by the caws of the cliff swallows wheeling above the ship. She had dreamed it would be like this, but she never allowed herself to believe her fantasies. In Paris, even in Normandy, she had never seen so much uninhabited, uncultivated land.

A woman could hide in such a place forever.

Oh, the girls were so full of children's bedtime stories. Savages, they told her, ruled these woods, men of bronze skin and

Two

André stepped out of the inn and collided with a cart full of eels. Limp, black fish lolled over the edge and licked his wide skirts, streaking them with slime. Waving the profuse apologies of the fisherman away, he absently scoured the stain with one gloved hand and stomped sullenly through the mud.

Good, he thought, as he noticed the black streak marring his clothing. He was wearing his best French outfit, an ensemble he had bought in Paris for the sole purpose of appearing in front of the officials responsible for holding back his inheritance. But the damned green coat fitted too tightly, the silver buttons were nothing but nuisances, and the seams dug into his skin and itched. The matching breeches strangled his legs at the knees, where they were gathered and gartered with a frivolous spray of emerald ribbons—the least feminine of his options at the time. He wanted nothing more than to toss his tight shoes, his wretched coat, and his damned breeches in the St. Lawrence River. Now, he thought, as he slid a slime-coated, gloved finger between his neck and the linen edge of his cravat, he would have an excuse to do it after today's deed was done.

He splattered out into the middle of the street, his red-heeled boots sucking deep into the mud, and headed toward Madame Jean Bourdon's house. A tepid breeze wove through the buildings clustered in the lower town of Quebec, carrying the tart scent of a recent rain. The sun glittered off the towering granite mass of the *Cap aux Diamants,* the cliff that thrust abruptly from the earth to form a backdrop to the town at its foot. Several warehouses nestled close to its base, and in and out of these flowed a line of settlers with the local currency—beaver skins—strapped across their backs. High above, in the upper town, the church bells gonged for the first Mass of the day.

André clutched the bulge straining out between the second and third button of his coat, and pulled on it so that the ties dug into his neck. Damn Indian magic. *Where's the rain? The thunder? The lightning?* A good Ojibwa shaman could read signs of a man's future in the wind and the weather, but André didn't need Indian wisdom to know what a blue sky and bright sun portended. A fool he was, to believe in such things. The sun had no reason to shine on this black day.

André knew which house belonged to Madame Bourdon the minute he turned the corner onto her street. A crowd of men swarmed around the door like bees scenting nectar. Several officers milled on the outskirts. One Frenchman, dressed in a brilliant silk doublet and breeches festooned with ribbons and lace, stood apart from the swarm.

"André!"

André lifted his plumed, wide-brimmed hat to shade his eyes from the glare of the morning. The sunlight glinted off Philippe's fair, corkscrew curls. "Christ, look at this, will you?" André said as Philippe stopped at his side. "Rutting season in Quebec."

"Last batch of the King's girls for the season." Philippe tucked his hat under his arm and snapped a familiar slip of paper out of his pocket. "Though I'm pleased you finally came to your senses, André, you could have decided earlier in the season to send me this message, and saved my heart the strain. I was sure I'd see you swinging by the neck before year's end."

André slid his gloved fingers under his cravat and yanked. "Can't you see the noose?"

André glowered at the crowd, at the closed door to Madame Bourdon's house, then he glowered up the black cliff of Quebec toward the palisades of the upper city. Nearly two months he'd prepared for this voyage, and too frequently he'd come up against something: *voyageurs* unwilling to sign on with him, merchants unwilling to accept his credit, provisions held in warehouses for "inspection" to search for secreted brandy, and bureaucrats turning away from the sight of gold gleaming beneath his hand, and all the while time sifted, sifted away. Now the first breath of autumn cooled the evenings, and every day another flotilla of canoes headed west—while he watched on the shore, grinding his teeth, inside thrashing like a mountain cat trying to find a way out of this trap.

"You've done the right thing," Philippe murmured, stuffing the paper into his pocket. "Marriage, even a reluctant one, has its benefits, hmm?"

"Not *this* marriage."

"Come, come, old friend." Philippe tapped his wrought-wooden cane into the mud, clinking on a block of stone beneath. "A warm bed, a willing woman—such things I've never known you to turn away."

"This will be a marriage of convenience." André slapped his hat over his dark wig, snapping one of the delicate ostrich plumes in the process. "When I come back in the spring, I'm getting an annulment."

"André—"

"I'm in no mood to hear you rhapsodize about the wonders of the conjugal bed." André rubbed his elbow against his side, trying to scratch an itch where a seam rubbed against his skin. "I'm marrying because I was given no choice: marry or give up the trip. So here I am. But there's no requirement that I *stay* married."

Philippe's smile faltered. He twisted away and gazed over the black waters of the St. Lawrence, watching a small boat navigate the currents to the opposite shore. An oxen lumbered by, strapped to a cart laden with ribbed green watermelons, fresh from the farm. One fell off and splattered into the mud, spewing its sweet rosy fruit over the ground.

"I suppose," Philippe began on a sigh, "that you won't consider a relationship with this woman."

"No consummation, no marriage."

"I suppose not." He reached into his pocket and pulled out a circular gold case which he snapped open with a click. The river breeze careened a whirlwind of dust off the contents. "To think, after I received your message last night, I entertained the notion that you might actually be coming around . . . My own folly. Old ghosts are rarely buried so abruptly, eh, *mon vieux ami?*"

Philippe pinched out a scruff of powder and pressed it against a nostril, snorting it deeply.

As expressionless as an Iroquois chief, the bastard, André thought, and all while he speared an old wound with a red-hot poker.

"So, what are you to do with her?" Philippe sniffed delicately, brushing his nose with the back of his hand. "I know you won't winter in Quebec with her, and I know you won't leave her here alone."

A murmuring began among the crowd of men as the door to Madame Bourdon's house cracked open. André turned away and shouldered into the crowd, blocking out the flaring of memory Philippe was doing his damndest to poke into flame.

But the crowd jostled, and did not move, and soon they were all herded into a ragged line. The orange scent of Philippe's strong perfume wafted over his shoulder.

"In rather a hurry, André, for a man so sullen about marriage."

"The sooner this is done, the sooner you'll get me my trading license." His nostrils flared as he glanced easily over the heads of the other men, toward the river. "The sooner I can be out *there.*"

"Marietta will be doubly disappointed." Philippe used his cane as a barrier, eyeing anyone who dared consider crossing it and cutting them in line. "She was looking forward to a woman companion over the long winter months."

"She'll get her heart's desire. Did you think I summoned you here just to be a witness?"

Philippe's blue eyes narrowed, and not against the glare.

"I'm giving you a governess for the winter, old friend."

"Governess." Philippe swung his cane in an arc and gripped its middle. "You wretched dog. I should have known you'd be up to something."

"You said you needed someone, a dozen times. Marietta is heavy with child. She'll need help with your three young ones when the babe is born."

"You wouldn't think of asking me, or Marietta, first, hmm?"

"I'm asking you now." André leaned closer. "You do want some return on your investment? You *do* want me to go west and bring back a harvest of beaver like you've never seen before?"

Philippe tapped his cane up the stairs as they came to the head of the line. "It's the beaver that you're leaving in my house that I'm concerned about."

Madame Bourdon, an imposing woman dressed in severe black, met them just inside the door. She reminded André of a pursed-lip nun who'd tormented him as a schoolboy in Aix-en-Provence.

"Your name, Monsieur?"

"André Lefebvre." He gestured to Philippe. "My friend only came to leer."

"It has been some time, Monsieur Martineau," she said, ignoring André's comment and nodding to Philippe. "It doesn't seem that long ago when your wife was housed here as a King's girl. How is she?"

"She's well, and expecting another child."

André swallowed his growl. Philippe puffed out his chest whenever he uttered those words, as if he had succeeded at some feat never before accomplished, when, to André, it was the prevention of conception that was the more difficult task.

"Send her my regards." Madame Bourdon turned her attention back to André and raised a quill over a yellowed book. "Monsieur Lefebvre, what is your means of livelihood?"

André told her he was a fur trader, and that he owned some land outside of Montreal that once belonged to his father, but had been neglected for several years. He told her that during the course of the next year his wife would be housed with the Martineau family. Madame Bourdon's nod was noncommittal. Philippe then interrupted to inform her that André's father had been a Parliamentarian in Aix-en-Provence, and André had just returned to France after collecting his inheritance.

Her demeanor changed entirely.

"If I had known, Monsieur, that you came from such a good family, I would have made sure you did not have to wait among the others." With a flutter of hands, she motioned for one of her domestics. "We have an exclusive group of women set aside especially for men like you. Well-bred women. Women of good family, who will grace your home with their charm and education."

André frowned. The last woman he wanted for a wife was some cold, high-strung, in-bred bitch. Before he could say anything, Philippe nudged him to follow the domestic down the hall. They passed a large room milling with young women in common dress, then continued on up a narrow flight of stairs. Midway, André turned to Philippe and muttered, "You left a few things out of my biography."

"Nothing of note, I'm sure."

"You forgot to tell the good Madame that I've already spent my inheritance."

"You'll be a rich man soon enough."

"You also neglected to tell her that my father was a rebel Parliamentarian, exiled here during the wars of the Fronde."

"That was decades ago," Philippe argued, waving it away like a gnat. "Besides, it wasn't your father's money you were claiming, it was your brother Leonard's."

"You know damned well that Leonard's money was my father's money. He hid it amid Leonard's affairs before we left France."

"Details."

"Those *details* kept me tied up in the royal courts for three years."

"I don't think it's necessary for Madame Bourdon to know that you came from a family full of rebels. Leonard appeared to be a good royalist, and it is all ancient history now." Philippe frowned. "It seems I must take charge of this issue of choosing you a wife. All you need is a trading license—but I'm getting a governess for my children. I want one with some intelligence and not some broad-beamed dullard." Philippe bowed mockingly before the open door, allowing André to precede him inside. "Of course, if she has any intelligence, she won't marry you, so obviously we'll have to settle for breeding."

The domestic ushered them into a bright room facing the St. Lawrence on the second floor of the three-story house. As he and Philippe entered, a dozen women turned and peered at them expectantly, fans fluttering like butterfly wings. André could guess their ranking by the richness of the ribbon edging their dresses.

"What am I supposed to do now?" he muttered, rolling his shoulders uncomfortably in the binding clothes. "Choose one as a butcher chooses his sheep for slaughter?"

"You have an open field, soldier." Philippe nodded a greeting to the one other men in the room, an aging officer of the Carignan-Salière regiment, which had fought in the Iroquois wars. "Any woman in this room would rather marry a fine buck like you than that aging stag."

He felt like a buck—like a buck facing a pack of hunting

dogs. "They'd be better off with the aging stag. At least he'll be home to rut."

"Don't choose the prettiest one." Philippe swept off his hat and bowed to the room. "Marietta will positively skewer me if I bring home a beauty."

"You sound as sour as an old whore." André extended one stiff leg in what he hoped was a courtly bow. "You and Marietta need a girl in the house. I need a wife to get a trading license. It's the perfect solution."

"Why then," he said through a frozen smile, as one woman approached them, "does it feel like extortion?"

André pulled on his cravat as the scent of sweet, light Parisian perfume wafted from the petticoats of a woman who stopped, boldly, before them. She snapped her fan closed to reveal a tightly boned bodice and wide, shoulder-to-shoulder *décolletage*. His fingers itched to pinch one of those fleshy mounds to test them for firmness. Certainly such an act would be allowed in this market. After all, one wouldn't take home a soft melon, would one?

"I am Renée Affillé," she breathed, bouncing in a pert curtsy, "recently from La Rochelle."

He bowed and felt his coat strain dangerously across his shoulders. "Monsieur Lefebvre."

"What sort of position do you have here in Quebec, Monsieur Lefebvre?"

Currently, an extremely uncomfortable one. "I'm a fur trader."

"A *coureur de bois!*" A second woman swept to his side and slid her hand up his forearm. She smiled at him like a doxy at the Marseille harbor, all wet lips and shining eyes, the melons rolling agreeably beneath a strip of yellow satin—firm and fleshy. "How romantic! Why, I've heard so much about men like you. Do you bring home many furs? Marten, mink?"

"Beaver."

"Yes," Philippe murmured, flexing a brow, "today he will surprise us with a live one, I think."

"Oh, I so much love mink. I had a muff of mink when I was in Rouen—"

"I understand that fur traders spend a great deal of time in the wilderness," Renée interrupted, her dark eyes flashing at the other woman. "The whole winter, sometimes. Is that true of you, Monsieur Lefebvre?"

He met a half-dozen pair of eyes, pair by pair. They all hung upon his answer, staring at him with various degrees of invitation in their eyes. Such *white* creatures, these Frenchwomen, all perfume and narrow shoulders, all pinched nostrils and fair curls and delicate satins; they looked like exotic butterflies trapped in a jar, imported here and totally ignorant of the harshness of the environment outside the glass.

It would be a wonder if half of them survived the Quebec winter.

Renée tapped her fan against her open hand. "Well, Monsieur Lefebvre?"

"I'm in Quebec so seldom," he said, suddenly, "that my house is a ramshackle bit of timber and moss, hardly worthy of . . . of a beaver."

Philippe snorted into his sleeve as the circle of women around them raised a collective, muffled sigh of disappointment and dispersed into random clusters around the room. Philippe elbowed him in the ribs. "You're supposed to be encouraging them."

"I'm not going to lie."

The woman with the gleaming smile was unmoved by his admission. She brazenly pressed her breast against his side. *Yes, yes, quite ripe.* She was not a pretty woman, but she had an earthiness about her that in another situation, he would willingly exploit to their mutual satisfaction. He made his first decision. This woman was too aggressive. He needed a quiet woman, a shy one . . . a *meek* one. He scanned the room. Several girls stood on the periphery of his small circle, avoiding his gaze. Further away, in a corner, he saw three women huddled together. They ignored his presence entirely.

Excusing himself with as much grace as possible, he extricated himself from the grip of the woman and approached the threesome. They talked quietly among themselves until he cleared his throat.

"Oh!" The three turned at the same time. One, a blonde with a spray of curls pinned fashionably on either side of her head, flushed as her gaze met his. She lowered her lashes. *Not her,* he thought. *Too young, too green, needs more time on the vine.* Besides, Marietta would unman him with her sharp Italian knife, if he sent this fair young beauty into her home.

A pitiful, retching string of coughs erupted from behind the ladies' skirts.

"What in God's name—"

"She's ailing, Monsieur." The blonde twisted her fingers together and glanced over her shoulder. "We only arrived in Quebec hours ago, and there's been no time to take her to the Hôtel-Dieu."

The bright skirts parted with a rustle to reveal a tiny woman curled up on a chair. Lank hair dripped from beneath a ragged linen headrail, darkened with perspiration. She blindly took the dry handkerchief André held out for her, dropping the sodden one to the floor. She yanked a blanket more closely around her, as she collapsed into a new fit of coughing.

The runt of the litter. He stepped back and scowled. Every year about this time, the ships from France unloaded a whole new crop of diseases into the colony. Only God knew what this poor woman suffered from. Her forehead gleamed with fever, and dark circles dug gray caverns beneath her eyes and cheekbones. Above the drooping edge of the blanket, the frail line of her collarbone jutted beneath her translucent skin. She was hacking out her life in his linen handkerchief, and the effort shivered the body swathed beneath the rough woolen blanket.

"She shouldn't be here." *Risking the spread of the illness.* "Why isn't she abed?"

"There are no more beds, Monsieur. So many girls are more ill than she, that they've claimed all the beds upstairs." The blonde shrugged prettily. "Marie will recover soon, I'm sure. She is strong. She tended me when I was sick aboard ship."

What were the officials in Paris thinking, when they sent such girls here? Simpering, frail Frenchwomen had no place in this new country—none. New France was a country only for the hardiest stock, and this chit looked as fragile and limp as a Provençal flower. He'd wager a barrel of brandy she'd be the first butterfly to die in New France. She'd never survive the autumn.

His eyes widened on the creature as an idea dawned.

She'd never survive . . . never survive . . .

"Philippe."

Philippe disengaged himself from a crowd of women and tapped his way to André's side. "What is it?"

"There's been a change of plans. You haven't got your heart set on a governess, have you?"

"Scarcely." Philippe glanced at the three women standing before them. The blonde flushed prettily, and a spark of surprise lit Philippe's eyes. "What the devil are you up to, André?"

"Later." He waved vaguely toward the door. "Get Madame Bourdon."

"Then you've chosen?"

"I have." He pointed to the woman curled up on the chair. Her coughs stopped abruptly, and she stared at him with red-rimmed, watery eyes. "Tell Madame Bourdon that I will marry Marie . . ." He glanced at the blonde for help.

"Duplessis, Monsieur." Disappointment sank a pout into the blonde's lip. "Her name is Marie Duplessis."

Taylor—made Romance From Zebra Books

WHISPERED KISSES (3830, $4.99/5.99)
Beautiful Texas heiress Laura Leigh Webster never imagined that her biggest worry on her African safari would be the handsome Jace Elliot, her tour guide. Laura's guardian, Lord Chadwick Hamilton, warns her of Jace's dangerous past; she simply cannot resist the lure of his strong arms and the passion of his *Whispered Kisses*.

KISS OF THE NIGHT WIND (3831, $4.99/$5.99)
Carrie Sue Strover thought she was leaving trouble behind her when she deserted her brother's outlaw gang to live her life as schoolmarm Carolyn Starns. On her journey, her stagecoach was attacked and she was rescued by handsome T.J. Rogue. T.J. plots to have Carrie lead him to her brother's cohorts who murdered his family. T.J., however, soon succumbs to the beautiful runaway's charms and loving caresses.

FORTUNE'S FLAMES (3825, $4.99/$5.99)
Impatient to begin her journey back home to New Orleans, beautiful Maren James was furious when Captain Hawk delayed the voyage by searching for stowaways. Impatience gave way to uncontrollable desire once the handsome captain searched *her* cabin. He was looking for illegal passengers; what he found was wild passion with a woman he knew was unlike all those he had known before!

PASSIONS WILD AND FREE (3828, $4.99/$5.99)
After seeing her family and home destroyed by the cruel and hateful Epson gang, Randee Hollis swore revenge. She knew she found the perfect man to help her—gunslinger Marsh Logan. Not only strong and brave, Marsh had the ebony hair and light blue eyes to make Randee forget her hate and seek the love and passion that only he could give her.

Available wherever paperbacks are sold, or order direct from the Publisher. Send cover price plus 50¢ per copy for mailing and handling to Penguin USA, P.O. Box 999, c/o Dept. 17109, Bergenfield, NJ 07621. Residents of New York and Tennessee must include sales tax. DO NOT SEND CASH.